IF BY CHANCE

D'Norgea Taylor

IF BY CHANCE

A Tale of Time Travel
and Generational Curses

A small Pacific Northwest community is so traumatized by tragedy, humiliation and outrage that the people don't talk about what has happened to them. Some of them keep the stories hidden inside even to their graves.

One of those affected is Byron Jr., who, while very young, began to see horrible visions of people who sort of looked familiar, just under his eyelids before he went to sleep and as he awoke each day. Now, after approaching middle age, Byron becomes extremely ill and near death when he discovers that a generational curse has infected all of the lives in his community.

One of Bryon's nurses has traveled through time to find him. She takes him on a journey to uncover the curses' origin so that the curses will not damage future generations, especially his children. First Byron must convince Maple, the woman he loves, to help him find all the victims, even though he is now a ghost.

They discover that there is one person who is directly connected to all the people affected by these curse. No one wants to come face to face with their secrets until Old Cup is found dead in the basement of the church house and the church burns down to the ground before authorities can investigate how he died, what happened and why.

Also by D'Norgia Taylor

STRING BEANS & CANDY CANES
© 2007

IF BY CHANCE

D'Norgia Taylor

Taylordlink, LLC
Portland, Oregon

ISBN-13: 978-0-9895103-0-1

Cover design by Alice Price

Published by:
Taylordlink, LLC
Portland, Oregon

Printed in the United States of America

ACKNOWLEDGEMENTS

Thank you to my Tuesday afternoon tea sipping critique group, Marlene Hill, Linda Smith and Jennifer Fulford, for their invaluable assistance, care and encouragement that helped bring this work of words out of its dusty box.

Thank you to Roseta Akin and Chris Poole-Jones who read and saw things I had missed in reviewing this book before going to press, and—told me so.

Thank you E'Njoni Café owners Michael & Sonya Damtew, who shared information with me about Eritrea, a Country in eastern Africa, on the Red Sea.

Thank you to my daughter Alice Price who contributed the beautiful artwork for the IF BY CHANCE cover design.

Membership in these organizations helped me tremendously:
    Oregon Writers Colony
    Willamette Writers
    Maya Angelou Writers Guild

Dedicated to:

My daughters, Leah Price and Alice Price
And my grandson
Anaru Jackson

This story will take you to a place where the ordinary is strange and the strange is ordinary. It is a place where people and spirits, watch and mingle.

History mingles with the present, where curses, spirits and real life touch, caress and then moves beyond reality.

Welcome to a new place in time in the millennium.

Beliefs change with two damaged souls in the present and they have to re-set the past for the future.

ENJOY THE ADVENTURE

Prologue

The room filled with the many fledgling spirits, brand new spirits whose energy had just gathered in strings of likeness. The new spirits were void of any cohesiveness but their familiars could recognize their energy anyway, when they wanted to. The fledglings hung there, darting vision to anything randomly mobile, while examining the spirits who wanted to live in human form again. The fledglings had no understanding of form.

Since everything on the planet is energy from the beginning of creation, there is nothing new under the Earth's sun or the entire universe. Energy constantly changes and mingles with different energy sources. Therefore, everything original lasts forever and can sometimes be disabled by extracting its main subsistence source.

The renegades, those who wanting to be in human form again, were the worst of these fledglings because they could become step-ins and alter a spirit's original purpose. Their decadence was hovering and the new spirits' positive energy, precious.

Some of the fledglings were unaware of those parasites that were actually the fallout scabs from curses. The cursed spirits hung on from generation to generation, long after the specific sin was forgotten yet continued committing the destruction of souls.

Enter Hannah who was true to her purpose. Abira Hanna, her given name, meant 'Strong Goddess of Life,' but she was just called Hannah. She appeared no older than five to seven human years old when visible but she held the wisdom of centuries. Hannah could watch and know where some situations were heading and squeeze her essence between the ideas that were causing signals of danger and the receptors of those to be consumed by the curse and disarm the affect. There was danger even to some souls who had not yet made an appearance. To those she could appear as anyone the viewer wanted or merely be dismissed as a non-entity.

Hannah scanned the end of Earth's twentieth century and found that there was one struggling soul and summoned Kaye, an ancient traveler, to calm the total situation and put an end to an evil from a curse that was still roaming earth's atmosphere. Her old soul didn't care much for attention, so she began to place certain things in order to start the process that would quarantine any derelict curse that resurfaced. The curse had to be broken before the twenty-second century or the whole planet would be garbage.

Chapter 1

"They found him in the basement at the church house. Somebody got him real good. He's been messing with people all his life and up until now nobody said anything to him," Luella let fly out of her mouth as soon as the rest of ladies began to show up.

The unofficial Golden Age Black Women's Collective was open for business, information sharing, and to put it politely it was time for the gossip crew.

"The boy's good and dead now. He can't hurt anybody else," Jessie Mae shouted.

"I truly believe he killed his parents. The police found them out in the woods with their hearts cut open. His folks must have wanted the old dog to do right, and he killed them," came from Fina who just sat down in the corner chair, hiding the last bit of cigarette she wanted to enjoy with her first cup of coffee.

"You think that devil is really gone?" she asked.

"I don't know about that, these kind of spirits and things come back quick in different skins," Jessie Mae smirked.

The ladies all stopped and turned to a set of eyes that met theirs. After a slight smirk or affirmative nod, exhaled their thoughts toward the floor.

"So what happened?" Each new bus group that came in the center asked as they started taking off their coats or tightening their sweaters around their chests and necks.

"Somebody's probably birthing another one of them demons right now," Miss Sugar chimed in.

"Yeah, you right," was part of an 'Amen' from the folks sitting close to the wall next to the morning treats.

The large, brightly lit room was filling up with seniors and people walking in with their canes, walkers and those almost sprinting in new tennis shoes. Stale donuts and fresh coffee fumes sprinkled throughout the room. Seniors who were seventy to eighty year olds and acting age eight filled the tables and argued about who could sit in which chair. Odds and ends of conversations stopped when Old Cup's name was heard above the buzz of other activities.

"That's the reason we have to pray for the newly departed, like Brotha Cup, so that their souls can rest and be peaceful till they come back and have renewed minds."

New smells of perfume, cologne, after-shave, Ben-gay and other salves or medicinal ointments mixed in with the Old Cup conversations.

"I hope that evil dog don't ever get back and renew nothing. He's probably sharpening up his fangs right this minute, stewing there someplace in his own slimy spirit," Luella said, loud enough to wake him if she could.

"Wasn't nobody there to pray for Old Cup—so ya know his butt is burning in hell at this very moment trying to make his way back. We have to keep him from finding his way back—he may have left a trail someplace," said Marcie.

"How do we do that, Macie?" asked Gerald one of the few men who would even speak up when the main crowd was mostly women.

"What do you know about this, Gerald? You knew Old Cup didn't you?"

"Not really he was kind of odd, that's all I know."

The ladies, now staring out the front window of the community center, started their morning update, trying to get into everybody's business to begin their day. But Old Cup wrapped around all their thoughts and questions.

Marvin looked at Gerald and said, "I heard that the choir rehearsal up at the church was just ending and the choir members heard six distinct gunshots. The men grabbed the women and children then ran them out of the church, away from the sound to safety.

Dorian rolled himself over to where the men had gathered to put his two cents into the consort, "One man was supposed to call 911 while the five men surrounded Old Cup and they locked arms in prayer, was told to me this morning. The Church leaders that were left behind slowly went to the lower level."

Gable, one of the church Stewards, said, "We felt the cold coming from the side door and heard slow moving footsteps crunching on the lawn out back. We closed that door and walked into the room where we believed the shots came from."

"Didn't nobody call the police?" Raynell asked, looking in her purse for a pen to take a few notes. She had to share this information when she got home to make phone calls, she thought. Raynell easily forgot everything so she always took notes, but still didn't remember to look at them later on.

"Said he had at least six bullets in him. One went right through his head, another one in the heart, one in each leg and each arm had a bullet, too," Macie blurted out.

"Sho you're right, I wonder what he did to rile up somebody like that? Seems like he got kind of quiet and settled for a long time. Didn't hear nothing 'bout him beating up his old woman or nothing." Luella tried to continue.

The workers began to serve the morning snack while several of the old folks removed their teeth, others watched to see if they could snatch a set that might fit their mouth, in order to chew better, without getting caught. They'd return the borrowed dentures to lost and found later.

"Well you know his woman, Sadie, that's her name, left town a while back to her country over in Africa to go check up on some of her relatives someplace back on the continent. Sadie must have known what he was up to, don't you think?" Jolina wondered.

"She probably knew, 'cause she had to know what he was, to stay there all that time," Luella said with her usual arrogant stance.

"Maybe not, some of those devil infected folks can hide all kinds of evil, especially from those who care about them, 'cause they don't want to believe the defects. You know that," said Miss Sugar.

The Bingo game was being organized in the center of the room that now seated close to fifty people. All had a word or two of input about Old Cup.

"He walked around with that simpleton manner like he had a layer of innocence wrapped around him; he 'looked' even childlike on occasion. But he was what he was," a deep voice came from the corner of the room.

"They say he used to mess with children, but nothing ever got done about it," said the woman reading the racing form off to the side by the window.

A hush kind of blanketed the space for a minute or two. One could hear long sighs and see heads shaking in disgust as each person grappled with the new revelation. When they could come to grips with that information in their own heads, they studied the floor quietly.

"Nothing got done 'cause everyone was scared of him."

"Not everyone. Look how he lured those innocent ones into his web. Why was it the kids and quiet ones who got took by him?" Jonnetta said.

"I wasn't scared of that old fool," Gerald almost yelled out and continued to grumble under his breath. He took out his teeth and put them in his breast pocket, then grabbed a donut and a scone.

18

"Maybe someone knew that he did things like that and was determined to get revenge," came a mousy voice from out of the regular morning group.

"You believe this was about revenge or was it just to stop him in his tracks, or was someone in his grip that was trying to get away?"

"You mean one of the children?" asked Fina.

"Sounds like he needed killing." Homer said as he palmed a set of teeth.

"Could be," said Miss Sugar.

"That's right, he needed killin'," Raynell confirmed.

"Naw, it looks like someone who came prepared. This place is so different from the way it used to be. Just look around and see what's happening here. A lot of the old folks are gone," added Gerald.

The town was changing quite a bit with new faces wrapped in different colors, and dogs dragging people by leash or chain to their desired grassy spot.

They all looked up at the sound of the siren and the fire truck raced down a one-mile stretch, past their morning perch and gobbled the attention they'd given to Old Cup.

"Wonder what's going to happen next?" Several ladies asked all at the same time.

"Hope it isn't none of our homes." That was the room buzz. Rolling eyes acknowledged each other when they each stretched their necks to see where the fire was likely to be. Those who were able rushed to the window; the others hollered, "What's happening?"

Just up the street a couple houses past the Senior center, Mrs. Chance crossed her arms and stood near her front gate to see what she could when the alarm startled her into going out to the front walk. It took her attention away from clipping her one rose bush. The 10:00AM sun was nice and warm.

The front of Miss Maples' house was closed up tight with drawn curtains as always, but the curtains moved a little; and

Miss Olive was peeking out her front door.

Everybody clandestinely watched and waited for the first word of what was happening right then, and the church burned completely to the ground before the firemen could exit the vehicle."

Chapter 13

K aye," the little girl voice shook and squeaked out a whisper, "That didn't really happen did it?"

"Oh, yes it did and nobody ever talks about it now," Kaye answered, brushing her tangled hair.

"How come?" Another squeaky voice asked.

"Well, folks believe that this whole area had a curse on it and when that man was found dead in the church they thought his spirit was still in there so, they had to destroy the curse by fire."

"Who did it?"

"Beats me, some say the spirit of the dead man made the church burn itself up, so that those crazy step-ins could continue to roam and survive even though they needed to go on to their next realm. I heard lots of stories about this area, especially about Miss Maple, who they said lived in that house with a real live ghost," Kaye told them.

"There is no such thing as a real live ghost. They are dead already," a soft voice said.

"Yeah, but people thought they were alive," Kaye said.

Kaye sensed the drawing in and tightening of the fledglings' energy from where she sat and motioned them to come closer. Kaye's job was to make the new beings ready to live in human form. She helped them practice and know about their future.

"From what I understand," said Kaye, "there were just twelve beautiful houses in this area and each family got pretty well acquainted. When one family moved away, the house was quickly filled with people who, even if they didn't know the rest of the community, became familiar immediately."

Shadow, the old satiny black cat that usually hung out with the old soul, Hannah, curled himself up on the overstuffed chair against the afghan. Brid, the ancient looking Cockatoo, sat on Shadow's back.

"Was there really a real live ghost?"

"Oh yes," said Kaye.

"Did he get killed too?"

"No, he got sick and died, but, he discovered something before he actually left his body, that he wanted to erase."

Just then Shadow stretched, then rounded his back. Brid, annoyed at being awakened again, opened one sassy looking eye and allowed a loud chirp to break the silence.

"How can they sit together and even sleep like that? I thought cats and birds were natural enemies, they are not supposed to be friends?"

Kaye smiled and told them, "Be open to things that come your way because anything is possible."

While holding one spirit in each arm and another attached to her back, Kaye marched the fledglings to their proper places to rest and she bid them goodnight.

"Will we see you again?" the Chance spirit asked. "Will we know you?"

"If that's your choice," Kaye answered as she closed their door and went back to a time she needed for the undoing of evil. She still had more lessons to prepare for them.

Right then she saw it all and tried her best to halt or undo some of the dastardly deeds that permeated many lifetimes. Even when she could, the cell memory was still present in the offspring of the doers, the step-ins, and the others.

The doers were the souls in real human form that committed awful sins, crimes and devastation to anyone the step-in chose. The humans had accepted the step-ins and were not solid enough to follow their own minds. They were afraid to stand up and say, "Stop," because they feared the consequences on themselves. The step-ins could leave a body for good or just temporarily. The temporary step-ins were usually those who do good, but not always.

Kaye labored to identify whom she could take back to find the original source of the curse. The third or fourth generation would be the best way to begin. Kaye decided to track the Chance bloodline. They would be just far enough away to know of their family legends and willing to find the truth. She decided to go back even further until at least a hint at the truth was evident.

Chapter 2

*Y*oung Byron came to Kaye's mind. She remembered her encounter, at least a generation ago, with his father. Kaye saw the elder Byron sitting at the pier watching for a fish to bite but he was also deep in thought. Byron Senior was a big man; wearing a sleeveless T-shirt, where one could see his smooth chocolate skin glistening in the warm afternoon sun. She remembered that he moved his family to the Pacific Northwest in 1941 so he could participate in the War effort. He lived with his wife across the Columbia River from the shipyard in Portland, Oregon.

After the war ended Kay again saw him at that fishing spot and warned him of ensuing doom, unless he moved his family to higher ground. Without question he immediately packed them up and moved north to the state of Washington. A few weeks later on May 30, 1948, a 200-foot section of the dike holding back the Columbia River in Portland collapsed during a flood, killing many residents. By nightfall the entire area was under water, leaving its inhabitants homeless. The people who survived said that the public officials neglected to respond to the destruction of heavily black populated communities. Survivors also said that racist attitudes contributed to the black community not being informed of the danger. The people, who lived there, except blacks, were told in writing to get their belongings and leave.

Knowing this, Kaye believed Byron Junior would probably be open to at least hearing her, since his father was receptive.

Kaye found Byron's tender times; times he was hurt, confused and angry. She saw his secrets while he slept. Kaye saw the moment that started his anguish and led to a troubled youth. His spirit embraced mistakes and poor decisions in young adulthood. He secretly hung out with those groups of kids his father told him to stay away from. He always seemed to escape serious trouble. Byron thought he had a guardian angel, so he continued to take risks until old Cup crossed his path.

Kaye invaded several years worth of his dreams starting with his very early days and smoothed some of the roughness from memory cells that held the hurts, humiliation and sadness. Since we all come back to human form in groups, mostly the same groups, she wanted to view his life encounters not have him relive them. The one thing she would see was who touched his life, for good or bad. Kaye found his turning point; the day he knew he could love someone. A brief encounter opened his heart to the spirit who loved him unconditionally, living or dead, in this world or in the next. Kaye knew it would take the strength of an open and glad heart to walk with him.

Kaye smiled when she saw Byron's heart open and the death that loomed in his body began to recede. The angels and Kaye would have time to locate the exact moment this group of people was infected. Kaye would facilitate the first encounter that was about to happen the very day she traveled to his car in the year 1986.

It was a dangerous time so Kaye had to be very careful in her travels now because she knew that approximately 234,000 meteors passed through the earth's atmosphere that year. Many travelers were thrown off course and could never re-enter their realm because of the interference.

Kaye arrived in the Pacific Northwest during the midst of an explosive shift in music and art. The Rock & Roll Hall of Fame launched in 1985 which inducted Chuck Berry, Ray Charles, the Everly Brothers and Elvis Presley among others that year. Tina Turner, after her fabulous music and troubled life, renewed herself and received a Star on the Hollywood walk of Fame; Luther Vandross' in video with "Stop to Love;" and Michael Jackson named the King of Pop when his music from "Thriller" was heard around the world. Renewal was definitely in the air. Although they'd all seen heartache and misery, each continued to walk on and reach for higher and better places in their bodies and souls. This was the music of the rough and tender times that Byron and Maple struggled through.

Kaye found Byron and as she stepped into his dreams she removed some of the poisons that were preparing his body to die before his time. She cleansed the energy of all the heart valves and vessels. The chambers were systematically cleansed of contaminants so that love energy within and 'round about him could nurture his being. The cells that held unhealthy and unnecessary memories were deprived of any life so that Byron could not hold onto those pieces of his history that caused pain and destruction within him. The cells that held fear, humiliation, and trepidation were examined and the energy redirected. She captured the cell memories for later study when she could piece together the story from his hidden DNA.

In Kaye's original realm it was well known that all living things on earth were made up of energy that survived best when at peace with the energy of its environment and itself. So she spent his dreamtime repairing his mind, body and spirit. Some areas of his existence only God could touch; therefore, she just made the repairs where she could. Because of Kaye's intervention young Byron survived years longer than he would have otherwise. The work had begun.

Kaye found a moment in Byron's life where he saw a boy he knew being beaten by a group of kids from school. His heart told him to go over and help. In the back of his mind he heard his grandfather's words telling him to 'stay out of other people's troubles.' He remembered his grandfather always said, 'walk the other way and avoid trouble in your own life.' From that point on he kept to himself, afraid he would get hurt and ignored the urge to help anyone out of serious situations.

Even when Byron married, he couldn't be bothered with hard decisions. That way if the wrong decision was made he could blame someone else. Byron and his wife had three children, two boys and one girl. Byron left most of the parenting to his wife even when the boys got older and wanted to play sports with him. Byron was always unavailable.

Byron had always wanted to run his own business. So he started with a small snack shop, near a high school. Business was pretty good and he enjoyed his work so his hours spent there became longer and longer. Now it was almost mid-June and he had to finish inventory and order less inventory because summer school brought in fewer customers.

That night after the last day of school he had to complete all his paperwork. It was quite late. He went home bone tired and he wanted to see if the kids wanted to go someplace to celebrate the end of the school term.

It wasn't dark at all as he drove home even after 9:00 pm. It was very close to the summer solstice and he saw that the sun had not fully set. Everything was quiet when he pulled into the driveway. *Hmmm, they must all be out for a while.* Then Byron entered the house and found it completely empty. There was no furniture, no pictures on the walls, no clothes in the closets, nothing. Except his personal belongings, everything was gone.

The note taped to the bathroom mirror said, "I cannot tolerate this masquerade of a marriage any longer. Your emotional and physical absence from me and from the children tells us we are not really a part of your life. We wish you the best and I will be in touch when we are settled. Bye."

Byron walked to the living room, sat on the floor and slumped against the wall. He still held and stared at the note. He could not think of one thing to think about. His mind was blank—as empty as his house.

Chapter 3

It was now 1987. All the 'Happy New Year's' had been said and school would be starting up in a few days for the winter term. Since his family left him Byron spent most of his time alone, except for working in the snack shop. Although he sent them presents through his mother for Christmas he received no response, no phone calls or anything from his children to say if their gifts arrived. Not even a card.

He spent Christmas and New Years' day at his parents' house and his mother told him "Byron, you closed your family out of your life and they needed you to be present. Now, I try to stay out of your personal business but you've shut everyone out. You should go get your family back or officially let your wife go. Your children will always be your children so make sure you support them, and their mother."

"Yeah, son. You better check yourself because people don't walk off for no reason," his father chimed in at the end of the conversation.

On January's first workday of the year, the cold, biting wind, whirled majestically around him as he stepped out into the early morning elements. He wrapped the 'hawk- protecting' scarf tighter around his neck. After Byron fastened the crackling leather jacket's top button, he tucked his chin in closer to his chest and charged down the driveway to the car.

I wish I'd known it would be this cold, I'd have put the car in the garage, he thought as he forged into the biting air, shoulder first.

"Man oh man," he said out loud while sitting, shivering, waiting for the car to warm up before taking off. The radio had some idiot contest on so he shoved a tape into the cassette player. The music reminded him of warmer, better days in the sun. As he pulled away from home, Byron's workday had now begun.

While he drove to work he thought about the crazy dream from the night before. The dream took him on a strange voyage through a highway-like system that was actually his own body. He could see cracked bones and gunk that stopped free flowing movement through a tangled system. Once he was aware of the bottlenecks in his system, he reached out to what appeared to be microdrils spouting out of the light essence that surrounded him in the dream. They were like tiny piranha creatures drilling through the blockages, which made all things flow. In the dream he had kept breathing deeply so he did that now and didn't cough nor did his chest hurt. *That is so weird.*

The light of day had just begun as he hurried to open the store on time. But, as he was about to enter his parking space on the side of the store, he saw her. At first she was just plain, ordinary, a bit spunky and she moved quickly. The energy in her movement, during those few seconds watching her, intrigued him and made him smile. Byron's eyes followed her walk to a dark green Ford parked at the end of the row, until an impatient horn blower got behind him. That brought him back to driving. He noted the make, model and color of her car and moved on. *If by chance I see her again, I will get up enough nerve to introduce myself.* Thinking of her, his face held a smile all day.

With no family responsibility to be physically present, Byron opened another store on the other side of town and it was doing very well now, his Last Chance Snack Shop. He hired a manager for the new shop and went back to the shop by the schools' first store until he could hire part-time workers for each store. This was the site of his first store. Not only did he have snacks for sale but also school supplies and since he put in the second copy machine, kids kept coming in to make copies of schoolwork, fliers about parties and other community events. The coin collector on each machine made it so much easier for record keeping and actually getting the money for the use of the machine. It was a win – win at both shops. Many told him that he was wasting his money, but he followed his own mind and succeeded.

He sold three of the shops when his wife left; eventually she sent him papers for a divorce. She said he was married to the business and didn't have time for a family.

In a way he was relieved, and knew he could rebuild from what the divorce cost him. He would miss the children and swore he would make time out of everyday to be in touch with them in some way. His wife never shared any of his dreams, wild as they were. He wanted to try to do more than work for a company or stay stuck as a bean counter for someone else's beans. Before they married he talked about how he wanted his own business and was going to work hard until he made it. Once they were married she didn't show any interest in wanting to work along with him like he thought she said she would.

The first shop worked out pretty well – it paid his bills and paid for some of the extras they had liked. He wanted to make things work even better. His children could reap the benefits, too. There had to be a system to break through to make the shop earn an even greater profit. He made almost a million dollars in the last three years with his ventures; unfortunately it cost him his family.

That early morning vision of *the woman* floated across and through his mind again, as he began to open the shop. But he had to work to make sure the students were able to buy what they needed. The music played just over the conversations in the store and he heard Whitney Houston's "How Will I Know." He smiled and just kept going until the day was through. After he locked up the shop that evening, the early morning vision of the woman and the green Ford hovered over him while he walked to his car.

Just then the full moon looked directly at him and, somehow reminded him of her, even though it was just an early morning glimpse of her. The tiny piece he could see of her face since she was almost totally covered except for one eye, which was unprotected from the cold, haunted his mind. He welcomed the thoughts of her.

See-through lacy clouds scattered around the brilliant globe so much so that the moon's light throbbed an enchanting glow. She sat there in his mind – only her profile and a body totally covered in a coat, and scarf covering most of her face. Still he could see something magical. He knew that right eye of hers had looked directly at him. As he drove home the veiled moon led him and sat regally atop his house. The glow that the moon left stayed with him long after he'd forgotten the rest of the day.

After almost five years in business, receipts from the Snack Shop were beginning to make a big difference. Byron talked to his friend, Grubbs, who told him to do more advertising targeting youth in the different neighborhoods. The school kids had money and didn't even think about how to spend it. He also asked the customers what else would be helpful to them to have in the store. He listened.

The shop didn't have much junk food… just some chips, candy, pop, however, he stocked predominantly fresh sandwiches, fruit and juice. The potato chips, candy and pop disappeared the quickest, so he would try to do what his friend Grubbs suggested and cater to their wants. He justified it by telling himself he wanted to be a better merchant and would rather sell junk food than watch them using money on drugs.

Several weeks went by and he tried to be outside the store during the same time of day as on that fateful morning, to get a glimpse of her in real life again. He had to find out her name. Byron forgot about hiring a new manager for that store just yet. So two part-time students would do for right now. He wanted to be there each morning inconspicuously and find out about her.

Most of the time her face held no expression whatsoever. Every once in a while she'd flush out a smile but her eyes didn't match the slight up curl of her mouth. Her smile vanished as soon as her gaze moved on when no one was watching her.

One day that very lady Byron had been thinking about walked toward her office while reading the memo she'd just taken from the front office. She walked passed the group standing in the hall without looking up, said, "Pardon me," and kept going. She was on the short side of average height and wore heels to compensate for what she perceived as small stature. With her cocoa complexion and dark full, lush, lashes surrounding large dark brown eyes she could captivate anyone's attention if she chose. But just didn't realize her power.

Byron Chance, part of the group standing in the hall realized that she was the same woman he'd seen months before on the early, almost daylight, bitter-cold morning in January. "Man, who is that lady?" he asked Hank.

"She's the counselor," he whispered blocking his lips with his hand from her view.

"Why'd you have to whisper?" Byron asked.

"She's kind of like, ah, ohm, ... a no joking around ...

kind of person. Ya know, politically correct and all that," he continued.

Byron smiled like a kid in Baskin Robins picking out his favorite flavor. His eyes filled with wonder and expectation.

"Why are you looking like that? Man, you want to meet her or something?"

"Yeah." said Byron.

"Her name's Maple, you know, like the syrup. She is kind of cute, though, but I don't know why you want to meet her, man, I know you got to see that rock on her left hand, don't you?"

"Awww, naw, I hadn't noticed it until you just said so," he said in a busted-bubble sigh.

Still, he watched her walk down the hall and wondered how he could just be able to say hello once in a while. His slightly goose-bumped skin helped him stay warm and tingly right where he stood, watching her and he owned that moment all to himself.

"I still want to meet her. Maybe she'll steer some of these folks who come in here to my store."

"I heard that. You always trying to get the hook-up to make a buck."

"What else is there?" Byron threw back at him.

"I haven't seen you down at this end of the block for a while, what's up? You could do some networking and make some hook-ups there. A lot of new 'honeys' are coming in there now, too. The women that come in there regularly, already know that I know you; and they even ask me when will I bring you in The Hangout with me," said Hank.

"Well," said Byron, "Maybe I should. What's the best time to be there?"

"Thursdays are good. Folks there are trying to get something going for the weekend. You still messing around with Lana?"

"Naw, that's over," Bryon answered quickly.

36

"Ya know, Thursday is also ladies' night out, so you might run into something for yourself."

"So that's why you're telling me about Thursdays, huh? Ya know the more I think about it, I'm not ready for that right now."

Byron stood tall and regal in his deep chocolate skin and a 'come over here' kind of smile that he tried to hide. He was dressed casually chic and appeared to have just stepped out of GQ. With his arms crossed in front of a sleek muscled chest and his feet spaced just right for a statue-like pose, he continued to watch Maple until she turned the corner at the end of the hallway.

"Okay man, I hear ya. Are you all right?" Hank asked.

Byron's expressions and words were not a match at all. The bullet-like pain marched right across the back of his eyeballs and he forced the words, "Yeah, I'm just taking it slow, that's all."

Chapter 4

Maple stepped into her bath and slowly sat and leaned back. This was the perfect temperature for her before daybreak meditation. It was her time to think about her day and plan what she wanted to accomplish—and to pray. Maple sighed as she thought about past life events and prayed that God would take the fear from her spirit of everything and everyone who frightened her. In her most dire circumstances, He had always brought her through to a better understanding and a light of contentment would appear. Maple wanted to remove the ugliness from her life. The ugliness she wore under a heavy cloak masked as peace. Even though she appeared content and aloof regarding her career and sometimes her family status or predicament, Maple held most feelings inside. Many saw her as cold to tepid by the way she responded, to their inquiries. She knew that and stayed out of people's way.

Maple wanted desperately to close her eyes and wish herself into a different life, but didn't dare for fear of the visions under her eyelids. They waited for her. The visions showed her things she didn't want to know. Dangerous, ugly, unheard of craziness was what she saw and sometimes felt at each corner she needed to turn. She feared so many things. She washed and continued sitting there as the water drained to allow all her worries to leave her with the dirty water of skin and sweat and vermin of others she encountered over her last twenty-four hours. Waste.

The kids, now ages eight and ten years old, would be waking up soon and Maple had to make breakfast and get ready for the rest of the day.

"Mom, Blossy took my socks," Omar, Jr. shouted. Maple heard the squabble as she set the breakfast table.

"No I didn't. I got my own, you lost yours," Blossom said. "He's always losing his stuff and blaming me for it."

"Put a stop to that mess, both of you, you hear me?" Maple called back at her children.

"I'm still gonna tell on you 'cause you had candy under your pillow, I'm a tell."

"Ok you two, that's enough!"

Maple had gotten out of bed over two hours ago and now felt the need to go right back. She couldn't figure why no one could find out what was keeping her so sick? *Maybe I should believe them and accept it's all in my mind.*

"All right darlings, it's almost time to leave. You don't want to be late for school do ya? Hurry up and finish your food." They shoved the food in their mouths, half wiped their faces and Junior wiped his hands on his clothes.

Maple dismissed that little sight and called them again, "Let's go. Let's go, now!" Maple put her coat over her bathrobe deciding to just be late for work. She would come back and finish dressing.

She pulled up close to the school's front door waved and smiled at some of the other moms dropping off kids, too.

When she got back home, Maple heard her husband, Omar, stirring around upstairs so she quickly finished her hair and make-up and threw on her clothes so she could be out of the house before he came into the kitchen. *Oh, damn, too late.*

"Hey, you make some coffee?" Omar asked.

"Yeah, there's some left on the counter. It's still hot. I

didn't turn the pot off, and I left you some breakfast, too."

"Say, you aren't feeling too good today huh? You look like hell; you going out like that?" he smirked after his daily put-down ritual.

"Thanks. You have a 'hellava' day yourself," she said as she slammed the door. His vicious quips that meant to cloud her day didn't sting quite as much as they used to. But she still felt the pinch in his cruelty.

She stood on the bottom step, breathed in as much new air as she could take in before walking out into her day. When Maple closed the gate behind her, the shackles left her body. She moved quicker and easier and her eyes began to smile.

Maple found herself thinking about the guy that was introduced to her a few weeks ago. *What was his name? Who was he? I feel like I've known him before, but where?*

Sliding behind the wheel of her old Ford Tempo she wondered what she could do to make her home better. She felt she was only the chauffeur, family bank, chief cook and bottle washer and whatever else the family needed. At work, the day held nothing special except when she walked past that spot in the hall where she had seen him the first time. She remembered that it was the place where Grubb, she knew him as Hank, had introduced her to that storeowner some weeks back. Later that same day after work she imagined she saw his face in the grocery store.

Continuing down the aisles she kept looking behind and upfront to see who was watching her, and the memory of his face entered her mind again. Maple knew there was a gentle prick in her spirit when she met him. A quiet chuckle went through her body and she shook her head, shrugged her shoulders and smiled. *Maybe it's just someone who knows how my heart feels and what it needs.* She kept moving

That evening as she started dinner and finished picking up everybody's stuff, her husband, Omar came through the front door leaving it open while he went to put his coat on the hook in the closet. The whole room chilled, not only the air, but also the spirit of the entire house soured. Maple studied his face and saw that he must have had a good day.

"Hey, how ya doing?" he yelled.

"Good, good, thanks." She almost woke up a smile to go with her response to his greeting, but decided, *why bother?*

"I'll get some ribs and stuff and bar-BQ this weekend and you think you could do the other stuff to go with it? Could you, huh?"

"You know it's about 30 degrees out there now? That's colder than usual for Oregon now anyway." She paused and said, "Sure, sure, is it just us or were you gonna invite someone else over?"

"I don't know, maybe some..." he left that hanging.

I wonder what this is about? While putting together lists of what she needed to do the next day. Maple continued to ponder her lists—her way of showing herself she accomplished something for the day. This erased those old recordings of Omar's comments, which stuck in her memory that said 'you can't do anything for yourself.' The rest of the evening went well, but her mind always watched for the unexpected. She moved through the house as if she were walking on eggshells.

They had once been happy and she couldn't put her finger on what happened or when it all changed. Maple thought in terms of before kids, surgery and afterwards. The tumors she had, kept showing up, all benign but frightening to her. She'd have to go back even farther in her relationship but it was before the illness started that the signs of change began. *But why. What is the purpose?*

Maple knew that she was doomed to this tragic marriage. She thought while driving to work that next morning about all the madness she'd seen in her life. The fog came toward her and rolled over the car as a song of a giant bird fluttering.

The sun tried to tear through a light fog, almost like lace over a lighted lamp. The fog looked like it did a little dance then the magic vanished. She tried to see the sky she'd just passed in the rear view mirror but by then it had all disappeared. The air was somewhat chilly but the smell of spring was making its presence known.

Maple rarely joined in the conversation or dished the dirt with the rest of the women on the job and the group stopped talking whenever she walked into the lunchroom. She pretended she hadn't noticed the abrupt silence, even though she usually heard what they were saying and believed that they meant for her to hear them.

"How's everybody's day going?" Maple asked while she reached for cream in the fridge. She heard coughing, throat clearing and rustling in seats as she walked through the lunchroom. "What happened? You guys must have been talking about me, from the way you're acting," she said with a muffled, almost closed mouth throaty laugh.

"Naw, Miss Maple you just came in when there was a lull in conversation. We were talking about how things are changing here and wondering if we are part of the RIF that's coming up. You know, 'Reduction In Force.'"

"Ah, you know they're cutting out a lot of jobs," said Jackie who wore bright green eye shadow that reminded Maple of signal lights.

"Oh... I... know... ohm... the organization is short on funds; I really don't know what's going to happen because some of the grants didn't materialize as had been expected," Maple continued, "I could be part of the RIF myself."

"Maple, how come you don't go out or anything?" Jackie asked. She was actually trying to get her to be a part of their group—mainly to see how much information she could garner.

"I go out sometimes, but I've got so much I have to do

when I get home. I'm too tired most of the time—I just rest. Then I've got to take care of my family; you know, dinner and dishes and baths for the kids and laundry and…" Maple said, telling a half truth. At that very moment Maple thought about how Omar never missed an opportunity to humiliate her in public so she preferred to stay where she thought it would be safe, home. But she knew that home was the least safe place for her to be.

"Hold up now. We all got those same things to do, too." Jackie chimed in.

Maple began to recognize their subtle cruel pokes so she made an obvious glance at her watch, then the clock on the wall at the back of the room and said, "My goodness I'm gonna be late. Gotta go," as she gathered up her half eaten lunch and left.

"She is so strange acting," said Cinnamon. "I wonder what she carries around all the time in that big old purse of hers?"

"No telling. But, who cares?"

"I certainly don't, as long as she don't cross my path."

"She's just odd, and not friendly to anyone except those she thinks she can push around."

Jackie stopped her and said; "Now you know she doesn't bother nobody. She's just a bit different and keeps to herself most of the time. She doesn't mistreat anyone. I think something's going on with her that she ain't saying." Jackie recognized Maples silent suffering but didn't know how to name it.

"Yeah, like that nut she got for a husband." Bella opened up. Immediately the two other women put their chins on their shoulders, with eyes looking up over their glasses staring at Jackie, asking 'what you know that we don't know?' Then they all began to whisper.

"Now I heard that…" the room froze for a moment as Hannah, Brid and Shadow, the cat, sauntered through. None of the gossipers' eyes recognized that 'visitors' had come through and engaged their lives. The chill broke when they left the room and Bella said questioning, "What just blew through here?" All conversation ended.

Kaye had been there, too, and watched from the corner of the room, but just to observe and to make sure that nothing had disturbed the office women's flow of conversation or meaning. She knew Bella and Jackie were at least two women there from the same circle that Cup had inhabited. Her mission was gathering steam as well as direction.

Chapter 5

1988

Crispy-cold and clear, the winter night held the moon captive to appear as a giant snowball in the late January sky. Byron pulled the collar higher and closer to his ears as he walked to his car. *There had to be a better avenue to greater financial success, there has to be a better way to do this,* Byron thought and startled himself when he heard his own voice say, "a better way to do this." He almost ran when he saw his car and quickly jumped in and drove off much faster than he should have. He looked around to make sure no one was close enough to hear him. While driving home he made a quick turn around so he could run into the liquor store. He waved at his old buddy who knew the exact bottle to hand him.

"Hey man, how you…?" the words were left hanging as the clerk saw another customer walk in.

"Doing fine," Byron answered. "Just wanted to stop in to pick up a little somp'em, to take the chill out of my bones."

"No, wait man." Plato, the storeowner said.

He stopped and turned around as his head felt like an ocean wave went through it and a cramp on his left side caused him to hang onto the open door.

"You okay man?" Plato asked as he leaped around the counter to help.

Byron hadn't felt well all that day so maybe his mind was playing tricks on him.

"Aw, yeah I just think I'm coming down with the flu or something. I got this bad headache and sometimes my head feels like I'm on board ship back in the Navy. This just started lately." Byron answered.

"You want to come on back in here in the room down the hall here and sit down for a while; it's warm? Man, you know we go way back and I don't want to see you out there sick, driving by yourself. You can wait a while and I can take you home or do you want me to call someone?"

Byron thought about that for a minute and realized he had no one but his folks to call on and he didn't want to worry them.

Funny how when we're out there, partying, clubbing and being with the in crowd, anyone could be your next call but then when it's something more you need, that's not a part of the fun and games, there may be few to no one out there to lend a hand. Yes, they say, just let me know and I'll be there… but actually you see who's there and it may be no one.

"Naw, I'm okay. I just need to get home, turn up the heat and get in the bed after I finish my nice hot toddy here."

"Uh oh, sounds like a love Jones to me, who's the woman that's got your nose open now?" laughed Plato.

"No, man, you got that wrong. I think I just might be better off by myself, at least for a while, Plato." Byron continued, "The womenfolk I meet out there are absolutely out of the last fragment of their minds, and I don't need no help on Crazy."

"So you and what's her face broke up, huh?' Plato asked.

"Yeah, I need to fly solo for a time. Ain't no one out there that ain't just looking for someone to be a Sugar daddy—and that's not who I am."

"I know exactly what you're talking 'bout man." Cush called out from the back of the line. "The women I meet are either too young, too old; too little, too big; too educated, too stupid; too 'real'; or phony as hell; can't cook, don't cook or don't want to know how to cook; got too many kids all ready, don't want their kids or want to make me their baby-daddy. That truly ain't me." Cush said.

Several men in the store chimed in, "You got that right, Bro' man."

"Yeah, you right. Some of those women out there are kinda hard to deal wit. So you doing some window shoppin' for a while, huh?" Plato said.

"Man you're going to go find that woman you been looking for and when you find her she's going to have you crying in the corner like a rat eating raw onions." Cush hollered out after he slammed his money on the counter for his usual half pint of gin.

The whole store laughed. "I ain't heard that in a while, you better go on and get that girl, she'll keep you warm and out o' that bottle." Grip, yelled out.

"Naw, man, now you the one's crazy. I'm going home and get rid of whatever this flu bug is that I got. Let me get out of here and pick up something to eat that's all ready cooked and work on this headache," said Byron as he put the money on the counter and grabbed his purchase.

"See y'all on the next go 'round." Byron said as he started out the store.

"Take it slow, man." Plato said as Byron left the store.

"You too," Byron called out as he walked out toward his car. He sat there for a minute or two while the car warmed. He could barely see the road in front of him. After turning the lights on he realized it was raining again and when he started the windshield wipers his vision was now fuzzy, too.

"Damn, what's the matter now?" he rubbed his eyes and checked them in the rear view mirror. *I better get me some glasses.*

Byron began to remember the time he had gone up to Olympia for his business license renewal. The time also came to mind when he had pissed off a lot of folks because he quit what the folks said was a 'good job' and was now close to broke. He'd had a lot of venture capital problems. He'd taken the train up there because there was supposed to be a storm coming that's why he didn't want to drive. He knew all would gel for him after the improvements he'd instituted to his balance sheet and the store operations. He'd sat there during the train ride looking out the window. The snow-dusted mountains captured his attention while the throws of his past flashed behind his eyelids like a movie projector stored in his head.

At that time his past was as gigantic to him as the mountains he saw while the rhythm of the train kept clicking into his thoughts. He had not been 'a good boy' was what his mother told him most of the time. Pictures came to his mind about his business prospects, as the mountains seemed to be blanketed by lime green velvet with sprinkles of white. The visions came faster and faster while his mood went from guilt to anger to sorrow to relief. The visions showed him what happy looked like, too.

He had thrown his hands in the air. *What else could I do about anything?* He then realized that other passengers on this trip north from Vancouver surrounded him. He was so deep in thought that he talked to himself loud enough for others to hear him so he pretended to look for something and went into a deep stretch and a loud yawn.

He left the thoughts of the past when he saw he was in front of the Chicken Shack before he knew it. Byron drove through and smiled thinking of hot food and a little booze.

Byron finally got home from the liquor store and the Chicken Shack without incident. Shaking from the chills and ravenous for anything to put in his mouth to eat, he was dead-bone tired. He'd been losing weight and everything he ate ran right through him. *I'll call Dad in the morning.*

Byron ate, drank and listened to music, then drank some more. Feeling cold again he turned up the heat even higher and lay down in his crumpled unmade bed. Restless sleep was his reward for the food and drink. He woke up several times for the bathroom and each time he felt worse.

The next morning he had to call someone, "Hey Dad, what cha doing?" Byron spoke into the phone that he couldn't even see.

"I'm just getting ready to go to the store," his father answered. "What you doing home this time of day? You sound like you got a cold or something?"

"Yeah, I think I might have the flu, I was just gonna ask you or Mama what you all think I should take for it? This headache is about to kill me."

"Hold on man, let me go ask your Mama what she thinks and I'll run by and drop it off. You need anything else, I mean did you eat all ready?"

"Naw I just woke up. I ate last night."

"I'll bring you some food, too. Your Mama will be in the kitchen trying to make you one of her concoctions. You been to the doctor?"

"No, I thought it would have stopped by now." Byron said. "Do you still have the key to my place?"

"I think so, I'll look," his father answered, checking his pockets for keys.

"Well, just in case you can't find it I'm gonna unlock the side door so if I fall back to sleep before you get here, you can just come on in."

"Son, you sound pretty serious. We'll be there within the hour."

He hung up and hoped that his Mother would come, too. Then Byron drifted back into an unshakable sound sleep.

When Byron woke up he heard the beep of what sounded like a squeaky moving rhythmic rocking chair. He was not in his own bed or even at home. The beeping he heard was a monitor attached to him.

"He's awake now," his mother announced in a whisper. And someone left the room as the spirit of another followed. Kaye was there too, watching over Byron.

Chapter 6

The fog, as thick as a Jack-the-Ripper-London-night, rolled over Maple's car like an ocean wave. Maple stayed her course trying to get home after a bullshit workday at her regular job and four more hours at her part-time job. Maple could barely see two feet in front of her windshield. She kept switching the headlights from high to low beams, trying to find which helped the best.

Not knowing what to expect from Omar, Maple didn't want to go home. But she had to check on the kids. The children loved him, with his comedic behavior and made up words and such. She had to make sure the children had their dinner. She had prepared a meal the night before. All Omar had to do was pop it in the microwave for a few minutes. But she always questioned whether he would or not. On more than one occasion, he'd seen the meals frozen, wrapped up and labeled and he'd thrown them in the garbage. So now she only prepared no more than two meals at a time. *Would this night be any different?*

Maple began to watch everything that went out of or came into the house. Money was sometimes missing and other things, too. So she kept a tight watch on everything.

Her camera from work, some of her embroidery projects, her paintings and her grandmother's gifts had all been missing at some point and some things had mysteriously reappeared. A small piece of a tag, like from a pawnshop was on one of her pieces of jewelry. Because of those incidents she now hid things that were precious to her.

Omar drank more and more beer and shaved and bathed less and less. She noticed him missing work and not taking care of a lot he had cared about before.

Maple noticed some strange accounts when they were closing a refinance loan on the house and a bill being paid off from a store she knew nothing about. It was for over $20,000 to a store and credit card where she never shopped and when she questioned it, he told her it was just for bills from 'his' credit card. He was not being open and honest especially about money. His philosophy was that he could do whatever he wanted with what he made. So she opened her own accounts at different banks.

In a sense she had a fairy tale-image in her heart and mind about what a true marriage relationship looked like. Everyday was magical and there would be challenges and disappointments but at the end of each day she saw that they would live happily ever after. So she sucked in her hurt, disbelief, and uncertainty, even fear and allowed her reality to be dictated by a fantasy.

This reality denial created a revolving door of disillusion and emotional pain because some people, maybe most people, are theoretically and naturally dishonest manipulators. She had once believed that people who said they were Christian and recited the words of the Bible could be trusted because she had thought they were true honest believers. Now she realized that like most everybody else, some who said they were Christian couldn't be trusted either. She began to see they were just as dishonest, greedy and manipulative backbiters as those un-churched. Those un-churched folks, pagans her mother used to call them, who said who they were and how they felt, constantly, right to your face, were a little more honest about their true intentions.

She continued to believe in the words of the Bible and its direct conversation to her while at the same time became more and more skeptical of people she saw around her. She lost a lot of 'so called' friends by staying away from people but felt protected by the shell she created around her heart, mind, body and interactions.

The comfort of being home no longer matched her dreams so she dreaded the time she left work for home. When it was time to return to work even though it too was toxic, she felt protected. At times she felt she had landed in a snake pit and could see no way out. Answers to prayers were silent. Still she prayed and hoped for and had faith that her life and the lives of her children would be better. Maple even re-examined some of her choices and wished she could reverse them, but knew better. She could only reverse the effects her choices had on her. She was not only entrenched in a life that included people who depended on her, but also people who were envious and wanted to see her destroyed. Maple felt trapped.

Chapter 7

Now driving close to her neighborhood, Maple realized she had forgotten to pick up milk, bread and coffee from the grocery so she turned the car around in the middle of the street to go back. She fastidiously checked the prices and weights of her purchases and after paying for the groceries she spotted the new coffee shop at the other end of the store. *I need to just sit for a moment. I'd better get a cup of coffee, too.* She picked up a cup and found a table in the corner near the window and sat, revisiting the thoughts of her day.

Nice things usually come sweetly when you least expect them. And it's doubly nice when you desperately need to have something good and wonderful in your life.

"Anybody sitting here?" she heard a voice behind her, which zapped her out of a quiet distance. She blinked and took a deep breath to break back into reality.

"Oh hi," she said to the almost stranger.

"Fancy meeting you here," said the guy she'd seen in the office hallway almost a year or so before. "My name is Byron. Remember?"

Stunned by the sudden interruption, she pulled her purse and grocery bag closer and committed a hesitant smile. He moved closer, directly across the table from her, flashing a let-me-talk-to-you, smile.

Hannah, with Shadow in her arms and Brid on her shoulder, watched the couple from outside the window. Maple and Byron didn't notice that there were several observers from another time watching them.

Not waiting for any response Byron rattled off a barrage of questions. "How are you? You remember me from the store next door to your office don't you? Mind if I join you, just for a minute?"

"Uhm, ah, oh yeah, please sit down." she said as she backed a little bit away from the table.

"I hope I'm not disturbing you. You looked like you were in deep concentration and nothing could be that serious," he said through a genuine hearty smile, then laughed.

She softened, "Oh … I'm … ah … this was a particularly trying day today. Please, have a seat."

"Do ya often stop for a cup of coffee at the grocery store?" he didn't wait for her to answer, "No. I'm just kidding," Byron smiled.

"You sure it's ok," he said. "Your husband won't come around the bend and knock my head off?"

"Oh no, you're fine."

He sat and stared at her eyes.

She broke the silence, "How's everything going at your Snack shop?"

"It's doing okay, ahm… always trying to drum up more customers. Paying customers that is," he pointed his left hand toward her and said. "You'd be surprised to know how many people come in for a meal with no money. I can't believe parents don't feed their kids before sending them to school. What's happening to this place in our society as a whole?" he said looking around the coffee area of the store and shaking his head.

"People are just overworked and frazzled, it feels like we are overwhelmed with so much. I don't mean we should stick our heads in the sand but there is a lot going on everywhere.

"I haven't seen you around lately, is someone else managing your store?"

While his eyes traced the marks on the table between them until he saw her fingertips and wanted to touch them.

"Yeah, I've been out sick for a little while," he said.

"Oh, I'm sorry to hear that," Maple said. "You're back in the rat race I see, huh?" she said with a smile.

"Yeah, it was a bit rough but my folks took over for me while I was recuperating," he said. "There's nothing like a good family."

She wanted to ask more but returned to his comment about how parents sent their kids off to school.

"There are so many people either out of work or working two and three jobs just to keep the rent paid. Sometimes there's very little left for food," Maple said.

"Well you know the economy is messed up because of the so called leaders—lining their pockets and making sure their buddies get bank, too," he continued, answering his own question. "And there always used to be some sort of program open for people who fell on hard times. People didn't have to stay that way. You know what I mean, don't you?"

She waited a minute in her thoughts then they both realized that they were staring at the same spot in the middle of the table. Maple jerked herself up and looked in his eyes just as he looked in hers.

"Yes, yes," replied Maple. "That's what our program is all about; helping people get new skills so that they can enter or return to the labor force. But we have to get them off drugs and other substances first. Well many of them—so we try to help them identify their goals and purpose. Some people are stuck in an ugly or angry space and they don't know how to get themselves out. Then there are those that have had catastrophic illnesses from accidents or worse. Especially women who have lost their husbands or husbands become disabled. Many times the woman has never worked outside the home," said Maple

"Yes I can see that would be a major problem but then, too, some people don't want to get out of their own way because they fear change." Byron said in a deep hard sigh. Maple noticed his chest puff up and his shoulders rise as if he were holding some great profound statement and he quickly backed down.

"Everything is changing so fast with these computers and all—it seems like now so much is operated with computers. Lots of people are getting knocked out of jobs," he said.

"But on the other hand you have to consider that there are fewer people entering the workforce now because everything was built up for all the baby boomers and now this new generation of workers is not enough," Maple said. "Or they are not training for the new employment trends."

"What do you mean not enough?" he asked.

"Baby boomers didn't produce as many babies as the generations before, so now there are about ten percent fewer job seekers as there are jobs to be filled. The other thing is that people haven't been keeping up with training for the skill sets needed and on top of that there's no formal succession planning by those now leaving the workplace to retire," Maple added. "Oh I'm sorry, I should stop talking shop everywhere I go."

"Wow! How do you know all that?" he asked

"I keep up with the trends and patterns that contribute to workers, it's my job, remember?"

"So that's what your program does then, get people ready for new jobs?" he asked, "While the high school kids are next door.

"Yes, and its too bad more people don't try to learn new things."

"I think the young people are impressed by the adults going to school. I've even seen some of the men getting help from the boys who know computer techniques and they are teaching them how to play games. To some of those boys these adults are the only father figures they have." That struck a hard nerve in Byron's heart and he immediately thought of his own children. Their mother moved out of state but they kept in touch with his parents.

Maple cleared her throat.

Byron quickly looked up and moved about in his seat and asked, "What about those people who are glad with what they do? I mean should they just turn away and go for new skills?" Byron wanted to know.

"We should all constantly be on a quest for knowledge. Even though folks are satisfied with where they are, they have to keep learning because things don't stay the same around them. Everything is in a state of some kind of change or movement, you see," she told him, "everything continues to evolve. I read someplace that even if you are in the right lane you still get trampled over if you aren't moving forward fast enough."

"But with the computers taking so many jobs and able to retain so much information, I do believe we are going to have some sort of insurgent underground group that will act as the Luddites in London regarding the Industrial Revolution. In this Information age we haven't quite figured out yet what and who will be left out."

"How do you think that's going to happen? These computer Gurus have this new information language wrapped up so tight only the smartest of smarts are going to be able to crack the codes and make a difference. Then we will have another elite group," he said.

"I believe it will be more sinister than that." Maple said with a wrinkle straight down the middle of her forehead.

"What I think is that greed is going to continue to rear it's ugly head and folks are going to find out how to take other people's information right off those computers and snatch their information right out of the air and make it so people can't get back to their own documents. You see, I hear so many people in businesses talk about paperless offices, and when their information vanishes into those little boxes, folks' work will be lost. During a recent meeting I overheard conversations in the corner about Y2K."

"What's that?" Byron's wrinkled brow came dangerously close to Maple's.

"From what I understand, it's that when December 31, 1999 ticks over to the year 2000, the computers are going to lose all the information they have amassed because there was nothing programmed into the binary code and time frame, for the machines to know what the next year is supposed to be. From what the experts are saying, computers control so many automatic functions now that they could take over and planes could drop from the sky and trains would stop working and high rise buildings would have no heat or elevator service and much, much more."

"Those are just scare-tactics, don't you think? He asked so she would keep talking.

Maple started to take a sip of coffee but it was iced cold when she brought it to her lips.

"Ohmagoodness!" she exclaimed. "Look at the time. We've been here talking over an hour. I have to get home to make dinner for my family."

"I'm sorry if I kept you, but it is so fascinating talking with you, you know?" he said helping with her chair.

She gathered up her bags and purse and began to clear her cup and table trash when he said. "Let me take care of that, you go on now. I've kept you long enough."

"Thanks, I really have to run. Bye now."

She left without hearing his goodbye. Maple stopped for a second and her heart told her 'what a nice man.' She left the store

Kaye stood right behind Hannah, Brid and Shadow, recognizing that Maple's tide was about to turn. She was growing, becoming stronger and there would be new challenges having to do with Omar. Her protector would have to come in some unlikely form.

Chapter 8

Maple entered the house through the front door with pleasant song bites going through her head. Omar saw a cheery spirit in her expression that angered him so he greeted her with, "What took you so long?"

"Mom's home, what'd you bring me?" Omar Jr., and Blossom now ages twelve and fourteen years old peeked in the bags of food.

"You brought us chicken already done, didn't you?" Omar Jr., said. "Did you get desert, too?"

"Shh. It was supposed to be a surprise, yes, I got ice cream."

"The kind I like with nuts in it?" Omar Jr. asked.

"Yep, the kind you like, go wash your hands."

"Ma, I don't want chicken, I wanted a hamburger and fries." Blossom whined.

"Well since you didn't give me your order I got what I thought would be best all around, so there."

"Why you so late?" Omar asked again.

"I left work a little late and stopped at the store. While I was there I ran into folks I know and started talking and decided not to try to cook anything so I bought take out at the Chicken Shack. Do you have a problem with that? Why didn't you go out and pick up something or cook something?

You know the kids need to eat just like you and I do." she threw back at him.

"Naw, I was just wondering. I needed to eat," he stood there and stared at her long after she turned away to set the table. The entire structure of the house felt her jaws tighten and her teeth grind as her nostrils drew in the air that allowed her to say nothing else. There were no other words between them the rest of the evening.

In fact, for better than three months or so, very little had been said. It was like each opportunity for Omar Sr., to strike out at Maple, to her relief there was some sort of interruption that diverted his attention.

Maple spent more time away from home in the evenings, working on committees and other activities with the children. She spent many evenings at the library helping the children get homework done. She volunteered to help older folks learn to read, when she discovered a literacy program there, too. She talked some with the people who were working on getting U.S. Citizenship and found out how good it felt when she learned they were successful. She and the children attended many of the swearing-in programs and their celebrations afterward. Maple noticed her children learning words in languages other than English and it felt good that they showed an interest in understanding differences.

Omar Sr., was also gone every evening now and even though no additional money was coming into the house he said he found a part-time evening job. She didn't ask any questions because it felt good that he was elsewhere.

For that short season there was very little yelling and no fighting. He hadn't called her a name or tried to bash her face in for quite a while so she stayed quiet. Then from out of nowhere Omar walked into the laundry room while Maple was separating clothes by color and tagging those clothes that needed mending. One load was in the washer and another load just started in the dryer when Omar began his tirade.

"Oh you're not running all over town today, huh?" he asked.

"What do you mean?" she said looking back over her shoulder at him.

"You're usually gone or about to leave by now," he growled. "I thought you'd have somebody to see or meet like you always do."

"I'm doing the family laundry as you can see," she said. "Do you want to do this instead of me?"

"How come you're washing all of your things first and not any of mine?" he yelled.

The wind-gates were opening and Maple tried to find the most reasonable response that would calm the tension erupting like an earthquake.

"Because I have to wash lighter clothes first and that includes the kids clothes, sheets and towels, so that color and darker colored fabric's residue won't make the light clothes look dingy or put steaks in them, why?"

All of a sudden he began to rant and shout and stomp through the house like he was ready to attack. He circled around her like a fighting bull in a ring.

He began to yell even louder. The children could be heard scampering for their rooms. "Cause you better take that crap out of the machine; I want all my clothes washed first, you hear me?" She didn't say anything but took the soaking wet clothes out of the machine and carried them to another tub.

"Hey, you come on back here and wash these damned clothes like I told you to do. You think you are so damned smart cause you got a job and can buy this crap you wear and …that over there ……"

Maple interrupted with "Wash your own damn clothes." as she walked away. When she went to put the soap and bleach away she didn't notice him right inside the door. Out of nowhere came the blow to the back of her head. She fell to the floor, stunned from being struck, she felt herself being pulled up by her hair to more yelling – most of the words weren't even clear.

She felt dizzy and smelled his beer-stank-breath when he threw her into the wall.

"Now get started working on my clothes right now, like I told you." He ordered as she held onto the side of the washer and picked up the pile of his clothes and threw them in the washer. Turning on the machine, she leaned over the washer, and stayed there while the hot water poured in. *This is never going to happen to me again,* she thought. The hum from her throat glued her teeth together so she didn't speak. The drum in her chest gave her cause to methodically wash the clothes.

"You gonna go call the police? They won't find a mark on you, but on the other hand my face just got scratches all over the left side. Strange, isn't it?" he said while scratching up his own face. Her silence infuriated him. "So what you going to do about that?" he fired at her.

"You gonna leave and try to take my kids with you, huh?" Omar's glare demanded an answer. Since she responded with silence he continued to belt out more insults.

"Well I'll let them know you're sick with whatever it is and you won't be able to take care of them cause you can't take care of your damn self. Your ass is on the way to the graveyard anyway." he spewed.

More venom flew from the demon who stood before her, but she half heard his ranting and just continued to lean over the washer. The warmth and the slight vibrations, kind of soothed the aches in her body after being knocked to the floor and into the wall a number of times.

Her almost inaudible hum of 'Wade in the water,' kept her insides calm. Again she thought, how am I going to get away from him and keep the children with me and how do I keep him from killing me? He had already reminded her that anywhere she could go, he could go. Damn!

His rampage was coming back into her earshot… "Just

68

remember," he said, holding the collar of her blouse ready to deliver his well-rehearsed speech. "Wherever you can go, I can go. And you think you can keep my children? I'll make them hate you, when I'm finished. And you know what else? You just gonna be a lonely old ugly stupid broad, ugly and stupid 'cause ain't nobody ever going to want you when I get through with you. So live with that, you hear?" He grabbed her by the hair and growled showing his teeth like a rabid dog. "I know I don't want you. Look at you, and who the hell else will want to look at the likes' of yo crazy slow-poke ass?" He was finished for the moment.

Maple continued to remain silent and began to believe that it was some sort of curse from the devil that surrounded her and half heard him when in her own mind she planned her next move, which would turn out to be 'no move at all.' A song played in Maple's head that drowned his tirade to a trickle.

More than four years had gone by since the washing machine incident and Maple had recuperated from another operation, and was planning to go back to work.

Maple looked forward to seeing some of her co-workers and friends she met from other places she'd worked and volunteered. Everyone had been so nice and helpful, phone calls and cards and gifts of fruit and books. She thought at first it was just because they wanted to get in her business but she began to feel that perhaps their gestures were genuine.

Maple remembered that during her hospital stay her coffee drinking friend had come to see her almost everyday. He came to drop off little gifts and special food, and great conversation about everything under the sun, fun stuff, some good, and some bad or just plain old news. After she was released from the hospital he called to check if she had eaten or if she needed anything. She always said 'no' but he'd drop something off anyway, or send it by a courier to her home.

Time passed with no improvement in the relationship between Maple and Omar. The children were growing up even faster now. Blossom was away at college and Omar Jr., was involved in every single sport they let him play while finishing High School.

When Omar Sr., acted even more bizarre from time to time, Maple would offer to make him coffee or some other drink or soup or cereal. She had saved the Valium, Vicodin and codeine tablets from all her trips to doctors and the meds came in handy. She would always ask for more medications for pain that sometimes was not as severe as she explained and even sometimes when her body really did hurt like hell, she didn't take any meds at all. She saved them to quiet the pain she lived with.

She'd save a third or even up to half of all meds—she just wouldn't take them. No, Maple ground them up and added the powder to whatever she served him. It was never enough to harm him, but enough to make him stop the cruelty, to calm his vehemence of negative feeling of himself which was caused by, what she thought, his cowardice to face and address his own demons. *I know I can't change him but I can make myself safer if I can calm his ass down.*

Now that she had a potion, there were fewer and fewer of his outbursts of aggressive-madness. Each time Omar would go out of town to visit his family or other friends, so he said, or even when he just went 'fishing,' she knew to be ready with a powdered drink the second he returned home. Her routine would last for several days, this time. She could see in his face, at first glare, that he had worked himself into a frenzy to get rid of whatever frustration he'd experienced while he was away. He planned to take it out on her.

Maple said as she rinsed the coffee pot and said she was going to have a cup of tea. "The kids asked about you everyday and I thought you weren't coming home until tomorrow so they will really be happy to see you."

"No, I want some coffee," he told her.

"Okay, I'll have a cup, too," she offered as she reached to the back of the cabinet for his special cup. A nice stiff dose of calm-his-ass-down powder was placed in the cup early that morning when she had a feeling he'd be back today.

She poured his coffee and asked if he still wanted cream and sugar. Maple set it down in front of him before pouring a cup for herself. She asked about his trip and told him how the kids had done the whole time he was away. It seemed he always wanted a day-by-day report but he began to nod so she asked if he wanted to go sit in the den in his chair and watch the news.

Omar didn't notice anything different he just went on and hollered back at her, "Give me another cup, ok?"

"Sure, I'll bring it right in."

Maple freshened his cup, dropped it off in the den and went back to the kitchen to start dinner. She didn't hear a peep out of him until the children came home. By then he was too sleepy to talk with them so he went to bed.

Chapter 9

Maple stared out the living room front window and smiled to herself thinking one more to finish High School and turn 18 years old. She could get away from Omar for good. A long sigh followed her thought. Her husband, Omar, would not then be able to just show up and find her. Find her like the time she grabbed her very small children up one morning after weeks of looking for an apartment, finding one and then taking the things she'd need to her new place little by little and she even filed a restraining order.

One day after a picnic at the park she took the kids home just as the sun was setting. Maple got the kids to bed and thought she heard something move in another room and dismissed it thinking 'I must be hearing things'. When she walked into the living room he grabbed her around the neck and said, "Who in the hell do you think you are; moving out on me and taking my kids?" he growled. "I told you, you aren't going anyplace until I say so. These are my kids and you got them out who knows where. You can't keep me from my kids." His loud whisper spoke to her soul and chilled her very being.

Then she felt the grip on her throat tighter. She began to fight to free her neck when she felt a blow across her face. She later found out that the court had given him her new address on the restraining order.

Maple brought her mind back to the moment, and continued to smile and know that the kids wouldn't have to see his gutter behavior unless they chose to go where he lived. But the best thing is she wouldn't have to take anymore of his cruelty.

It was like the time he threw her onto the front porch barefoot with only a slip on and it was twenty-five degrees outside and ice was on the ground. Omar didn't care. He just grinned, when he finally let her back in the house and puffed his chest to show how he felt about his benevolent act of rescuing her, even though his act created the danger. Every inch of her body ached from cold. Frostbite had even started in her bare feet.

Maple reluctantly opened up to a few of her friends about the craziness in her life, but she felt no one really believed her. She remembered what he'd said to her that 'wherever she could go he could go, too.' He was so charming to everyone else and extremely accommodating to her, in front of company. But all things changed when they were alone.

Months passed quickly and she knew that she'd be out of the hellhole with no strings tied to him in the not-too-distant future. She saved money and began taking her really valuable and special things to storage. Otherwise, she knew he'd destroy them or give them away.

Omar was changing. He was getting more and more weird talking about how women tricked men into doing what they wanted by taking worn underwear of theirs and using it to dust the house then burying the garments somewhere in the house in flower pots or in the yard outside certain doors.

He got that from his crazy mama, Maple thought. So she didn't think it strange when he stopped wearing underwear and she began noticing that some of hers was missing from the dirty clothes hamper at each washday. She laughed each month or so when she bought more new undies while noticing her old pieces were disappearing. *I guess he believes his relatives' folk-lore,* she smiled and kept going.

Her coffee friend, Byron, was usually someplace near, at least by phone, when she needed an ear to talk to. But sometimes he'd disappear for months at a time and no number, home or work was available. When he'd surface, Maple teased him about his finding a girlfriend. But this day it had been a long while and they backed into each other looking at coffee creamer to purchase when they each said "excuse me" then turned around and recognized each other. They embraced in the biggest hug anyone could imagine, and then quickly moved away from each other when they realized other shoppers were staring at them. That magical moment's embrace suspended them in a time they could each go back to whenever they needed the bliss of that moment again. They talked for a few minutes and exchanged phone numbers and that was that.

Maple realized that, although she was delighted to see Byron, he really didn't look well. I'll call him in a few days, she thought, but so much was going in her life that calling Byron slipped right out of her radar.

"Omar, did you move the sewing kit and boxes of cookies and things I just brought in? Where did you put them?" Maple looked down and saw her things in the garbage. "What are you doing?" Maple asked. "That's my stuff, it's not bothering you."

Maple saw the monster develop in Omar right before her eyes. His cheeks blew up like a blowfish; his eyes grew big and bulged, in their sockets, the veins to his head looked like electrical cords running up through his neck.

Before Maple got a chance to make a call she found her-self in the fight of her life with Omar. She looked for the box and bag of items she'd just bought and laid them on the kitch-en counter. Maple turned away when he grabbed her around the throat. Her head barely grazed the edge of the table when she felt like a hand had been there and held her head so she quickly tried to run to safety, slipping and sliding all the way into her room and still feeling help from out of nowhere.

Then the monster, Omar, grabbed and twisted her arms while forcing her into the stairwell. Omar let go and then pushed her down the stairs. She slid down the stairs as if she were on a schoolyard playground slide. Again, she felt as though a hand stretched out to carry her the entire stairway flight. There was no thud when she landed on the floor, but a springboard that lifted her past the areas where she left her purse and her phone. They were magically lying right on top of the hall table.

This time she left the house and called the police, the first time she'd ever done that right after one of his tirades. It was so humiliating and she was totally drained of feeling, of reason or anything. When the police arrived Omar was at the house and they took him away.

Maple followed all the steps the domestic violence advo-cate told her she could take. He finally was completely gone. He was forbidden to come anywhere near her. He tried and she warned that she would report him if he ever bothered her again.

He hung around the grocery store she frequented and other places she'd be and when she saw him, she'd walk away and pretend he wasn't there, even though he looked straight into her eyes. That stare no longer had a sting.

Her close friends, the ones who truly cared about her, came from out of town and packed up all his stuff. They helped her get things out of the house and change the locks. They thought of things she needed to do that she had never imagined to be important before. Her whole life changed for the better. She kept remembering the hand that held her in those split second encounters at the time of her greatest fear on the stairway.

People gave her all kinds of messages from him and she'd comment, "That's interesting, thanks for telling me." She knew they just wanted a reaction from her that they could spread around.

The moon's glow graced the night sky and Maple breathed a sigh of relief. Now she could really begin to uncover those wild dreams from childhood that kept nipping at her memory. They weren't that far fetched, after all. She wanted to travel and see other cultures and go to magical places like the Eiffel Tower, the Vatican and the pyramids.

Maple wrote out a travel schedule that went 25 years out. So that meant every two years, she planned to go to three places either with a friend, a group or by herself. She was just beginning to realize her value, and a commitment to take care of herself and protect her spirit and soul as well as her body.

She filled her home with colorful pictures and beautiful music. Maple smiled at her reflection and said to her image, "I am open and receptive to all good." She said this to herself each morning in the bathroom mirror. She'd read that in Louise Hay's book You Can Heal Your Life.

But at night when it was time to rest she kept seeing strange images under her eyelids. The dreams she sometimes dreamed caused her, to some extent, to be afraid to close her eyes and sleep.

Chapter 10

Maple continued to build the life she wanted. She met new people, saw new places, found new interests, discovered adventures through world travel and flew her kite much more. Her main priority was safety. She didn't feel safe because Omar still lurked in her vicinity. She made decisions based on her wants and needs, even her wildest dreams.

Months, then years quickly passed. Maple watched her daughter, Blossom, transition into beautiful womanhood that her daughter had designed for herself. Maple was delighted and laughed and cried at Blossom's graduation, then wedding. Her daughter's husband, Jeremy, was a kind, gentle man who loved Blossom completely. Maple eagerly waited for grandbabies to come.

Maple stood proudly in applause when Omar Jr. walked across the stage to receive his University degree. What a great day it was for Maple because she believed her son would be successful with his fierce drive to be the best. He landed a great corporate job, the same place he had interned, but Maple didn't know exactly what it was he did. She believed it had something to do with computers. He earned enough money now to purchase his own condo and take care of himself.

All was pretty much right in her world. Work was okay and she was active in community events and volunteered to teach adults to read. From time to time she heard from Byron, her coffee friend, and they went to the movies, and theater performances and dinner. His business was going really well, and he spent a lot of time traveling the country, making deals, distributing products and keeping his stores going.

Maple followed her dreams to travel and found places and people she adored and appreciated the similarities as well as differences in everything. She noted the differences in the air, smell and landscape of those places she discovered. She loved Rome, Paris, Brussels and Madrid. Maple would often take side trips to smaller communities outside the major cities and once she saw a man in Dinont, Belgium, who looked enough like Byron that she could almost swear it was he.

The pictures of troubled people under her eyelids appeared again and Maple felt that even though everything was going well, she was standing on a cliff's edge. *Something is about to happen that is either going to push me over the edge, give me wings or test my strength.* Maple went home from her Brussels vacation not only invigorated by all the sights she'd seen but also uneasy about a heightened fear of some impending fright. It was something like walking through a doorway and a spider drops before your eyes. That happened to Maple once while in grade school. She told a friend about the incident that caused her to almost wet her pants. After that some of the other kids scared her with toy spiders and other bugs, so she stopped talking about her fears with anyone.

A few weeks after she returned one late spring like afternoon the phone rang and it was her coffee friend, Byron. They laughed and talked for quite a while when she said, "Where the hell have you been? I've searched everywhere. I thought you had left town," she said, in a sarcastic tone, but she was really glad to hear his voice.

"Oh, I've been around, just a bit under the weather though."

"What's wrong? Did some hoochy mama walk into your life and rip up your feelings and finances again?" They both laughed and mentioned a couple of Byron's other escapades.

"No, nothing like that. Thanks for reminding me," he answered, with a chuckle stuck in his throat he couldn't hide.

"Do you need anything? Why didn't you get in touch with me before now? I see that you still have phone skills," she said and they both laughed again.

"You say the damnedest things," he threw right back at her. "That's a lot to answer all at one time, but first I want to know how you're doing?" he asked.

"I'm fine. Just straightening out all my financial stuff and looking out for the kids as they begin their careers and lives on their own and... I just got back from Belgium. It is a beautiful country." Maple's voice went to a happy squeal.

"What are your doctors saying? I want to know about how you are feeling," he asked.

"They say I'm doing better. You know stress has a way of making health issues worse. So now that Omar, my EX, and I put great emphasis on EX is out of my world, I'm feeling better health-wise. Now what about you? What's going on in your life? You must have someone new in your life, in your atmosphere on the planet, huh?"

"No, nothing like that" he answered softly. "Like I said, I've been a little under the weather."

"A little under the weather. What does that mean? Can I bring you something? Chicken soup? Are you still living back at your folks' old place?" she asked.

"I'm not at home, I'm being cared for and I don't think there's anything anyone can do."

"What do you mean 'cared for'? What's going on? What's wrong? Where are you?" Maple searched her mind for the right words to exit her face and asked as she frantically looked for a pencil to take down any information.

"I'm in the hospital."

She took a deep breath, "What hospital... what for?" she waited for what seemed like forever, before she heard,

"Saint Anthony Hospital," he answered.

"I'll be right there. Is that ok? What's your room number?"

"Yes, yes. I'd like to see you. I'm having an operation tomorrow."

"Tomorrow!" she screeched, trying not to.

"Room 522," he said just before he dropped the phone.

"I'll be there in a few minutes," she hung up the phone as she put on her shoes and grabbed her purse.

Before walking out her door she stopped for a minute to say, "Dear Lord, Jesus, my friend, Byron, says he is sick, Lord. Please heal his body and his spirit, in the name of Jesus." That's all she knew to ask for. Maple ran out the door and quickly jumped in her car.

Before she knew it she was parked and running through the hall to his room. Just before walking into the room she paused, took a breath and said, "Dear God, make my friend okay. Bless him Lord. Please heal his body from whatever it is he's not telling me, Lord, but you know. In the name of Jesus I pray that you heal him to wholeness."

Maple entered the room and saw her friend surrounded by machines and tubes coming from every part of his body. She had no idea from their conversation a few minutes ago, that anything like this was going on in his life. *He sounded good; or was that wishful thinking?*

She put her hand to her stomach just to assure herself that she was taking a breath. "Hi."

He opened his eyes and instantly produced his ever familiar, giant sized smile. "Hey, you. You made it. How many small animals, curbs and bushes did you hit?"

"You know I had to come and see about my number one coffee Bud. I ran over all of them and a couple people jumped out of my way, too. Damn, I just missed them."

They both laughed.

"Can I give you a hug or would I break you?"

"Sure," quickly came from his lips and he reached both

82

arms, attached to plastic tubes, out to her. Byron and Maple just stayed in the hug, neither of them said a word but consoled each other being together in this 'why didn't you tell me, why weren't you here so I could help you,' kind of hug.

Maple moved away saying, "I brought you some cashews cause I know you like them and they've been in my cabinet, hermetically sealed since the last time I saw you. Want some now?"

He shook his head, and just stared at her eyes. She took his hand and he lightly held onto hers.

Again trying to find the right words she broke the silence with, "I remember how great you made me feel the times you visited me when I was in the hospital. I'll never forget that time I had pneumonia after surgery and they made me sit up and take deep breaths into that plastic thingy even though it hurt like hell. I saw you back into the wall and you looked terrified."

"I was," he said. "I never wanted to see you in any kind of pain."

"Just like I don't want you to be in any kind of pain. Are you hurting now?" she asked.

"Naw, they keep me pretty well sedated. You know they got some real good drugs here."

They both laughed and Maple said, "We got to share them."

"I bet mine are better than yours," he said and wagged his head.

Laughing again, she said, "How long have you been in the hospital? What surgery are you having in the morning, AND why the hell didn't you tell me about this before now?" Maple's voice tone sharpened with each word.

"Slow down, slow down." he told her, half smiling.

"Oh I didn't mean to …" she began to apologize.

"Stop, Stop! I've been here for a while," he almost whispered.

"Why did you wait so long to call me? I never kept you waiting to know about me, did I? That is when I can find you," she laughed.

"No, so now you're going to jump on me about it?"

He said poking his lips down in a frown—then laughed.

"Yeah, well, of course not, it's just that you were always there for me. And I was always glad to see you. You would really pick up my spirits just walking into the room."

"That's what you just did for me," he smiled while saying it.

"I'm glad," Maple told him

"Now what about this surgery you're having? You don't have to tell me if you don't want to. But I'm going to stay as long as you let me."

"I'm very fortunate, I'm a … I'm having a transplant. A kidney transplant."

She moved her chair closer to his bedside.

"I'm so sorry, I didn't know," she said

"I know I didn't tell you or anyone, well, except my folks know."

"You found a donor so quickly?"

"Yes, it's a relative who is donating it."

She took in a deep breath and exhaled slowly, even though she wanted to ask more she tightened her lips and looked at the floor.

"After the surgery, what happens? I mean how can I help, you know, make things easier for you? Will you be going home or do you have to go to one of those rehab centers?"

"Probably I'll go to a center for a few weeks, then home."

"I'll be as close as any telephone, or right at your bedside, so let me know if you need anything or want me around to talk to or you can let me beat you at scrabble."

Maple took a breath but didn't want to stop talking, afraid that if she quit talking she'd burst out in tears. "Or I could just stay at your house a few days or even longer while you are recuperating, and make sure you get the proper food and get to the doctor and stuff," Maple said in a matter-of-fact as if she were rattling off an ordinary list of things to do.

"Naw, you would come in my house and start changing things around and then, I know you would try to take liberties when I needed a bath." He laughed through the whole comment.

"Now you know I wouldn't do that. I tell you all the time, 'I don't want to see your business. You got to keep that to yourself," she told him. "I just think that's on your crooked little mind, trying to get me in your room when I'm just going to cook and serve you food. Your boys can come over to help with bathing. But I might just pinch you a time or two, if I get an opportunity when you aren't looking." Smiles broke in both their faces as they saw each other's watery eyes. She held onto his left hand with both of hers.

"See, I knew all this time, you've been after my bod." he told her.

"You wish," she said just as the nurse came in and put something in his IV with a syringe. She must have hidden it behind her back because Maple didn't see it in the nurse's hand when she first entered the room.

"Ma'am, visiting hours are over," she said to Maple.

"Okay, I'll go."

"No. Can she stay till I go to sleep? She has to tell me a bedtime story first."

"That will be fine," the nurse said as she winked at Maple.

Maple stood up to put her jacket on and tidy up around his bed and the windowsill. He was almost asleep when she touched his hand as her gesture to bid him goodnight. When he spoke, it startled her.

"Can I hug you?" he said.

Maple bent down to touch his shoulders as he reached out to her. Their faces touched when he whispered a question in her ear, "Will I see you soon?"

"Of course I'll be back tomorrow. You behave yourself, ya hear me?" she said.

"By the way, if you could go anyplace and be anywhere, where would it be?" he asked.

"Anyplace?"

He nodded.

"A place with a warm sun near a waterfall with birds singing, walking on cool sand and your hand holding mine," she answered.

The smile lay across his face long after his drug-induced slumber began.

Maple gave another squeeze then patted his hand and kissed his forehead right above the distinctive mole over his right eyebrow. It was the eyebrow that Byron would raise or lower whenever he was either surprised or in deep thought.

"You forgot to tell me a bedtime story," he mumbled.

"Yeah, I know," she whispered. "That's for tomorrow, rest now," she said as she stood at the door for a minute before she turned the light out and slowly started the walk back through the hospital and to the car.

On her way out the nurse stopped her and said, "You must be Maple, the very person Byron's been waiting to see." The nurse reached out to shake her hand. "My name is Kaye."

They both nodded.

Kaye continued. "He kept saying he wanted to wait until he looked better so you wouldn't be shocked to see him. I dialed your number for him. I am so glad you were available to come here to see him. You made his day."

Maple nodded again with a half thank you smile and ran down the hall, out the door and to her car where she sat for a while then drove off and cried all the way home.

Chapter 11

Maple went to the hospital everyday after work to sit near Byron. Some days he was more lucid than others. Kaye came into the room on several occasions to comfort Maple and find out more about their friendship. Maple told Kaye that she thought of him as a dear friend, not a lover.

"Byron needs me to be beside him right now, he is like that person I wish I had grown up with, who lived next door. Someone who'd help me find tadpoles in the creek, or tell the guy that sits two rows in front of my desk that I liked him. But none of that ever happened between us. I only met Byron about ten or so years ago."

"A good friend?" Kaye asked.

"Yes, he is a true friend, someone with whom I could share secrets and heartaches. Also the kind of person who'd bring me food when family members including my spouse didn't think of making sure I ate for three or four days after a long hospital stay."

On this particular day while Maple and Kaye chatted when entering Byron's room he opened his eyes. Maple smiled at him and Kaye disappeared.

"How long you been here?" his gravely whisper broke the sudden sterile silence.

"Everyday for about a week."

"What'd you do that for?"

"I couldn't just let my best friend and partner in coffee crimes spend the day without someone to watch over him. I had to make sure you don't get into trouble or make sure nobody had an opportunity to take liberties with you."

"What kind of liberties you talking 'bout, girl?"

"Well you know those meds really knock your ass out and I've just seen all your business and your butt is kind of cute. I know the nurses have been pinching on your buns when they give you your shots—you probably don't even need all those shots. They just like feeling on you," said Maple.

Byron tried to laugh but instead he coughed with a grimace that took over the moment. Maple's eyes filled her whole face as she searched her mind for a way to help him. Then the moment left and he really laughed right out loud. It was only a second but she saw and heard it. *My friend is back.*

"Those are professionals and they are not paying any attention to my butt or any other part of me, except what they are supposed to be paying attention to. Now put that in your pipe."

"Well, I guess I've been told off?" Maple said giggling.

"Naw, naw, I'm just defending myself. You know, I've been thinking about you?"

And I've been dreaming about you too. Maple thought.

"Oh yeah? What did I do?" she asked.

Byron was fully awake now and even trying to rev up his macho image.

"Just being here," then he quickly changed the subject. "Hey, I picked up this CD a while ago before they put me in this hospital. I like the music a lot and I want you to tell me what you think of one of the songs. It means a lot to me. Will you do that? Listen to it, I mean," he said.

"Sure, where is it?" she asked.

"It's up in the cabinet over there, tell me what you think of the sixth song," he said. He tried to rise up quickly, and groaned. He lay back down and more or less said to himself,

"Yeah. Song number six."

"Look in the top pocket of my backpack. I stuck it in there with your name on the envelope. Okay? I want you to tell me what you think of the song. Yeah, song number six," he sort of said to himself for reassurance.

"Okay," she went to the cabinet, "Oh, here it is, hmmm it's brand new," she said and read all the names of the songs on the back.

"All I Am. What is it jazz, singing or instrumental?"

"I want you to tell me what you think when you listen to it. Okay?"

"Okay."

"All I Am. Hmmm, George Benson. I like him. Does he sing or just play guitar on this one?"

"He sings and plays. This song—it really speaks to me."

"I want you to tell me what you think when you listen to it. Okay?" He asked again.

"Sure, okay," Maple answered. She had lots of questions about why but left them unsaid.

"Will I see you tomorrow?" Byron looked intent about her answer.

"Of course you will, but not until late."

"But tomorrow is Saturday and I know you are not going to work on a Saturday, are you?" he asked.

"I know. I have to wash my clothes and pay bills before they start cutting off stuff at my house. Then too, I have to go to the store and pick up a few things."

"Like what do you need?" He sarcastically remarked and winked.

"Let me just start with … say, toilet paper, you know my kids come by and think they can just take anything they want—and they do, just like I'm the local neighborhood free store or something."

"You let them do that," he said as a matter of fact.

"Yeah, I know, but…"

He interrupted saying "You know I might leave here in a couple of days."

"Where you going?"

"To my brother's house I think. I really don't think his wife wants me there. It's a bitch getting sick like this. You know, I have insurance that pays for everything and I have my own house, but that's not enough when you're sick."

"Tell me about it. I don't know what I would have done without your help when—all the times I was so sick."

"I think the doctors will tell me if I have to go to one of those rehab centers while I get my strength back and see how the transplant works. I know they don't want me at home by myself."

"I can stay there with you if you want to go home, until you get back on your feet. You have an extra room for guests, don't you?"

"Now, see. I told you, you just want to take advantage of my body, while you help me bathe and everything," he said laughing.

"'Now, see.' Maple mockingly repeated. "You didn't even have to go there, did you? You cut that out. Make believe I never said that. But you know I'd help if you want me to."

"I know," he said almost in an apology giving her a puppy-dog-eyes stare.

There was silence as they both stared into space at the same spot in the air.

Maple broke the silence, "How does it feel, I mean with somebody else's parts in your body? I mean can you tell it's... not, yours yet?

"Right now it hurts like hell."

"Should I call the nurse?"

"NO!" looking frightened he almost shouted the word.

Chapter 12

Maple drove up in front of her home, and checked to make sure the same lights were on that she'd left burning. She surveyed the whole area until it felt comfortable stepping out of her car. With house keys in hand, a raced to the front door and almost in a perfect dance step she unlocked her doors completing a full circle. Then she continued to turn as she entered the house and locked herself in. She stood there listening for quiet.

Her dreams that night were filled with Byron in conversations about and in exotic locations all over the world. They were in places she had never heard of, beautiful, wonderful, glorious places and scary ones, too.

The next morning, she noticed that the day didn't look too bad. The sun was shining and it wasn't supposed to be because the news mentioned that there would be rain all day. After completing all her errands and while on her way home, she noticed smoky looking clouds above. They were see-through. Uneven sunlight peeked from behind them staring down on her. For a second she felt she'd been floating. Maple checked her watch and saw that an hour had passed by without her noticing it. *Where does the time go?*

Maple finished her projects for the day and was about ready to go visit her friend when she remembered the CD he'd asked her to listen to. "Hmmm, Benson and Jarreau?"

This should be good. It was a beautiful, but, haunting song. *Life is not about getting things. It's about knowing things and identifying your options based on what you believe and already know. In the song Benson sang,* "I'm just someone who loves you, that's all I am." *Was this a message to me that he couldn't say in his own words?*

"Hello, how are you this evening?" the nurse said as Maple walked past her station.

"I'm doing okay. How's my buddy in there?"

"Nervous, scared, apprehensive and all those things that go along with it. He is always so much better when you come to see him. Have you known each other long?"

"Yeah, since our kids were little and we were each married—to other people that is," Maple said with a wide laugh and an inner chuckle that she kept to herself. "Will he be going home soon?"

"Yes, very soon."

"What will he... ah... will he need special... ah... equipment... or... what kind of quality of life will he have?"

"That's up to him and those around him and those who love him." Kaye left the sentence hanging—as if there were more questions that hadn't been asked and more answers she wanted to share—dangled in her head trying to surface.

"So, he may heal completely? I mean go on with his life? He told me he was going back to work as soon as possible," said Maple.

"I'm getting off in a couple of minutes. You want to meet me in the cafeteria, before you talk with Byron, for a cup of awful coffee?"

"Okay, ahmmm, sure." Maple answered and proceeded to the elevator for the cafeteria on the lower level. She wondered what this was about.

Maybe the nurse wanted to give her more information than she was supposed to. That was all right with Maple, but why? Maple sat at a corner table out of the way of foot traffic. She believed it awfully strange that this woman wanted to talk with her. Wild questions ran through her head. She did not understanding why the nurse suggested this chat, then she heard a cat purring. That was Shadow watching her.

"Sorry it took me so long. A new person just started to work here today, came in after my shift and I had to brief him a bit more. Did you already get your coffee?"

"No, I think I'll get a cup of tea."

"Ya hungry?" Kaye inquired.

"Not really. I have a taste for something but can't imagine what. It'll come to me later on, I'm sure." Maple said.

"I'll go get tea for both of us." Kaye said as she put down her jacket and book on the chair.

"Oh, okay." Maple said hesitantly.

The moon was brilliantly full. She stared through the window from the corner where she sat. Her friend was so sick and Maple thought about what else she could say, not so much to cheer him but to help ease the worry and fear, she had read in his eyes.

Maple wondered if he realized how much she cared about him. She never said it out loud, even though the 'love yous' flew back and forth all the time. But, neither receiver took the other seriously, she believed. The senders only heard their parts. He'd whispered in her ear "I love you" or was it? She wondered why he was more or less motionless, after her declaration, and she couldn't read his mind to know if there was more to be said.

Kaye came back and set the tray on the table that held tea and cookies and other odds and ends for snacking. Maple placed a cup in front of her with both hands sort of corralling its placement. Kaye recognized her pensive stare into the contents of the cup and asked, "What's wrong? You appear to have something troubling on your mind," said Kaye.

"Yes, but it's something that I want to keep to myself right now."

"Oh?" Kaye questioned.

Right then, there were fifty years of silence that went through both their heads. Silent hurts permeated the flashes of sorrow that ended in one long hard sigh from both.

Kaye made the first attempt at a real conversation. "I know you're right. Some words when put together don't come out to be fully understood by the hearer. Sometimes, those words are trying to find their conscious meaning. But we do wear our unspoken thoughts on the outside.

"The words I'm wearing right now, would take many life-times to say." Maple commented as her mind drifted back from her daydreams of Byron.

"These are the words that you massage while you go for a walk," Kaye said, "or write a poem or story, a novel or a play; even an argument with a friend or a beloved pet. Ya know, the spoken word is powerful; when uttered it gives the thoughts credence and can create a wall, a cloak, and mask so that neither the speaker nor the hearer can escape its meaning. Is Byron the reason you are holding onto these words?" Kaye asked.

Maple sat up taller in her chair, her neck allowed her head to turn a click at a time to square her view of Kaye's face.

"Why are we here talking about Byron?" she asked Kaye.

There was a bit of a smile on Kaye's face and she looked over her glasses and stared for a minute waiting for more questions. Not really answering, Kaye said, "There are many ways to help him . . ." she stopped. "Tell me something." Kaye paused while her expression told Maple she was trying out a proper phrase in her head.

"Do you read your horoscope daily, weekly or just sometimes?"

"Sometimes, why?" Maple answered.

"What do you know about other… dimensions?"

"I'm not following what you mean," Maple said as her eyebrows squeezed together.

"Well, Byron and I have had plenty of talks about a lot of stuff that I didn't think he knew or even cared about," said Kaye.

"Like what?" Maple asked.

"Like, out of body travel and out of dimension travel in general."

"What has that got to do with anything here?" Maple asked.

"Well, I've introduced some interesting theories to Byron and he was wondering how he could possibly get there from where he is now," Kaye said.

"I don't understand a thing you're saying. What is this about?" Maple began to gather her purse and jacket and started to rise up from her chair.

"Please, no, wait." Kaye said. "I want to share with you what I mean. It would be a lot easier than you running away and always wondering, don't you think? Some patients who come through here become very special to me. I don't know why they catch my attention and . . ." she paused for a long while again. "I know this isn't the proper term but I feel for them; not sorry for them, but just… I want to help, that's what I'm trying to say, especially when I can see greater possibilities," Kaye said.

"So what are you, a seer or something? A fortune teller or what?" Maple's goose-bumped face and arms revealed an attitude adjustment. She was about to let Kaye have a piece of her mind when suddenly she felt different. When the feeling stopped, she was in another place. She heard a bird chirp and the cat's purr, again.

"What the hell is going on? What did you do? Are you some kind of black-magic witch?" Maple almost screamed in fear.

"No, no. I want to show you something that may help you through this."

"Did you drug my tea or something? Where have you taken me?" Maple noticed she was right in the middle of Byron's hospital room. She had just raised herself from his hug and she heard him say, "Please don't continue to run away from me."

Maple was stunned and stuck right in her tracks, motionless.

Maple stopped fighting and realized this was out of her control, and said to him, "What is going on here? What do you mean?"

"You know what I just said and what you just said back to me. Why are you running away, again?" Byron said.

Maple looked all around and thought, *how did I get here?* Then her spirit settled into that moment and stayed.

"I've never run away from you."

"Stop!" he said. "Did you listen to the song that I asked you to?"

"Yes."

"What do you think it was saying to you?" he asked.

Maple backed up to the footboard and held on to the bed's metal frame. She felt tears racing to her eyes. Her conscience self was trying to keep them from showing her feelings. Her mind tried to return to the table with Kaye but she couldn't find herself there.

"You know Byron, I could sing that same song to you and mean it. But I …" she stared at the floor and slowly raised her eyes from the foot of the bed to the start of his hairline.

"But I … what?" he asked.

"I don't want this to happen. I just don't." Tears were dropping to the floor like from a faucet in her eyes.

"Don't I deserve a response, Miss Syrup?" he asked, his mouth offering a trembling smile.

They both chuckled, remembering the time he had told her back when they first became friends when he thought of

her name, Maple, he thought of Maple syrup on his pan-
cakes. With the smiles planted firmly on both their faces
they stared at each other. She had told him that her mother
wanted to name her something that was truly God's gift and
that she thought of sweetness and good. The name Honey
came to mind but Maple seemed extra special. She had told
Byron that she was glad her mother didn't name her Honey.
So Byron's name for her became Miss Syrup, to remind him
of her sweetness.

"Yes, you do deserve a response." A calmer Maple continued. "Can I hold your hand?"

He nodded.

"Now don't stop me from what I have to say, okay? You
promise?" she asked.

"Promise. You want me to place my hand on a stack of
bibles or something?"

"Nope," she smiled, "a promise is good enough. Also, you
cannot comment until I'm through with what I have to say,
agreed?"

"Agreed." he said. "Well, I'm really scared right now," he
said and raised forward.

She held up her hand and said, "Remember you promised
and agreed. I'm scared about your health and I don't want to
lose your friendship and, combined with my own health issues, I fear I would be a burden to you."

"Wait, stop!" he interrupted.

"No, don't talk, you promised," she reminded him.

By now his eyes were also watering and he turned away
and said, "Okay, Okay." then looked back at her.

Both of them took a deep breath and gave each other that
silent almost grin they each knew so well.

"Now, are you ready for me to continue without inter-
rupting?" she asked.

He nodded again and sucked his lips inside his mouth
showing just one straight line across his face. She stroked the
hand of the arm that held the IV.

"You know, this is hard for me to say because I've kept it in for so long," and right then she saw a strange kind of sadness in his eyes.

"What I've kept inside is that—" she held his hand with both of hers. "That I fell in love with you, or at least began to, on that day we first met." She stared at the blanket as she talked. "I looked forward to those days when you stopped by to ask me about some of the clients who needed food, I truly looked forward to those visits, no matter how brief. Then that day we had coffee, which I thought was purely by accident, but now I believe you were following me."

"I was," he interjected followed quickly with, "I'm sorry, my bad, I won't talk," he said with a smile in his eyes. Looking at her, he saw that a dream of his was coming true. Maple was a delicious eyeful only for him.

"Please let me ask just one question. It's not a comment I promise?" Byron asked.

She nodded.

He tried to pull her closer. "Why didn't you ever say anything to me?"

"I just couldn't. I couldn't because I could not disrespect my family. My children, I mean. I was married, and I thought you were too. I felt, back then, it was highly inappropriate."

He gave her a long, loving stare and she wished he'd break his promise again to tell her what was on his mind. But he didn't, so she continued.

"Then all those times when you helped me and when we played tennis together and when you visited me in the hospital and when I'd see you arrive at work and I was afraid that I was just some silly, discontented spouse who didn't have the courage to get out of that devastating, degrading, charade of a marriage. I thought it would be good for the children because they loved their father. And… "

He finally interrupted, "You knew if I'd had any clue that you cared even a tiny gnat hairs' worth for me, I… would…

have … acted on it and, yeah, yeah, some people may have been hurt or at least discontented. I would never hurt you, you know that, don't you?"

"The time was just not right for us then and now we are two creaky-hinged, starry-eyed old folks, and I believe now, the reason why I'm so scared is that I would be a burden to you and we couldn't have a quiet little cottage someplace off by ourselves, and… " said Maple.

"We could," he began talking right over what she was saying.

"We could what?" asked Maple.

"Find a place that is just for you and me. We could live our clanky, clunky, creaky lives, with Ben-gay and aspercreme and whatever other liniments are on the market. I understand WD40 works on the joints, too." They both burst into laughter, and just then the nurse came in.

Kaye was suddenly back and Maple's whole body cringed into a full muscle spasm.

"Oh this sounds good. Sounds like fun and laughter going on and what decisions have you come to?"

"What do you mean, decisions?" Byron asked.

"Well now that you've been honest and let your guard down—both of you—where do you go from here?" Kaye asked.

"What do you mean?" he asked.

"You know that tomorrow is not promised to you, to either of you?" Kaye said looking back and forth from one to the other.

"Yes, so what does that have to do with now and what we've discovered?"

"You both knew in your hearts what the other felt, you each were too afraid to venture out and say something. I do mean both of you."

"But that was the right thing to do since there were others with whom we had commitments," Maple said.

Byron nodded in agreement.

"Neither of you are committed now, nor have either of you been 'involved' or 'committed' in quite some time," said Kaye.

"Yes, but then we were each working out our individual issues including health problems," Maple said

"But when you didn't say that to each other you walked through those 'issues' alone, each afraid of being a burden to the other. That was the burden." Kaye said.

There was so much joy and enthusiasm between Byron and Maple that they felt they were riding into the sunlight where it would hold them in splendor forever.

"You have a decision to make, right now," Kaye said.

"What?" Maple asked.

"Go back to the time when neither of you were committed, or you will only be able to communicate across realms that you have never been aware of or... believe."

"What is this craziness you're talking about?" Maple blurted out.

Byron grabbed her hand and squeezed it until Maple turned and look directly into his eyes and he said to her, quietly, "Let's go ... now."

"Let's go where?" Maple cried out through a face riveted with fear, anguish, and a faint hint of love that she still had a problem openly admitting.

She wasn't sure what had just happened, but life felt good holding Byron and him holding onto her. "What's happening? Where are we going? What is this?" she cried. "That nurse did this didn't she?"

"Calm down, calm down." Byron reassured her. "We will be fine. I want to show you some wonderful things that you've never seen before and they have been right here all the time."

They clung to each other and found their suspended realm and decided to stay, at least for a while. No one knew they were gone, except Kaye. But then in a soft breeze Hannah,

Brid, and Shadow went with them.

"Where are we?" Maple looked wild eyed at all the beauty that surrounded her.

There were flowers and perfumed air and glorious trees well supplied with fruit. Also there were golden honey dripping pots and soft grass and sunshine and the spirit of happiness coming from all directions. The wonder of it all was spectacular and she buried her face in his chest and grabbed his arms, "Tell me, tell me, what is this place? It feels like love in every breath. Where are we?"

"This is Forever."

"Forever?"

"Well… yes, but, let me put it this way. This is the beginning of the journey to Forever."

"But no one else is here. Why?" Maple asked.

"The world, the entire universe is so vast, so gigantic and has always been. When you look from the ground up to the sky you are seeing it. It's the air, the water, the sun, the flowers, the foliage, the grass, the earth, the stars and the moon. It's everything God made." Byron tried to explain.

"Okay, but that's everything we already have, isn't it?" Maple asked.

"What I'm trying to say is that it's the process everyone has to go through to truly know their purpose and help others to start their inward quest to find their own."

"So Forever is not a place?"

"In a sense it is a state of being, like everything is. We are all energy. Everything is energy. So your energy-self is anywhere you put it." he said.

"So whatever happens to me it's my fault if it's bad or good?" Maple asked.

"You put your energy where you want it to be, so, yes?" he answered.

Just then, spirits surrounded them and they knew they had a hard corner to turn.

Byron held Maple close as they danced to the melody ringing from the bells of angels' wings. Even when smoky clouds wrapped around them and whisked their journey into a fantasy that enveloped them in lilac essence and peppermint drops, they just stayed in their newest reality. They understood that their relationship was on the verge of something that neither one knew nor had any idea of what it would be.

"Is that why Kaye wanted me to be here with you now?" Maple asked.

"I wanted you to be with me now, Kaye didn't feel you were ready yet. But I knew it was time. It is our time, right now." Byron tightened his lips not wanting to tell more. He wanted her to stay with him right in their moment before his rapture. Everything was unfamiliar and familiar at the same time. Everything revolved around elements of their lives and community for which there had never been an honest recognition that those curses were there. But they knew, deep down inside, they both knew. The madness of the curse they tried to deny was hair strands from this, their utopia.

Chapter 13

Kaye didn't believe Maple was ready to hold onto the knowledge she'd just gained on her journey with Byron, so she re-directed all that Maple had seen to her dream-state thoughts.

When Maple stepped up to the nurses' desk she was out of breath and sweaty.

"How's my friend doing in there?" Maple asked fanning her face with a newspaper she picked up from the desk.

"He's doing pretty good, but sleeping most of today."

"Is Kaye in there with him now?" Maple asked

The nurse turned around to look and said, "That's so strange, I thought she was just here."

"I'll just go on in for a few minutes, if that's ok?" Maple said.

The nurse scratched her head and said, "Sure, sure."

When Maple walked into Byron's room, a funny feeling came over her. She felt she had just been in Byron's room but he was sleeping soundly and his breathing was heavy, almost labored. She noticed beads of sweat on his brow and picked up a tissue to wipe the perspiration away. His whole face smiled when she touched him. She used the same tissue to blot her own face then stared at the totally dry piece of tissue in her hand.

Byron slept through her visit. Maple busied herself by re-organizing the flowers and get-well cards so he could see them all. Finally she sat next to him with her hand resting inside his. Every once in a while he'd squeeze her hand and smile. But his eyes didn't open. She thought that was good because he was no longer troubled by the visions he'd seen under his eyelids.

Her visions were similar but she had never told him. For some reason she thought if anyone knew what she saw they would think she was crazy. After Byron had validated the visions she had when he told her about his vision, she didn't see the visions, hardly at all, anymore. But her dreams grew strange.

Maple stood up to leave but stared out the window for a while. Her head played the love song Byron had asked her to listen to. She looked around and his face still smiled. So she placed a kiss on his forehead and said, "I'll see you soon."

Byron responded, "I love you and I'll see you first."

Maple backed away slowly not taking her eyes off his face until she reached the door. For a minute she stood there holding onto the door listening to him breath. *I will come back to-morrow.* The song, 'All I Am,' kept playing through her head. She left the building slowly, not rushing as usual to get to her car.

After Maple arrived home, she fed Buster, watered the plants and checked her messages. Everything seemed to be in order so she went to bed. Sleep came easy that night. Then, way past midnight, the silence was so loud it woke her up. Even her television had turned itself off. Maple sat straight up in bed and crossed her arms over her heart, feeling as though something had touched her. A moonbeam crawled across her bedspread. Then it seemed to walk and dance which charmed her into a sudden giggle. By the time the beam of moonlight filled her entire room she was fast asleep, snuggling into her warm fuzzy covers. Maple's face held onto a smile the rest of the night.

On the other side of town where Maple had visited her friend a few hours before, the sterile crispness of the sharp alcohol and antiseptic whiff vanished as the nurse left the room. Byron, lay in a stone like pose with machines assisting his breathing and tubes attached to plastic bags filled with life comforting fluids entering many parts of his body. The only sound was the rhythmic flutter of the respirator and nothing else moved. Byron's spirit searched for Maple and found her sleeping.

Mr. and Mrs. Chance sat huddled in the corner watching for, waiting for, and praying for any sign of life in their youngest child. There were no more tears left, only vise-like clenched teeth and blood-stopping holds on their hands. These hands had held onto each other for more than half a century now. Byron's parents could not believe they were witnessing the exit of their baby. They didn't dare look in each other's eyes and have the other see their own pain double. The Chances couldn't share that kind of torment.

"Mr. Chance, Mrs. Chance, will you please come to the next room with me for a moment?"

"No!" said Mrs. Chance, "I'm not leaving him to transition without me right by him. Even though he's a man now, he will always be my child, first. Say whatever you have to say, right here. He already knows what's happening to him, and so do we."

Dr. Rossi looked at both of them and said. "Mr. Chance, Mrs. Chance, this is very hard for me to tell you." she paused. "I'm terribly sorry to have to say this but a cancer developed in the transplanted kidney. That's not very unusual in someone taking the medicines required to prevent rejection. If it were just in the kidney, we could take it out, but… the cancer has spread to his lungs." Mr. and Mrs. Chance reached for Dr. Rossi's hand while she continued.

"At this point we can only keep him as comfortable as possible. Again, I'm so terribly sorry. I wish there were something more we could do."

The Chances nodded, and she turned and left the room.

Mr. Chance looked away from his son, so as not to see the pain directly and reflected on the little boy who had jumped on his legs when he got home from work; and the bike—still in the garage, on which he had taught Byron Jr., how to ride. Byron Sr. worked hard all his life just to make sure his son's life could be better than his own.

Byron Sr., had wanted to join the Army but they would not accept him because four of his toes were missing. It happened when he was working on the little farm his father developed out of a-nothing-piece-of land in eastern Georgia. His father had grown tomatoes, greens, peppers and watermelons. At the end of each summer he had driven that old truck of his up to New York and sometimes Chicago where he sold everything off the truck to make enough money for the family to live during the winter. He also bought his seed while in the north so he could pay out less money. On one of his trips Byron Sr. stepped on something sharp and it cut into the boot on his left foot. A sharp thing like a nail, or piece of broken glass had made a scrape on his foot but it didn't hurt so Byron Sr. didn't mention it to his father. By the time they got home his whole foot was infected and the doctor, who was also the local veterinarian removed his toes so the rest of his foot could be saved. Since he could not join the Army, he and Nelba, his girlfriend from Forever, ran off and got married. He decided to make a contribution to the war effort by moving close to Vancouver, Washington to work for the military in the shipyards. When the war was over they moved further north and found work. They made a life for which their family grew, two boys and a girl. They had moved away from Vanport (a small community of shipyard workers in North Portland, Oregon) just about a month before the big flood occurred there. The move took place right on time; because the flood destroyed that entire area a few weeks after they moved.

Nelba thought her husband was the smartest man in the world by knowing that they should move right when they did, even though she was kind of being slow about wanting to leave there, moving to another unknown place.

Bryon Sr. cherished his family and prayed for their success in life and helped them all whenever he could. He brought them up good, sturdy and never thought he would outlive any of them.

His mind came back to the hospital room. Byron Sr. swallowed hard or cleared his throat or coughed whenever he felt tears coming because Nelba could not see him cry. He wanted to be strong for her.

They stood there and sat there, then walked over and touched his skin, and Byron Junior's mother rubbed a warm cloth across his face while holding one of his hands. She kissed his forehead and walked backwards not wanting her eyes to leave him. Byron's parents' breathing was shallow as if an inward voice was telling them to give him all the air in the room. The machines stopped beeping as Kaye's foot crossed the threshold of the room. None of the three moved, even when attendants came rushing into the room.

Mr. Chance sternly spoke, "Stop. He wants to leave now."

Right then Byron's essence filled the room and lingered there to help them grieve. The three of them, Mr. Chance, Mrs. Chance and Kaye stood there in a tight huddle as Byron covered them with his love before leaving.

Chapter 14

A jagged edginess disturbed Maple's spirit from the moment she opened her eyes and recognized morning had come. She first thought of all the things she had to do that day and decided to call Byron later in the afternoon to see how he was doing and follow up on their conversation. Her smile that grew out of the space in her heart she made for him caused her to feel he was sitting right there in the room with her. She chuckled and looked toward the foot of her bed. *Wouldn't that be nice?*

Maple grabbed her list of things to do and ran out of her house to finish all errands she had to get through. She then went home to shower and change for her visit with Byron. She was glad she hadn't disturbed his peaceful sleep the day before.

At around 3:00pm Maple received a strange call from a man she didn't know asking if she knew Byron and that her name was on his list of people to contact. She smiled thinking he was ready to go home or to an assisted-living center until he recuperated. She asked the caller to wait for a minute and she got paper and pen out of the drawer.

"Hello," she said, "I'm back, so you have a message from Byron, do you have his new phone number? Whom am I speaking with?" She asked

"My name is Avery, and no it's not that," he answered.

"His new address, you mean?" she replied.

His husky robust voice was wavering and slightly softer with a questioning tone.

"No," he said.

"Well what is it then? A message from who . . .?" She left her words dangling.

"No, please I have to tell you something and that is he, Byron died this morning and you were a person I am suppose to contact. His family is busy now making the arrangements and I'm helping by making some of the calls for them." He continued to blurt out the rest. "I'm sorry to be so blunt over the phone and all, but anyway, after I find out when and where the services will be, I will call you back—are you there?"

"Yes, yes, I'm here—what happened? Can you tell me?"

"Well, ah—from what I understand, his body rejected the transplanted organ. He wanted to stand up and walk a little and passed out after about two maybe three steps. So, then, well I was there and he mentioned your name a few times.

"Anyway, me and the guys made sure he didn't fall on the floor; the nurses and other medical folks came running but we'd already sat him in the wheelchair. They put him on a stretcher and took him away. We stayed with the family most of the evening and his parents spent the night. He was comatose and the doctor came in and told his folks that he… he… he well, that there was nothing else they could do. You there?"

"Yes. Yes, I'm here."

"Miss Maple, I'm sorry to be the one to call you but… ah my wife is home most of the time during the day and you can call here and she will have all the information or as soon as I have anything to tell you, I will be sure to call you. Is that okay with you?" He said and gave her his number.

"Yes. Yes. That's fine."

"I'm so sorry, I know you were good friends with Byron and he thought the world of you."

"Thank you. I'm sorry, I forgot what you said your name is."

"My name is Avery. That's okay, I understand."

"Thanks again and don't forget to let me know where and when. Good bye."

"Bye now."

Her mind went completely blank when the phone clicked off. She sat there, like a stone.

Even though she never closed her eyes for more than twenty-four hours, her face recognized the sunshine that moved across her skin while her head continued to shake from side to side and she heard herself saying "No, no, no, no, no."

The next day Avery's wife called her with the funeral details. The service would be in three days. Maple continued her life duties in robot form.

When she walked into her room she saw Buster, her arrogant, wacky old cockatoo. He had shown up on her roof one-day several years ago immediately after she moved in and he never left. He had taken over her room but now he appeared to be occupied by the little bird that had been sitting on the ledge outside her bedroom window. She fed him and refreshed his water dish and sat in her chair with all the lights on in the house.

Chapter 15

The funeral for Byron was solemn with many of his friends whispering how they could not believe he was gone. They talked about how good he looked and they made small talk. The truth was, who looks good in a coffin? Very few people talked to each other but sat stoically and could hear others saying, "why didn't we realize he was so ill?"

One lady said, "Byron was so secretive he never told anyone his problems." Some people got up and said nice things about how he influenced their lives and what a good person he was.

When Maple walked up to view his body, she almost fell in a little stumble, but caught herself when someone touched her hand. She didn't see who it was. Prayers were said, the obituary read, and there was a short sermon, she didn't hear a word of anything. She noticed he looked peaceful lying there and looked as though he was getting ready to speak. When she looked down at his body she thought she heard his laugh, which just had to be in her head. She would never forget what his voice was like or his laugh or anything about him.

The minister was very matter of fact and didn't show any emotion or sincerity, which helped the attendees who all seemed to be holding their breath.

Byron was kind of an oddball friend to most of them. He wasn't a close, good buddy to anyone in particular. He preferred to keep his life to himself. He'd just show up from time to time and wherever and whoever it was, Byron was welcomed.

Maple wondered where he had been when he disappeared from time to time. Now she wished she'd gone places with him when he'd invite her to go out with him. Maple sat quietly in the back of the sanctuary while others filed out, so that she could continue to reflect on her friendship even though his body had been covered, his coffin closed and removed.

She walked out of the church and heard her name, "Maple. Maple you want to ride with us out to the cemetery? We know you guys were real buddies. Come go with us so you don't have to go by yourself," said Avery.

"Thank you, I'm not going to go to the cemetery. I'll see you later at the church house." she said.

Maple passed the group of people some of the people who went in and out of his snack shop, which was also gone.

Maple noticed that Kaye was there with a strange little girl and others she had never seen before who looked a bit out of place. They weren't family or friends or anyone from the community. The little girl had a bird in the purse she carried. *How strange.*

A million disconnected thoughts were going through her head when she dashed to her car as quickly as possible without being noticed by anyone else. She wanted no one to see her let go the ocean of tears that she held behind her eyes. His scent filled her car and quieted the drumbeat that was her heart. A familiar voice in song on the radio sang "find me in your dreams, " several times. When Maple parked the car she realized that the radio had not been turned on.

Chapter 16

A few years passed and people were busy and settled into new routines that filled the spaces Byron once held. Byron's brother, Gabe, didn't have the passion for business that Byron held dear, so the snack shops all closed. Their father tried to help but he was nearing 85 years old, without a 'quickness' in his step nor thought process. His joints made cracking sounds at times or would sometimes swell. Byron Senior managed to sell what was left of his son's businesses and property then sent the proceeds to Byron's children. The senior Chances sold their big old rambling house to downsize into a little two-bedroom ranch. Nelba loved planting flowers and watching them grow while her husband believed he was supervising all the landscaping, and horticulture projects. They miss their energetic baby boy.

They went for short walks each evening after the dishes were washed from dinner. One time they met and talked to a lady up the street who they realized was a friend of Byron's named Maple. She had visited him in the hospital and they remembered he'd said he liked her. She was pleasant, and had a good smile thought Nelba.

The older woman walked past them on several occasions and nodded or just looked away. Her name was Olive. She had finished raising a relative's children because of a terrible tragedy whereby four children were orphaned.

The other neighbors had filled them in about what had gone on in her life. Olive had to finish raising a relative's children, because there was also something about abuse and murder. The Chances tuned that story out of their listening pleasure. The children were grown now but oh so sad. Mr. & Mrs. Chance continued to tend to their gardens and meet their new neighbors.

The late summer evening crisp air told Maple there would be an early autumn and cold winter. She pulled her jacket a little tighter as she arrived home and the air instantly changed all around her. Stepping up onto the front porch she heard the clank and tingle of her keys hitting the concrete, which brought her out of the walking daydream that visited her constantly since Bryon's death. She stopped and retrieved her keys. With too much stuff in her arms, she fumbled with the door to get it opened and then checked to make sure she hadn't lost any keys.

Maple opened the door dropped all the packages, purse, newspaper plus other odds and ends right next to the entryway. "Whew!" she said aloud.

The back of her hand wiped her forehead and another sigh escaped her. She could barely remember when keys and locked doors became so important to her. Maple was dog-tired. It always seemed like there was so much to do. The house was quiet, as if you shouldn't even make noise breathing. She flopped down onto the closest chair to the door. Maple looked back to reassure herself the door was locked and looked at the box beside the entry and saw that mail was delivered today, nothing of any consequence just bills it appeared, so she turned away and stared out the window.

She hadn't quite completed her ritual of checking the house yet, so she tested every window and all the doors before she could settle in. It was a thing she learned since the first time she tried to leave her ex-husband. He must have sneaked

116

in through a window or an unlocked door of her new apartment. She didn't put anything past him even now after all this time and all he put her through. Then again, she felt stupid at remembering all the things he did that she didn't know how to escape. A loud sigh ended those thoughts and she moved from the chair to begin her evening. Everything was secure.

What shall I do this evening? There really wasn't anyone she wanted to call or hear from, maybe except her children who were off doing their own thing. Maple got up and walked into her bedroom where Buster opened one eye then ignored her. He probably hadn't heard her come in or just pretended not to.

"You mad at me boy because I didn't get home early?" she said to the large white Cockatoo perched on top of its cage. He opened both eyes and turned his head. "Huh, the damned bird I feed everyday isn't even speaking to me." she told the lavender plant in the corner. She felt the soil and left the room for water to give Lovie a drink.

When walking through the doorway she almost jumped out of her skin, because a funny feeling caused her to look around the room. Right then she noticed an indentation on the bed. She backed away from the room because she had not sat on the bed since she made it this morning and no one else could get in the house. She told herself to calm down "there's no reason for me to be afraid" she said over and over.

Suddenly, "If you're in here, I've got a gun," she shouted. "I'll shoot you!"

Maple thought to call the police but the phone was in her purse next to the front room chair. Again she looked at the place on the bed towards the imprint, but it was gone. She laughed out loud. "Don't tell me I'm losing my mind," she said to Buster. She went to get the water. There was still something about what she believed was on the bed.

Maple busied herself the rest of the evening with opening

mail, writing out checks, dating the spot where the stamp was to go, reading her email and playing her games on-line. It was close to one o'clock in the morning and she still hadn't gotten ready for bed. Again, she checked and re-locked the doors. But the eerie feeling didn't leave her.

The television was keeping her company but she noticed the time and had to prepare for work the next day. The house seemed mellow she noticed as she put on nightclothes. She then turned everything off, checked the doors and windows again before slipping under the covers in bed. Maple changed the TV channel and said goodnight to Buster.

The Andy Griffith show, an old rerun was just starting and Buster whistled the tune right along with the TV. Maple lay her head down on the pillow and asked sleep to hurry. Her mind drifted as her eyes closed seeing pictures in the undersides of her eyelids. Maple hadn't seen those pictures in a long while. She opened her eyes but didn't sit up. Barney was telling Andy that Ernest T. was a nut, on the TV; Maple remembered that episode from long ago. She tried to close her eyes again, but Buster was still whistling. She looked up and realized how light it was outside and saw a beautiful, brilliant, golden full moon. A brighter one than she ever remembered seeing.

Looking at the sky, she thought about her friend, her Coffee friend, Byron. He was gone. He looked good the last time she remembered him but he died a couple of days later. She got out of bed and looked through the window again and again at the moon, the sky, and stars and even saw a shooting one. *Maybe that's him. Why couldn't I sense that he was so close to death?* She thought, *When I'm dreaming, I wish he could talk to me.* "Come to my dreams," she said out loud to the moon for Byron to hear her.

She lay back down but left the TV on and found sleep. A pleasant drifting sleep. Quiet slumber it was, yet with a hint of uneasiness.

Later during the night, the bed moved near her feet she tensed then relaxed, the smell of lilies in full bloom unfolded and rolled across her senses. She opened her eyes and he was sitting there.

Her eyes filled with tears she wanted to scream but her entire self was frozen, paralyzed.

"Don't be afraid." he said, keeping his distance.

"You're dead, how can you be here? Am I dead too?"

"No, no you are not dead. You invited me to your dream, remember?" Byron's spirit answered.

"I don't understand this," Maple said. He began to move away from her bed, "Remember the last words I said to you?"

"Yes, you told me you loved Me." she said not quite audibly.

"Then what did I say?"

She looked up towards the ceiling from side to side trying to pull the words out of the air. "That was the last you said," she said still shaking in fright.

"No, I guess you've forgotten me already," he jokingly remarked.

"I haven't forgotten you. You were a dear, dear friend why didn't you tell me before things got so bad, how very sick you were? I told you I'd see you soon and you also said you'd see me first. So that means I'm dead, because I know you are, I went to your funeral but I couldn't go to the cemetery."

"I know, I missed seeing you."

There was a long pause – *I'm dreaming this, I have to be*, she thought as she stared at the apparition. "Other than the fact that I invited you to my dream why are you here, now?" Uncontrollable tears dropped on her folded arms.

"Do you have something to tell me? Are you here to take me, too? This is getting scary. What do you want?" she heard his laugh, a laugh that ran right out of his heart to hers.

"Please don't be frightened I just wanted you to know that I'm here for your—ah protection, if nothing else."

"Protection from what?" she snapped.

"Of all the things you've been afraid of for most of your life and in this house."

"What do you mean, what are you talking about?" she pulled the covers closer around and crossed her arms in front, now sitting up scooted back to the headboard.

"You've left lights on all over the house until a few months ago. Sometimes you put books and cans in front of doors, and noisy toys below windows. You have metal doors and windows. Who are you trying to keep out? Or should I ask who are you locking in?" his voice sort of drifted off and danced in the air.

"Stop that! Stop it. Stop it! How do you know this? Have you been watching me? You're a ghost and you're stalking me!" she almost shouted

"Go ahead call the police," he folded his arms and a second later they both busted out laughing.

"Let me get this right," she began again. "You are a ghost, in my dream and you're here to, to, to do what?" Not waiting for his answer, "I'm sitting here—covered up in my bed, the moon shining like daylight in my room, that's usually always dark—mind you—I'm talking to you, a ghost, who was a friend that died several years ago." She looked up to the ceiling. "Lord, have I lost my complete mind?" she said in a whining sigh.

"Can I say something, will you hear me? I know things have not been as you would have liked, can we start there?" he asked

She said nothing just looked at her feet twirling in circles under the covers.

"Can I?" he repeated the words that came out as a plea. She nodded

"You don't leave lights on all the time anymore, and you can walk through the house and not be afraid, right?"

Right, she nodded.

"You've been okay, by yourself and haven't needed anything you couldn't get or didn't just suddenly appear. Right?" he paused.

"Right?" he questioned again.

"Right." as she nodded

"You can be in the house at night and go down into the basement to wash clothes, to look for something, or just for any reason at all right, or go up to the attic anytime you want? Even when you're alone, right?"

"Right?" he questioned again.

"How do you know that?" she grumbled as she sunk down into the covers up to her chin.

"I've been asking angels to keep you safe, to open happy doors for you and to close the sad and scary ones. You have to begin to recognize that there are some people you must keep away from you. There are destructive people who don't want to see you or anybody else with any kind of happiness, or pleasure or love. I don't have to tell you who, do I?" Byron asked.

A questioning look came over her face. "How do you know those things? You're dead."

"Rest now I'll see you later," he said

"No wait, I thought you said this was a dream, so you don't have to go until I wake up."

"Do you want me to stay?"

"I don't know. If this is a dream I'm asleep," she added, "but it doesn't feel like I'm sleep," Looking around the room with a questioning look took over her face.

He repeated, "So, do you want me to stay until you wake up?"

"Yes"

"Why?"

"Then I'll know it really is a dream and . . ." she stopped and tightened her lips.

"And what?" he asked

"The room feels better," she looked around the moonlit room, *yes better*, she thought.

"Is there something else you wanted to say?" he asked.

"Yes, and I've missed you, too." She suddenly felt that she could embrace a dream and her heart convinced her head that this very moment was a first step into a new journey, she smiled. *I'm dreaming a good dream.*

She closed her eyes and when morning came she woke up smiling. *Today is a good day* she thought and she remembered a piece of a dream from the night before. She'd dreamed she danced with Byron, but he wanted her to call him by another name. They had danced in every room in the house until all the rooms felt better. But it felt as if they were in another kind of space.

The morning sun shone bright throughout the house and she opened all the shades and curtains. Maple made coffee and raisin toast, then, sat at the dining room table to recite her favorite Psalm.

"The Lord is my Shepherd, I shall not want." She thought about that statement for a minute and looked around her. "Thank you, Lord God, Thank you." she said out loud, "I am so blessed. Thank you Lord," she said again and again.

Buster started squawking so she had to feed him and take the cover off his cage. He'd been quiet most of the morning *how odd* she thought.

Maple showered, dressed and gathered her things to leave for work.

Off and on that whole day she caught snip-its in her mind of a strange visitor in her dream. A friend who had died and one she mourned, not so much his passing because she could see the pain he suffered, but she grieved the loss of his spirit close to her. A spirit that had not been this close to her since his funeral was now beaconing her. She wrapped herself in those dream snip-its and waltzed through her day making decisions, catching up on work and identifying new projects.

Others noticed that she was in an upbeat mood.

One of the girls in the lunchroom commented after she sashayed out of the door, "I wonder what's got her gear shift cranking?" They all laughed. Maple heard a bit of the comment and laughter as she continued down the hall.

Kaye and Hannah watched as Maple's spirit expanded and searched for more understanding. They knew then that Maple could end the curse. The battle was on.

Chapter 17

That evening when Maple arrived home she walked into her front room and again the house felt loved and loving just as she'd left it. The plants were watered and with the rest of her routine home entry chores completed, Buster was heard calling her.

"Hey you! Eat, eat, eat!" Buster shouted.

"Ok, ok, don't ruffle your feathers, I'm coming!" Maple told the bird.

She hesitated a minute before going into her room, remembering what happened yesterday and the imprint on the foot of the bed. She'd smoothed out everything when she made her bed this morning and checked it before she left the house. Buster had free reign of the house but he couldn't make an imprint that size unless he rolled around on the bed, *not likely* she thought.

She entered the room, no imprint. *I am just being silly,* she thought, so she filled Buster's dish and brought fresh water, then continued with what she needed to do for the evening.

There were three phone calls to return, one call needed to be made to the phone company because of the hang up calls she'd received lately. They bothered her so much that she hesitated to go near the phone each time her home phone rang.

Looking around in the kitchen Maple realized how much clutter was everywhere, so she began throwing things away.

She stacked papers with notes to herself in an old cardboard box and put it near her computer. She just continued through the house picking up everything she felt needed to leave. Just surface stuff, she hadn't begun any deep cleaning. The garbage was taken outside right away so that it wouldn't continue collecting in the house or find its way back to its old resting cluttered space.

Outside emptying trash she noticed how her yard was dry since there'd been no rain in quite a while so she turned on the sprinkler. Maple went into her office area to check her e-mails then just stopped and thought while she sat there staring out the window.

The phone rang and she didn't recognize the number so she waited for the ringing to stop. She had been getting several hang-up calls lately and remembered that's what Omar used to do. Maple found a tablet and listened to every message she'd saved and erased all of them except her children's voices. I've done a lot today she thought as she fixed a quick sandwich for dinner. So she turned everything off, locked and checked the doors and went to her room to get ready for bed. Maple turned on the light and Buster was sitting on top of the cage, silent.

As she slowly turned to scan the room from the corner of her eye there it was, the imprint on the bed. She stood there frozen, not knowing if she should be excited or frightened, to scream or smile. She picked up her nightclothes and went to the bathroom to change. She rolled her hair, and scrubbed her face and dabbed a hint of cologne behind each ear and her wrists, then laughed out loud at herself.

Maple went back into her room and saw that the imprint was gone. She sucked her lips into her mouth and thought; *I'm being silly, why am I fantasizing this?* She picked up one of the books in her stack to read and tuned the volume down on the TV, as she started to put the cover over Buster's cage, but realized he wasn't in there, so she got into bed.

Buster had left his cage and sat on the top of the drapery valance then when Maple settled in her bed, he flew downward and landed on the pillow next to her. Then got onto her shoulder and tried to start a conversation.

"You want me to read to you?" She asked Buster and he matched the rhythm and number of her words in his own language. He kissed her on the ear and gurgled. She turned over and tried to start reading the same sentence several times but it just wasn't working. The moon wasn't as bright as it had been the night before but it was still brilliant. She tried to remember the little singsong poem kids used to say 'star light, star bright, tell me who I'll see tonight; I wish I may, I wish I might make this wish come true tonight.' *No, it wasn't working*. She thought because she couldn't remember all the words. Nothing else came to mind so she turned to the TV and there was a dance program; and the announcer mentioned Alvin Ailey. She thought, *Alvin... dancing. He was in my dream and he told her to call him Alvin, his real first name*. She invited Buster to go back to his cage but he wanted to stay there on the pillow.

"You poop on my pillow, you're going in the washing machine with it. Do you understand me?"

"Ya, ya, ya, ya," said Buster.

"Stop getting smart you big bag of feathers."

Maple turned the light out and Buster got on Maple's shoulder and walked down her body and stopped at her knee. He just stood there. Maple closed her eyes and half listened to music coming from the TV. She began to doze off.

The smell of lilacs filled her senses. She opened her eyes and sat up quickly.

"Welcome back to dreamland," he said.

"What's going on? This is not a dream, I wasn't asleep yet."

"Oh, but you are. You asked the star who you'd see tonight and the universe answered you."

"No, that was just the TV, a coincidence," she snapped.

"There are no coincidences or accidents, everything happens for a reason and on purpose. Sometimes we discover what the reason is and sometimes we don't." said Alvin.

"What are you doing, why are you here?" she asked.

"You've been looking for me all day," he answered.

"I most certainly have not!"

"Yes, as a matter of fact, when you first entered the house you came in this room to check if I'd been here." he said.

"You're spying on me? What do you want from me?" she said close to tears.

"Please don't' cry, I'm sorry if I've upset you. Tell you what."

She looked over at him and held the covers to her bottom lip.

"What?"

"Do me a favor?" Alvin formerly called Byron asked.

"What?" she grumbled.

"Go to the hospital where I was, before... you know... and talk to Kaye, the nurse.

Chills ran up Maples body from her toes clear up to and exploded at the top center of her head. She rested both hands on the top of her head as if she were holding her essence inside to keep it from leaving her body. She held her breath.

He continued, "Tell her that you've had a dream about me and you want to understand why."

"Is she a witch or something?"

"No, nothing like that, please do that, promise me?" he said.

"Why should I? You are not real, I'm losing my mind." she responded.

"No you are fine, it's a dream that's all. Okay?"

"Okay." She said. Hesitating to tell an out and out lie, she wasn't okay.

"I see Buster is standing guard for you. He loves you, you know that don't you?"

"He's here and likes—hear that again, LIKES me because I feed him."

"You should hear and know what he's really saying to you."

"Do you know what he's saying?"

Alvin nodded.

"You're telling me you speak bird, too?"

They laughed.

"Now put your hunkles down and relax," he said.

"If this is a dream, I am relaxed, right?" she wanted to know.

He started to move away toward the door.

"Wait." she called.

"Do you want me to stay?" he hesitated.

"Yes, it's cold in here and I've got goose bumps all over me and I don't know why I'm talking in my sleep," she told the air.

"Relax. How did your day go?" He already knew, but inquired anyway, to calm her.

"Very well. I don't know why but I had a burst of energy and I got so much done today.

"Are you still isolating yourself from everyone and everything?" he asked.

"What do you mean?" Her dry somber query shot right back at him.

"You know, you had phone calls to make and people to see, did you do that?"

"Why, why are you here?" she asked.

He turned to leave.

"Where do you go?" she wanted to know.

"No place in particular. Listen, I'm not here to hurt you, or alarm you, or frighten you."

"I miss the talks that we had and the ones I always wanted to have with you. I missed touching your hand and hearing you laugh," she said. "But you're gone now, and this isn't real."

"And I miss never having taken you in my arms to kiss you." he remarked.

"Stop! Wait, don't go any further." she snapped.

"I miss never having cared for you openly." he stopped and looked down at his folded hands. "Tell me more about those talks you always wanted to have with me."

"Alvin?"

"Yes?"

"It's really hard for me to call you that. Why can't I just say your name that I know? You know, I've missed you, too. Why didn't we see this before?" she said

"We each thought we had lots of time, and didn't focus on important things," he answered.

"Like?"

"Love and friendship that's real."

"We had that? I thought you cared about me like you would a sister or cousin even."

"Naw, it wasn't anything like that," he said with a soft, deep friendly growl.

"Why are you saying this now?" she asked.

"Well, I thought I had, and then I tried, and then it was too late," he answered.

"So why now?" she wanted to know

"Because you need me," he said. "Remember when we ran into each other at the grocery store---coffee shop?"

"Yeah, why?"

"I waited for you to be there." he said.

"You mean that was no accident?" she asked.

"No, I saw you drive into the parking lot and I walked through the store and watched for you," he told her. "As a matter of fact, I knew it was our appointed time to talk." he responded.

"You dirty old geezer, you stalked me!"

"Yes, I'm guilty, and I knew you were miserable. I wanted you to have any kind of caring I could give you," he said.

"Oh. You were near when I needed a friend, huh?" she said softly.

He was afraid to answer so he asked, "How's your health? Have you been taking care of everything?"

"Yes, why?" she said through clenched teeth.

"I don't want you to end up like me," he said.

"You suffered so," she said as they both looked away from each other then at the same spot in the air.

"I know, but I could have taken a little better care of myself. And I didn't."

"I could have helped," she said, "if I'd known."

"You did help."

"No, if I had known I would have been right there for you," she said. "Nagging the hell out of you," she said laughing.

"Maybe you would have, but will you talk to Nurse Kaye?"

"Well," she searched her mind for any excuse, "Yes," she said reluctantly.

"When?"

"You have to answer my question first, the one that you side-stepped about your name."

"People will see me with you, maybe, so it will be easier if I have another name. So folks find it really hard to believe that a ghost is in their presence, so they can just believe that I'm a relative of the person they knew as Byron. Make sense?"

"Makes sense." She said and tightened her lips. "So you are really here. You are not in my dream?" Maple asked.

"Only when you need me in your dreams," he said. "I promise I will keep you safe. Will you meet with Kaye, for me?"

"I'll go on Friday."

"How about tomorrow?" he asked.

"Tomorrow?" Maple said with a question in her voice.

She couldn't think of one excuse to delay the meeting.

"Yes, tomorrow."

"Okay," she said.

"Promise?"

"Promise." she answered.

"Where do you go when you leave and where have you been since you ---?" Maple suddenly realized what she was asking and could not quite ask her complete question. Thoughts of his death raised tender emotions that she stuffed inside as far as possible.

"I've been lot's of places, learned lots of things, and found some of my mistakes." He was trying to reassure her.

"That's interesting but it's not a place to be," she said.

"Yes, I know," he paused trying to find what needed to be said. "It's on my way to Forever," he smiled through that statement.

She didn't hear it because she was suddenly into a deep sleep and he lay across her feet and she didn't know he was still there. Buster quietly went to his cage, and closed the door, and the scent of lilacs spent the night with them.

Chapter 18

Maple ran inside to catch the phone by the fourth ring. "Hello," she said in an out of breath hoarse whisper.

"Hey Mom, how are you? You sound out of breath," said Omar Junior.

"I'm fine, I was in the yard so I had to run to get the phone. How are you doing?" Maple answered.

"Mom you can't be running, I would have called you back. I'm doing good, where have you been I've been calling and calling you for days and you're never there. Did you just quit answering your phone or are you ignoring messages, again?"

"No, I've been here. But I've been outside a lot lately trying to get some flowers growing in the front yard and tending to my vegetable garden in the back. I still have some weeding to do"

"Why don't I come over and help?"

"Sure, come on over now if you want. Don't wear your good clothes," she said. "I'm putting you to work."

"Ok, I'll be there in about half an hour."

I wonder what's going on now? Maple thought, since there was a puzzling sound to his voice. *My child, my child, I wonder how much money he needs this time? I've got to stop that.* She quickly changed her thoughts to 'how great it would be to have her son drop by and chat while finishing up the yard chores with her.'

"Knock, knock. The door's open so I'm in the house." Omar Junior yelled.

"Come on in," Maple yelled back.

"Don't leave your house open like this, Mom, somebody could just come in and steal you." Junior joked.

"Nobody wants me except the hain'ts." she remarked.

"Now, I know I've heard you and daddy use that term before. What is a hain't?"

"A ghost or spirit that's kind of mischievous more so than devilish."

"Ain't no hain't gonna take my girl away from me." Junior grabbed his mother and gave a big hug and then kissed her on the forehead.

"I don't know; sometimes they are all around hawk watching me. You know, I'm an old timer now anyway so they might be waiting on me."

"Cut that out. You ain't going no place." Junior said.

"To what do I owe the privilege of your fabulous company today?" Maple asked her son.

"Dad hasn't been feeling too good and wanted to have some family over for a barbeque," Junior's mood changed quickly, "and, he was wondering how you were doing."

"He's wondering about me, I wonder why?" Maple said.

"You are in a chipper mood. Have you been sipping on the sherry?" he asked.

"I'm just feeling good. I feel like doing more, I'm getting more things done for myself so I don't have to pay somebody else to do things around the house."

"Oh, yeah?" he said.

"Yeah," she answered. "That's too bad, about your father. Anything serious? He's got folks to look out for him doesn't he? Wait, why are you telling me this about him?"

"Well, he asks about you all the time. I thought it might be nice to have a barbeque or something before the summer's

134

gone. It would just be good to have all of us together for just a few hours. That wouldn't hurt, would it?"

"Who do you mean when you say, 'all of us?' Where is all this coming from, Junior? Why would I want to do that? Your dad has his life and I have mine. You know that. I'm too old to be tossed around like an old rag doll."

"Mom, he's not like that anymore."

"Lets let sleeping dogs lie," said Maple

"I'm trying to start planning a wedding. I want both of you involved in all of it. Can't you put your guard down and crack that fortress around you where he's involved just for a little while?"

"Whew!" Maple sighed, "Who's the girl? Have I met her already? Or is she the one you're hiding out with lately?"

"You met her a while ago. We kind of got back together and it's working this time."

"Who is it?"

"Remember Retrea?"

"Yeah, I remember. She's the one you had a lot of disagreements and drama with isn't she?"

"Yeah, but that was a long time ago and I've learned my lesson for good. That will never happen again. I mean it."

She gave him her best – 'don't-lie-to-me-boy' look. "You were fighting her in her apartment and the police were called."

"Ma, don't start."

"What do you mean 'Ma, don't start?' Didn't you get enough of what I had to deal with while you were growing up? What did your dad say about this? Does he know you are getting married to this girl?"

"Yes, he knows. Dad kind of read me the riot act, so to speak. Well, he said don't let what happen to him, happen to me."

"What does that mean?" she asked.

"Well, he said how wrong he was. He knows how wrong

it all was and there's not enough 'I'm sorry' in the world for him to say to you and finally he told me to go to anger management classes. He told me he'd go with me if it would help."

"Oh really?" She sarcastically replied.

"Now, can we have the barbeque here at your house? Your house, well, it's a lot prettier? I want everything to be nice for Retrea."

"Oh, so that's what this is about, having a party at my house, huh?"

"Mom, please think about it," he asked.

"Okay, I'll have to think about it," she commented with a deep sigh.

"Oh, thanks Mom!"

"Now wait. I didn't say, yes."

"But you didn't say no, either."

"Listen, son, do you have plans for dinner?" Maple asked.

"Not really, I was going by Retrea's and we were going to pick up a bite somewhere."

"Call her and see if she wants to come over here with you – you can pick her up while I get some food ready. This won't take much time at all."

"Okay, great, I'll do that now." Omar Junior left just before Alvin appeared.

"Are you going to let his dad back in your life?" Alvin asked.

"Were you standing out there listening to my conversation?" Maple asked.

Alvin smiled and nodded.

"No, that can't happen because I know his tricks. Remember?" said Maple

"He will try to make you miserable again, believe me. I have seen it."

"You've seen my future?" Maple said opening the door to the back yard. She began to clear off the table to prepare it for the meal.

"No, but I've visited your past. I looked at some of the good things and bad you told me about. Like the time when the dog showed up and blocked your front door, at that moment I knew, your husband was in a very bad, nasty mood. He was ready to pounce on you for any reason. I asked an angel to be there for you." Alvin helped Maple clean off the table. The air was quite warm and nice to sit outside and enjoy their evening meal.

"The dog was an Angel? I remember that time. Whenever Omar came near me, the dog would growl and show his teeth. The dog even followed me to the bedroom and lay down on the floor at my side of the bed," said Maple.

"Omar was quiet for the rest of the night, remember?" Alvin added.

"I do remember that. The next morning after everyone left the house, I let the dog out and he just disappeared. I'd fed him. I thought he'd come back, but he never did." Maple said as she rubbed her bare feet in the grass.

"Omar had planned to take his bad day out on you. He could have killed you that night. I believe he was planning to, but for the angel."

Maple looked down at her feet, breathed in deeply and said, "I know.

"And the last time he pushed me I felt someone was there because my head almost hit the corner of the dresser. I would have been a goner, but it was like I felt my head being moved forward or held."

"That's all you remember?"

"Was that an angel, too?"

"Angel. You could have died that day, but you called out for divine help. The Angels came. They are all around. All you have to do is ask. They will come to your aid. Maybe not always the way you think it should be, but the way that is best for the circumstances and Divine Order."

She sat down on the lawn bench and looked at all her gorgeous flowers in full bloom and smelling luscious. "It's been a long time since I've thought about the ugliness I endured."

"Why did you endure it?"

"I didn't believe I had a choice, and I didn't know what choices to look for. I didn't want to displace my children or lose them entirely and I believed that could happen so I waited until they were close to adulthood."

"Do you really think that was best?"

"Now that I look back on it, no. But at the time, I just didn't know what else to do. There were no classes on the subject and it's a topic people don't readily talk about," she said.

"So why let him into your life now?"

"The kids will be here soon. You can stay if you like." Maple paused a minute, then said, "Oh no, what will they think if they see you, and know you are the ghost of Byron? A person they know has been dead all this time?"

"Why not be a relative of... yourself?" She laughed and so did he.

"I'll come back around the end of dinner, ok? And to them I'll be my cousin, Alvin."

"I'd better finish making the food."

He kissed her forehead and hugged her tight, sealing everything that had just been said.

Instantly he was gone. Alvin then came right back with a bag full of food already prepared.

"Lets just set the table, and everything else is done," he told her. "Time travel fixes a lot of quick dilemmas."

"You think of everything don't you? Now, when will you show me how to do that?"

"When you are ready."

She finished the table and put the food in proper dishes and platters when she heard Junior come in. Alvin left.

"Hey, Ma. I'm back. I got Retrea with me. Where are you?"

"I'm here in the kitchen, Junior."

"Hi Retrea," Maple said as she walked into the room to greet them.

"Hi, Miss Maple," Retrea said.

"I hear you and Junior are talking about jumping the broom here pretty soon. When's the date?"

"We haven't set a date just yet. There are some things we want to do first," said Retrea.

"Come on out on the patio and tell me about your plans and how I can help." Maple said.

Maple led them outside to the back yard hoping they'd comment on how beautiful the garden was.

They ate and talked and ate some more, then paused when the doorbell rang.

"Excuse me. I'd better get that." Maple said.

"No, Ma. You sit down. I'll get it," she sat as Junior went to answer the door.

"Retrea, what kinds of 'things' are you planning to do before you set the date?" Maple asked.

"Well, Miss Maple, you know our relationship had been a rocky one and I didn't want to end up like my sister or my mother."

"What do you mean?" Maple asked.

Retrea stared at the nothingness of the tablecloth. Then she continued. "My sister is in the penitentiary for killing her husband after years of him beating her. When she couldn't stand it anymore. She got a gun and shot him."

"Oh Retrea, I'm so sorry." Maple said.

"It started a long time before. I mean we saw my daddy hit Ma whenever his day went bad, and that was most of his days. One day he started in on her and she didn't say anything back. That was unusual cause she usually did. So, anyway, she was making candy out of something like molasses, berries and sugar. He went to lunge at her with this big old knife in his hand and she threw the pot of boiling liquid in his face."

"Oh my God. What happened then?" Maple asked.

"Well, it looked like daddy was trying to outrun the hot boiling sugar and missed the top step and fell through the back railing that was loose—all the way down and landed in the yard which was concrete," she paused, "broke his neck and it killed him."

"What happened to your mother?'

Retrea sat for a minute not saying anything, just looking at the vacant air.

"Daddy threw the knife just before the hot pan hit him and it stuck in Mama's chest. She died on the way to the hospital." Retrea said that sentence as if it were one word.

The room filled with the grief of Retrea's memories. Maple understood what was happening and Retrea re-lived that moment again. The same hurt touched her heart again, from years ago.

They both looked up as Omar came barging in, "Ma there's a man out there that looks like your old friend, Byron, the one who died a while ago?"

"Calm down, boy. Its Alvin... he's a cousin, a distant relative to my old friend, Byron."

"That's what he said, but if I didn't know that Byron was already dead, I'd swear he was back"

"Stop that, yes, he does look like him," she told Junior.

"Come on in, Alvin, we are just finishing dinner," said Maple.

He walked in and bid everyone a good evening. Junior's eyes were as big as saucers shooting out from his face.

"Junior, are you all right? You look like you've seen a ghost." Retrea said.

"I feel like I have." Omar Junior said.

"Don't worry about it, son. I get the same reaction from a lot of people who knew Byron." Alvin said.

"You could be his double," Junior said while he shook his head back and forth.

Junior's whole body tensed up. He balled up his fists and ground the heel of his left foot into the lawn to make the point that he was right.

Maple watched and felt she had just seen a demonstration of her ex-husband's behavior whenever anything happened that he couldn't name. She saw Retrea's right eyebrow rise as she looked at Maple and nodded as if to say, see what I mean?

It was getting dark now so they went into the house and sat down in the dining room for coffee and dessert. Alvin didn't eat anything and Junior was as antsy as if there were several spoonfuls of cayenne pepper in his drawers.

As they said their goodnights, Retrea told Maple she would call her next week and finish their conversation. Junior asked Alvin where he parked his car and Alvin told him he'd walked.

"Well, let me drop you off at your place. You staying close to here."

"Thanks, but that's okay I'm going to sit for a little while with Maple, here."

Maple saw the tightening of Junior's jaw.

"Omar, we'd better be going. I've got an early day at work tomorrow," said Retrea.

"Yeah, yeah, lets go." he said abruptly.

Junior kissed his mother on the cheek, said goodnight to Alvin and grabbed Retrea's arm.

Retrea looked back at Maple and winked when they said their final goodnights.

As Junior and Retrea walked to the car, he said, "I don't like this, I don't like this at all." He helped Retrea into the car.

"What are you talking about, Omar?" Retrea asked.

"That guy that we left at Mama's house, because YOU just had to go."

"Well, you can drop me off at my place and come back here and sit with the two of them." Retrea snapped.

"What's gotten into you, Miss high and mighty?"

"Nothing. Lets just go, please."

The drive was silent and long. He pulled up in front of her house and said nothing as she got out. Before she closed the door she looked at him and said, "Your Mother is a grown independent woman and if she feels like keeping company why should anyone else have anything to say about it?"

He simply looked straight ahead and drove off, leaving Retrea on the sidewalk.

She shook her head, slowly walked to her door, then quickly went in, locked the door, and set the alarm. She saw the wedding plan books on the table, picked them up and threw them in the back room, saying, "I am not going to live like that."

Back at Maple's house the mood was not quite as tense, but close. "It looks to me like your son has a very short fuse," said Alvin.

"Yeah I know. Just like his dad. I've tried my best to get him to think things through before he reacts or at least weigh the consequences of his behavior. But he just ramrods his way through life and the predicaments he gets himself into. The aftermath is that he looks for whomever he can blame. Nothing is ever his fault, to hear him tell it." Maple said.

"Lets just change the subject, can we? You are sending your blood pressure through the roof," said Alvin.

"Thank you" she said with a smile.

"For what?"

"For stopping me from dredging up old stuff."

"Sometimes dredging up old stuff can clear up old-stuff issues. But you do have to work on those issues when emotions

142

are not wrapped up in the old stuff. Those are the emotions that protect your old view from what the issues really are."

"Enough said," Maple said through tight lips that moved from side to side on her face so she wouldn't say anything else that could open her old wounds.

"When will you go to talk with Kaye?" Alvin asked.

"Tomorrow."

"That's what you said last time I asked you."

She hesitated because she feared the unknown, hidden doors that were about to open. She took a deep breath and then another one. "Tomorrow for sure," Maple said.

Chapter 19

Maple stopped at the first nurses' station and asked, "Can you tell me how to find Kaye, she's an intensive care nurse?

"Are you a family member of someone she's working with today?" A faceless desk clerk said.

"No, well she was working with someone but he's not here now, I would just need a couple minutes of her time."

"Just let me check. What's your name?" she asked with her face turned to the computer screen the whole time.

"Maple, Maple Pomaroy, thank you."

The desk clerk pushed a button on the console and said, "Hey, is Kaye Neely up there? There's a lady down here at reception, wants to talk with her for a couple minutes. Name's Maple Pomaroy," there was another pause so the clerk picked up the receiver. Then said without looking up, "Ms. Pomaroy, she's going to check to see if Kaye Neely is available."

"Thank you," said Maple to the clerk. The rude clerk who wore her attitude like an ugly dress, never even looked Maple in the eye.

Maple found a comfortable chair because she didn't like the plastic one's. She sat and waited for what seemed like a few lifetimes. She crossed her legs from left to right then changed to ankles right to left. When she was just about to get up to leave she heard, "Oh, there you are." It was Byron's old nurse, Kaye.

"Hello." Maple reached out her hand.

Kaye took her hand then hugged her around the shoulders.

"How are you doing, dear?" she asked Maple.

"Fine, fine, thank you. Is there someplace we can go and talk privately?"

"Well," she took a quick look at her watch and told the woman at the front desk whose eyes never looked up, that she'd be back a little later. "It seems I'm not needed this evening after all." Kaye told her. She then switched her attention to Maple saying, "Sure let's go to the nurse's lounge."

Maple was too nervous to sit comfortably – she chose a straight-backed, wooden chair and sat on its edge, like she was getting ready to jump up and run any second.

"Are you all right, dear?"

"Yes... ah uh, I think so." She looked down at her purse strap that she'd twisted into a knotted mess.

"Please don't think I'm out of my mind... because I do," she paused. "Anyway, Alvin, well that is ah, Byron, he changed his name. He has appeared to me in three consecutive dreams and when I asked him why he changed his name and why he was there, he said that I had asked him to be there in my dreams. Each dream we've talked and he asked me to promise him I'd talk to you.

"It was the craziest thing because one day he just showed up when I wasn't asleep. He reminded me that I had promised to talk with you." Maple rambled. "Did he leave me a message with you or something?"

There was complete silence. Neither looked at the other.

Maple couldn't stand that kind of silence.

So she got up to leave saying, "I'm so sorry I bothered you."

"No, please wait, I do have a message for you," said Kaye.

"He told me I was in a dream but it seemed as real as you and I are talking now," said Maple.

Kaye smiled. "You are about to break the strap on your

purse. You don't have to be so nervous, I don't bite."

"I feel like I have lost my mind with what's been happening, it's almost like watching a movie and I am a part of it." Maple sighed. "Maybe I caused it."

"Did he tell you there are no accidents or coincidences?" Kaye asked.

"Yes."

"You know I was on duty working here the last three days and today I was supposed to be off but someone called in with a child care problem and I agreed to cover and take her place. Then half an hour ago just before her shift was to begin she showed up saying everything worked out, so you see I was supposed to be here to talk with you today."

"About what?" Maple asked.

"What else happened in the dream?" Kaye asked.

"He just showed up at the foot of my bed. I mean just showed up out of thin air."

"Scared ya, huh?"

"Hell yeah, it scared me. Then he quickly told me I was dreaming and..."

"And?" Kaye leaned forward for the answer.

"I did kind of, well, make a wish on a shooting star that I could talk with him again, but that stuff never happens for real. It's just wishing like when you wish for a million dollars or something else impossible."

"Oh, but it does happen. Your life is quite interesting you know." Kaye said.

Maple watched a bumblebee land on rose petals right outside the window, and nodded, then shook her head.

"There have been some very great highs and almost equally great lows in your life, but through all of it you never gave up even though you never saw the real purpose in it all."

"What do you mean?" Maple said.

"What's been the worst part of your life?" Kaye asked, wanting Maple to concentrate on her own self-actualization.

147

"People leaving." Maple shrugged her shoulders.

"Deaths you mean?" Kaye asked.

"Not just death, but people disappearing from my life and I never get the reason for it. Some of them I looked for and the few that I found had lost that magical essence I once saw in them, which meant the person I thought I knew was gone."

"Your former lovers, you mean?"

"Well, no I mean family members and friends and just people that make me think of family. Yeah, ya know."

"Yeah."

Kaye got up from the table and went to pour two cups of coffee; Maple sat and tried to find words to break into the desert of silence. She pulled a cough drop from her purse after unraveling the strap.

"Does Alvin know about things you have gone through?"

"Some of them. The things I've told him over the years we've been friends," Maple said.

"You know he's going to try to fix them for you?" Kaye said.

"What do you mean, fix?" she asked.

"Change it. Each of us are in the space and time we should be in, however, sometimes we can escape to or visit another time in the past." Kaye said.

"Just the past not the future? You mean like time travel? I've dreamed about that almost like I was there." Maple said.

"You can only escape to the future when someone who's already there takes you or opens portals and banishes the barriers for you to pass through."

"So what you are saying it's like the Time Machine, that old movie?" asked Maple.

"The concept of journeying into other times is the same but . . ." Kaye paused.

"I saw this program where a physicist named Merrill studied the possibility of time travel to go visit his father who died when he was a small boy. His studies found that even Einstein researched the subject and inferred that inter-dimension travel could be related to the black hole or worm-holes. I don't know what those are. At least I hope it's not going in the ground like earth worms do." Maple smiled.

Kaye laughed right out loud and said, "I don't think so."

"So what's happening with Alvin now, is he past or fu-ture?" Maple quietly asked.

"Matter of fact, he's both," said Kaye.

Maple went inside herself and couldn't find a point of ref-erence to grasp that would give her a footing or hold on her next utterance or move. Not her intellect, spirit, body or soul gave her a clue. She felt she was hanging in the middle of a midnight story all by herself.

"Oh let me illuminate some of this confusion for you. Have you had dinner?" Kaye asked.

"No, I came here right from work. I wanted to keep my promise to …"

"Let's go get some food," said Kaye.

"Okay, but, I'm not really hungry." Maple said.

"Humor me, I'm starved." said Kaye.

They left the building and once outside Maple walked to her car and Kaye followed.

"Why don't we each take our cars and then we won't have to come back here?" said Maple.

"Oh, I didn't drive today so I'll just ride with you. Okay?"

"Okay, where to?"

"Take I-5 south over the Marquam Bridge then exit at Multnomah I think it's near there. I have to get my bearings when we get to that point."

Maple hadn't heard a word Kaye was saying, until…

"Exit I-5, now!" Kaye squeaked. "Here we are."

"Wow that was quick. Where are we?"

"Don't worry about it we're here. The food is great even if you only taste the appetizers," said Kaye.

They walked into the restaurant and Maple was amazed

at the elegance of it all. She never knew this place existed. The waiter who seated them appeared to know Kaye very well.

"I'll have a glass of red wine please and I'm not sure about what to eat yet," Maple said.

"My treat, so get what you want."

"Ok, in that case I'll have the salmon even though it doesn't go with the wine," said Maple

"Me, too," said Kaye as she looked directly in Maple's eyes and said, "so what do you think is happening?"

"I don't know." Maple put her right index finger in her mouth and tried to chew on her cracked fingernail. She couldn't bite through the gel caked under the nail it had a tiny jagged edge since she last went to the nail shop. The jagged edge was caused by Maple biting her nails when she was nervous which was now to the extreme!

"Remember we talked about travel before. You know, visiting time, you remember, and you wanted to see what you missed or just relive it?" Kaye reminded her.

"I vaguely remember that." Maple said starting to squirm in her seat, a chill went straight through her body and her shoulders jerked upward.

Kaye watched intently.

"When did things start going bad for you and your last love?"

"I guess when I realized he had no regard for my feelings, my family, my friends, my belongings, my work or my dreams."

"He could be a violent man, couldn't he?"

Maple sighed twice and held her lips tight together so that the words in her mind wouldn't escape into the conversation. She nodded.

"You know, that wasn't about you. It was about him. There was nothing else in his life that he could control except someone who trusted him wholeheartedly. So when you realized he was controlling and questioning your behavior, he had nothing to fall back on but the violence he'd been taught and what he knew." Kaye commented.

"If it was about him then why was I the recipient of his tirades, his punching bag; the one he could belittle, humiliate, criticize and blame? Ya know, I was lied to, lied on and lied about; I don't understand."

"Is that why you stayed?" Kaye asked, "because you didn't understand?"

"No, it was because every place I ran to I felt I was an intrusion on someone else, and I had so much to sort out I couldn't get to any of it in my head. I believe that I had made bad choices that I had to live with and take care of." They stopped talking while the waiter poured her another glass of wine. Maple noticed that the waiter smelled like ancient spices. Familiar.

"The scariest thing was the threats. Threats that he would keep the children and I'd only see them when he said so. Because I was not capable of taking care of them, he'd say. He was cruel enough to do that. Then, unexplainable things would happen." Maple said.

"Like?"

"He'd be really nice, easy going, agreeable even, and we did things together as a family, then out of nowhere he would explode." Maple said. "Never again."

Both glasses of wine were instinctively raised

"Cheers," said Kaye.

"Cheers," replied Maple. "I never talked about this because people think you're nuts when you have problems that you can't handle, or they feel you cause yourself."

"So what happened that you finally walked away?"

"Something pricked my spirit so that the last time he pushed and hit me was the last time! Period! I made up my mind that I'd survive on my own. And I did."

"Where did Alvin enter the picture?" Kaye asked.

"Oh, he was there, always, a friend, a dear friend. I guess

he was there from the time I began to see that I would be okay no matter what happened with my marriage. I still had to wait until the children were old enough for me to go to work everyday and they wouldn't need me."

"Nothing more? I mean with Alvin?" Kaye asked.

"No, we respected each other and we enjoyed nice conversations and we talked for long times just about our lives, our children, our jobs and most of all our health. He didn't reveal that his health condition was as bad as it was for him. Or maybe I just didn't see it or didn't want to acknowledge it. I don't know."

"If you could do anything over again what would that be?" Kaye asked.

"One day I was in the grocery store and I hadn't seen him in a long time and we bumped into each other. We both smiled from ear to ear and grabbed each other in full embrace and realized we were in the middle of the isle in the frozen food section and almost apologized; I should have or I wish I had said lets go have a cup of coffee or a drink or dinner or any reason to talk about what had just happened when we hugged. I could have told him I missed him."

I was at my wits end that day and needed a friend who would not take advantage of the situation. That was Byron, I mean Alvin."

"Let's go there," Kaye said.

"What. What do you mean? " Maple asked.

The room changed from dark to light and Maple found herself with the shopping cart and Bryon right to the left of her going in the opposite direction. Maple began to re-live those moments.

"Hello, how are you? I haven't seen you in ages."

He grabbed her and said, "I've missed you, how are you doing." The hug became magical and electric.

They stood there for the moment.

"Are you buying ice cream?" she said

"Do you want some?" he replied.

"No, I just thought that maybe we could have a cup of coffee and catch up if you didn't have any groceries that would spoil or melt."

They laughed.

"How about meeting at the coffee shop on North whatcha macallit?" he snapped his fingers trying to remember the name of it.

"All The Time Saturday Morning," they said in unison.

It was a funky little café located near the south side of the Interstate Bridge. Serving breakfast all day and night.

"I can meet you there within the next half hour."

"Me too," she agreed.

In a blink of an eye, they were there.

They talked and their talking continued for days it seemed and they walked and talked and his hands covered hers and her fingers intertwined with his.

"I want you with me always. You've left him, I know." Alvin told her.

"You – you, can't say that. This is temporary. You know we will have to go back to real time." Maple said.

Maple felt that this was part of Kaye's magic and not real at all. She thought she was in a trance.

"This is real for right this moment. Live here with me as if there were no tomorrow or yesterday, just right now." He wrapped his arms around her and she followed his lead. She raised her head to look up to him and he was already looking, relishing in the love he had for her and at that very moment they kissed for the very first time. They each felt suspended in the middle of the sky. Their moments in time ended but not before their lives were intertwined into her world and his.

"Will you still come to my dreams?"

"Whenever you want me there, yes."

Suddenly, Kaye was there and tugged at Alvin's arm,

"You have to let go now." Kaye said.

He left with one strand of her hair and a tiny piece of fingernail she'd started to chew on and it broke off in his hand, her energy attached to his.

The jolt of sitting quickly brought Maple back to the table. She looked across at Kaye.

"I was there with him wasn't I?" Maple sheepishly questioned. "I wasn't asleep! I wasn't, was I?"

"Yes, but be careful, you were with him. He can't survive for long in your realm and you can't go to where he is now," said Kaye.

"No you were not asleep," said Kaye.

"Ladies, what would you like for dessert?"

"Ice cream." Maple announced.

"Make it two." Kaye said.

A friend of Kaye's came to the table and introduced himself to Maple. He spoke like he knew her. Maple saw how he looked at Kaye so she mentioned she had to get going and Kaye's friend said, "I'd be honored to see you home Kaye."

Maple left Kaye in the restaurant and drove the long way home through the woods. There was still daylight but she noticed the fingertips of trees were inviting an early autumn, while the sunlight cascaded through their branches.

She arrived home not quite knowing what to think. As she opened the door Buster was cackling, she put down her things, locked the front door and went to see what was going on with her bird.

She saw the note she'd left on the spot where Alvin sat in her dream.

The note said only, 'hello.'

"Tell her I said hello." Buster repeated, over and over. Maple didn't even try to quiet him; she just got ready to dream.

Chapter 20

Maple, looked up from deep slumber. "You really are here," the smile in her voice broke the cool summer breeze just before daybreak silence. Alvin stood by the door.

"I are here," screeched Buster.

They looked at Buster and then each in unison, "Buster needs a new room."

"Buster new room," the bird repeated.

"I'm going to fix some coffee, can I make you a cup?'

"No, but, thank you," Alvin said.

By the time she showered and completed her early morning personal care, dressed and walked in the kitchen, she noticed the coffee was there and so was toast and a bowl of fruit.

"You amaze me," she told him. "Teach me how to do that."

"Do what?" he asked.

"Go to different places and times, whenever and get things done easily."

"When it's time I will be glad to teach you," he said.

Do I have to die first?

"No, you don't." he said.

Oh, no. He knew my thoughts!

Alvin burst out laughing. So did Maple.

"Ok, where do we go from here? I mean you're here but you're dead? Am I back in a dream again?"

"No you are right here with me this moment," Alvin said.

"When do you allow other people to see you like the other evening when Omar was here with Retrea? Do other people see you?"

"Not the way you see me. Those who knew me before only see the image I project which is similar, but not exactly as they remember me."

"Why me, though?" she asked.

"Because I've loved you forever and I couldn't leave you with all that's going on around you," he said.

"There will always be something going on around me, good or bad, but, something. So why now?"

"Yes, I guess you're right," he said in a somber tone, not wanting to say more just yet.

The steam from her first sip of coffee fogged up her glasses so she took them off to see Alvin eyeball to eyeball.

"You told me you are here to protect me. I guess I don't understand, from what?"

"Maybe from yourself or someone close to you, I'm not sure," he said

"So does that mean you're my angel?"

"I wish I could be, but no, I'm not an angel."

"You sure I'm not still dreaming?"

"I'm sure."

"Well, now, what happens next?"

"I'm not fully sure, but you requested me and I came to you. Believe me, you are a joy, my joy," he said.

"So, you've died and gone to heaven?" she asked.

"You don't know how true that statement is. I feel that I have... being here with you," he said. "But heaven isn't a particular place, it's a state of being, of existing. It's the place my energy is near."

They each stared at the table between them.

"Maybe I still have lessons to learn, and I know it's not time yet for you to escape the earth."

"What do you mean?" she asked

"For you to walk out of your shell, your body, your burdens, your physical pain, your anguish." he said reaching for her hand. "There is more for you to do, but first you have to find your true happy place." He struggled to find the exact words.

"When you find it you wait, especially in quiet times, until someone calls for you to help, to hear, to show them something they need."

"So is that different from the travel through to different times?" she asked.

"Most definitely."

"How?" she said.

"Traveling is your earthly spirit wanting to know things, but when you actually leave you hope you left enough love and caring behind for someone that you may not even know will be needing. At that time you can do as much good as you can or feel is necessary. Some people have done so much good before they go that there is no wait time for them. Do you know what I'm saying?"

"Yeah it's like Clarence in that movie 'It's a Wonderful Life,' trying to get his wings."

"In a sense, yes, you could say that is sort of how it is but the wings aren't the prize, the help you render is."

"So again, where do we go from here?" Maple asked.

He sidestepped the question again. "There's a turn that someone or some people have to make. I don't know what it is but it's your link to them.

"Tell me Maple, after you finally got your freedom, why didn't you date anyone or get into another relationship?"

"I was waiting for you. But you never said anything to imply an interest and I was afraid to say anything to you for fear of causing you to run away. It was only after you were gone did I realize I could have said something to make a difference. Then it was just better to close up my heart shop and concentrate on work and prepare myself for growing older." She said squirming in her chair.

"Me too, I didn't know how to approach you without losing our friendship," said Alvin.

Maple paused to wait for Alvin to confirm her thoughts she'd just revealed. He kept his head down and traced the pattern on the tablecloth design.

She continued, "I don't want to be a burden to my children or anyone else and I want to be able to take care of myself until there's nothing left of me. I preferred the isolation to the misuse of my spirit. Maybe my bullshit radar never matured, I don't know, but I never quite got to the point where I could understand people's games of jealousy and trickery."

She stopped and looked away as she remembered some of the crap that had been thrown at her, in order to start a smoke screen enough to throw attention to someone else and get the heat off them, crap throwers, were the real villains.

"Do you want to say more?" he asked.

"No, enough said." Maple replied.

"Okay."

"I am worried that my son is showing the same abusive characteristics as his father. His past girlfriends have left abruptly now there's one who's had a troubled life and I believe she loves him. But I'm glad that she's taking care of herself first."

"Do you mean Retrea?" he asked.

"Yes, I believe she will do very well in her life," said Maple

"How about your daughter?" Alvin asked.

"She's doing fine. We have lots of talks and she has a lovely family, a nice husband who loves her and their beautiful, precious children."

"I believe you're right about your daughter, she is a lovely person and her spirit is sweet and loving especially to her family. I think it has to do with your son or someone in his life, that causes me to wonder," Alvin said.

"I worry about my son. He is so angry all the time. Sometimes prayer helps but I can't pray away his anger and I don't know why it's there. I wonder what is going on now," she said.

"Oh, what is going on now? Do you know?" she asked.

"It's not a short term fix I'm talking about. This is a long-range plan we, meaning you and I, have to help initiate. You never know when you will be called on to help someone else out of their suffering," he said.

"Oh look at the time, I have to go to work. If I lost my job I'd be in trouble. I just need to work one more year, and then I'll retire and plant tomatoes and beans and peppers and help rescue injured birds."

"Is that something Buster asked you to do?"

"In a sense yes. He was a rescued bird but now that I think about it, he actually rescued me. Buster even has a bird friend that comes to the window to visit with him. The bird started showing up after you . . ."

"My body gave out?" Alvin tried to lighten the moment.

"Yeah," she said looking toward the window.

She waved her hand at Alvin. "Scoot now I have to get going."

A few minutes later she ran out of the room and Alvin was waiting for her.

"I'm late, I can't believe the time escaped me like this." Maple told Alvin.

"I can drop you off so you don't have to worry about parking. Unless you're scared some of those busy body co-workers will tease you, I can hear them now, 'who's that man driving you to work this morning?' They will ask you that, now take my word for it." Alvin, told her.

"Don't worry about me. I can handle them. What will we do this evening?" Maple asked.

"You and I have to do some traveling soon but there are a few things I have to talk with you about first," Alvin said.

"Let's talk this evening."

"What's troubling you, Alvin?"

"Some of the travel has to wait until I find out more from Kaye. She's my guide, you know." Alvin touched her face to bring it closer to his and his lips could meet her own. The air she breathed warmed his spirit.

"About what?" Maple questioned and tenseness echoed around her.

"I thought you knew everything," she said attached to a coy smile. "Take me to work."

"Your wish is my command," he bowed.

Chapter 21

Maple measured out the exact number of spoonfuls of coffee to brew three cups. She put all else on the table to establish her morning. Her food, her list of things to do and now she could finished her ritual to get the day started.

She thanked God for waking her up in her right mind and for all she had been given. Maple was not rich by any means nor could you say she was well off. She was able to sustain herself with a few things she cared to have around her. A small and very nice place to live, let's just say that she felt she had enough. Maple continued to thank God for everything that came to her mind. She asked for wisdom and mercy for herself and her children. The others in her life were included in prayer, especially Eritrea, called Retrea. A faint whistle off in the distance and a fragrant spray of lilacs filled the room where she prayed. Maple's face smiled from the inside; outwardly she continued to wear her expressionless mask, which she thought hid her feelings.

Alvin was someplace near.

"Prayers done?" he asked.

"Oh no. Never. I'll always have something to be thankful for and... "

"I know, I know," he replied before she could finish.

"I've been thinking about Retrea and she just jumped into my prayer this morning. I wonder if she's okay, I mean it seems overwhelming that as young as she is, she's taking on so much responsibility."

"What do you mean?" he asked.

"I mean she's going through the court system to get custody of her little sister and ..."

"Her life from what I've been told, has not been, ... sunshine, picnics and barbeques," he said.

They both laughed an uncomfortable chuckle.

"You come up with the craziest statements," she told him, as her hand appeared to throw something at him.

"I know... " he left that floating in the air.

"Alvin, what do you suppose it all means?"

"I don't know how to start," his eyes traced the pattern on the floor.

"Anyplace would be fine," she saw a struggle come across the image of his face.

"You are so deep in thought, what's the matter?" she asked.

"Have you ever heard of people being cursed?" he asked while staring straight through her eyes into her spirit.

"You mean, witchcraft and voodoo stuff?" she said.

"Oh no, far from it. Very far from it," he said holding the table as if it were about to fly away.

"In your Bible there are several conversations about curses. The first curses belong to Adam and Eve, for Adam's disobedience."

"But they both ate the fruit," she commented.

"Yes, but God gave Adam specific instructions, and he disobeyed."

How could this conversation be coming from him? Her right eyebrow went up almost to her hairline while her left eyebrow kept its place.

"It's for real, Maple," he said with sad eyes.

"From the very beginning we've all been struggling between right and wrong: good and evil, heaven and hell.

Right?" he didn't wait for her answer.

"It's all in the Good Book, God's Word of blessings and curses. We tend not to openly talk about the curses, but they exist, too, right along with the blessings."

"Are you cold?" he asked as he watched her wrap her arms around herself and all but folded up in a ball.

"No, just a bit of a chill in the room," she lied.

"I don't mean to frighten you but," he let that hang out in the air for about a minute. He continued with, "I had to search out the curses in my core. They are real Maple, and maybe Retrea is trying to survive while living under a generational curse, or many of them, too! It could have started four, seven, twelve or more generations ago."

"I don't believe you," she said as she sucked in a full body of air and held onto it. How can you say such a thing?" she began to get up to walk towards another room.

"Will you let me show you something?" he asked as he reached for her hand.

"What?" she snapped, digging her heels into her own mindset?

"Where is your Bible?" he asked

"No you can't use my Bible for this nonsense you're talking about!"

"Please, let me show you something. You can interpret it however it suits you. Okay?"

Maple stiffened her lower jaw and said, "Okay," through clenched teeth.

"Let's look up Mount Ebal and see what it tells us."

"Deut 11:29, Oh, a place to proclaim curses. Is this the only place it's mentioned?" Maple asked.

"No, there are many curses mentioned in the Bible and they are really for all of us to pay attention to. Read the whole book of Deuteronomy and maybe we can talk later. Or at least read the entire twenty-eighth chapter. Will you do that?" Asked Alvin.

163

"Okay, yes, I'll do… that," she said through a deep sigh where she could almost see steam coming from her nostrils.

"God tells us over and over, throughout the Bible, what He will do for us but then we also have an obligation," said Alvin.

"And what's that?" Maple asked

"Obedience. Obedience, to His word. That's it," Alvin said.

"But what about… " she stopped.

"No, it's obedience to God's law, we are not supposed to change it. Like in the Book of Samuel, I think it is − 'Obedience is better than sacrifice.' I'm not kidding you, it is right in there."

"I don't understand how this stuff affects us now. I mean I don't check everyday but I don't break commandments, not intentionally."

"Not even a little?" he asked.

"No, I don't think so. Why?" she said.

"I went back as far as I could to find everyplace any of my ancestors were out of line with what God said, and… " he stopped and looked away.

"And?" she said questionably.

"I found some pretty ugly stuff," he answered.

Maple saw an overwhelming sadness coming from his spirit through his eyes.

"What'd you do?"

"I went back, and back again through several generations and found my people in a small country in Africa named Eritrea."

"You mean there is a place in the world that Retrea, Omar's girlfriend, is named after?" Maple asked drawing herself into a ball.

"Yes, and I believe she is one of the first links I've found to uncover the curse," he said.

164

"So I was not surprised when you introduced me to Omar's girlfriend." He paused. "I saw some of the things they did or didn't do and I prayed to God to release my ancestors from the curses for their disobedience. Then I prayed for all of them until I got to me."

"To you?" Maple asked.

"Yes, to me. I had to pray for forgiveness that was a carry through from my forefathers and mothers, so that I could free my spirit and the spirit of my children. I don't want their lives to go through life the way mine did."

"How do you know?"

"I've seen my kids and they look … well … they look new, happy and they are doing better and so are their children," he proudly declared.

"So, what does that mean for me?" she asked.

"It means that this feeling of guilt and paranoia has been sizzling out of our very souls."

"Think about your life and disappointments, sadness, fears, and sorrows. You can release these so they don't continue in your 'life account.' You don't have to hold on to what someone did hundreds of years ago. They just happened to send their DNA through bloodlines to you. This gall vexes the Laminin in your physical self and permeates through to your soul. The curses came with the DNA."

"This is craziness!" she huffed gasping for more air.

"No, it's not. Keep your heart and mind open until you read it for yourself, so truth can unfold before your eyes," he assured her.

"A closed mind can't grow or learn." Alvin said.

"None of the churches I've ever attended teach this, this madness," she almost shouted.

"Who wants to hear about the ugliest part of life? There would be no regular congregation, all the pews would be empty, or mostly empty," he laughed.

165

"This is too unbelievable and hellish." Maple said.

"As long as the preachers are talking about blessings and favor, prosperity and goodness, people listen and identify themselves in that category. But when the congregation hears about the consequences of behavior not within God's will, they look at others. They look at their neighbors, associates and friends to identify their faults. But they disregard their own misgivings."

I know that's why so much goes on right under our noses and we don't see it," he said.

"Why don't we see it? Is it some magical place for our minds or something?" she asked waving an imaginary wand.

Maple's eyes tightened almost shutting entirely and Alvin saw an anger rise up in her he'd never seen before.

"No," he said solemnly. "We don't want to see it, recognize it or account for it. If we do, it becomes real and we have to take responsibility for it," he answered.

Maple noticed how his mood changed to a sadness she didn't quite know.

"Is that where Kaye took you in time. So you would know your past and that of your bloodline?"

"Kaye took me to places where I would be open to knowledge that I didn't know existed, and because of it, I had to go on a journey to find out about my past. And once I knew, I had to act."

"So what about me?" Maple asked

"People knew something was wrong about your marriage, not to the whole extent but we saw pain in your eyes. We saw your spirit screaming and fighting to stay alive."

He paused then said, "Some of your acquaintances even tried to take advantage of you when they saw a vulnerability. Vulnerability, meaning that there was a lot going on in your head, mind and spirit that meant you couldn't keep up with everything.

Maple was unnerved by now and sat speechless until she could change the focus back to him.

"Did you find out about your illness and why was that a choice you made?" she asked.

"Yes, I made some foolish decisions and contributed to all that happened," he said. "And everything that happened to me I helped create it by not searching for truth. Everything that happens in our lives is directly correlated to some choice we've made, even when we do nothing, that is a choice," he continued.

Maple tried not to show the disbelief in what Alvin was telling her.

In a soft voice, almost inaudible but with a taste of sarcasm, "So why did you choose to die?"

"I chose to die after I realized that … that… my physical self would be useless to everyone and I didn't want to be a vegetable and … you needed an angel."

She immediately wanted to grab that last question out of the air and stuff it back in her mouth and down her own throat. Instead she just looked at him with very sad apologetic downcast eyes and said, "Thank you."

At that point, they held onto each other's hands while the essence of all they each were, melded into one heart, one purpose, and one love.

Their search for the curse's origin began at that very moment.

Chapter 22

Alvin and Maple, along with their silent partner Kaye, began the journey to find those places that better choices could have been made. When they found those choices they intervened to undo the chaos that could continue to happen.

"I've learned a lot about how to break generational curses but how does prayer work when things have already happened and chaos is a part of our lives?" Maple asked.

"You cannot truly change the past but you can ask for forgiveness for yourself or for someone else." Kaye told her. "This can change future outcomes."

"What do you mean, someone else?" Maple asked.

"There's a great example in the bible, 'Forgive them for they know not what they do;' its in Luke 23rd chapter, the 34th verse," said Alvin.

"You know some people who are struggling in their lives, careers and within their families, their finances, their health, don't you?"

"Yes, I do." Maple said as she lowered her eyes to the floor.

"They are, in fact, in a spiritual poverty; so pray for them." Alvin said intently. "Pray for them now! Because a lot of those horrific choices come from cell memory that has been passed down for as many as seventy times seven generations."

"I don't know what or how I should pray for them."

"You don't have to, just pray that their lives get better in Divine Order and ask God to help them with whatever is making them struggle. There is also a verse in the Bible that you can pray, Jeremiah 33:3; God will answer." Alvin smiled as those words left his mouth. "God says, 'Call on me and I will answer you,' telling you things you do not know," he said. "So ask God what you should say or pray about, he will show you."

"I'm afraid to look at my own relatives or ancestors, because I know something is lurking around me. My health condition is one of them, and then there are my relationships. There are some other things too that I'm not yet ready to talk about. My son is having trouble with relationships, too. I don't want to spy into his life, but there is this young lady that I know he likes or maybe even loves, but they keep getting into fights. I know that must have something to do with the way my ex-husband and I couldn't get along and I didn't know where that came from." Maple turned her eyes to the window while she talked.

"Maple, you know you'll be amazed how most of our lives have crossed even before we were born. And then we come back to this world in groups, most often with the same spirits from other times. Let's go see how we can unravel some of the webs in our lives."

Alvin grabbed Maple's hand and Kaye opened the doors they needed. "We are all connected in some way."

Their actual journey began at that very moment.

They searched for places and followed people and found ugly hearts and longing souls. Souls encrusted with enough bitterness to sour an ocean. The people they found were broken by damaged old souls and walk-ins. Yes, walk-ins whose souls were troubled so they looked for good luck to make things better or searched diligently for revenge—it was mostly for revenge.

Kaye knew about many of the lost spirits but there was one thing she could not alter and that was a person's free will.

One by one they began to unearth damaged spirits and asked God for healing. It was ugly and earth shattering and mysterious and awesome and not just frightening but bone-chilling anguish materialized. They found all the deadly sins and more. There was creepy crawling evil throughout each and every timeframe. It was a constant overhang in all societies. Even those that appeared to be pristine and pure were soaked in sin and corruption and mayhem. There was murder and lust and lies and pride and gluttony—not just for food. The acts of coveting and rape and pillaging were everywhere—Alvin and Maple saw it all.

The trouble that they found vexed their very souls and skyrocketed their spirits to action. They covered themselves and prayed and continued praying throughout as many generations as could be found. They found themselves in Eritrea, a small country on the African continent, and saw themselves. They prayed for their own souls.

Chapter 23

Maple went back to a closer time to their own and found Olive first. They realized that her spirit was part of their same circle of curses.

They watched when Olive turned the crank at the bottom of the box that played her song almost every day since the child was born. It was the tinkling notes of 'Love me Tender.' Olive didn't know if the child was a girl or boy, no one told her. And she was told not to tell a solitary soul. So Olive obeyed and kept the ordeal inside her spirit.

She arranged her wig on her unruly head of hair staying clear of the mirror but watched her shadow on the wall aside the door. Her shadow was the only image of herself she dare observe.

Her long-legged angry strides were slow and almost cumbersome at times so she stopped for a minute to catch her breath from time to time. The late afternoon air, cooled suddenly, but not enough to chill her ebony skin. Her legs and arms fully covered by the extra large old outdated ankle-length dress. The dress covered the creepy white skin that had begun to eat the dark and continued to spread.

She hated it. As a child, she wanted white skin and even wished for it, when the phrase 'Black is Beautiful' entered the 1960's culture revolution, she walked taller in her dark and lovely skin. She became use to the dark and made friends with it. She remembered smiling at herself in the mirror and touching her smooth luscious dark chocolate skin and fluffed her un-processed, naturally cork screwed curly crown. She was happy, lovely and beautiful back then.

Most of her hair had vanished now due to processing then no processing, then coloring and now gray covered her head like a ball of cotton. A wig, uncombed and nearly dreaded like strands covered her oversized head—a crown. Nothing else really mattered anyway.

Olive marched through the neighborhood to the market with combat soldier precision to get groceries for her brother's children who'd be staying with her for a while. No one recognized her grief for the brother she rarely spoke to over the last 25 years.

Her brother died after falling from a third floor back porch, right after he killed his wife, they said. She wanted to believe that his wife had killed him and his last effort was to get her, too. That thought gave his action reason, although in her deepest heart thread she knew what he was.

She claimed no children of her own because her husband, whom she loved dearly way back when, ran off with the make-up assistant he met at the theater when the big show was in town. He worked as a janitor at the building. The head janitor, she said proudly back then.

Olive kept to herself over the past years not involved with family or friends. It felt to her like every person she trusted had betrayed her in some way. There was very little she felt she could offer to any kind of friendship so she didn't.

There had been happy times when she was a little girl. She played in the street with the other kids. Not many girls in the neighborhood mostly a lot of boys. Olive remembered her mother saying to the ladies who sat on the front porch with her that since there were so many more boys than girls, there would be enough men to send off to war. The lady from next door said she thought the government put something in the water or in the air so more boy babies could be born during certain times. She said wars were planned twenty years out and the government picked certain areas so that they could take the resources by force and the big cats could get richer while the poor boys fought the war. The big government boys saw them, the poor, as expendable.

Olive thought, *that sure was about fifteen to maybe eighteen years before the war started from the times we would all play together down by the creek.* Many of her childhood friends from back then were dead now. Dead because of wars fought in foreign countries or wars they fought on the streets or homes or work or drugs. There were so many walls built to keep some people from any kind of success or better life, whatever that was. Her skin instantly chilled because she also remembered the old man that used to sit around and watch them play.

The old man told the boys they should go swimming in the creek because it was such a hot day. He said they should take all their clothes off so their mothers would not be mad if their clothes got messed up in the water. After a few times the boys didn't go to the creek anymore.

Olive had been planning her thirteenth birthday party at her friend's house and started her walk home. *I'm going to be a teenager.* She used the path by Willow creek as a short cut to get to and from her best girlfriend's house to play mud-pies or make skirts out of grass and leaves for their dolls. One day she walked home through her short-cut path and the old man was there. It was like he just showed up and acting like he lost something. She heard what sounded like change dropping on the wooden walk board. Then she heard keys drop, too. Olive went to pick up the change to help the old man but when she turned around his face looked clown like and he didn't have any pants on. She got up from the ground to run but after two

175

or three steps he'd grabbed her around the waist. Olive yelled for her mama, but her voice was muffled by an odd smelling towel over her mouth and nose. She felt a pain then nothing. She slept.

Olive's mind kept going back to all the drama in her life and how hard many of her years had been. However, she continued her march to the store.

Hannah, Brid and Shadow waited outside until Olive finished her shopping and left the store. They had been keeping up with her all day. When Olive reached the exit she stiffened her back to ready herself for the march home. It was just a few blocks but she knew the stares and smirks would be aimed at her as she tried to focus on going home, home to nothingness.

She had a dog once but it died at about fifteen years. The dog was kind of funny looking; Olive was, too. The canine was a mutt, mixed with everything, a true mongrel. Continuing to look back she remembered seeing some kids with a three wheeled wagon that had lots of jovial looking, playful puppies. She had watched them for a while and noticed one that seemed to be shunned by the rest of the litter.

She asked the group of kids, "What are you going to do with all those puppies?"

One kid, the leader probably, said, "My Mom says we have to get rid of them today or they go to the pound. Do you want to buy one, they only cost a dollar each?"

"What's wrong with the little runt over there in the corner?" Olive asked while rummaging in her purse for a dollar bill.

"She's a weakling and her mother would have eaten her alive but we got to her first. She doesn't eat much like the others, they just push her away."

"Okay, that's the one I want," she said handing the leader a one dollar bill.

"Lady she's nothing but skin and bones and mama said she probably won't live long and she's just a waste of dog food."

176

"That's all right," said Olive, "I'll keep her as long as she lives." *I'll call her Bones.*

"They will be company for each other," Hannah told her traveling buddies, Brid and Shadow, as they were with her even back then.

While Olive was deep in thought about her precious dog, Bones, she walked passed the 'Just-For-You' Beauty Shop. She stood there for a moment to catch her breath and listened to some of the shoptalk.

One of the ladies seemed to be talking about the sermon at Church the other day.

"Yeah, the preacher last Sunday was delivering the sermon and it was about who we are in this world and one of the comments was 'we are but dust.' Ya know that's in Bible in Genesis 3:19 after Adam ate the apple. Well as we were walking out of church after services, this little boy asked his mother "Mama, what is butt dust?" Fina said.

"All around there you could hear snickering and throat clearing, then she told him "I'll tell you when we get in the car."

Edra lay back while Gladys washed her hair and shouted out "I could have answered that. It's what folks leave on the commode who don't wash their ass."

Another customer waiting on the side, said, "wait now Edra, that is not what it means."

Edra yelled back "What does it mean then?" as her beautician lifted her head wrapping her hair with a towel.

"He was saying that our bodies are just dust and dirt and that's what we shed every day, and when we die our bodies go back to being dust, ashes and dirt. That's what our shells are and the real person living in these bodies are what's permanent," Jonnetta, from the Women's club, stood right up and said.

Edra shot back at her saying, "Aw, girl, you are just trying to clean it up." Edra then stood up with the towel wrapped on her head, "Gladys, let me run to the rest room before you put me under the dryer."

Edra began to walk toward the back bathroom and Tallia who was working on another head of hair called to her, "Hey Edra, don't leave none of your butt dust in that bathroom, 'cause I plan to go in there next."

"Don't mess with me now," Edra shouted back.

Gladys looked up at the window and said, "Hmm, there goes old Olive, she's a strange old duck. I bet she was listening to our conversation."

"Stop that now, girl, you know she's had a lot of sadness in her life."

"Yeah, a lot of butt dust, too!"

By then the shop was on fire with laughter and new conversations. Olive continued home, with a chuckle in her brain. She thought, hmm, but dust.

Chapter 24

The alarm clock buzz brought Retrea out of a great dream of a loving family all around her. Then the reality of Omar leaving her at the curb and driving off released her spirit. She smiled. Her soul felt relieved that she had dismissed him from her life. Many fears just dropped out of her mind. Fears of how Omar might treat her sisters and brother once she could help them with a safe place to live. Junior didn't want to understand why Retrea was so set in her mind on rescuing her baby sister, Ginger, from the foster care system. All those apprehensions of not knowing, when he'd blow up about something she'd decided to do, that he didn't agree with, were gone. She breathed hard and long and felt the freedom that her mind had just confirmed.

Now the real work was ahead. Her little brother, Geleb, was still living with Aunt Olive, but she didn't believe that would last much longer. Retrea felt his restlessness whenever she was near him. Aunt Olive was strange and they had never heard of their father's older sister before he died. Her name was never mentioned as far as she could remember.

In her mind Retrea believed all this drama, heartbreak and loss would fall down behind her when she could get all her siblings safe. However, she didn't know how she could help Hazel. There was no one else she knew of who could come to her rescue. So Retrea forged ahead on pure gut. She prayed the prayer that Miss Maple told her. Miss Maple told Retrea to concentrate on the Psalms---particularly Psalm 59. Kaye watched Retrea from a distance and knew that her healing had begun.

Several miles away, Retrea's older sister, Hazel, looked around her small space as an ant crawled out from the crack in the space between where the floor and wall met. There were no fancy baseboards, just an off–white painted wall sitting on a gray concrete painted floor. The three inch thick mattress gave no comfort in sleep or sitting to daydream. It was a resting place for her butt that was better than the cold, hard floor.

Hazel thought about the choices she'd made. Being here was the best thing, she thought. Better than everybody knowing what happened to Ginger. "Yeah," she said out loud. Then she thought about how she met her husband Deacon. Deek, everyone called him. He was far, far away from anything his name made reference to. He probably hadn't seen the inside of a church since he was old enough to run away from home 'bout twelve years or so. She now realized that every problem in Deek's life was always somebody else's fault, he claimed.

She met him at a quarter party she wasn't supposed to attend, three weeks after her seventeenth birthday. He was nice looking and all the other girls liked him but he asked her to dance. That made her feel special and she hadn't felt special since her mama died. Her father died too, but she didn't care about that, *he needed to die.* She shivered when she thought about how mean he was to everyone in the house especially Mama. Her mind went blank but tears crawled down her face without her knowledge, or permission, with the same pace as the ant that crawled up the wall.

Her mind quickly went back to thoughts of Deek when

she saw her own tears splash onto the cold gray floor.

She remembered their first apartment, just one room and a let-out couch for a bed. The bathroom and kitchen were about the same size, tiny. It only cost $165 a month so they could afford that. At least she could.

Hazel wanted things to dress up the place, like curtains and pictures for the walls to bring color to her space but he would talk her out of everything she wanted for herself or surroundings. He needed the money always for the good deals he could get for this or that stuff she never saw or knew about. She realized she must have been frightened of him even then.

She thought back and remembered the day she went to her girlfriend's house, Cinnamon, who was getting ready to go to work. Hazel asked her if there were any more jobs there and Cinnamon told her she'd find out and gave her a number she should call that very afternoon at about 2:30PM.

"Girl, Deek don't want you out of your place especially to work. You'd be out there with the rest of his no-count friends, knowing what he's up to all the time." Cinnamon said.

"Now, I don't want to be the one to spread rumors but... he's a liar, and a hustler. I do believe those words were made up, just for him." Cinnamon told Hazel.

Hazel kind of looked down at the floor and her tight lips said, between her almost clinched teeth, "I know what I got and what I'm up against." She turned to leave and as she reached the door she thanked her and said, "some things just need to be left alone." Cinnamon handed her the number on a small piece of brown paper torn off a grocery bag.

Hazel made the call and was scared of what Deek would say or do, but she had to help her brother and sister get away from that crazy Aunt Olive they all had to live with since their folks died. If Ginger ran away one more time she was going to a home for bad girls and Hazel knew she wasn't a bad girl just an unhappy, grieving little child. The call was productive and she started her job the next day.

181

It didn't pay much more than minimum wage, her job was sorting things for shipping, but it was her money and she could get things that she wanted to get.

Chapter 25

Maple smelled the hint of growing tomatoes just outside the kitchen window. She stopped washing dishes and hunted for a bowl to see how many were ready to pick, for eating or just windowsill ripening. Other than the fresh smell of new growth, the air was too warm and damp for her liking. She took only shallow breaths while she poked a stick through the bushy tomato leaves to be assured that no snakes were hiding to strike if her hand ventured into the wrong area. The bowl filled quickly as she raised up to get a good look at her treasures she heard him off to the left, just in the way of the sunlight, and the smell of lilacs filled her head.

"You're out early today," Alvin said while holding out a hand to carry the bowl for her. "Good crop this year, Angel mine, now how are we going to make sure you get to do all you want with these?" he teased.

"Stop that! I think you are trying to make fun of me." Maple said with a half smile and a sparkling eye staring down toward his feet.

"What do you want today, old man."

"What do you mean, 'old man'? If you recall, I stopped 'being' at age 51," he quipped.

"Don't remind me. You are still a being." Maple said and they both laughed so hard the birds started chirping.

"I know I've asked you this before, but I guess what I

183

want to know is what happened to you, your spirit?" he asked Maple. "Your laughter would brighten up my whole day, and I rarely hear that anymore," Alvin said.

Maple began with, "My philosophy used to be 'Laugh as much as you breathe and Love as long as you live.'"

"Isn't that still true?" he asked. Alvin bent down to take the second bowl of tomatoes from Maple.

"No, since then I've discovered that those silly sayings were impossible in real life," said Maple. "I also believed that you give what you have and trust life for the rest." Maple paused as though she were trying to roam through her thoughts to find the exact words she needed. "Now, I know that is also hogwash."

They walked into the house and Maple filled a large plastic bowl with water so they could wash and examine the tomatoes.

She sat down at the table and Alvin moved his chair closer to hers, "What happened to the happiness I saw in your eyes when we first met?"

"I laughed a lot because I still held onto the dream that things would get better. They'd be different. I'd escape to those special moments in my head when things were good, just to keep me going. But I knew life would never be good again."

"So where is your happiness and joy now?" Alvin asked.

Maple looked up from her wet and dirty hands and said, "the happiness and joy escaped through the wounds I was left with." She grabbed a paper towel to wipe some dirt off one of the tomatoes then folded her hands and lowered her head.

Alvin immediately wrapped his whole essence around her and rocked her in his soul.

Chapter 26

Olive arrived home and sat down to remember more of her little girl days. She wondered what went wrong, what did she do that was so bad? It was a warm day and the ladies of the community didn't believe they had anything else to do but discuss what they saw going on right on their block. Mostly they eyed the little girl, not to help her, mind you, but to speak disparaging words into the air that contributed to her lot in life and dampen her spirit and they scorched her soul.

"Look at that fast-tailed gal out there, her mama ought to call her in the house and tell her how to behave like a little girl should," said Alba.

"Yeah, somebody going to 'get her' sure enough, with her tussling with all them boys like she does. 'Cause you know it looks like she's starting to develop and everything."

"It'll probably be one of those same boys out there trying to 'experiment,' or something." Callie chimed in.

"No telling, it may be one of these old men out here been hawking her like she's something to eat." Grindelia said. "You know she's one of the oldest of all them kids over there and don't nobody watch what they're doing. Pretty soon we going to start finding her drawers in the weeds or bushes. Just you watch. Them boys out there developing, too, it'll probably be one of them or all of them – you know they do crazy things these days."

"I've been watching and wondering why they pay so much attention to that gal. I'm seeing Mr. Cupboard hawk-watching her now too. He has been watching her from the gangway pretending he's doing something to his yard. It's been looking like a trash bin since they moved in over there 'cross the street."

"She's always got her butt showing and just out in the street showing off, Olive is."

"Yeah, I seen his old lady, watching, too."

They both kind of half turned to the side, faced each other then looked back at the window, tightened their lips and said "Hmmm, hmmm," in unison. There was no need for anymore of an explanation.

Just then Mr. Cupboard was walking home from the job. Up the back alley and then through the gangway right before he walked into the front of the house he saw her gyrating like a little loose woman in one of those clip joints he frequented.

He stood and watched as the boys picked her up and tossed her around. Her legs opening and bending to wrap around the guys and hold on and then get flipped by another one of the boys.

Cupboard stood mesmerized by the action in front of him. He wasn't even aware that his mouth watered and his hand went instinctively into his left pants pocket; happy to be in the shadow of the house just under the window box, out of sight from where all the neighbors had been sitting and talking about the little girl. The little girl, Olive, came to his mind in the space where he stood. Leaning on the side of his house, holding onto the wall of the building next door to his. He watched her until he felt the air escaping from as far down as his gut, then up and over his tongue, he blew all the air out of his whole self and felt the little girl that he had wrapped around his fantasy. He gasped for breath as the scene he lived in his mind culminated in an earthquake of a body shudder.

Mr. Cupboard pulled himself together when the voices of the little boys and that one little girl finally reached his ears. He went to the backyard for the hose and was glad the handkerchief was in his pants to cover the hold in his pocket and could catch anything that needed to be caught. The drink from the hose dripped down the front of his clothes and rinsed out the hanky then he used it to wipe the beads of sweat from his forehead, all the other fluids and the drool mingling with the nappy beard he was trying to grow.

Sadie heard Mr. Cupboard out in the back of the house. "You home already?" she said.

"Yeah, we worked an hour less today, that's all the work was there."

"Go wash up, look you spilled stuff all down your pants, I'll have to wash them," she said.

"No, it's just water from the hose out back, it's really hot out here for October and I wanted to feel something cold on my face, I must of stood up too quick."

"Hang 'em up so they don't wrinkle and you can wear them for tomorrow. Go wash and change your clothes and I'll meet you at the table.

They sat and ate without a word. He'd stare at the salt-shaker and she would hand it to him. When he'd just about finished his first helping of anything on his plate she would jump up and replenish it.

She sat and focused on different patterns of the table-cloth. The butterflies seemed to be waving at her while she waited. After he belched, stood up and said "not bad," she was allowed to leave the table.

Chapter 27

Maple laid the book down on her lap and said "Hello," a bit startled because the phone rang at such a late hour.

"Maple, how are you doing?" the familiar voice said.

"Just fine," came Maple's ice-cold reply.

"This is Omar."

"Yea, I know," she said.

"Listen, Junior came over to my house telling me he had dinner with you the other night and he could have sworn that a ghost showed up at your door. Now isn't that a kick?" Said Omar Sr.

"Did he really? Why would that matter to you?" Maple asked.

"I was just calling to make sure everything was all right for you. You know, I'm just looking out for you still, like I always did," Omar's voice got real soft, as he seemed to cower, pleading her assistance or at least some friendly acknowledgement.

At that moment you could have heard a mouse piss on cotton—all she could think of in the absolute silence.

"You still there?" Omar asked.

"Yep, I'm still here. What are you calling me for?" The dusty words lunged out of her mouth.

"So you aren't seeing anyone, huh?" he asked.

"What do you want?" she said in a disgusted, tight-lipped tone.

"Well, Junior told me that he and Retrea were talking about getting married. Since she don't really have no folks to speak of, I thought maybe you and I could kind of help out with the wedding."

Maple cleared her throat, "You know, I really don't want to presume that they need my help, Retrea is quite capable of doing the things she wants and if she wants my help she knows how to ask me. Junior also knows how to ask," Maple said.

"I was telling Junior that maybe you and I could get together and help them with the planning and all the things they need up front. What do you say to that?" he continued, paying no attention to what she'd just said.

"I just told you already, that may not be necessary," said Maple. She raised her voice a bit trying desperately not to spew out what she wanted to say.

"You see, there you go, I'm trying to be nice and have a conversation about our son getting married and you want to start something." The old man's childishness was revving up so he could get the response he wanted.

"There goes my doorbell, I have got to go. I'll call you later," Maple lied and hung up without any goodbye.

There was no one at the door, but Alvin walked into the room as if right on queue.

"You doing okay?" he asked.

"Yep," she snapped and then her whole face relaxed into the warmest, gentlest, inviting smile anyone had ever seen, then said, "I'm doing good," while nodding her head.

They held onto a long and pleasant stare in each other's eyes. Then smiled at the visions before them.

"Why didn't we meet when we were young and innocent? Ya know what I mean---before the ways of the world took us off focus and beat us up so badly?" Maple put her book down that she was still clutching since the call when she heard Omar's voice. She stood up and began straightening up the room.

"We should have met," Alvin said.

"So many people put their information into us. All that knowledge of what's supposed to be good or bad, right or wrong gets stuck in our brains. You know there are all these do's and don'ts . . ." Maple rambled.

"What's got you all wound up?" he asked her.

"I just hung up on my ex."

"Anything else bothering you?" he asked.

"Before that call from what's his face, I was trying to read and then just started to think about what Retrea told me regarding her family. You know she's going to try to get custody of her little sister?"

"Yes, and she will do a wonderful job with her just as you have done a wonderful job with Retrea."

"What do you mean by that?" Maple asked.

"By telling her the truth," he said

"How do you know? Have you been stalking me again?" she said through a coy smile looking up. Let's go outside and sit a while." Maple said while closing the curtains and blinds.

He smiled and said, "I love you. I will follow you anywhere."

She grabbed his pinky finger with hers and they walked out to the back yard.

"Look at all those stars, aren't they magnificent?" Alvin said in awe of the blanket of lights dangling in the sky.

"Hmmm yeah," she answered. "A wonderful sight for any eyes."

"Want to go on a adventure?" he asked.

"To where?" she asked.

"Any place you want to go," he said

"Can you take me to the place that brought us to this point in our lives, excuse me, in my life and yours when you were . . ."

". . . Alive," he said. "Now I'm just in a different … realm," Alvin said with a smirk.

"I do want to find out about the curse or curses, but at the same time I'm afraid."

"Me, too," Alvin admitted.

"You know the little girl we found last time? I now realize that I know who she is," Maple blurted out.

"Who?" Alvin asked.

"She's related to Retrea, in fact, Olive is the one who took her and the siblings in after their parents died."

"We've prayed for Olive, remember? And we will continue to pray for her and all those connected with her. However, I do believe she is the link to where we need to go." Alvin said.

"Are you ready to go now?" he asked, standing up to leave.

Maple stuck her neck out and said, "I really want Kaye to go with us… I'm truly afraid of what we will uncover," she said with eyes staring at the ground, and carefully not allowing herself to look up even though she wanted to see his expression. Maple didn't want to make him think she didn't trust his ability, but she didn't, totally.

"Let's go," he said and right then Kaye appeared and led Maple and Alvin to a little village right on the outskirts of Asmara, which was the capitol of Eritrea in the Horn of Africa. The place was near what ancient Egyptians believed was a sacred place called Punt, which meant 'Land of the Gods.' Since Eritrea had a long coastline on the Red Sea, it was a Mecca for foreign trade. The trading posts imported and exported a variety of special goods. Their gross domestic produce included gold, aromatic resins, wood, ivory, incense, perfumes and gum. People from around the world traveled there for trade. Some were from an evil time and the step-ins had overtaken many of them and assumed the identities of locals.

Hannah with her bird, Brid, and cat, Shadow, led Kay through the devastation and destruction of the people, their resources and the land of Eritrea. European countries had overtaken the country of Eritrea, many times. One country after another occupied their homeland. Then the border wars with Ethiopia, Egypt and Sudan created even more struggles for the people living there.

Each time Maple and Alvin traveled, beginning at around 1800, they saw what appeared to be three sometimes four of the same children. One, the color of midnight stood mighty, like a strong noble prince who found solace in big kitchens – especially in cupboards and cabinets where food was kept. The second child was round and bubbly and unafraid like a bear cub and took chances to make his way out of hunger and solitude. The third child who hid herself in caverns, caves and dirt holes, scampered about at daybreak for food, water and cloth to cover herself and locked herself away from the evil of intruders beginning at mid-day. The fourth child was Hannah, who kept the other three alive. The three were the offspring of one or two of the unnamed invaders, the carpet-baggers, who wanted to control this land, and perhaps at least one was a step-in.

The first child who hid himself in kitchens and could sleep on the shelves after filling his knapsacks with food would empty jars for water when he could find it. The second child risked his life everyday and only Hannah could keep him alive because of the chances he took without thinking of the possible consequences. The little girl who hid herself felt safe in the hollow of trees or in dirt caves on the side of a hill. The three children always found each other and even though they were captured many times, they endured and stuck together.

Whenever the invaders or traders found one of them open and unprotected they would kidnap them for their sick pleasure but the children's watchful eyes could most times make an escape. All the while the children were making their way to the coastline. Upon arrival the children found plenty of everything including freedom and more opportunities. At the coast the children were not hungry or beaten or in the hands of scoundrels, they were together. Hannah saw to that. The boy who took chances led the way. He always kept a piece of flint and something metal so he could start a fire to stay warm, to scare away an enemy including animals or for cooking food.

One day while trading their incense and resins an older man saw them and recognized their mother's eyes in each of them and knew that they had to be his offspring. They saw him as a letch and steered clear, but he followed them and without their knowledge he boarded the boat that they stowed away on. He was determined to make them his slaves in some form.

Hannah blinded the man to the children's whereabouts on the ship and during the entire journey to the United States, Kaye, Alvin and Maple prayed for them. They prayed that the damaged DNA given them by the old man would not overtake their purity in spirit, mind or soul. They prayed to God without ceasing, during the entire journey. Nothing touched the little ones of any muck and mire consequence; they just hid themselves and listened to the different speech patterns and languages and learned, while making plans for their lives. The year was 1841 and they were listening to talk of a pure rich land, an open land where they could survive.

Kaye, Alvin and Maple went to find the origin of the generational curse that plagued so many lives. And they found him. They knew that their actions would not change what each of them had gone through up to this point in their own realm; however, the lives of their children and children's children were changed at that very moment in their own natural time.

Chapter 28

It was early on a Saturday morning while Maple was trying to plan out her day when the phone rang.

"Hello," said Maple, crunching as she finished the last of her breakfast cereal.

"Miss Maple, hi, this is Retrea, how are you?"

"I'm fine dear, how nice of you to call," as she wiped the crumbs from her face.

"Well I just wanted to apologize for what happened at your house the other night. Junior just gets like that when anything crosses his path that he doesn't either agree with or understand."

"I know he's a chip off the old block, shall I say?" said Maple.

"Miss Maple, I am in your neighborhood, I don't want to impose on you… I would really like to talk with you face to face, if you have time right now?"

"Sure, dear, come on over and I will start the coffee pot," Maple said.

"I'll bring some pastries, okay?" Retrea asked.

"Great, I will see you soon." Maple quickly began to spruce up the place… picking up papers and things she hadn't put away. The doorbell rang and she threw some papers behind the sofa.

"How are you," Maple said opening the door with out-stretched arms.

"Thank you so much for seeing me," Retrea was cut off with . . .

"Come, sit down," said Maple.

"No problem at all. I rather like company from time to time."

The table had been set for their visit with Maple's 'good' dishes.

"Thank you, I brought some chocolate and lemon scones, I should have asked you if you wanted anything special."

Maple smiled at the comment and could hardly wait to open the package.

They sat at the kitchen table and almost head-to-head, Retrea began to try to make sense of what was going on between she and Omar Junior.

Maple poured the coffee and made sure the napkins and everything they'd need was on the table.

"Do you want sugar and cream in your coffee?" Maple asked.

"Yes, please," said Retrea.

"If we could have finished our conversation right then the other night, I was going to tell you that Junior and I would have had to go through counseling before we set a date to get married. He keeps saying that he doesn't want people in his business," Retrea said, "But I tried to tell him that it is my business, too."

"I do understand. After our talk I wondered about a few things." Maple said.

"You did?" Retrea questioned

"Yeah? I know you want to discus Omar but I'd like to know more about you. After your parents died, who raised you and your sisters?" said Maple.

"There are four of us, I have two sisters and a younger brother, and my Aunt Olive took us in. She was my dad's older sister," said Retrea as the corners of her mouth turned all the way downward before she spoke again.

"How was that growing up?" Maple asked.

"Not too good, we constantly heard Aunt Olive say that my mother made my father misbehave like he did but that's not what I saw or believe. So Hazel went off and got married just to get away from there." A tear filled one eye but did not fall on her face.

"I went away to school on scholarship as soon as I was out of high school and worked like a crazy woman. My younger sister started running away and was put into foster care several times, and my little brother may have to go into foster care or a reformatory."

"So, I'm going to get all of my family under one roof and we will be together. Maybe we can help each other heal." Retrea sighed.

"Hazel, my oldest sister is in jail for a crime that was unavoidable and I'm helping her get back to us, too."

Neither said a word for many heartbeats.

"How did you stay so long in your relationship? I know there was violence going on, Junior told me you were always getting on his dad's case." Retrea asked.

"I don't really know. I think at first I was in shock and didn't know what to do when he began to change into a monster. Who would I ask? When I asked the Pastor he said that it's up to the woman to keep the household strong. Then I was too humiliated to tell anyone. When I started telling people after it got worse, no one believed me. So I endured while I tried to prepare myself to live on my own and take care of my children," said Maple.

"How did you take it? I mean I've seen some of Junior's tirades, too, and he even scares me watching a basketball game on TV." Retrea said.

Maple tried to continue without feeling the memories of the awful times.

"I was numb most of the time to any feeling whatsoever. Then when I tried to go he threatened me that anywhere I could go, he could go, and how he could make sure that he got the children, because he had connections. So I waited until they were practically adult and then when the last straw snapped I no longer cared about how I was going to break away, I just wanted to be free." Maple sat a minute to reflect on how much she should say.

"Oh, it was difficult because everyplace I turned for attorneys and other help they favored him. I lost a lot financially, friends, and other areas but I got **me** back. **Me**! You know sometimes what you care about gets all used up and goes away, forever. And the person I once knew indeed went away, Forever. I finally realized how important I was and that I should value myself. But in the process of being numb, I became very ill and of course he used the illness against me, too," said Maple.

Retrea wrapped her arms around herself as if she had a child in them.

"Those people who stepped out of my life were supposed to be gone including him. The money I lost came back to me ten fold. Not so much in dollars but in many other ways." Maple folded her hands for a minute then poured each of them a fresh cup of coffee.

"Retrea, if my son is showing you a behavior that you don't like, don't get into a marriage. Believe every behavior that turns your stomach now, or it will haunt you in retrospect. Not all guys hit. If you are seeing stuff now that is unworthy of you, think what it will be like when he thinks he owns you? Sometimes 'goodbye' is the best thing you can say to save yourself," Maple said in her motherly voice.

"Thank you, Miss Maple for your honesty. I'm trying to get certified now as a foster parent for my little sister and brother. I want them to know love and caring. Can I stop by and talk with you from time to time?"

"Of course, I'd be glad to hear from you anytime, anytime at all." Maple said.

"I have decided not to get married right now. There is no need for any kind of celebration." Retrea said with a smile.

"Believe me, I do understand and know you're right," said Maple.

"Now Ms. Maple, I just want to get nosey, how is Mister Alvin? I saw how he was looking at you, like a great big protector."

"He is just fine. We are good friends, well, the best of good friends." Maple said with a devilish smile.

They laughed and Maple remembered something that had been gnawing at the back of her brain so she asked Retrea about her name.

Retrea said, "It was kind of a strange event to hear my mother tell it. Seems she was all set to name me after some kind of flower or plant and this strange looking nurse picked me up and I started laughing and giggling and she told my mother I should have an exotic name." Retrea paused. "Said that I could even rule a country or at least be named after one. So she mentioned this tiny little country in African – I think they call the area the Middle East now, but as far as I'm concerned it's all Africa; well, anyway the name she said to my mother just kind of 'danced,' that's what my mother said, out of her mouth. Then she said it sounded pretty and smart like she wanted me to be, so... that's what she named me. Eritrea, but everyone has always called me Retrea."

She said that I was the best thing that ever happened in her life and I should always strive for the best."

"Did your mother ever tell you anything more about her? The nurse, I mean? Or did you ever get to meet the nurse when you were older?" asked Maple.

"Naw, because mama said she went to look for her to thank her and no one had ever heard of her. Strange, isn't it?" Retrea said as she sort of looked off into the air like there was a private movie going on in front of her eyes.

"What was her name, do you remember?"

"Oh, yes, I'm not likely to forget her name it's Kate, Kaye or one of those, and we couldn't find any nurse named that who worked there at that hospital around the time I was born."

Maple shuddered at the thought then relaxed when Retrea stopped staring into space.

"My mother thought she was some kind of angel or something and that from time to time she thought she saw her in the distance or in a passing car or bus or walking down the street. Isn't that crazy?"

"No, not crazy at all. We never know when we will run into an angel, so our best bet is to pay attention to what and who we meet," Maple said ending their visit as she heard Alvin near her.

When they reached the door, Retrea turned to give Maple a hug and said, "Thank you, you make me feel like I did when I could sit and talk with my mother."

Maple knew the feeling, and was happy to know that she made a difference in Retrea's life. She knew she'd be seeing more of her later.

When the door closed Alvin was standing behind Maple. A big hug was waiting for her.

"He whispered in her ear, "We have someplace to go, now."

And they left to search for clues.

Chapter 29

Maple and Alvin arrived in the State of Georgia during early summer, at the end of the nineteenth century and they could smell the magnolia trees, feel the sun-baked air and see remnants of a July sunset. This time Alvin and Maple came back again to a later date, searching for souls. These souls they found were believed to be linked in someway to each one who lived in Maple's time.

Alvin knew that the souls they had to follow left Africa sometime during the early eighteen hundreds. They watched as the three they found in Eritrea, disappeared and returned in the same order at least three times continuing in the same group, spanning more than two centuries. Alvin and Maple watched as their ancestors' lives unfolded in front of their eyes.

The year was 1867 and Baron Chance was hard at work on his private garden. The space Maple and Alvin found themselves was part of the land Baron bought and was developing to grow a crop he could transport up north to sell. He made it just over the Mason-Dixon line. Baron planted watermelons, Collard and Turnip greens, tomatoes and an assortment of herbs. He transported most of the produce to northern cities and always sold the entire stock. The money he made was enough to take care of the family all winter and with funds left over to buy more land, seed and crop supplies. Enough was left over to save a little, too.

When Baron believed he was good at farming and selling he let others who were a part of the Choctaw and African family rent plots on his land for $5 a year. That way all who wanted could use it for their families to share, barter or sell their produce, too. He did have stipulations for the renters, that's why he charged them. It was that they had to care for the land all year round and harvest on time as well as fertilize during non-growing times.

Baron's wife, Iris, was secure in who she was and knew that they had each chosen the right person for lifetime partners. She felt that they were one spirit, not just kindred. She was fascinated that his family came all the way from Africa, not as slaves and found themselves sheltered by a group of people who cherished the land. They, the Choctaw, were her people. They cherished their land just as his family had wanted to fight for their Eritrea. Except that they had no parents since they were old enough to have memories. When they arrived in the United States they were wonderful children with old souls and angels were all around them, so the Choctaw Tribe took them in. They all prospered once everyone developed trust in one another. Baron was taught to speak English and Choctaw when he first arrived.

Baron and Iris Yellow-Bell, her complete name, were comfortable in the house Baron, his brother, and her brothers build for them. They had three children and they were so happy with two boys and one girl. Baron was especially happy to have and be family. At last a family he could provide for and protect.

Alvin and Maple observed Baron and Iris Yellow-Bell's days throughout the lifetime and Alvin realized that he was actually seeing his great-great grandparents. It was now the year 1912 and their children now had children. Three more houses; houses build by family now graced their land to make sure all the family stayed together and they always wanted to care for and be available to counsel and support their children. Any child that was orphaned or abandoned was welcomed into their home. Iris' conversations with newcomers always ended with telling them that they themselves had to find their own way to what made them happy. "You make your own path to happy," Iris always said.

Alvin was so enamored by actually watching his ancestors he was blinded to any hint of a curse. The evil was all around and Maple knew that. It was revealed to her on the trip before this one, Kaye told Maple what to look for and said that Alvin's spirit would not be receptive to that truth. Even though he would already know that the specific evil was in his own soul, his spirit would attempt to deny it.

Baron was successful at farming and at business. He understood the properties of trade, negotiation and trend. But he was not fully convinced of the deep seeded roots of racism and any idea of a superior race other than the human race, which included all men and women. Baron and his wife promoted that each and every person who lived among them had to find and develop their own plan to an enjoyable and successful existence. Each night after supper Baron walked around his property to greet his neighbors and take stock in what was there, to see if anything needed repair and if he could find out who was doing damage to his fences. Also, he knew someone had been killing some of his livestock.

While repairing a hole in the fence at the edge of his property one evening, the wind gave him pause to listen to the words in the air.

"Who does that nigger think he is up there?" said Dusty, the group's leader who had carrot-red hair, sweat soaked to his head that dripped down his mangled dusty beard and a funky cigar hanging from his lips.

"He ain't never been owned by no one, because he came to this land after the slaves was let go. He don't know our ways out here, " said Old Doug who had done business with Baron.

"We've been cutting down the posts and slats of the fences but he keeps putting them back up, like he knows that we're there. We're gonna have to teach him our ways. What you think, Sandy?" Dusty said.

Sandy, a thinning blond haired chubby man, sat over in the corner chewing on straw said, "Let's just kill him and put him out of his misery, we can tell the town's people he stole from the bank, because we don't know where his money is coming from to buy all that stuff he got, and the land, too."

"Nobody here is paying him anything, we can just take what we want. The law's on our side." Dusty said, pointing to the Sheriff pouring a glass of spirits.

"Well, if you believe he stole something then we can just go get him." Sheriff Green replied.

Baron heard bits and pieces of the raucous talk and laughter from down the hill, that house on the edge of his property. It was adjacent to the Choctaw reservation and none of the whites wanted to be that close to them. Baron's land was between the two. The white sharecroppers and farmers feared that the chants, the spiritual ceremonies and the rituals would make the Choctaw and coloreds overtake them and they would be treated the same or even more harsh than the whites had treated the Choctaw and the Coloreds. The white sharecroppers could not fathom the notion that working together would help them all.

Baron caught wind of their intentions by finding a circle of dirt just big enough for him to sit and speak with the Heavenly Father. The one he was told about at the one and only time he attended church in his homeland. The Elder preacher said, "The Lord says 'Call on me and I will tell you things, things you do not know.'"

Baron never forgot that. So he asked his Heavenly Father to help him and keep his family safe and tell him what steps to take.

Their spoken words came flying at him. Baron saw in his mind's eye the destruction to Eritrea when other nations took over their land. He remembered indeed.

"This is no different," he heard his own voice say. He looked to the heavens for the answer and a chill wrapped around him when he saw a ball of fire flare across the sky and toward him. Baron closed his eyes and saw pictures of things he knew under his eyelids. His body was wet with fear of how he could eliminate the giants he had to conquer.

"I can help you accomplish your goal," came a voice from out of the dark. Baron believed it was the old man who had followed him from when he first began to remember anything when he was a child.

"You are more like me than you are willing to admit," the old man said. "I know how to remedy this problem and you will never be touched by them again."

Baron was a big man, all muscle from hard work. His hands were power tools of strength, and his mind held determination of steel. But his heart hurt for fear those words he heard would materialize and he would not be there for his family. They would kill him, those men at the bottom of his hill.

Baron went back to finish repairing his fences.

The family he had, who depended on him were the only thing in life he loved. Baron did not want to believe that he, too, could be a monster. He finished the repair of the last length of vandalized fence and stood up seeing that he was eyeball to eyeball with this diabolical quasi-stranger.

"I see you've taken a royal name, Baron."

"Who are you, I mean, what's your name and what do you want with me?" Baron said, as he stood transfixed by what he felt could be his nemesis. "Again, I say, what are you called?" Baron insisted.

"I am called Cup, as in cupboard," he said while hunting for more words in his head to put Baron at ease, at least a little.

Hearing those words gave Baron a prick in his spirit. His body tightened to stone and he remembered the feeling of sleeping and hiding in cupboards when he was a boy. "Why are you called that? Baron asked.

"I was a thrown away, abandoned as a child and I raised myself by sleeping in cupboards where the flour and grain bags were kept. It's where I was able to get food and stay warm when the air was cold. I learned to endure anything to stay alive and if I held the hammer of power I knew how to strike. Then while I was still in my teens I witnessed an unbelievable phenomenon." Cup stopped for a moment and looked around.

"Phenomenon?" "Unbelievable?" asked Baron. "What are you?"

"What am I, you say?" Cup acknowledged. "Hmmm, I was born once, and then growing up as I did, a step-in found me during a vulnerable time in my stream of consciousness. You also have encountered many step-ins, your energy has been positive and strong so that is who you attract," Cup paused again. He stared at Baron and then at the structure down the hill.

"You cannot go with me this time, but in the future, you will do quite nicely. Right now there are too many monsters living in the shadows, your shadows."

Baron had not been able to comprehend the entire conversation, but he remained stuck on the term 'step-ins.' "What actually is a step-in?" Baron asked Cup.

"A step-in is a spirit whose body no longer serves it properly and must leave it to find a new and sometimes willing host." Old Cup waited and watched Baron's expression change and it even began to relax.

"In some cases," Cup continued, it's temporary in that the

step-in needs the body just for a second or two. This is when a message or deed needs to occur and the step-in's current host body is unable to carry it out. Sometimes it's spontaneous, to keep the body out of danger. Or, for example, a message to someone who will only hear it from a certain mouth," said Cup

"What are the other cases?" Baron asked.

"That is when the host body needs to change into a complete new paradigm. I mean that the host will now promote whatever the step-in decides it wants or needs to do. Now, stay here, I will return in a minute. I will be different and I will let you know who I am. You and your family will be safe. I'll be right back."

Baron was frozen with the idea of what would happen next. He lost all track of time but it seemed like just seconds had passed and within that time the house down below caught fire and burned up. His next breath was filled with cloth burning smoke as the figure walked toward him and said his name.

Chapter 30

The showdown of the curse began to unfold before Alvin and Maple's eyes as they watched in horror. Their jaws dropped when another figure walked towards Baron. Just as Alvin took a step forward to help his great-great grandfather, he and Maple felt Kaye's hand on their shoulders.

"Don't be afraid," Kaye said.

Kaye held onto Alvin and Maple until she felt their spirit energy begin to calm. Kaye then told Maple to breath slowly.

"You are here to observe and then pray, remember that," said Kaye.

Again she told Maple and Alvin, "Don't be afraid. Alvin, remember when we talked about the curse that surrounds your familiars? You said you wanted to be the vessel to break the curse. You asked me to show you what to do." Kaye said.

Alvin's spirit wavered. Maple watched and tried to reach out to Alvin in love and understanding. She could not reach his hand.

"Alvin you know the verse in the Bible that says, 'God is Love. There is no fear in Love, but perfect Love casts out fear.' That's in first John chapter four, verse eighteen. So don't punish yourself. Baron has to make a choice and when he does, you will know exactly what you must pray."

Alvin, Maple and Kaye heard the demon call Baron's name. The demon was wrapped in a different body. He had stepped into Doug's body but did not become him. Doug had a spirit of goodness, fairness and love in his countenance. But Cup was what he was. The three of them watched. Maple wanted to breathe but continued to try to hold her breath instead. She still felt like the smoke singed her nostrils.

"Baron, come out of your ground circle," Cup commanded. Baron remained motionless. The crickets made no sounds, nothing moved, dark bitter silence encompassed the hot humid air. Alvin, Maple and Kaye remained in their own bubble of conflict, and defiance. Love entered the circle when Maple began to pray for all the living who had come through Baron's bloodline. She prayed without ceasing as other spirits surrounded her and joined in the prayers to break the curse. Each time Cup commanded that Baron come out of the ground circle God had provided for him, Cup took a step backwards... Cup could sense the prayers that targeted him even though the prayers were silent. The hillside filled with a multitude of spirits who could evoke the annihilation of the curse. All the curses God spoke to Moses recorded in Deuteronomy 28:15-68, were in the lives from Baron's descendants. Baron did not move from God's haven, the circle of love.

Kaye broke the silence of intercessory prayer while the host of spirits surrounded Baron.

"The first time this event took place there was no one here to assist Baron. Cup overtook him for a time long enough to injure his spirit. So a bit of his poison was infused into Baron's spirit and it impacted his future and those of his bloodline," said Kaye. In one quantum moment, the air-dried itself up. Alvin and Maple saw it but could not feel the impact.

Maple was shaking and wondered what would happen next. Alvin felt her quiver and wrapped his spirit of love around her. He knew that Maple had to be a part of breaking the curse. She had gone through a hellish situation and survived.

"We live in a fear based world which I hadn't thought

about until just this moment. We live our whole lives in fear of almost everything. Most people have a fear of un-experienced pain, of unknown danger and unrealized loss. The marketplace advertises products, on a large scale, based on fear of consumers unwanted circumstances," said Maple.

"Kaye, what happens next," asked Maple. Before Kaye answered, Maple was distracted when she recognized some of the praying spirits. The spirits included her grandparents, Omar's older brother, then she smashed her hands into her face to block anymore visions which were similar to what she'd been seeing under her eyelids most of her life.

Alvin appeared to be weeping because he, too, saw the devastation in the spirits all around them. He knew them by name.

Kaye knew what was happening to both Alvin and Maple and said, "You know, we all come back in groups because we can always recognize our familiars." Kaye looked around and shuddered. Hannah grabbed her hand and waited there with her. A bird chirped at the darkness.

"Maple, in answer to your question, what happens next is that the last remnant of the curse must be destroyed."

"How does that happen?" Maple asked.

"Cup will determine his own destruction, that's something that all of us have to do," said Kaye.

"Oh?" said Maple. She was not ready to wrap that information in her brain, her thought was, '*did Alvin bring on the disease that killed him; did I bring about my own miserable health condition?*'

"We can return now and leave Cup to call on the energy he needs to complete his ending," Kaye told Maple and Alvin. She knew that not only did Cup have to destroy himself but he also had to make sure that those still living who'd been hurt by him had to know of his destruction.

Baron remained in 'God's circle' and regained his strength, as Cup stood stark still, acknowledging his defeat.

211

Kaye recognized steps-ins interspersed in the spirits' circle. In an instant Maple, Alvin and Kaye vanished. Kaye and Hannah made sure they were safely hidden.

Hannah instructed all guardian spirits to be on alert with familiars so that they could have some sort of closure in whatever the individual endured at the hands of Old Cup. There were at least six individuals still living in the community. The others died from accidents, illness, suicide or murder. Among the living were Olive, Gerald, Byron Sr., Miss Sugar, Omar Sr., and one more that had not yet been identified. Everyone else in the community was indirectly impacted by the devastation brought on by Cup over his subjects.

Chapter 31

The middle of the room was the best place to sit comfortably and be able to look out all the windows. Maple saw the trees glisten when she stood up. A burst of setting sunlight shocked her eyes, sudden like.

"Are you alright?" she heard Alvin off in the distance.

"Oh, yes, yes, I'm okay that sunburst just startled me for a moment."

Alvin rocked back on the energy mass he created for feet. "What sunburst? The sun's been down for over an hour now. "

"Since you showed up in my dream," Maple began.

"Don't you mean when you invited me to your dream?" he interrupted.

"Well whatever, but since then so much has happened, I mean so much has come to light." A puzzled look came across her eyes, which led her focus to the oatmeal colored carpet. Her mind took her back to what she began to think created the madness that haunted her thoughts. *The times I saw movement out the corner of my eye, I knew there were messages I hadn't grasped quite yet. Somewhere out there is an energy I have to find.*

I heard some soapbox preacher in the Park speak of an emotion code and my body took me through many magnetic fields. At the time I didn't quite know what had happened to me. I will speak to Alvin about it when I can find the right words for what is going on inside my head.

"I'm tired of the way things get all messed up. I'm trying to piece all this 'traveling' stuff together. There is a key right before my eyes and I'm missing it. I need to find some answers," said Maple.

"Have you ever seen the inside the pyramids?" asked Alvin.

"No, why would I?" she asked

"Maple, many answers are there."

"Why don't we? Come on, let's go."

And they did. Alvin and Maple were shown new thought and learned solution techniques. Puzzling messages Maple had received, now easily untangled.

When they arrived back at Maple's house in her own time, she said, "Alvin, it felt like we were there for a month and look it's almost the same time as when we left."

"I know. Kaye showed me how to do this. She said I could help influence some fledglings and not lose any of my own time. For me the time doesn't matter much but it does for you, so I have to be careful."

"What's a fledgling? Are they young spirits just starting out on their own?" Maple asked.

"Fledglings are newly formed spirits, balls of energy, who desire human form," Alvin said.

"Do you think Kaye will show me how to travel and not lose any of my own time too?" Maple asked, "Or could you show me? I was afraid of her at first because she took me back to the last time I saw you in the hospital. I was afraid because I didn't know what to expect." Maple said.

"Tell me, were you still afraid when I met you in your dream and asked you to contact her?'

"Yes, I was shaking in my boots."

"Why'd you go to see her then?"

"I was more afraid of not seeing you again, even just in my dreams." Maple fidgeted with her fingers. She tried to attack a cracked cuticle with her thumbnail.

"You seem preoccupied what is it?" Alvin inquired.

"Retrea's sister is out of prison and she was staying with Retrea until she secured a job. Now Retrea doesn't see much of Hazel, that's her sister, said she met a new person in her life and they were getting closer, too."

"That was quick."

"Well, not really, you know time marches on and the girl lost a few years of her young life for defending herself against a batterer. I don't believe she should have gone to prison at all for it."

"So you believe it was okay to just kill him?" he asked.

Maple quickly got up and went into another room without a word or even a glance his way.

Alvin followed and tried to get close to her.

"Do you realize how many women are raped and beaten and killed everyday? Every three seconds! Just this last couple minutes, 20 to 30 women have been abused or killed by someone who has pledged their love to them," Maple said.

"You were married once weren't you, you know what I'm talking about, Alvin?"

"Yes, but we are not talking about me."

"Did you ever hit her?"

"No, but I wanted to."

"What stopped you?'

"Something my father said to me the day I got married, he thought we were too young. He was right."

"What else did he say?" asked Maple.

"Don't ever try to punish a grown women, don't hit her or nothing else just when you get to that point of anger you need to walk off. If you got children make sure you send her enough money to take care of them and enough for her, too." Alvin said mimicking his father.

"So that's what you did?"

"Yep. Well, let me back up a bit and say, she left me an empty house. I got home from work and everything was gone.

I was ready to go track her down and bring her and the kids back to our house, but my dad was a big guy and I don't think I was ready for a battle with him. I've never regretted being out of that tense marriage situation. What I did regret was missing out on the kids and later missing you." He grabbed her face and tried to melt into her essence.

"I lost out in both of those relationships because I didn't take care of what I should have."

"Do you mean all of that was your fault, even your death?" Maple asked

"Yes!" he changed the subject. "How's Retrea's little sister doing?"

"Can you believe it? They are preparing to send that baby to college. After Retrea got her out of the State system the child never ran away again. And her grades went to the top. I'm going to the child's high school graduation coming up soon."

Now that's the best news I've heard today," Alvin said.

"Retrea is making a little more money now so she's trying to buy a house. She's got a new boyfriend, too. Seems like a very nice young man. I met him in the grocery store when I ran into Retrea there a few days ago. She is also caring for her little brother."

"Oh, really, how did that happen I mean how did Retrea and the guy meet?"

"Well, she was going back and forth to State buildings to do all the paperwork for her sister and brother and she kept seeing this guy and realized they were trying to do the same thing which was to get their relatives out of harms way and take care of them. He has similar tragedies in his life. His brother killed his sister-in-law and then himself. They left a baby boy, six months old. So Doug, worked to get the baby out the State system and then adopted him. They started talking and just liked each other—then they fell in love."

216

Alvin's energy tightened almost to a boiling point when he heard that name, Doug.

"What has Omar Jr. said?" Alvin asked.

"I don't think he knows. It's none of his business anyway. That girl is going on with her life and I believe that's wonderful. I am so happy for her."

They continued their constant adventures and Maple stayed on her job and no one seemed to ask anymore about where Byron's cousin, Alvin came from. He just blended in with everyone else. Blossom and Jeremy had four children now and Jeremy's dental practice was doing well. Blossom took care of the home front and Jeremy took care of his family and patients.

Alvin and Maple were satisfied with the calm in their loved ones' lives but knew they had at least one more trip to finish their quest. Neither wanted to go back to the event where Baron met Old Cup, even though they had no choice.

Chapter 32

Maple had some funds tucked away and a few stocks that were doing very well so she checked with her financial advisor. Maple realized that all was well and she decided to retire. The party was on. Just about everyone showed up, past co-workers, old friends, long lost friends that owned her money and some people she wasn't quite sure who they were. These friends and even new acquaintances continued arriving and leaving into the evening at her house where there was plenty of food, drink, music and dancing.

Hazel came up to her and said "congratulations on your retirement, Miss Maple I'm sure happy for you. Now you can catch up on that traveling you like to do."

"Yes, yes, I can, thank you for coming; now who's that person hiding behind you?"

Hazel paused for a moment because she didn't really know how people would take her new life. Apprehension wrapped around Hazel like a cloth coat on the coldest day of the year and she still shook from the frost, so Hazel decided to just blurt it out.

"This is my ... partner, her name is Temple, I didn't want to cause no trouble, and so I can go."

"Hush, hush, Hazel." Maple turned to the other young lady and said, "Temple, welcome to my home. Hazel I'm glad for you that there's someone in your life. We all need that, don't we?" Maple welcomed them both.

She hugged them as each said thank you in her ear.

The party was a fabulous success that Retrea, Blossom, Ginger and Hannah, the little girl next door put together. Kaye even poked her head in to just see how everyone was doing.

There were smiles, laughter and sweet music throughout the evening, and lots of funny work stories.

Omar Jr. came late and he was already a bit inebriated.

"Who's that guy Retrea's with?"

"That's her husband," Maple said.

He went and sat in the corner for the rest of the party. He was mad enough to chew up the entire lawn. His dad, Omar Sr., came in strutting like a peacock with a young woman less than half his age. You could notice some bruises on her arms and a swelling by one eye. He hadn't seen the light yet.

Retrea and Hazel's Aunt Olive was invited even though she was still in court for the way she handled the children's money, but she was a neighbor and she was family. So now even Retrea's little brother, had straightened out and was living comfortably with Retrea and Joseph—Joseph Douglas, called Doug—and the baby, Joel.

"So when are you going to start all those vacations you've talked about?"

"We are leaving on a cruise around the world tomorrow, so take the food with you as you leave."

Omar came up to Maple, "I'm glad for you, Mom, you seem so happy and all. But how could Retrea just get married on me like that? And on top of that it's a gray dude!"

"Junior, where were you when she was trying to pull her family back together?" Maple said.

"I told her not to do that, that they needed to work their own problems out. I thought I'd wait til she came to her senses."

"She came to her senses and she did exactly what she wanted to do. And I'm happy for her."

"See you always do that, you're on her side, what about me?"

"You need to look at your life and decide how you want to live it, who you want in your life and how you plan to behave. In order to keep people you say you love in your life, ya know, you have to take responsibility and take care of your relationship. Sometimes it's better to be happy, than right. Let me see my guests out. I'll talk with you when they all go."

She walked in the other room leaving Junior there with his fists balled up and ready to jump up and down like a Jack in the Box.

"Hey son how's it going? I see your old girl picked up on her a white boy, married him, too, now you don't have to be bothered with that one anymore."

"Goodnight Pop." Omar, Jr., said and walked away.

Back inside the kitchen Omar Jr. ran right into Alvin, "Hey man I'm sorry I guess I wasn't paying attention."

"It's okay, son, looks like you got a lot on your mind, are you okay?"

"Me? Naw I'm cool."

"Yeah? Sure?" said Alvin.

"How could she just run off with somebody and then have the nerve to come into my Mama's house with him? How could she?" He ranted loud enough so that everyone could hear.

"Wait now Omar, you really have to look at the entire picture. She's been dating this young man for quite some time. Are you saying she owes you something? An explanation? Why? You are the one who stopped seeing her, remember you didn't want to be involved with her family issues? She needed someone who wanted to be involved so he found her and loved her enough to make a lifetime commitment to her immediately."

Alvin leaned back and studied Omar Junior in a silent prayer.

"So why are you mad at her or him? They both just followed their own hearts. Neither of them is in control of the other. They seem to be true partners. Be happy for them. Retrea attended those anger control classes she talked to you about, did you go?"

"Naw, man I don't need that stuff." Said Omar Jr. as he shoved his hands in his pockets.

"Omar it's like hunting jack rabbits. You know you're chasing them inconspicuously through a pasture you've got one in sight and you step in a pile of cow dung. Who are you mad at the rabbit because he got away? The cow because he crapped in the pasture or yourself because you did not pay close enough attention to what was going on around you? There's a lesson in all those things that … confound us. Take it from me, I've been there." said Alvin.

"Wow, Alvin, thanks, man that's pretty deep. I'm going to think on that tonight. Y'all have a good trip and watch Moms."

Alvin knew Omar, Jr., didn't mean a word of it.

"She's in good hands and I'll see to it that she gets lots of rest and sunshine and great food."

Omar reached out his hand to shake and Alvin gave him a big hug instead.

Maple and Alvin sailed and they saw and they loved and counted their blessing while helping others see their own. Finally Maple said, "I'm ready to go back and finish our job."

"How about tomorrow?"

"Yes, I've got to call Blossy and Retrea to let them know."

"I'll take care of all that." Alvin said.

Being home was good, everyone dropped by to see how their yearlong trip had been. Although it had been truly many lifetimes for them. They had seen the world. They toured Europe, Asia, Africa, South America and every place they could think of in the United States and Canada. They even peeked at historical events and felt the buzz and exuberance of the crowds and sometimes the hurt and sadness of the victims in world events.

"Blossom, while I was gone I had some papers drawn up for you to hang onto like my will, and insurance and stuff like that, here it's in this pouch, put it in a safe place will you?"

"Sure Mom, but let's talk about this later I'm just so excited to have you home."

The days got slower and slower, Alvin and Maple continued their short jaunts around the world to near and distant lands. After one of the trips in particular, the mood of the air became heavy. Maple had prepared a nice family dinner. Blossom and her family, Retrea and family with Hazel, Temple and one of the ladies Maple had worked with who was also now retired, her name was Jackie. She'd been kind to Maple.

Mom, how are you doing?" asked Blossom.

"I'm doing okay, just moving a little slower than usual. So glad you could come to dinner. We have to do this more often, don't you think? Can I get you anything?" asked Maple.

"No, you sit there and let me serve you. I'll get the coffee and desert. Also, I agree we should have family and friend get-togethers more often. Next time I want everyone to come to my house. Will you be there?" said Blossom.

Ginger got up and helped Retrea clear the dinner table, and Hazel with Temple began to clear off the table in the kitchen. They all shouted, "I'm coming, too."

"I wouldn't miss it," said Maple.

"Maple, where did you get these spices? Wow! The flavors

were magnificent. Wish I could cook like this."

Maple smiled and thanked them all for raving about the meal and her cooking.

"My special people deserve special treatment. I'm glad you liked what I prepared."

The evening wound down and the guests began their goodnights and headed out the door. When Maple closed the door she heard Buster chirping in the bedroom. *I wonder what's going on with him?*

Entering her bedroom she saw Alvin and Buster looking out the window at another bird that was pecking on the glass.

"I think you guys have some kind of rhythm going on in here." Maple and Alvin laughed and the birds chirped louder.

Maple wrapped a sweater around her shoulders, then looked at Alvin and said, "I'm tired. I am going to sit in my favorite chair out in the yard. You want to come with me?" Maple, not waiting for an answer left and walked out the back door. Alvin followed.

"Alvin, what's troubling you? Your spirit is restless and almost explosive."

"I'm okay," he said.

"No, I don't believe that. Tell me what's wrong." Maple said, feeling the confusion in his presence.

"I cannot believe that my ancestor turned away from God and followed Old Cup. He was supposed to stay strong, but he got scared and it seems like he lost his faith."

"We all get scared sometimes, Alvin."

"But he gave up his soul."

Maple felt the heart of Alvin's spirit cry out as though a piece of his essence nestled inside her chest.

"At that point in his life Baron believed he was taking care of his family. Remember Old Cup tricked him into believing he was his friend and rescued him from certain death. Some things that are in a man's heart don't show up anyplace but in his eyes or behavior."

"Yes, but God told Baron to stay in the circle and when he heard Old Cup's voice coming out of Doug's body, who he stepped into, Baron listened to Old Cup, the devil himself," said Alvin. "He sunk to the bottom of the barrel."

"We all make poor choices. Sometimes it's because we want to believe what is convenient, familiar or immediate," Maple said.

"So now where does that leave us with the curse?" said Alvin.

"Well, now we know what happened," she said.

"I'd like to go back to that moment in time when Baron made that choice." Alvin said.

"You know we cannot change the past in anyway, don't you? Kaye taught me that," said Maple.

"Yes, I know but we can say prayers so that the curse is stopped at least in your real time, right now."

"We can?" Maple said.

"Yep, ya game?" Alvin said. "The spirits will hear us, and our energy will be mingled into the atmosphere and will travel up to your present day."

"What will I have to do? We are not supposed to interact with those long ago dead spirits, don't you know that?" Maple asked.

"Yeah, I know, we just pray.

Maple and Alvin traveled to the site of Baron's ground circle that God had prepared for him. Maple looked to the sky and saw the colorful underbelly of the clouds at sunset. They were red and pink with streaks of sky and deep purple. The cloud's quick movements made the heavens appear angry. Maple shook from the chill that sight gave her. Alvin smoothed a place for Maple and she sat there as Alvin wrapped his spirit around her.

A high-pitched cry of grief resonated from deep in the ground while the earth shook, quick like, without disturbing their peace. Maple's skin cried as Alvin clung to her every cell. Hannah and Kaye brought their angels to also wrap around Maple as she and Alvin offered their souls to God. Maple was the only human bound soul that could be given to God for this purpose. Her faith was strong.

In the melee, Maple saw her mother. In tears, she was, because Maple had run off with that boy. Her mother knew of his meanness and watched her daughter's sweetness dissolve into panic and fear. Maple's mother didn't know what she'd done to lose her child to that monster so she caved in on herself and drank her heart to death.

Instantly the clouds were no more and the stars laughed, twinkled and danced in the turquoise blue sky. God accepted their offer and blessed their souls.

"Are you okay?" Alvin asked.

"Yes, I believe I'm more okay than I've ever been." Maple said.

"Pray for me." Alvin said.

Maple prayed and the shackles fell from his spirit.

She also prayed for all the ones she knew about to have clean hearts, spirits and souls in Divine Order.

They both saw their pasts and mistakes and triumphs.

Maple laughed, "Ya know all the time I thought that Omar was so wonderful and he took my breath away, I realize now that he was suffocating me."

Alvin wanted to counter her new reality with his own in that he, too, had buried himself in work to avoid the things he didn't understand. He told Maple that he'd given his power away by following and not leading. Then hiding in his work he never asked the Almighty for help. The spirits of the dead lit up the sky in gratitude to God.

Their angels were still all around and Maple realized for some reason she was supposed to go to choir practice that night. She hadn't done that in a while, but she promised the Pastor and Gerald, and suddenly remembered that he was Kaye's friend from the restaurant.

"Alvin, please take me back to a few minutes before choir practice starts."

"Sure, sure," he said as the huge fire which started inside Baron's circle shot up to the sky.

Chapter 33

"Hey Girl," came the shout out as Maple entered the choir room. The choir members were about to meet with the Pastor and discuss the songs for next Sunday's sermon before rehearsal.

This was the children's service week, which meant that the youth would serve as ushers and take the lead in reading announcements, they would distribute literature and welcome guests. The Pastor went through the highlights of his message, which were always subject to change. The Pastor told them that he would talk about the prayers we teach the children. The last one he would recite and discuss would be:

'Now I lay me down to sleep
I pray the Lord my Soul to keep
If I should die before I wake
I pray the Lord my Soul to take.'

Several choir members began thumbing through hymnals.

Maple waited and watched to choose the right moment when there was a lull in the conversation, she said, "What about the last song being, "It is Well with my Soul?"'

"Yes, that's a good one, Luella, who was now the assistant choir director, said.

"What about Jesus loves the Little Children?"

The Pastor requested a few more and then left out the side door. The choir members moved into the sanctuary and found their individual spaces knowing that Luella would probably move some of them in the process of singing each song.

"Look at her, she wants to turn everything into a major production," Fina told Maple.

"Girl, you ought to quit. She's just doing what the pastor wants," said Maple.

"Hmmm hmm, not just for the choir either," Fina said, looking over her shoulder at Luella and the Pastor deep in conversation.

The whole choir sang all the selections with only minor adjustments as to who would sing which solo part.

"Well, it's a wrap, saints, so go get your choir robes and take them home. The men are painting the church tonight and tomorrow and you know sometimes things get messy and we need our choir robes, without paint drippings all over them."

Maple checked her robe and as she turned to tell Fina something, she noticed some of the choir members and the stewards were following the Pastor down to the basement area.

"Fina, did you see that? I wonder where they're going?" Maple said.

"I don't know 'cause I'm looking at that fine drink or water coming in the room to see you," said Fina.

Maple turned to see Alvin coming in as Fina continued with, "he sure reminds me of Nelba and Byron's boy who died back some years ago, don't he?"

"Fina, stop that! Where'd everybody go?" Maple asked.

The sound of at least six firecrackers resonated through the church.

There were no other sounds for quite a while except soft slow footsteps on the grass in the back.

"Some kids must have been playing in the basement, we're trying to help these kids and look what they do." Fina said.

Gerald came running into the choir room and yelled,

"Y'all men grab the women and children then help them out to the front lawn. Don't go in the back parking lot, something is terribly wrong. Stay safe and help each other. I will be out front in a few minutes."

Alvin grabbed both Maple and Fina, took them out to the front of the church and they all stood stark still.

Gerald ran back down the stairs.

"We have to stand right here and pray," Alvin said to Maple. Alvin could see signs of the hovering spirits even those who 'stepped-in' to some of the church members. He walked Maple and Fina away from the church and away from the crowd. Fina's husband joined them and escorted his wife to their car and drove off.

Alvin looked down at Maple and said, "Pray."

"Pray for what?" Maple asked.

"Anything that comes to mind," Alvin said.

Alvin heard Maple's whispered prayers and kept her safe.

Packed moving crates and boxes were in the parking lot and the men of the church hitched them to trucks and a caravan moved everything away. They had taken all the wall hangings and precious things from the church earlier that day so that they would be safe from the painting job and those painters who would also be working the next day. The men of the church drove everything to a rented storage unit.

Maple was watching the commotion and looked left and right then behind her and stamped her feet like a prelude to a bathroom run. "What's happening?" she asked.

An animal howling sound came from up under the church building. The men were standing guard at each entrance and at all the low windows.

"Let's go home," Maple said.

Alvin walked her to the car, which was parked two blocks away.

"You know about what's happened or happening here don't you?" asked Maple.

"Yep, I do," said Alvin.

"Want to tell me about it?" Maple said.

"Not yet." He said, "Everything will be revealed in the morning."

"I'm tired, I want to go home and get some rest." Maple said.

"Can we meet in your dreams?" he asked with a sweet loving smile, he knew that his time to be with Maple was winding to an end.

"Only if there's a full moon," said Maple

"I can arrange that." Alvin remarked

Alvin drove Maple home.

Chapter 34

Maple was silent the whole drive home. She knew deep inside that the commotion in the church basement had something to do with Old Cup and the curse. Maple took a deep breath and emptied her lungs with a long heavy sigh. Alvin put the car in the driveway and came around to help Maple out the car. She turned to him and said, "I feel like it's over now."

"What's over?" Alvin asked.

"The curse, it's gone. Everything around me feels like my heart can sing and at this very second my children's lives are theirs. It's gone, isn't it?"

"Yes." He said. "It's gone."

"What happens now?" Maple asked.

"You can go back to your life and enjoy retirement with all your dreams of seeing the world, you can spend more time with your grandchildren and your children too, if they can find time for you. Or, is there someplace you want to go now?"

"Now, that was a cold statement," a rasp in her voice said.

"What cold statement?" he said.

"My children just have busy lives, that's all, and I can respect that. I have a life too, you know."

"No, I believe I interrupted your life. I needed you to help me… to find and eliminate the curse. Ya know, you were the only one."

"What do you mean, the only one?" Maple asked.

"The only one alive that believed me, accepted me unconditionally and loved me enough even in my death to walk through the pain and sorrow with me. What made you do that?" Alvin said.

"God talks to me too, you know," she said.

"Oh yeah?"

"Yeah. I was sitting in the yard one evening as the sun was resting on the horizon and God's warmth wrapped around me and His message soaked through my skin, bone and my breath. It soothed my heart when I was aware that I had to walk with you and be the flesh needed to end the madness of the curse to keep it from multiplying."

"How did you know?" he asked.

"God asked me who I believed Him to be and I knew from His Word, He is the Alpha and the Omega. He blessed me and at that second I felt that the shackles and guards I'd woven around the core of my being were shattered and dissolved. That's the only reason I could enter and remain in Baron's circle and I knew I can do all things through Christ who strengthens me."

Alvin moved through the room in a ceremonial dance, the entire essence of his spirit exuded joy that ignited the room.

"Alvin, do you know what I mean?"

"Yes, I do," he said in a joyful yell!

They stood together without touching, wallowing in their newfound presence of love.

"Is there anyplace you want to go?" he asked again.

"We've visited every continent and witnessed their most spectacular sites. You've seen many of your ancestors and talked briefly with a few. So what next?" Alvin asked.

"Well, how about we go to where Forever is?"

"Forever?" Are you ready?"

"Almost. Blossom will have her baby any day now and you are about to witness the birth of your grandchild's baby yourself through your eldest son. So I want to wait until these blessed events take place, don't you?"

"Yes, I hope I can be there when my son's grandbaby is born. I'm in awe of how much I've been able to witness since—you know," Alvin said, "How wonderful it has been that I've seen several hundred years of my ancestors and soon it will be two generations of my off-springs."

"I feel that I am truly blessed." Maple said.

"Yes, we are blessed," Alvin said.

The air twirled, dipped and danced through the sky. The full moon stood watch while the stars darted across the heavens. Morning arrived with a bright red sky and people began the hustle and bustle of their day. A siren interrupted everyone's concentration in the neighborhood. It was almost 10:00 in the morning, the sirens were blaring and the church burned completely to the ground, while the firefighters could do nothing but watch.

"My purpose has been fulfilled. I've completed what I was supposed to do. I know that now," she said. The curses are truly over. There were no disturbing visions that frighten my sleep last night.

Maple peeked out the window.

"Thank you. I have fulfilled destiny, because of you."

"Me, too."

Both Maple and Alvin saw the births of their grand and great grandchildren and showered them with blessings and love and knowledge.

"Forever?" he said.

"God showed it to me, I know it is time now," she said.

Forever?" he smiled.

"I want to sit outside in my favorite chair and watch the stars dance until I sleep. Is that alright with you?" Maple sat down, lay back and sighed a sound too deep for words.

Alvin's spirit leaped with joy and he held her hand until her spirit met his forever.

Chapter 35

Nobody wanted to believe Maple was gone. Family and friends sat quietly as Kaye helped orchestrate the service schedule and the program. "Blossom, Kaye is the one who found her lying back in her favorite chair. Kay told us that she could even see a smile on her face, just so peaceful," said Blossom to Fina her mother's friend.

They looked around for Alvin but he never showed up, Kaye told them he had to take an unexpected trip and may not know that Maple was gone yet. She said she would find the right time to let him know.

Blossom pulled Kaye to the side and asked her about why her mother wanted everything done at one time, the wake, the funeral, and the reading of the will and last but not least she had written a statement so she could have the last word.

"Kaye do you know what the will or the statement say?"

"No, she left specific instructions that each had to be opened at certain times, and her attorney had to be present. So we can now go to the cemetery, and have her laid to rest the way she wanted."

"Can I help you with anything?"

"She left a seating chart, too, so if the funeral director needs to know who's who you can do that or maybe just sit with your family so we can help comfort you," Kaye said.

"Okay, let her know that I can identify who sits where if she needs me," Blossom said.

The long black cars rolled out to the cemetery and to the site of the Mausoleum Maple had paid for her exact spot and even visited there from time to time just to feel the peacefulness.

The family sat quietly and watched as they put her casket in its proper place, when it was securely in place they saw that the left bottom corner there was an inscription and a sketch in the metal of Maple smiling, they stood there in sadness and one person commented "That Maple thought of everything didn't she? Even her goodbye."

The workers began to take the shrouds that covered the other doors of those interred around her. One by one the mourners saw the picture next to hers. There was an inscription that said, "Forever" underneath her etching. They were even more confounded by closely noting that Alvin had passed away many years earlier. It was who Junior thought it was. The nameplate read Alvin Byron Chance (ABC).

Chapter 36

Epilogue

Attention everyone – there is one more request from Maple. It's a statement she prepared for you to hear after the will is distributed to each of you," said Kaye.

"It reads:

'Dear Ones,

I love you all for the goodness I feel in each one of you. Thank you for being a part of my life to the end. I have such joy having transitioned into 'Forever.' I will continue even now to pray for you. Please also keep me in your heart. Life takes you through lots of twists and turns and roadblocks. It's up to you, individually, to make the path easier to travail for each other. You also have a responsibility to make the trail easier for others you don't even know, if you can. Make your life mean something to those you come across. If it's only a smile, I bet it makes a difference. Be tolerant, be gentle, and be loving and kind.

Life is precious and our hearts are tender – when we touch we must do it to greet, to help, to teach and to show love. A touch should never hurt.

Care about each other; I've made decisions of how to dispose of all my belongings based on my heart, soul and spirit. Sometimes the most needy also need courage and the ability to trust. Sometimes the strongest or most powerful need encouragement and a taste of humility. All of you strong, or needy, and those in between, want someone who cares about you and someone to care about. So love each other with your whole heart. Otherwise, Forever won't let you in."

About the Author

D'Norgia Taylor's writing career began with a great interest in English and Journalism. During that time she began technical writing for local publications and medical programs. Over the next few years she continued freelance writing with her own company, Designer Publications, creating brochures, newspaper articles, billboards, political materials, grant proposals, and marketing materials for small business and non-profit organizations.

Maya Angelou Writers Guild, Willamette Writers and Oregon Writers Colony helped prepare her for this new work. Taylor is known for her community involvement. She has directed several non-profit organizations that benefit the Portland community at large, including Domestic Violence awareness, education, working with seniors, and disaster preparedness.

Made in the USA
San Bernardino, CA
19 January 2016

GREAT FICTION!

WANDA HICKEY'S NIGHT OF GOLDEN MEMORIES AND OTHER DISASTERS

Also by Jean Shepherd

IN GOD WE TRUST, ALL OTHERS PAY CASH
THE AMERICA OF GEORGE ADE

JEAN SHEPHERD

WANDA HICKEY'S NIGHT OF
Golden Memories
AND OTHER DISASTERS

DOUBLEDAY
NEW YORK LONDON TORONTO SYDNEY AUCKLAND

A Main Street Book
PUBLISHED BY DOUBLEDAY
a division of Bantam Doubleday Dell Publishing Group, Inc.
1540 Broadway, New York, New York 10036

Main Street Books, Doubleday, and the portrayal of a
building with a tree are trademarks of Doubleday, a division
of Bantam Doubleday Dell Publishing Group, Inc.

*All of the characters in this book are fictitious,
and any resemblance to actual persons, living or dead,
is purely coincidental.*

DRAWINGS BY RAYMOND DAVIDSON

These stories originally appeared in *Playboy* magazine.
Copyright © 1966, 1967, 1968, 1969, 1970 by HMH Publishing Co., Inc.

ISBN 0-385-11632-2

25 24 23 22 21 20 19 18

CONTENTS

To little Leigh with love. I hope it's been worth it all. . . .

WANDA HICKEY'S NIGHT OF GOLDEN
MEMORIES AND OTHER DISASTERS

THE GRANDSTAND PASSION PLAY
OF DELBERT AND THE BUMPUS HOUNDS

"'Mah-ree Elena, yore the answer to mah prayer. . . .'" The familiar twangy moan of old Gene Autry seemed to be coming from next to my ear. It was the first time I had ever dreamed in sound. Or *was* I dreaming?

"FER CHRISSAKE, WHAT THE HELL IS THAT RACKET?" The bedsprings clattered in the next room, as my old man cursed and leaped out of the sack, his feet thumping the floor in the dark. Instantly, I was wide awake.

"'MAH-REE ELENA. . . .'" It was even louder, now that my mind was working again. The tinny plunking of a guitar cut through the darkness. My kid brother sat up in his bed across the room from me and began to whine, his usual reaction to any outside stimulus.

A guttural grunt of intense pain, followed by a high-pitched bleating wail, as the old man once again un-erringly cracked his big toe against the leg of the dresser. He had done this so many times in the past, in

13

the dark, that all the varnish was now worn off the leg, and my father's toe was permanently shaped like a small tennis ball.

"Now what?" My mother joined in the chorus, her hair curlers rattling in the gloom.

"'WHEN IT'S TWAALAHT ON THE TRAY-ULL. . . .'" Autry had launched into another favorite of simple-minded millions everywhere.

"What the hell *time* is it?" muttered the old man. He was always an aggressive sleeper. Sleep was one of the things he did best, and he loved it. Some look upon sleep as an unfortunately necessary interruption of life; but there are others who hold that sleep *is* life, or at least one of the more fulfilling aspects of it, like eating or sex. Any time my old man's sleep was interrupted, he became truly dangerous.

"It's almost three-thirty. Who the hell's playing those goddamn records at three-thirty?"

Someone was, indeed, playing records at full blast. It was then that we first became aware of another sound— one that was to become more familiar and ominous in the weeks to come: a kind of snuffling, scratching, moiling, squealing, squishy turmoil.

"'. . . THAT SILVUHH HAI-UHD DAH-DEE OF MAHN. . . .'" Doors slammed. Twangy voices argued indistinctly. Gene Autry keened on and on. The snuffling squeals rose and fell. The old man reconnoitered silently through the bedroom curtains.

"HOOIICKK-PATOOOEY!" Something juicy splatted against the side of our house.

14

"Holy Christ!" The old man hissed a rhetorical comment to no one in particular.

"GRRAAAHHKKK! BROWWK!" A window-rattling burp boomed out over the scratchy Gene Autry disc.

My mother was finally galvanized into action. She had fought a lifelong battle against obscene noises of every variety. I could hear her pattering feet, as she joined my father at the window.

"Who *are* they?" she asked, after a pause to survey the scene.

"Damned if I know!" the old man answered; but I could tell from the sound of his voice that he knew trouble had arrived. Big trouble. The Bumpus crowd had moved in next door and was already in business.

Ours was not a genteel neighborhood, by any stretch of the imagination. Nestled picturesquely between the looming steel mills and the verminously aromatic oil refineries and encircled by a colorful conglomerate of city dumps and fetid rivers, our northern Indiana town was and is the very essence of the Midwestern industrial heartland of the nation. There was a standard barbershop bit of humor that said it with surprising poeticism: If Chicago (only a stone's throw away across the polluted lake waters) was Carl Sandburg's "City of the Broad Shoulders," then Hohman had to be that city's broad rear end.

According to legend, it bore the name of a hapless early settler who had arrived on the scene when the land was just prairie and Indian trails. Surveying the sparkling blue waters of Lake Michigan, he decided that

15

Chicago, then a tiny trading post where land was free for the asking, had no future. Struggling through the quagmires farther south, for some demented reason now lost to history, he set up camp and invested heavily in land that was destined to become one of the ugliest pieces of real estate this side of the craters of the moon. Indeed, it bore some resemblance to the moon, in that the natives were alternately seared by stifling heat in the summer and reduced to clanking hulks when the fierce gales blew off the lake. Our founding father set the pattern of futility for all future generations.

My old man, my mother, my kid brother and I slogged along in the great tradition. The old man had his high point every Wednesday at George's Bowling Alley, where he once rolled a historic game in which he got three consecutive strikes. My kid brother's nose ran steadily, winter and summer. My mother made red cabbage, peanut-butter-and-jelly sandwiches, meat loaf and Jell-O in an endless stream. And I studied the principal exports of Peru at the Warren G. Harding School.

Delbert Bumpus entered Warren G. Harding like a small, truculent rhinoceros. His hair grew low down on his almost nonexistent forehead, and he had the greatest pair of ears that Warren G. Harding had ever seen, extending at absolutely right angles from his head. Between those ears festered a pea-sized but malevolent brain that almost immediately made him the most feared kid below sixth grade.

He had a direct way of settling disagreements that he established on the second day of his brief but spectacu-

lar period at W.G.H. Grover Dill—our number-two-rank-
ing thug, right behind Scut Farkas, who stood alone
as the premier bully of all he surveyed—challenged
Bumpus to a showdown the first time he laid eyes on
those peculiarly provocative ears. It was recess time
and, as usual, we milled about aimlessly in the stickers
and sand hills of our playground. It was too early for
baseball; football had been over for months; we didn't
have a basketball hoop; so we just milled.

Spotting Bumpus in his worn blue jeans and black
turtleneck—tiny, close-set eyes almost invisible under a
thatch of jet-black, wiry hair—Dill opened negotiations,
his own slitted eyes glinting in anticipation of a little
action:

"What's yer name, kid?"

Bumpus pulled his head lower into the turtleneck and
said nothing.

"I SAID, WHAT'S YER NAME, KID?" This time in
a loud, trumpeting voice that alerted the rest of the
school ground that spring had come and Grover Dill
felt the sap rising. Bumpus, a full head and a half shorter
than Dill but built along the lines of a fireplug, muttered:

"Bumpus." It was the first word we had heard from
him, his accent redolent of the deepest Kentucky hills.

"BUMPUS! What the hell kind of a name is that? Holy
Moses! Didja hear that? Bumpus! What kind of a name
is that?"

Dill's humor, while extremely primitive, was refreshingly
direct. He began to sing in a high, feminine voice:

17

"Bumpus Schlumpus, double Crumpus—" He broke off, advancing on Bumpus, sandy hair abristle.

"D'ya have a first name, runt?"

Farkas watched with Olympian disinterest as his protégé moved in for the kill. Schwartz huddled next to me, ashen-faced, while Flick attempted to blend into the sand. There wasn't one of us who had not, at one time or another, been dealt with by either Farkas or Dill.

"I said, what's yer first name, kid?" Bumpus, backed up flat against the school wall, finally spoke up:

"Delbert."

"Delbert! *DELBERT!*" Outraged by such a name, Dill addressed the crowd, with scorn dripping from his every word. *"Delbert Bumpus!* They're letting *everybody* in Harding School these days! What the hell kind of a name is that? That must be some kind of *hillbilly* name!"

It was the last time anyone at Warren G. Harding ever said, or even thought, anything like that about Delbert Bumpus.

Everything happened so fast after that that no two accounts of it were the same. The way I saw it, Bumpus' head snapped down low between his shoulder blades. He bent over from the waist, charged over the sand like a wounded wart hog insane with fury, left his feet and butted his black, furry head like a battering-ram into Dill's rib cage, the sickening thump sounding exactly like a watermelon dropped from a second-story window. Dill, knocked backward by the charge, landed on his neck and slid for three or four feet, his face alternating green and white. His eyes, usually almost unseen behind

18

his cobra lids, popped out like a tromped-on toad-frog's. He lay flat, gazing paralyzed at the spring sky, one shoe wrenched off his foot by the impact. The schoolyard was hushed, except for the sound of a prolonged gurling and wheezing as Dill, now half his original size, lay retching. It was obvious that he was out of action for some time.

Bumpus glared around at the hushed faces, then spit a long stream of rich-brown tobacco juice onto Dill's left tennis shoe. The buzzer sounded for the end of recess, but it was the beginning of a new era.

That's the way the whole Bumpus crowd was, in one way or another. Overnight, the entire neighborhood changed. The Taylors, a quiet family who had lived next to us for years, had moved out and—without warn-ing—the Bumpuses had flooded in. There were thousands of them! The house seemed to age in one week. What had been a nondescript bungalow became a battered, hinge-sprung, sagging hillbilly shack.

I remember only brief images of various Bumpuses. They never mixed with anyone else in the neighborhood, just moiled around, hawking, guffawing, kicking their dogs and piling up junk in the back yard. They drove an old slat-sided Chevy pickup truck that was covered with creamy-white bird droppings and a thick coating of rutted Kentucky clay. It had no windshield and the steering wheel looked like it was made entirely of old black friction tape. It roared like a tank, sending up clouds of blue smoke as it burned the sludge oil that the Bumpuses slopped into it. It seemed to be always hub-deep in mud, even though there was no mud in our neighborhood.

Old Emil Bumpus was kind of the headman. He was about eight feet tall and always walked like he was leaning into a strong wind, with his head hanging down around his overall tops. He must have weighed about 300 pounds, not including his chaw of navy plug, which he must have been born chewing. His neck was so red that at first we thought he always wore some kind of bandanna. But he didn't. He had an Adam's apple that rode up and down the front of his neck like a yo-yo. His hair, which was mud-colored, stuck out in all directions and looked like it had been chopped off here and there with a pair of hedge-trimming shears. And his hands, which hung down to just below his knees, had knuckles the size of pool balls, and there was usually a black, string bandage around a thumb. His hands were made for hitting things.

The Bumpuses weren't in town three days before Emil cleaned out the whole back room at the Blue Bird Tavern one night. They said somebody had given him a dirty look. Another time, Big Rusty Galambus, who had heard about that incident and felt his reputation was at stake, busted Emil's gallon jug over the back of his head. They said that Emil didn't even know he'd been hit for a couple of minutes, until somebody told him. Then he turned around, stood up, looked down at Big Rusty and said:

"Ah'd be mo' careful with that thar jug a mahn ef'n

ah was yew. Ef ah didn' know bettuh, ah mighta tho't yew was spoilin' for a fight."

There was something about the way he said it that persuaded Rusty, a scarred veteran of the open hearth, who had once hoisted the back end of a Ford truck with his bare hands when the jack busted, to apologize and say that the jug slipped.

Emil let it pass; after all, he had 9000 more jugs at home, of all sizes and shapes, sitting on various window sills. We wondered what they were for, until we saw the Bumpuses carrying in pieces of copper tubing—and until we got our first whiff of a mighty aroma from their basement that overpowered even the normal neighborhood smell from the Sinclair oil refinery a half mile away. It got so bad at times that starlings would sit around on the telephone wires back of the Bumpus house, just breathing deeply and falling off into the bushes and squawking. From time to time, there would be a dull explosion in the cellar, and a Bumpus would run out of the house with his overalls on fire.

One afternoon, with a snootful of whatever they were making down there, Emil came reeling out onto the back porch. He was yelling at somebody in the kitchen, his deep molasses drawl booming out over the neighborhood.

"WHO YEW THANK YO' TAWKIN' TEW?" With that, he grabbed ahold of the back porch and pulled it right off the house. He just grabbed the porch and yanked it out by the roots:

"AAAuuuggghhh!"

From that day on, the Bumpus house had no back porch, only a door about eight feet up in the air and a rusty screen. Once in a while, one of them would jump out—and land in the garbage. And every so often, one of the skinny, red-faced sisters would fall out accidentally, usually carrying a pail of dishwater or chicken innards.

"Lawd a'mighty. Amy Jo, ef'n yew cain't watch them clodhoppers a yourn, we gonna have to chain yew up!" Another raucous round of harrooping. They sure loved one another.

From the day they moved in, the house was surrounded by a thick swamp of junk: old truck tires, barrels full of bottles and tin cans, black oil drums, rusty pitchforks, busted chicken crates, an old bathtub, at least 57 ancient bedsprings, an old tractor hood, a half-dozen rotting bushel baskets overflowing with inner tubes and galoshes, a wheelbarrow with one handle, eight or nine horse collars and a lot of things that nobody could figure out—things that looked like big tall water boilers with pipes sticking out. For some reason, they loved wire; they had all kinds of it—chicken wire, baling wire and rolls of barbed wire, just sort of lying around. And in between the big stuff, there was all the little stuff: sardine cans, old batteries, tire irons, old blue tin cups, corncobs, leather straps and a lot of tire pumps. They were always bringing home license plates, which they nailed up by the basement door. The Bumpuses went to the city dump two or three times a week—like art patrons to a gallery—to stock up on more of the same.

The sea of wreckage spread like a blight onto the surrounding yards, first an ironing board on our lawn, then a bicycle tire in our bushes, then a few odd corncobs on the front porch. And one day, a gust of wind covered my mother's flapping laundry—her pride and joy—with a thin, indelible coating of chicken dung, pigeon feathers, rabbit fur and goat droppings. After that, her jaw was grim, her eyes thin slits of rage, every time another burst of hawkings or blattings reminded her of the Bumpuses. The night my old man tripped in the dark over a rusty radiator in our back yard, causing him to drop his bowling ball on his left foot, didn't help things, either. He grabbed the radiator and flung it into the dark, back into the Bumpuses' yard; it crashed into the rubble, and for five minutes, an avalanche of sound rumbled on and on, like Fibber McGee's closet. Emil stuck his head out of the kitchen window, quickly followed by the barrel of his trusty shotgun. When the old man stood his ground, Emil hissed, "Sic 'em, Luke!" Instantly, 17 dogs roared out from behind the garage. The old man barely made the kitchen.

A few days later, Schwartz, Kissel, Flick and I were trudging up our driveway when Flick stopped in his tracks, pointed and said, with a touch of delighted wonder, "Hey, look at that funny little house."

"Yeah, look at that little moon on it," replied Schwartz, likewise with some wonder.

"What the hell is it?" Junior Kissel chimed in.

Suddenly, Delbert Bumpus shot around the side of the house, dodging his way through the junk yard like a broken-field runner, and hurled himself headlong into the tiny pine shack and slammed the door, disappearing from our view—but not, unfortunately, beyond our earshot. It was then that we found out about little houses with moons, a new concept for all of us. Devout believers in eternal verities and ancient traditions, the Bumpuses obviously distrusted newfangled, citified contraptions such as that white-porcelain doohickey beside their upstairs bathtub, which didn't get much use, either—except, rumor had it, for the aging and storage of white lightning. From that day on, there was an endless stream of Bumpuses beating a path through the back yard at all hours of the day and night. The outhouse also solved for them the problem of what to do with last year's Sears, Roebuck catalog.

With the Bumpuses—and the outhouse—came the rats. They must have brought back a couple of thousand from one of their trips to the dump. Emil would squat out in back and pop at them with a long-barreled single-shot .22. You could hear the ricochets bouncing off the oil drums, and then Emil yelling:

"Gahdamn, Ima Pearl, ah missed that varmint agin."

"Emil, yew kin go out huntin' after supper. It's time we et."

The Bumpus hounds, who had their own problems with an even larger population of ticks and lice, had no interest at all in the rats. Once in a while, you'd see a hound sprawled flat on his back in the dust, legs spraddled, ears spread out, mouth hanging open, tongue lolling, sound asleep in the sun, with a rat lying beside him like they were the best of friends. The rats had no such nonaggression treaty with the Bumpus chickens, whom they ganged up on now and then, but their losses were too heavy to make it a regular thing. The Bumpuses had *mean* chickens. One big gray hen with a ratty tail and demented yellow eyes chased Schwartz all the way to school one day and waited in the playground for him to come out at recess. He wisely cowered in the locker room.

They also had rabbits—and pigeons. For some reason, hillbillies dearly love pigeons. They kept them in chicken-wire pens when they weren't out dive-bombing our yard and roosting on everybody's laundry. And the Bumpuses had one animal nobody could identify. It was kind of round, with blackish fur and claws. It weighed about 30 pounds or so, and Mrs. Kissel told my mother it was "a swamp bear." Nobody believed her, until one time it tried to eat Mrs. Gammie's Airedale, Rags, who had a nervous breakdown and had to be sent to the country. But the only atrocity it ever actually committed was to devour all my mother's iris bulbs. Emil used to holler at it once in a while, when it got to chewing on the truck tires. Its name was Jack.

The three goats never gave anybody much trouble; in fact, they kept our lawn mowed for us. They didn't smell too good if you got downwind of them on a warm day, but nobody complained about it—what with all the other indescribable smells that drifted our way day and night. My old man would peek out of the kitchen window with a Montgomery Ward spyglass to try to

25

see what the Bumpuses ate when they were all squatting around the trough in the kitchen, with a yellow light bulb hanging overhead amid the wriggling flypaper. There was one smell that really used to get him. He could never tell what it was—a kind of smoky, greasy, gamy animal scent. Then one night he got it. He was watching them wolf it down, the way they always did, slurping and crunching, throwing off a thick yellow spray.

"By God, they're eating possum! That's what it is. Possum!"

My mother, who was always interested in cooking, asked: "Possum, what's that?"

A *Field & Stream* subscriber, the old man immediately answered, "Possum—you know, it's kind of a big rat." My mother, who was putting tomato paste on top of our meat loaf at the time, dropped her spoon and ran into the bathroom. After that, she didn't ask much about what the Bumpuses ate.

"I wonder where the hell they get it?" the old man continued. "I never heard of a possum around here." Where they got possum was just another of the Bumpus mysteries.

Every five minutes or so, someone threw something out the back window into the yard. My mother would be standing at the sink, peering out the window that looked right into the Bumpus house just across the driveway from us. A soggy paper sack filled with coffee grounds and apple cores would sail out and land amid the rubble.

"Tch, tch, just look at those pigs!"

She was right. We were living next door to a tightly knit band of total slobs, a genuine gypsy family. The Bumpuses were so low down on the evolutionary totem pole that they weren't even included in Darwin's famous family tree. They had inbred and ingrown and finally emerged from the Kentucky hills like some remnant of Attila the Hun's barbarian horde. Flick said that they had webbed feet and only three toes. It might have been true.

Delbert Bumpus, the runt of the litter, came to school about three days a month. It was three times too often. Whenever he showed up, there would be a lot of yelling, and they'd throw him out. Delbert never played with anybody and he hardly ever talked; but he spat a lot. Since he lived with the goats and rabbits and chickens, he didn't smell exactly like the rest of us, either—and *we* weren't any bargain.

One time, Miss Parsons, our gym teacher, made the mistake of putting Delbert in a volleyball game. I guess they never played volleyball in Kentucky, because at first he didn't seem to understand what was going on. But when he got the hang of it, everything changed. He stood there, watching them knock the ball back and forth, for maybe five minutes, and then somebody hit one toward him. He left the ground about three feet and gave the ball an overhand shot that sent it screaming over the net; it caught Schwartz just below the left eye and knocked him flat. Bumpus' side cheered.

Miss Parsons said, "No, Delbert, you mustn't hit it that hard."

Bumpus spat on the gym floor and glared at her for a minute, and then growled, "What the goddamn hell is this game 'spose ta be about?"

While Schwartz crawled around on the floor, crying, Miss Parsons—who taught Sunday school at the Baptist church—tried again.

"You mustn't use those bad words, Delbert. Now, let's begin the game again, shall we?"

Miss Parsons believed in law and order. Schwartz, who had been removed to the nurse's office, trailing blood, had been replaced by Roger Beanblossom, who, at the age of seven, was already six feet tall. Beanblossom, famous for his serve, sliced a whistler right at Bumpus, who stopped scratching just in time to slam the ball back over the net. This time, he got Jack Morton in the pit of his stomach, knocking the wind out of him like a deflated beach ball. He slumped to the floor, the color of Cream of Wheat.

"No, Delbert." Miss Parsons was back in the fray. "Here, I'll show you."

She tapped the ball delicately into the air, to show how the game was played. Bumpus, watching this exhibition, came out with a line that soon became legend at Warren G. Harding School.

"Who the hell wants to play a goddamn silly girl's game lahk that?"

Miss Parsons, now beet red and faced with a question many of us had privately asked, since volleyball was a hated game among the males of the school, could do only one thing. "Delbert Bumpus, you go to the office this instant!"

Picking his nose, Delbert slouched toward the door and muttered, with classic simplicity: "Screw you."

And he left. It was lucky that Miss Parsons didn't know what he meant by that, or there would have been real trouble. He was kicked out of school for only a week.

Then there was the time Miss Shields opened up the day by reading us a chapter of *Raggedy Ann and Raggedy Andy*. Miss Shields was tall and thin and wore rimless glasses. She was a very kind lady, who believed that all children were basically good.

"Boys and girls," she began, after setting the book down, "are there any questions?"

Bumpus, who had never asked a question, spoke up. He had a very deep voice for a kid; already it sounded a lot like old Emil's, rich and phlegmy.

"Yeah." That was all he said.

"Oh, you have a question, Delbert?" asked Miss Shields, obviously pleased. She felt at long last she was *reaching* him.

"Yeah." He was a kid of few words.

"Well, what is your question, Delbert?"

"Was this guy Raggedy Andy a bohunk?"

"What was that?" Miss Shields was caught off guard.

"Mah Uncle Cletus knew a bohunk onc't named Andy."

Miss Shields, who did not know Delbert Bumpus the way the class did, gamely replied: "Well, no, Delbert,

Raggedy Andy was not of Bohemian extraction. He was a doll."

"Well, ah'll be goddamned," he snorted.

"What was that, Delbert?" Miss Shields felt the class slipping from her grasp.

"You mean a doll that walked aroun'? Shee-it!"

"Delbert, you mustn't use words like that in class. Yes, Raggedy Andy was a doll who walked around, and so was Raggedy Ann."

Delbert snorted again in disbelief and, as he sat down, said in a loud voice, "Ah nevah did heah such a crock a hog drippin's."

"Delbert," said Miss Shields with an ashen face, "report to the office this instant!" We waited for him to say what he usually said when he left the room, but I guess he liked Miss Shields. He just stalked out and went home.

The only time Delbert ever said anything to me directly was one day when I made the mistake of throwing him out at first base. He looked at me real hard for a long time and then said: "Doan' worry, piss-ant, ah'll git yew someday."

Little did I dream at the time what form his revenge would take.

Delbert was the only Bumpus kid in my grade, but they infested Warren G. Harding like termites in an outhouse. There was Ima Jean, short and muscular, who was in the sixth grade, when she showed up, but spent most of her time hanging around the poolroom. There was a lanky, blue-jowled customer they called Jamie, who ran the still and was the only one who ever wore shoes. He and his brother Ace, who wore a brown fedora and blue work shirts, sat on the front steps at home on the Fourth of July, sucking at a jug and pretending to light sticks of dynamite with their cigars when little old ladies walked by. There were also several red-faced girls who spent most of their time dumping dishwater out of windows. Babies of various sizes and sexes crawled about the back yard, fraternizing indiscriminately with the livestock. They all wore limp, battleship-gray T-shirts and nothing else. They cried day and night.

We thought that was all of them—until one day a truck stopped in front of the house and out stepped a girl who made Daisy Mae look like Little Orphan Annie. My father was sprinkling the lawn at the time; he wound up watering the windows. Ace and Emil came running out onto the porch, whooping and hollering. The girl carried a cardboard suitcase—in which she must have kept all her underwear, if she owned any—and wore her blonde hair piled high on her head; it gleamed in the midday sun. Her short muslin dress strained and bulged. The truck roared off. Ace rushed out to greet her, bellowing over his shoulder as he ran:

"MAH GAWD! HEY, MAW, IT'S CASSIE! SHE'S HOME FROM THE REFORMATORY!"

Emil grabbed her suitcase and Cassie, the ripest 16-year-old ever to descend on northern Indiana, kissed her father in a way that clouded up windows for blocks around.

"Mah Gawd, Cassie, yew sure filled out!" he boomed,

slapping her none too paternally on the backside. Maw Bumpus, drying her hands on her apron, yelled from the porch:

"YEW GIT IN HERE, CASSIE, AN' LEAVE YORE PAW ALONE. LEASTWAYS TILL WE'VE ET."

After that, my father stepped up his spyglass work considerably, since they had no window shades and Cassie liked to dress very casually around the house. She also liked to lie in the swing on the front porch and suck jawbreakers when the weather was hot.

On Saturday nights, even before Cassie arrived, a roaring fleet of old cars would park around the Bumpus house and a mob of slope-browed, slack-jawed friends and relatives would crowd into the place. All night, paneless windows needlessly flung wide, a thunderous square dance would shake the crockery for blocks around. Hawking and spitting and swilling applejack, they yelled and sweated and thumped up and down, while old Emil sat in a corner and sawed on his fiddle. On those nights, hardly anyone dared leave their homes. These parties always ended one way—with a sudden crash, a prolonged scuffle and then:

"EF'N YEW LAY ANOTHA FINGA ON MAH WOMAN, AH'LL SLICE YEW UP LIKE HOG BACON!"

"YEW AN' WHO ELSE, YEW SONOVABITCH!?"

Followed by screams, crashing bottles, running feet; then a distant wail of sirens. A tremendous roaring of ancient motors, a cloud of gravel and they were all gone, leaving a trail of blood and sweat behind them.

Then there were the dogs. They had at least 745 dogs. Now, our neighborhood had always had dogs—walking-around, ordinary dogs, with names like Zero and Ralph. Once in a while, one of them would knock over a garbage can, but they were dogs that knew their place. The Bumpus hounds, on the other hand, didn't seem to be dogs at all, or maybe they were such *total* dogs that no one knew how to handle them. They were the most uninhibited animals you ever saw in your life. They had absolutely no sense of privacy. They did everything in the bright sunlight, and I mean *everything*. They were just a great churning mass of tails and tongues and flea-bitten bodies. You could almost see the smell. On a warm day, a sort of bluish-greenish-yellowish haze hung over the Bumpus house, and even the haze had fleas.

Every day, one of the Bumpus women would swing down from the back door to feed them. She strode amid the slavering pack, carrying a greasy dishpan full of obscene table scraps and chicken gizzards.

"COME AN' GIT YO' VITTLES!"

The mob would charge, rolling over her in a tidal wave of heaving flanks, bloodshot eyes and mangy fur. Snarling and squealing, they stormed over the littered back yard, a heaving ball of yapping curs. The Bumpus woman, fastidiously shifting her wad of tobacco from one side of her mouth to the other, would then kick her way through the pack and back into the house.

They dug holes continously—under the porch, in the back yard, in the middle of our scrawny lawn and under the car. Five of them took up residence beneath our garage. They slept there in shifts 24 hours a day. Every time the old man would drive the Olds in, we'd hear under the floor: "ROWFF OUFFF ROWWFF!" and they'd run in mad circles around the garage.

"Shoo! Beat it! Lemme alone!" my father would shout, as he hopped up and down amid the hounds, fighting his way toward the kitchen door. We'd see the eyes of the Bumpus family peering out, waiting for him to make a wrong move. They were a real hillbilly family when it came to their dogs. You could say anything you wanted about anybody in the family, but you didn't dare insult one of their dogs. You didn't say anything against Old Blue or Big Red. *All* the dogs—with the exception of those 17 named Luke—were named either Big Red or Old Blue.

Half a dozen times a week, my old man would come sprinting up the back steps just a stride ahead of the leader of the pack—a wiry, scarred battler named, of course, Big Red—baying the way Kentucky hounds always do when they've got a bear up a tree. Every time this would happen, there would be another wave of juicy guffaws and wheezy backslapping from the Bumpus mob. This really burned the old man up. After a hard day at the office and the Olds' acting up again, fighting off Big Red to get into the kitchen really got him. He'd sit at the kitchen table, his face sweaty, gulping down a bottle of Atlas Praeger. Finally, after catching his breath, he'd say, "Goddamn it, did you see what those lousy hounds did to the hedge?"

My mother, who had long since given up caring, always shrugged her shoulders and continued stoically scouring her pots.

When there was a full moon, the Bumpus hounds, feeling some ancient canine urge, would treat the neighborhood to a nightlong serenade.

"OwwwwwOOOOOOOOOOOOOOOO. WOWOOOOO-OOOOOooooooooo. Yap yap yaoooOOOOOOooooooooo-oo."

One after the other, they would take solos; then, after a blessed moment of silence, a full chorus, 15 or 20 strong, would howl to the inconstant moon:

"Yipe yipe yaaWOOOOOOOOOooooooooo. Ow Ow OW-OOOOOOO. OOOOOOOoooooooWOWOOO WOW! WOW! WOWOOOooooooo."

All over the neighborhood, in darkened bedrooms, hairs rose on reddened necks, children whimpered in fear. The Bumpus hounds bayed on, interspersed with Gene Autry—"MEXICALI ROSE, KEEP SMILIN', AH'LL COME BACK TO YEW . . .'"—and the running commentary of the Bumpuses themselves: "HOICK-PA-TOOEY."

Months went by. We were in a state of siege. Only after you've lived next to a family like the Bumpuses can you understand how anyone could carry on a lifelong feud with his neighbors. My mother and father were just standard-type people. The old man would flip his cork once in a while when the furnace went on the fritz; he'd threaten to blow out his brains when the White Sox traded away the only ballplayer they had. But he never got mad enough to throw rocks at people—not until that fantastic day when the rumbling volcano of his temper, roused from dormancy by the arrival of the Bumpuses, finally erupted.

Every three of four months—roughly three times a year—we would make a major food investment. I suppose rich families don't even think about this kind of thing, but ordinary families in those days spent their lives eating canned corn, meat loaf, peanut-butter sandwiches, oatmeal, red cabbage and peas. In such a home, the great meals that came along every few months stuck out like icebergs in the Caribbean. Buying a turkey was a state occasion. The entire family would go to the market to inspect all the turkeys; they'd discuss the relative merits of each, press the breastbones down, wiggle the legs, until finally they'd take a vote and decide on this particular 12-pounder, which is borne home with honor and prepared for the big day, like a virgin for the sacrifice. It's a ritual almost as cherished and time-honored as the moment when the tribe hunkers around the ceremonial campfire to devour it.

For weeks afterward, the theological debates continue: "That was a very good turkey. Very good."

"It was almost as good as the turkey we had in Thirty-three."

"But it wasn't quite as tender as the one we had in Twenty-nine. Actually, this year's was a little dry."

These feast days are always associated with major holidays: turkey for Thanksgiving and Christmas, roast chicken for birthdays and, in our house, Easter always meant ham. My father was totally ape over ham. The week before Easter, usually on Friday night, he'd say, "I'll tell you what let's do. What do you say we all pile in the car, drive down to the A.&P. and pick out a great big ham for Easter?"

He said it almost nonchalantly, but his eyes would be lit with a wild and ravenous light. It was no small thing he was suggesting, since "a great big ham" meant about half his pay check in those days.

My mother almost always would come back with, "Well, gee, I don't know. Can we afford it this year? We can always get a nice little pot roast."

"Ah, come on! What the hell. You only live once. What do you say?" And she would always relent.

Quivering slightly, he would throw on his coat and rush to the door. He could already see the ham half eaten, rich and red, weeks of magnificent pickings. Nothing goes with Atlas Praeger like cold ham after a session at the bowling alley.

We'd race to the A. & P. All the hams would be laid out, wrapped in white paper, some marked Armour Star, others Swift; not to mention Hormel. There were always great arguments as to which was really best. These were not dinky little canned hams but weighty monsters smoked darkly and tied with greasy, twisted twine.

The old man would go up and down the case, poking, peering, hefting, sniffing, occasionally punching, until, eventually, *the* ham was isolated from the common herd. Somehow, it looked a little different from the rest. It was *our* ham.

We would leave the market with at least four giant

bags of groceries, our fare for the week: loaves of Wonder Bread, Campbell's tomato soup, Ann Page pork and beans, eggs, a two-pound jar of grape jelly, fig bars, oatmeal, Cream of Wheat—real *people* food—and the ham. *The* ham.

When we got the ham home, my mother immediately stripped off the white paper and the string in the middle of our chipped white-enamel kitchen table. There it lay, exuding heavenly perfumes—proud, arrogant, regal. It had a dark, smoked, leathery skin, which my mother carefully peeled off with her sharpened bread knife. Then the old man, the only one who could lift the ham without straining a gut, placed it in the big dark-blue oval pot that was used only for hams. My mother then covered the ham with water, pushed it onto the big burner and turned up the gas until it boiled. It just sat there on the stove and bubbled away for maybe two hours, filling the house with a smell that was so luscious, so powerful as to have erotic overtones. The old man paced back and forth, occasionally lifting the lid and prodding the ham with a fork, inhaling deeply. The ham frenzy was upon him.

After about an hour, the whole neighborhood knew what we were having for Easter. Finally, the next phase began. Grunting and straining, my mother poured off the water into another pot. It would later form the base of a magnificent pea soup so pungent as to bring tears to the eyes. She then sprinkled a thick layer of brown sugar, dotted with butter, over the ham. She stuck cloves in it in a crisscross design, then added several slices of

Del Monte pineapple, thick and juicy, and topped it off with a maraschino cherry in the center of each slice. She then sprinkled more brown sugar over the lot, a few teaspoons of molasses, the juice from the pineapple can, a little salt, a little pepper, and it was shoved into the oven. Almost instantly, the brown sugar melted over the mighty ham and mingled with the ham juice in the pan.

By this time, the old man, humming nervously to himself, had checked his carving set several times, to make sure the knife was honed, the fork tines sharp—while in the oven, the ham baked on and on, until late Saturday night, when my mother finally turned off the gas, leaving the oven unopened and the ham inside. She said, as she always did, "Never eat a baked ham right after it's baked. Let it sit in the oven for twelve hours at least."

All night long, I would lie in my bed and smell the ham. The next day was Easter: Easter eggs and chocolate bunnies and all that. But the ham and only the ham was what really counted—not only for itself but because it always put my father in a great mood. We would play catch tomorrow; he would drink beer and tell stories. For once, the Bumpuses would be forgotten. Who the hell cares about a bunch of hillbillies, when there's baked him on the table? I lay in my bed, awake, the dark, indescribable aroma of ham coiling sinuously into my bedroom from the kitchen. In the next room, my father snored lustily, resting up for the great feast.

Immediately after breakfast the next morning, while my brother and I crawled around the house, looking for Easter eggs, my mother turned on the oven to heat the ham ever so slowly. This is important, she told us. The flame must be very low.

By 1:30 that afternoon, the tension had risen almost to the breaking point. The smell of ham saturated the drapes. And on my trip down to Pulaski's for the Sunday paper, I found that it could be smelled at least four blocks away. Finally, at about two o'clock, we all gathered around while my mother opened the blue pot—releasing a blast of fragrance so overwhelming that my knees wobbled—and surrounded the ham with sliced sweet potatoes to bake in the brown sugar and pineapple juice.

We usually had our Easter meal around three. Everything was timed carefully around the ham and the Parker House rolls. About 30 minutes before H hour, my mother took the ham out of the oven and laid it out on a big sheet of wax paper, right in the middle of the kitchen table, to let it cool a bit and set—the thick, sweet, brown molasses and sugar oozing down over the sides, the pineapple slices baked brown, the cloves like tiny black insects soaking in the hot ham gravy.

Easter that year was the way all Easters should be but rarely are. Spring had come early, for a change. There were years when winter's hard rock ice was still visible along the curbs, blackened and filthy, coated with steel-mill grime, until late in May. But this Easter was different; gentle breezes blew through the kitchen screen door. Already the stickers in our yard gave promise of a bumper crop. The air was balmy and heavy with spring passion about to burst.

The spring sunlight slanted in through the kitchen window and bathed the ham in a golden, suffused light, just like any good religious experience should be lit. The old man was in an exalted state of anticipation. Whenever he really got excited, he would crack his knuckles loudly. On this fateful day, he was popping them like a set of Brazilian castanets. He had on the new white shirt that he had gotten the week before at J. C. Penney.

While the ham sat basking in our gaze, my mother busily spread the lace tablecloth on the dining-room table and set out our best china, which was used only three or four times a year at the maximum. My father picked up his carving knife again, for one last stroke on the whetstone. He held the blade up to the light. Everything was ready. He went into the living room and sat down.

"Ah."

His eyes glowed with the primal lust of a cave man about to dig into the kill, which would last us at least four months. We would have ham sandwiches, ham salad, ham gravy, ham hash—and, finally, about ten gallons of pea soup made with the gigantic ham bone.

When it happened, he was sitting knee-deep in the *Chicago Tribune* sports section. I had been called in to wash up. My mother was in the bedroom, removing the curlers from her hair. My Aunt Glenn and Uncle Tom were on their way over to have Easter dinner with us. Uncle Tom always gave me a dollar. It was going to be a day to remember. Little did I suspect why.

I had just left the bathroom and my kid brother had just gone in for his fumigation, when suddenly and without warning:

BLAM!

The kitchen door flew open. It had been left ajar just a crack to let the air come in to cool the ham.

I rushed to the kitchen just in time to see 4293 blue-ticked Bumpus hounds roar through the screen door in a great, roiling mob. The leader of the pack—the one that almost got the old man every day—leaped high onto the table and grabbed the butt end of the ham in his enormous slavering jaws.

The rest of the hounds—squealing, yapping, panting, rolling over one another in a frenzy of madness—pounded out the kitchen door after Big Red, trailing brown sugar and pineapple slices behind him. They were in and out in less than five seconds. The screen door hung on one hinge, its screen ripped and torn and dripping with gravy. Out they went. Pow, just like that.

"HOLY CHRIST!" The old man leaped out of his chair. "THE HAM! THE HAM! THOSE GODDAMN DOGS! THE HAM!!"

He fell heavily over the footrest as he struggled to get into the kitchen, his voice a high-pitched scream of disbelief and rage. My mother just stood in the dining room, her face blank and staring, two aluminum hair curlers still in place. I ran through the kitchen, following my old man out to the back porch.

The snarling mob had rolled across the back yard and was now battling it out next to the garage, yipping and squealing with excitement. Occasionally, one of them would be hurled out of the pack, flipping over backward in the air, to land heavily amid the barrel staves and sardine cans. Instantly, he would be back in the fray, biting and tearing at whatever moved.

The ham didn't last eight seconds. Old Grandpa Bumpus and a dozen other Bumpuses stuck their heads out of various windows, to see what all the yowling was about. Without pausing to aim, he reared back and spit a great big gob of tobacco juice—a new long-distance record— right into the middle of the pack. It was a direct hit on our ham—or what was left of it.

He whooped wildly, wattles reddening with joy, spraying tobacco juice in all directions, while Cletus, his dim-witted grandson, yelled from the basement door:

"GAHDAMN, GRAN'PAW, LOOKA THEM HOUN'S GO! LOOKA THEM OL' BOYS GO! HOT DAMN!!"

Delbert, meanwhile, circled around the roaring inferno, urging them on, kicking dogs that had given up back into the fray. Suddenly, he looked up at where I was hiding, a sadistic grin on his face, his hair hanging low. Our eyes met significantly for a fleeting instant and then he went back to kicking. A paralyzing fear gripped me. I remembered! That time I threw him out at first! Was this what he meant? Was *I* responsible for this tragedy? Oh, God, no! I slunk back into the shadows.

Bumpus women, their lank hair streaming down over their red necks, cackled fiendishly. Emil Bumpus, who had been asleep under the front porch, came reeling out, trailing his jug of white lightning. He took one look

43

and practically passed out, wheezing and harrumphing and gurgling with hilarity.

My old man just stood stock-still on the back porch for a long moment, and then he blew his stack. I had never seen him do anything before that came near what he did now. We kept bottles on the back porch to be returned to the grocery store. He reached down and grabbed a milk bottle. His face white with rage, he wound up mightily and, with a sweeping, sidearm motion, hurled the bottle against the side of the Bumpus house with a deafening crash.

Grandpa Bumpus stopped in mid-spit, a big juicy gob hanging down over his chin. Emil dropped his jug to the ground, eyes lighting up with joy. This was back home for Emil. He was in his element. Turning around as if to run for his shotgun, he paused when he saw the old man standing there unmoving—radiating the clearest and most beautiful rage I'd ever seen in my life.

I cowered next to the railing on the back porch. Even the dogs felt his hatred. One by one, they fell silent. The bare, shiny bone of the ham lay in the sun. Big Red licked his chops.

After a long, pregnant moment, the old man turned, walked back into the kitchen and slammed the door. He stood for a minute by the kitchen table, looking down at the big sheet of wax paper dripping warm ham gravy. The heavenly aroma still hung heavy in the house. The old man just stood there—and came as close to crying as I'd ever seen him come.

Finally, he spoke, in a low, rasping voice: "All right!

OK! Get your coats. We're going to the Chinese joint. We're going to have chop suey."

Ordinarily, this would have been a gala of the highest order, going to the chop-suey joint. Today, it had all the gaiety of a funeral procession. The meal was eaten completely in silence.

That was the beginning of the bitter Shepherd-Bumpus feud. Relentlessly, the old man beleaguered the Bumpuses at every moment. He had tap-dancing cleats put on his shoes, which proved to be quite a nasty surprise to Big Red the first day he tried his usual ankle grab and caught a cleat behind his left ear. The old man took up tobacco chewing and arched long, undulating gobs onto the Bumpuses front porch when the wind was right. Every time the Bumpuses cranked up for a Gene Autry record festival, the old man countered with *In a Persian Market* played at full blast on our Sears, Roebuck Silvertone phonograph.

He took to throwing beer bottles out of the kitchen window and hurling coffee grounds onto the roof of the Bumpus truck when it bellowed by, taking the Bumpuses down to pick up their weekly relief check. He put bottle caps and tacks in the driveway and laughed uproariously every time one of the Bumpus women fell out the back door. He planted stickers in the cave that the Bumpus hounds lived in under the garage and took to jumping up and down on the garage floor late at night, when the hounds were asleep. Once he even bayed at the moon louder than all the hounds put together. I still remember the startled look on Big Red's face when the old man let out a long, drawn-out, quavering howl that he had learned from 20 years of watching Tarzan pictures.

The only trouble was that nothing he did—but *nothing*—made the slightest dent on the Bumpus way of life. They didn't even seem to know he was doing anything. The bottle caps and tacks he threw in the driveway never even scratched their feet, horny-hard after generations of shoelessness. The only thing that came of it was that we got two flats in one day on the Olds. His pitiful tobacco juice added as much to the sea that the Bumpuses themselves produced as a raindrop in the ocean. Nothing he could do had any effect. One night, he told my mother he had concluded that the Bumpuses *planned* the ham raid, the dogs carrying out their orders like guerrilla fighters. He hinted that he had something up his sleeve that he was working out in the basement that would really settle the score once and for all. He was biding his time.

The Bumpuses, meanwhile, went on with life as usual. There wasn't much they could do to us that they hadn't already done without intending to. Grandpa Bumpus jacked up his output of tobacco juice a little, but the rest of them just went about their business—collecting junk and piling it in the yard, tossing potato peels out the window, brewing moonshine, hollering, hitting each other and scratching themselves.

Then one night, without warning, everything changed forever. I awoke suddenly about three A.M. with a strange feeling that something was wrong. It was. For a couple of minutes, I couldn't focus my mind; then, gradually, it became clear to me that something was up. I heard my father in the next room. He had apparently awakened about the time I had.

He said hoarsely to my mother, "Hey, wake up!"

Then a long period of silence, while he listened in the darkness. We were always having alarums and excursions, but this was really different.

The bedsprings squeaked and the old man's feet pattered across the bedroom floor; the usual thump and groan of excruciating pain as he stubbed the foot of the dresser. A rustling silence as he peered through the curtains into the blackness of the night.

"Shhhhh!"

Another pause. I waited, scared and anxious in my bed, my kid brother mewing softly across the room.

"I'll be damned!" the old man said aloud in wonder. "You'll never believe it."

"Believe what?" whispered my mother, who had gotten up and joined him.

"Just take a look out there," he said with disbelief. "They moved out! They're gone!"

I realized why I had awakened. For the first time in many months, the sound of Gene Autry records had ceased; the continuous whine and yelp of the Bumpus hounds had been silenced. Everything was—*quiet*.

My father sniffed noisily.

"The smell is gone. Even the smell is gone!"

It was true. The air in my bedroom was clear of cabbage, dog urine and corn whiskey for the first time in six months.

47

The next morning, the truth was there for all to see. The Bumpuses had packed up and moved on, leaving behind a sagging shambles of a house, the back yard rutted and ground to gray dust by the endless clawings and scratchings of the Bumpus dogs and the Bumpus chickens, with great, tangled rat's nests of rusting junk and weather-beaten barrels, and smelly gallon jugs and empty bean cans that told everything there was to know about the way the Bumpuses lived out their days. They just ran up a big enough rent bill and then moved out in the middle of the night. We never heard another word about them.

At first, my father seemed to be glad. Then, about a month later, a nice old couple moved in next door and soon had the house and yard looking like an illustration for an insurance company that sold retirement plans to nice old couples. They went to bed every night at 8:30 and had a canary as a pet.

One night at supper, after a couple of beers, the old man finally said it:

"You know, they cleaned out just when I was going to hand 'em my crusher. I'll bet they did it on purpose." He got kind of moody for a while after that. We never found out what he had planned.

COUNTY FAIR!

I struggled frantically to my feet, spilling Diet Pepsi over the front of my brocade smoking jacket as I flailed about. There wasn't a second to lose. Lurching forward, grasping for the knob, I fell heavily over the coffee table. On hands and knees, I scrambled forward, hoping to kill the TV set before it was too late. With a groan, I realized that once again, I had lost. The late-late-movie curse had struck again. I sat back to accept my fate.

I was trapped by one of the worst ever, a bucolic horror that I had taken care to avoid, when it was first released, by walking on the opposite side of the street from any moviehouse that played it. In a sky-blue suit and straw skimmer, Dick Haymes stood framed against the movie version of the Indiana countryside, dotted with quaint corn shocks and tinted with lurid oranges and greens, at the entrance to an archetypal Hollywood state fair. A few minutes later, there was the mandatory Old Gramps perched atop a sulky in the big trotting race, and The

Girl, rosy-cheeked and beribboned, who watched walleyed while Dick soulfully serenaded the Indiana moon.

Vainly I watched for a single glimpse of the Indiana fairs I had known—the Indiana fairs nobody makes movies about—but it never came. As Haymes warbled on, his eyes twinkling with boyish sincerity, my own grainy movie of a real Indiana fair began to unwind in memory.

As the scene opens, Schwartz, Flick, Junior Kissel and I are standing around back of the Sherwin-Williams paint sign in a misty drizzle. We are discussing current events, as was our wont. Schwartz had found half a can of Copenhagen snuff in the weeds, which we had all tried. After sneezing and gagging violently for 15 minutes, we took up our conversation where it had been interrupted by Schwartz' discovery. The dialog begins:

"My old man says if you ride on the whip too often, it scrambles your brains and you can't think good anymore," said Flick, whose nose was running copiously as a result of the snuff. "And it stunts your growth."

"That must have been what happened to *you*, Kissel," said Schwartz, spitting out a shred of snuff between his teeth. "That's why you're such a shrimp. You musta rode that thing fifty times last year."

Kissel, a full half head shorter than any of us, said nothing at this, realizing that it was the truth.

"Well, I don't care what your old man says, Flick," I said. "I'm gonna ride on the whip—and the caterpillar, too. There are so many things that stunt your growth and make you crazy, you might as well do it that way as any other." My wisdom, as usual was profound.

The rain drizzled down steadily, carrying with it its full load of blast-furnace dust and other by-products of the steel mills and oil refineries that ringed the town like iron dinosaurs. We wandered down the alley, kicking Carnation milk cans into imaginary goals as our conversation dragged on.

"One thing I'm gonna get is one of them red taffy apples!" Kissel shouted as he rooted around in somebody's garbage, looking for another can to kick.

"My old man says they stunt your growth, too. That red stuff clamps your teeth together so you can't grow good," said Schwartz as he pretended to sink an imaginary basket against a sagging backboard hanging on one of the garages that lined the alley.

"Yeah, well, your old man should know. He's about three feet tall," Kissel lashed back, cackling fiendishly, as Schwartz threw a half-eaten potato in his direction.

The next scene is a couple of hours later. My old man, my mother, my kid brother, Randy, and I are sitting around the kitchen table eating meat loaf, mashed potatoes and red cabbage. The old man takes a swallow of his beer and says, "It doesn't make any difference to me if you want to look at the quilts and raspberry preserves, as long as we get to see the first heat."

"Then Randy and I'll meet you two after the races," said my mother as she got up to put the coffee on. My kid brother immediately began to whimper piteously.

"You can have a taffy apple," she said to him from the stove. He stopped sobbing.

"One of those red ones?" he sniffed.

53

"Any color you want."

That was enough for him.

"Well, kid. . . ." The old man batted my arm.

"We'll watch Iron Man Gabruzzi give 'em hell to-morrow." As far as he was concerned, county fairs *were* dirt-track races. All that farm stuff was for the birds.

I went to bed happy. My brother and I whispered back and forth about the great stuff that would happen the next day. He was a Ferris-wheel nut who would have been glad to spend his whole life going around and around on a big wheel that creaked. Come to think of it, that's as good a way to spend it as any.

"I'll get that son of a bitch yet!" my old man's voice hissed suddenly and venomously through the darkened house.

Gawhang! Whap! Gawhang! Whap! Gawhang! Whap-whap!

My parents' bed squeaked dangerously as he leaped up and down on it, batting away at his old enemy. Every night in the late summer and early autumn, mosquito squadrons flew miles from the swamp to seek him out. The minute the lights were off, they dove to the attack. Flying in tight formations, they strafed again and again. The old man loved every minute of it. Fighting mosquitoes was his favorite sport. He slept with his personal fly swatter always at his side; he also had a loaded flit-gun, but he preferred the swatter. It was more sporting, somehow.

Whap! Whap! Bang! Something crashed in the darkness.

54

"Got the bastard!" He laughed exultantly. The battle was over—until the next hot puff of air brought in reinforcements. Our screens served only to keep the more enormous mosquitoes out of the house, allowing the smaller, lither, angrier types free access. During the second lull between attacks, I drifted off to sleep.

ZZZZZZRRRRIIIIINNNNGGGGGG!

The alarm clock blasted me hysterically into consciousness. Gray Saturday-morning light filled the house. The old man cursed and muttered sleepily as my mother padded out into the kitchen in her bathrobe and curlers to get the scrambled eggs started.

An hour later, we were in the Pontiac on the way to the county fair. The ill-fated Pontiac was an inexplicable interruption of the old man's lifelong devotion to the Oldsmobile. He was an Oldsmobile man the way others were Baptists, Methodists, Catholics or Holy Rollers. He later recanted after this episode of backsliding and returned to the fold with the purchase of a 1942 Oldsmobile station wagon that appealed far more deeply to his flamboyantly masochistic nature. A block or so ahead of us, Ludlow Kissel's battered Nash, loaded with kids and Mrs. Kissel (who weighed 360 pounds and read *True Romance*), struggled toward the fairgrounds. His Nash laid down a steady cloud of blue-white exhaust that hung over Cleveland Street like a destroyer's smoke screen. Junior Kissel peered out of the grimy back window, grinning wildly.

"Old Lud is sober. That makes the second time this summer," said my father as he struggled with the Pontiac, which had started shimmying again. It had bad king-pins.

Ten minutes later, we were out on Route 41, bumper to bumper in the great tangle of cars all headed for the fair. The sun rose higher over the distant steel mills. Steadily, the temperature and humidity rose until the sky was one vast copper sheet. We inched along like an endless procession of ants across a sizzling grill.

In the front seat, my mother fanned herself with a paper fan marked ORVILLE KLEEBER COAL AND ICE—REASONABLE. The flat fan was cut in the shape of a lump of coal. It had a wooden handle. She always kept it in the car for days like this.

"WHAT THE HELL YOU DOING, JERK?" barked the old man, head stuck aggressively out the window, at the driver ahead of us. His neck was red from sweat; his pongee shirt clung limply to his wiry frame; and his drugstore sunglasses dripped sweat as he glared through the heat waves and exhaust fumes at the idiot ahead.

"SLEEPING JESUS, YOU GONNA PARK THAT WRECK OR DRIVE IT?"

"Little pitchers have big ears," my mother intoned automatically, gazing placidly out her window at a Burma-Shave sign. The old man's latest curse—one of an endless lexicon—was a new one to me. I filed it away for future use. It might come in handy during a ball game or an argument with Schwartz.

It was now well past noon, but we were getting close. Far ahead, we could see the enormous, billowing cloud of dust that rose from the fairgrounds. Excitement mounted in the Pontiac as we shimmied closer and closer to the scene of action. Suddenly, with a great hissing, scalding roar, the radiator of the car ahead boiled over. Drops of red, rusty sludge streaked down over our windshield and spattered on the hood.

"OH, NO! FER CHRISSAKE, NO!"

The old man pounded on the steering wheel in rage as the lumbering Buick wheezed to a halt. The driver, a beet-faced man wearing a stiff blue-serge suit and a Panama hat, stumbled out of the car and raised the hood. A white cloud of steam enveloped him from head to toe.

"Goddamn it! There goes the first heat. Son of a bitch! Gimme a bottle of pop."

Silently, my mother opened a bottle of Nehi orange and handed it to him. She passed one back to me and gave my kid brother another. I felt the stinging carbonation sizzle through my nostrils as I guzzled the lukewarm contents.

Ahead, the other occupants of the Buick had gathered around the car and were fanning the hood with somebody's white shirt. The steam rose higher into the heavens. The car behind us began honking; then others joined in. This only bugged the old man even more. Out the window went his head.

"SHUT UP, YOU JERKS!" he yelled at the line of cars. They honked even louder.

The Buick was not the only car giving off steam. Several others had begun to percolate in the heat around us. The crowd ahead had begun to push the Buick off

57

the road, like some great wounded whale. There is nothing deader than a dead Buick.

Finally, we were able to squeeze past the stragglers and once again move on toward the fairgrounds. A biplane towing a red-and-white streamer droned over the line of traffic: FISH DINNER ALL YOU CAN EAT $1.69 JOE'S DINER RTE. 6.

We were so close now that the sounds of the fair began to drift in over the roar of motors: calliopes bleating, whistles, merry-go-round music, bells ringing, barkers. Two cops in short-sleeved blue shirts waved the cars in through the main gate and past a cornfield to the jam-packed, rutted parking lot just inside the grounds. Flushed and sweaty, these two men faced the pressing horde of hissing, steaming, dusty rattletraps with the look of men who are struggling with a totally uncontrollable force that threatens to engulf them at any moment.

One blew his whistle in short, sharp blasts that matched every breath he took. With his left hand, he seemed to gather the cars in a steady hooking motion that pushed them on past his right hand, which moved like a piston in the air, shoving the heaps through the narrow gate. The other cop, taller and sadder, stood astride the center line of the asphalt road and glared slowly and deliberately at each car as it rolled past him.

The old man, by now totally hot under the collar, muttered barely audible obscenities as we drew abreast of the first cop.

"What was that, buddy?" The cop's voice was level

and menacing, cutting through the racket of the Pontiac's piston slap like an ice cube going down your back on a hot day. Instantly, an electric feeling of imminent danger whipped through the car. Even my brother stopped whining.

"Uh . . . pardon me, officer?" The old man had turned on his innocent voice, which always sounded a little like he was slightly hard of hearing. He stuck his head out the window with exaggerated politeness.

"Did I hear you call me a son of a bitch, buddy?" The tall cop was approaching the side of the car, his eyes piercing the old man like a pair of hot ice picks.

"Uh . . . what was that, officer? Sir?"

"You heard me." A hamlike hand rested authoritatively on the door handle; a heavy foot clunked solidly on the running board. The line came to a halt behind us.

"I'm sorry, officer. What was it you said, sir?"

"Did you call me a son of a bitch?"

"Oh, heavens no! Mercy me! Why, good gracious, you must have heard me sneeze. I am troubled with hay fever." The old man sounded amazingly like an Episcopalian minister.

He sneezed loudly into his sleeve as a demonstration. I had seen the old man get out of many a tight squeak before, but this performance topped them all. I drank it in, knowing what I was seeing a master at work. My mother said nothing through it all, just looked nervously pathetic, which seemed to help the old man's act.

"OK, buster. Just watch yer lip, y'hear?"

"Why, bless my buttons, officer, I certainly will. Yes,

59

indeed! That is fine advice. Heavens to Betsy, I certainly will."

With a flick of his wrist, the cop waved us on. The emergency was over. The old man let the clutch out so suddenly that the car jerked heavily twice before lurching forward.

An elderly, toilworn Chevy pickup truck carrying a farmer, his wife, seven kids and a Bluetick hound had stalled just ahead of us. The old man, out of pure reflex, muttered: "Son of a bitch!" Realizing he wasn't yet out of earshot, he covered it with a loud, juicy sneeze.

It grew hotter and hotter in our little oven as we waited for the farmer to get the Chevy moving again. At last we got inside the chicken-wire fence and past the little box office where they took the old man's two bucks, the price for an afternoon of untrammeled bliss.

My father shoved his hat onto the back of his head while he fished frantically inside his coat pocket for his pack of Luckies, a sure sign that he was reaching the boiling point.

"Holy Christ, wouldja look at that!"

Ahead of us, waves of heat rose from a long line of motionless cars that stretched toward the distant parking lot. They had the look of cars that hadn't moved for maybe two hours. People sat on running boards; fat ladies fanned themselves in the shade; kids ran in and out past spare tires and around radiators; and guys with pushcarts selling hot dogs and Fudgsicles moved up and down the line, doing a roaring business.

Two cars ahead of us, a lady was unpacking a lunch

basket and spreading bowls of potato salad and jars of pickles on a blanket that she'd laid by the cornfield. A tall man in shirt sleeves and a straw hat chomped contentedly on a sandwich.

"Would you kids like a peanut-butter sandwich?" My mother began rummaging in the paper bag that held our lunch.

To the left of the line of cars was a high board fence plastered with red-and-yellow posters. From behind it, suddenly, surged a tidal wave of deep-throated roaring, followed by clouds of dust and the smell of burning rubber and castor oil. My father hunched over the wheel in excitement. This was his home ground, and he could hardly wait to get in on the action.

SSSSSKKKKKRRRRREEEEEE . . . KABOOM!

For an instant, something blotted out the sun. One of the picnicking ladies stood frozen, holding a bowl of cole slaw. The sandwich eater stared heavenward, his mouth poised open in mid-chomp. The old man, who had just tilted a can of beer toward the sky, stopped short, foam dribbling down his shirt front, eyes bugging out in amazement and delight.

The top of the board fence disintegrated with a stupendous crash and there, gracefully airborne high above the line of jalopies, a bright-blue racing car with a big number 12 on its side arched overhead, trailing smoke. The white-helmeted driver, his green goggles glinting in the sun, looked perfectly calm. It was all in a day's work. One wheel flew crazily ahead of him on a solo flight.

"JESUS CHRIST! THERE GOES IRON MAN!" the old man yelled as his favorite member of the racing fraternity disappeared in a cloud of dust and oil spray into the cornfield off to our right.

A great cheer came from behind the shattered fence as the crowd roared its approval of Iron Man's spectacular crackup. That's what they came to see, and Iron Man gave it to them.

As the line of cars inched toward the parking lot, we could see a tow truck dragging Iron Man's lethal Kurtis-Offy Special back into the fray. Iron Man himself, wearing blue coveralls, sat nonchalantly in the cockpit, waving to the crowd. Dirt-track racers are not ordinary mortals.

"GO GET 'EM THE NEXT HEAT, IRON MAN!" bellowed the old man.

"Boy, ain't he a pisser?" This was my father's highest compliment.

"Little pitchers have big ears," my mother said again.

"Well, he is." My father knew a pisser when he saw one.

At last we were parked, between an ancient Willys-Knight and a Cord owned by a prominent local Mafia finger man who ran a mortuary on the side as a kind of tie-in.

"We'll meet you by the band shell," said the old man. He was in a hurry to get inside the arena.

"Now, you be careful," my mother told me, as she did so often. It was a phrase that ran like a litany through her life. She dragged my kid brother off in the direction of the quilt tent. My old man and I headed for the track.

Five minutes later, we were in the stands, immersed in the roaring mob that had come from miles around to cheer the mayhem and carnage on the dirt oval below. I sat hunched next to a gaunt, stringy, hawk-faced farmer who wore a broad-brimmed straw hat low over his eyes. His Adam's apple, as big as a turkey egg, bobbed up and down in excitement as he watched the racers. He rolled Bull Durham cigarettes automatically with his left hand as his elbow dug into my ribs. His wife, a large, pink, rubbery woman, breast-fed a baby as the races roared on.

Dirt-track racing is as much a part of an Indiana county fair as applesauce, pumpkins and pig judging. Down below us, Iron Man Gabruzzi—back in action, his famous blue Kurtis-Offy a little dented from the previous heat—battled it out with his archrival, Duke Grunion, who drove a battle-scarred yellow blown Ford special, and a field of lesser competitors. Round and round they careened, throwing up sheets of yellow dust laced with the blue smoke of burning oil and scorching tires. From time to time, a car would leave the pack, slewing sideways, and bounce into the rail, trailing even more smoke than usual. The mob leaped to its feet, bellowing bloodthirstily, and then squatted again, waiting for the next near catastrophe. Over it all, the tinny voice of the P.A. announcer kept up a running commentary of feeble jokes and trivial observations. Hot-dog vendors squeezed up and down the rows, passing out the franks as fast as they could slap them between buns.

The old man was in seventh heaven, cheering wildly every time Iron Man moved ahead of Duke Grunion on the far turn to come whistling down the straight, his battered old Offy screaming. The 100-Mile Dirt Track Championship Race is as fiercely fought as any Grand Prix, and in some ways is far more exciting.

The last lap saw Iron Man and Duke battling it out on the homestretch, both sliding high on the banked oval, flat out, with Iron Man zooming across the finish line a half car ahead of Duke. The checkered flag rose and fell; the crowd cheered insanely as Iron Man, waving jauntily from his cockpit, took his victory lap, saluting the crowd. He had won 150 bucks for an afternoon's work in the hot sun.

We filed out of the stands and headed straight for the bandstand, which was at the center of the fairgrounds. Inside my head, the roaring of the race cars continued, blotting out the sound of the crowd. I would be hearing them in my sleep for at least a week. My nose burned from the gasoline and alcohol fumes.

"I gotta have a beer." Racing always made my father very thirsty.

We stopped at a stand while he guzzled a bottle of Blatz and listened to the other dirt-track fanatics yelling about how great the race had been. I drank a Nehi orange, my fifth of the day. Already my stomach was starting to ferment.

My mother and kid brother were waiting at the bandstand when we finally showed up.

"I gotta go to the toilet!" whined Randy. My brother always had to go to the toilet, especially when there was no toilet around. On either side of us, open sheds filled with rows of soft-eyed cows and jostling farmers stretched into the distance.

"Go behind that truck. I'll stand guard." The old man had handled this situation many times. My brother scooted behind the truck and emerged a couple of minutes later, sheepishly.

"I wanna see the pigs!" he said.

"So do I," I seconded him. I always liked to look at pigs, and still do, for that matter. There is something very satisfying about the way a pig looks. They were housed in a tent next to the cows, which were kind of dull. Row on row, the porkers lounged casually, completely at ease with the world. I have never understood why the pig is an animal whose name is used in derision. He is intelligent and kindly, often benevolent, in fact; in short, totally with it.

In the center of the tent, under floodlights, an enormous white hog with black spots graciously accepted the applause of his admirers. GRAND CHAMPION, the sign read, and above his bed of straw hung a large, trailing blue ribbon attached to a blue-and-gold rosette. Below it was a plaque: BIG HORACE. He had eaten half the ribbon. His tiny red eyes peered out at us jocularly. He was a champion and he knew it. Lesser pigs grunted and rooted in pens all around, but Big Horace was the star. We stood silently before this regal beast for several minutes.

"I bet that baby'd make great bacon," my father finally said in a quiet voice. A look of reproach flickered over Horace's mighty face as he glanced in our direction.

We moved on with the crowd into the prize-goat tent. Photographers were popping flashbulbs around a luxuriant, silken-haired Angora with a set of wicked-looking horns. Beside him stood a short, fat 4-H girl wearing a green beret and holding up another blue ribbon. The goat tent was among the gamier exhibits, but exciting. Goats are unpredictable, and from time to time one would try to climb out and go after some kid's taffy apple. Goats always have fancy names. This one was Prince Bernadotte Charlemagne d'Alexandre of Honeyvale Farms. The 4-H girl stared solemnly at the cameras while the bulbs popped on. The goat just chewed and looked bored.

We wandered along with the dusty crowds, looking at turkeys, ducks, rabbits, sheep, guinea pigs and chickens. It was in the chicken tent that an enigmatic event took place. In one corner, a heavy-set lady wearing a green shawl sat on a camp chair next to a large, fancy cage containing a single white, efficient-looking chicken. Atop the cage was a sign: ESMERALDA KNOWS.

"Would you folks care to have Esmeralda tell your fortune?"

"Yeah! Yeah! I want my fortune told! Waaaaaa!" My kid brother went into high gear. The chicken hopped around in the cage and clucked knowingly.

"How much is it?" asked my mother warily.

"Only a dime. Just ten cents to learn the little boy's fortune."

The chicken pecked at the cage, waiting to go to work. My mother reached into her carryall with the picture of Carmen Miranda on it, fished out a dime and handed it to my brother, who grabbed it eagerly.

"Put the dime into the slot, little boy, and watch the chicken tell your fortune."

My brother walked up to the cage, his face inches away from the chicken's beak. The two stared at each other for a long moment.

A small crowd was beginning to gather. He dropped the dime into the slot on the side of the cage. At that, a ladder dropped from the roof inside the cage. The chicken scurried up rung by rung, clucking madly. At the top of the ladder was a box containing folded slips of paper. The chicken picked one out with its beak, hopped back down the ladder, eyes rolling wildly, and dropped the slip of paper into a chute, releasing a half-dozen grains of corn.

Cluck-cluck-cluck waaaaaak! It gulped them down hungrily.

"There. Esmeralda has told your fortune," the lady said to my brother. I noticed that she had a mustache.

The slip of paper had dropped into a small tray outside the cage. My brother grabbed it and read the message aloud:

"'You are unwise in your in-vest-ments. Care in the future will ensure your success.'"

My mother laughed. "Esmeralda was right. You spent your entire allowance last week on Fudgsicles. See?"

My brother glared angrily at Esmeralda. After that, I had no desire to hear any smart talk from Esmeralda about *my* life.

"OK, you've had your fun. Now there's something *I* gotta see," said my father. "Wait'll you see this. I read about it in the paper."

"What now?" asked my mother as we started after him. She knew better than to fight the inevitable.

"Hairy Gertz saw it yesterday and he said you wouldn't believe it."

"Well," said my mother, "if Hairy Gertz said that, it certainly *must* be something!"

"What do you mean by that?" my father shot back. Hairy Gertz was one of the old man's bowling buddies, famed throughout the county for his collection of incredibly gross jokes. My mother didn't answer.

"Anyway, I want to see it." He went over to a dozing cop and asked him directions.

My father came back, beaming. "OK, here we go. Follow me." We did, and a couple of minutes later were waiting in line in front of another tent.

"Wait'll you see this. You won't believe it!" My father rubbed his hands together in anticipation. The crowd snaked into the tent in a long line. Finally, we were inside.

Big floodlights hung from the tent poles. In the middle of the sawdust floor, there was a roped-off square.

"What is it?" my mother asked as soon as she got a look at what was on the platform.

"What do you mean, 'What is it?' Can't you read the sign, stupid?"

A sign hung over the astounding object that had moved even Hairy Gertz to speechless wonder. The crowd stood in reverent silence. Occasionally, someone snapped a picture with a Brownie, hoping that there was enough light to enable him to preserve this magnificent exhibit forever in his book of memories. The sign, hand lettered in gilt on fake parchment, was draped with an American flag. It read:

THIS GIANT 47-POUND, 10-OUNCE INDIANA PUMPKIN, BEARING A STRIKING LIKENESS TO OUR BELOVED PRESIDENT FRANKLIN DELANO ROOSEVELT, WAS GROWN BY HOMER L. SEASTRUNK OF R.F.D. 2, NEW JERUSALEM, INDIANA. MR. SEASTRUNK PLANS TO PRESENT THE PUMPKIN TO PRESIDENT ROOSEVELT.

"How d'y like that?" my father said softly as the four of us stood before the great pumpkin.

Someone behind me muttered angrily, "That nut is ruinin' the country. I know what *I'd* do with that pumpkin!"

"Shhhhh!" several indignant patriots hissed back.

There was no doubt that it was one of the high points of the fair. Another sign said that Mr. Seastrunk himself would make a personal appearance at three P.M. to give a short talk on how he figured God had created that pumpkin in honor of the President. He would also give free autographs.

"I told you this was worth seeing," said my father as he wound one of the knobs on his trusty camera. "Now, how wouldja like to go next door and see the world's biggest cheese?"

The same cheese, I have no doubt, has been on exhibit at every fair I ever attended. It wasn't much to look at; when you've seen one, you've seen them all, even if it weighs two tons. A sign read: THE MILK FROM 2000 COWS FOR ONE FULL YEAR WAS REQUIRED TO MAKE THIS CHEESE. IT WOULD MAKE OVER 422,000 CHEESE SANDWICHES.

This kind of stuff really got to the old man. He snapped more pictures and walked all the way around the cheese, examining it from every angle. All it did was make my kid brother hungry again.

It was late in the afternoon now and the crowd was really warmed up, moving in straggly columns around huge, black-wheeled tractors, cultivators, threshing machines and other agricultural exotica. Salesmen, the collars of their shirts opened, ties hanging limply, shouted over bullhorns as we wandered dazedly amid the shuffling throng, kicking up bread crusts and paper cups as we eddied on.

"I'm hungry," my brother droned, his voice barely audible above the uproar.

"You've just gone. You'll have to wait," said my mother, pushing the damp hair back off her forehead.

"I don't have to go! I'm *hungry!*" Randy never gave up.

"You heard what your mother said." My father got into the act.

"I said I'm HUNGRY!"

"You're *what?* You've had three taffy apples, four hot dogs and two root beers. That's enough for a while."

"I wanna PICKLE!"

As it happened, we were passing a stand where a guy in a red vest and a white chef's hat was selling giant dark-green pickles from barrels. People eat strange stuff at county fairs.

"I want one, too!" I said.

We all bought pickles in wax paper and rejoined the moiling mob. My pickle must have weighed two pounds. Every time I bit into it, it squirted down the front of my shirt.

It was getting dark now and 50 times more exciting as the bright lights began to flash on. I washed down the tart, puckery taste of the pickle with some cold buttermilk from a paper cup with a picture on it of a red cow wearing a green hat. My knees had begun to ache from the endless trudging through sawdust and over piles of debris. On either side of us, a sparkling ribbon of spinning yellow wheels, blue-white neon lights and hot orange flames under cooking grills stretched to the horizon. Guys with leather jackets and great mops of carefully combed, greasy hair ranged through the crowds, looking for fights and girls.

71

On a high platform, two blondes wearing silver helmets sat on the saddles of enormous bright-red Harley-Davidsons. They gunned the motors deafeningly sending thin blue exhaust smoke into the crowd that stood around the platform with glazed eyes and gaping mouths.

"Dee-fying death every second, straight from the world championships in Paris, France, Melba and Bonnie stare into the very jaws of eternity!" yelled the barker.

BBBBRRRROOOOOOOMMMMMMMM!BAAAARRR-OOOOOOOMMMM! Another cloud of acrid smoke drifted out over the mob.

The barker spieled on: "There is time for just one more big show tonight, just one more! Never in your life have you seen anything to equal THE DEVIL RIDE!"

BAAARRROOOOOOM! BBBBBRRRRRRROOOOOO-OMMMMM!

"Bee-ginning in just one minute. In just sixty seconds! Beautiful Melba and lovely Bonnie stare into the jaws of death!"

The two blondes, thin-faced and pallid, peered out from under their spectacular helmets, chewing gum steadily as they gunned their Harleys.

"I gotta see that!" This act was *designed* for my old man. Anything that had to do with roaring motors and crash helmets hit him in the vitals. Add the fact that these were skinny blonde women, another weakness, and you had bigtime showbiz, as far as he was concerned.

With a couple of final, provocative roars, the two raced down the ramp and disappeared through a doorway outlined in yellow with a string of colored light bulbs festooning a blood-red Devil's face with green eyes.

We followed close behind my father as he elbowed his way through the sweaty throng of daredevil fans to the head of the line inside the tent. We found ourselves standing at the rim of a circular pit ten or fifteen feet deep. The noise was deafening; the wooden floor vibrated and creaked under our feet. The air was thick with burning gasoline. Down in the pit, the two motorcycles boomed round and round, chasing each other madly in faster and faster circles, rising up the curved walls until they were riding almost horizontally under the chicken wire that separated the Harleys from us.

A white-faced, blue-veined minister, his high collar spotted with catsup, stood next to us in tense excitement. Kids ran wildly in and out of the crowd, throwing peanut shells at the riders as they screamed round and round in their tight spiral. The old man peered down into the maelstrom, pounding the rail in excitement as the motorcycles accelerated faster and faster.

"DEFYING GRAVITY ON THEIR SPECIALLY BUILT HARLEY-DAVIDSONS, MELBA AND BONNIE WILL NOW PERFORM A DEATH-DEFYING FEAT NEVER BEFORE SEEN IN THE UNITED STATES!" shouted the voice on the P.A. system over the racket. Down in the gloom of the hell pit, the exhausts trailed smoke as the motorcycles rode abreast.

"MELBA AND BONNIE WILL CHANGE MOTOR-CYCLES AT TOP SPEED!"

The crowd hunched forward with expectancy. Even the kids were quiet. The thunder of the motorcycles had reached the point where no more sound could be endured. The whole structure—the floor, the guy wires, the back teeth, everything—vibrated to the scream of the Harleys. Down in the pit, there was a quick shuffling of bodies and it was done.

"Fer Chrissake, how d'y like that! I wouldna' believed it!" said the oldman to no one in particular. The minister, his black hat hanging at a rakish angle, applauded frantically.

Once again we were out on the midway, 50 cents poorer but infinitely richer in worldly experience.

My mother, who was eating a piece of watermelon, said plaintively, "I haven't seen the quilts yet."

"I wanna go on the Ferris wheel," whined my brother for the 298th time.

"I thought you were gonna see 'em when we went to the races," said the old man, ignoring him for the 298th time.

"We went to the cookie tasting instead."

"The what?"

"The cookie tasting. Over by where they were having the artistic flower arranging."

The old man said nothing and headed for a three-story-high orange face that laughed madly under a sign that read FUN HOUSE. He hoped that by not answering, she would forget the quilts.

"Mrs. Wimple has a quilt in this year," she persisted. "Bernice Wimple, from the club."

74

My mother belonged to a dart-ball club that staged mysterious contests in the church basement every Thursday. Bernice Wimple played for the La Porte, Indiana, Bearcats, a legendary dart-ball team.

"It's a Thomas Jefferson quilt," she continued, wiping a watermelon seed off her chin with a paper napkin that said HAVE FUN in blue letters over an American flag.

My father, realizing he'd have to say *something*, stalled for time: "What the hell kinda quilt is that?"

"Well, it's a patriotic quilt that has the face of Thomas Jefferson on it, done in cross-stitch."

"Oh, well! *That* I gotta see!" said my father sarcastically.

After a ten-minute search, we finally found the tent with the quilt exhibit, under strings of yellow light bulbs. The quilts were tacked up all around, stretched tight, so that their designs could be admired respectfully from behind a rope by the motley throng of art lovers. Mrs. Wimple's entry was among them. We stood before the 6'×9' portrait.

"He looks a little cross-eyed to me," the old man observed accurately.

"I think it's very pretty. Mrs. Wimple worked seven years on it."

We peered at the third-place ribbon it sported and moved on to look at the others. The winning quilt had a stand to itself. It bore a spectacular portrait of Old Faithful on a yellow background framed by purple mountains and surrounded by a herd of animals: a moose, an elk, two bighorn sheep, a bunny with pink eyes and what appeared to be a hippopotamus. Above this scene in Old English-style red, white and blue letters was the following profundity:

The Beauty of Our Glorious Land Is Surpassed Only by God's Blessed Handiwork.
—Roswell T. Blount, L.L.D.

"Now, that's what I call pretty," said my father solemnly, reading the inscription. We all agreed that it was pretty.

Most of the quilts ran heavily to such patriotic themes, except for one that had a ribbon for UNUSUAL SUBJECT—HONORABLE MENTION. It was a full-color portrait done on a background of grass green. The eyes of the subject, staring beadily out from under his familiar cap, stopped the old man dead in his tracks.

"Well, I'll be damned. I'll be a son of a bitch!"

We stood in awe before this transcendent work of art.

"I never thought I'd see Luke Appling on a *quilt!*"

Sure enough, it was a ruddy likeness of old Luke himself, the foul-ball king of the American League. My father, a lifelong Chicago White Sox fan, was visibly moved. Under the picture streamed the legend, woven in golden thread:

BATTLING LUKE APPLING
ALWAYS FIRST IN OUR HEARTS

(I wonder what a genuine Luke Appling quilt would go for today in the chic, high-camp *boutiques* along Third Avenue in Manhattan.)

"Let's go, all you great lovers, all you he-men," barked a man in a purple derby at the next concession. "Let's see what kind of man you really are. Show that beautiful girl you're with just what kind of man you really are. Here you are, here you are, here you are, here's your chance to get up and really ring the bell. Everybody wins. It's good healthful exercise and everybody wins. Ring the bell. I said everybody wins. All right, you lovers, show that little lady what kind of muscles you really got. Ring the bell."

We joined a circle of gawkers at the foot of a 30-foot pole that had a wire running up its length, with a big gong at the top. At the bottom was a round metal plate. The pole, candy-striped red and white, was marked with gradations. Beginning at the bottom, they read:

CASPAR MILQUETOAST

LADIES' DIVISION

BETTER EAT YOUR WHEATIES

AVERAGE

NOT BAD

WATCH OUT FOR THIS GUY

And way up at the top: WOW! A REAL HE-MAN.

A huge, rosy-cheeked, curly-haired tractor-driver type, wearing Sears, Roebuck pants and a checkered cowboy shirt, stepped into the arena.

"Let's see how the young man swings. Look at those shoulders, folks, look at those arms! Swing the hammer nice and smooth; hit it right on the button. Let's see you ring the bell."

The barker handed the behemoth a big mallet. His friends jeered and snorted noisily in derision.

"Belt the hell out of it, Caleb!" one yelled.

"Aw, come on. He cain't make it past the LADIES' mark. He ain't got no lead in his pencil!"

The crowd snickered contemptuously. Caleb grabbed the handle and swung wildly. K-THUNK! The iron weight rose feebly up the cable and fell back with a clank.

"No wonder yew cain't make out with Minnie!" hooted one of his friends.

Caleb spat on his hands, swung again. The hammer whistled. KER-THUNK!

The weight rose higher this time, almost reaching the AVERAGE mark halfway up the pole. Caleb looked thoughtful, as the distant sound of the merry-go-round calliope switched from *Alexander's Ragtime Band* to *The Valkyrie*. It was, indeed, a Wagnerian moment, the twilight of the gods.

He peered upward at the gong, which now seemed twice as high as it had before. He kicked the dirt like a batter digging in at the batter's box, wiped his hands on his trousers and once again grabbed the mallet. His biceps rippled under the tight-fitting cowboy shirt. Dark circles of sweat stained the armpits. His back arched. This time, he swung the hammer from the ground, then up in a great, swinging arc. K-THUNK! The metal weight drifted up the wire, slowed and stopped at CASPAR MILQUE-TOAST.

"Man, yew better quit before that thing don't move at all!"

Caleb dropped the hammer, his face bathed in sweat and red from humiliation, paid the barker and left the arena, a broken man. I had a suspicion of what was going to happen next. If there was ever a sucker for that kind of thing, it was my old man.

"I think I'm gonna try whacking that thing," he whispered.

"Now, don't make a fool of yourself." My mother was always afraid of his making a fool of himself. She had good reason to be.

"Aw, just for fun. I mean, what the hell."

"All right, you lovers, you saw cousin Caleb get all the way up there to AVERAGE. Let's see how you can do. Ring the bell, ring the bell, who can ring the bell?"

As Caleb snarled at the Greek chorus of hisses and boos from his corn-liquored buddies, the old man stepped into the clearing without a word, gave the guy a quarter, grabbed the hammer and swung. K-THWACK! He didn't hit it with anywhere near the thump that Caleb got into her. But: ZZZIIIIIIIP . . . BONG!

The iron weight raced to the top and rang the bell so loud it could be heard a block away.

"Y'see that, Caleb? That there guy's got lead in *his* pencil!" The nasal bray of rustic wit opened up again.

"The little man wins a box of genuwine Swiss-chocolate bonbons. All ya gotta do is have a good swing. Who's gonna win the next big prize, all you lovers?"

My father, stunned at his totally unprecedented success, grabbed the box of chocolates amid the applause of the rabble.

The last we saw of Caleb was the hammer rising and falling at two bits a swing, being milked by that barker for every cent he owned.

This moment was to become a sacred gem in the family archives. The more it was told, the greater the feat became. Caleb grew into Paul Bunyan, and the old man's hammer swing rose to Olympic proportions. It wasn't until I was 16 that I read an article in *Popular Mechanics* and discovered that the barker operated the thing with his foot. The old man, fortunately, never found out.

As we moved from one marvel to the next, my brother and I began to list heavily to starboard; we hadn't stopped eating since we stepped onto the fairgrounds: homemade popcorn balls, red, white and blue, made by the 4-H; girl-scout cookies; French fries; boiled corn on the cob dripping butter; Nehi orange and Hires root beer; peanuts; pumpkin pie; hot dogs; pickles; American Legion Auxiliary crullers; baked beans on paper plates; lemonade; Ladies of the Moose angel-food cake; taffy apples; and a thousand free samples, including Purina Chick Chow, which my brother and I both ate avidly. Added to this was the real specialty of any Indiana fair—homemade black-walnut chocolate fudge, displayed in thick, fly-crawling slabs at stands operated by beaming Kiwanians wearing funny hats and badges. We also scoffed down about five pounds each of peculiarly native candy called vanilla angel breath, an airy concoction so cloyingly sweet that a bite-sized portion could rot teeth at 50 paces. A fundamental ground rule of the county fair was that kids could have anything they wanted to eat, just this once. Steadily, we chewed our way toward Armageddon.

Barkers on all sides hawked everything from horse collars to Mystic Mohegan Indian Squaw Korn Kure. We paused briefly while my old man hurled lumpy baseballs at battered wooden milk bottles, his blood rising visibly as the balls bounced off the canvas at the rear of the tent. Other athletes strained and grunted, their hard-earned cash winging into the canvas with dull thuds. A shelf held the possible booty: cerise Kewpie dolls with enormous red-feather fans, stuffed pandas, shiny china panthers with clocks in their stomachs, souvenir ashtrays in the shape of mother-of-pearl toilets—a veritable king's ransom.

The proprietor, a short, round man with a gray chin, played them like rainbow trout. "Y'got a nice arm, son. Let's see you lay it in there. Show the little lady how the big-leaguers do it. Look at that arm, folks! He's tossin' a real knuckler. Three balls for a quarter. How 'bout you, little lady? Try yer luck."

While my father was winding up, the man handed three baseballs to a skinny girl about 11 years old. She quickly bowled over three milk bottles and still had a ball left.

"Pick any prize y'want, little lady, any prize!"

The sweating yahoos threw with renewed vigor, dollar bills cascading across the counter. The 11-year-old picked a Kewpie doll and left. It wasn't until the next day that we found out she was the daughter of the guy who ran the joint. We saw them in Joe's Diner eating shredded wheat.

It was getting late. Our feet were coated with chewing gum and popcorn, and we were covered with a thick layer of finely powdered yellow clay. I knew that somewhere on the grounds Schwartz and Flick and Kissel were doing things that they would lie to me about the next day.

Now we were deep in the heart of the thrill-ride section of the fair. The Ferris wheel reached high up into the dark sky, its spokes outlined in colored light bulbs, jerking upward and stopping and jerking and jerking upward again. It loomed over us like a huge illuminated snowflake.

"I wanna go on the Ferris wheel!" Randy whined for the 317th time. This time, he was not to be denied.

My father bought a ticket from the man in the little booth. Off my brother went through the turnstile and into a wobbly car the color of a grape. A minute later, he was laughing down at us and sticking his tongue out as he swept up ecstatically into the night. Every few seconds, the wheel would stop and unload a car. We stood around and waved every time he went past.

Finally, the grape car stopped at the bottom. We could see the attendant in blue coveralls swing the gate open. He seemed to be arguing with the occupant. The attendant finally hollered out to the guy in the box office:

"HEY, JAKE! THIS KID WON'T GET OUT!"

"Oh, fer Chrissake, what now?" the old man muttered.

"NOW, YOU GET OUT. YOU HAD ENOUGH," said the attendant.

"WHAAAAAAAA!"

The attendant reached in and wrenched him out, fighting and kicking every inch of the way. My father took over the battle, dragging him out into the midway.

"I WANNA GO ON AGAIN!!" he screamed, but to no avail.

The big wheel started up without him as we moved on to the next attraction, Randy struggling at every step.

We tried to hurry past a merry-go-round swarming with little kids and mothers, but it was no use. Randy threatened to throw himself under it if he didn't get to ride on it. I stood with my father as he whirled round and round beside my mother, sitting on a black swan with a yellow beak. He tried to do a headstand as *The Man on the Flying Trapeze* played over and over and over and over. After the sixth ride, we managed to pull him off. He emerged slightly pale but still game. We ate a red candy cane apiece, thus setting the stage for total disaster.

My father never went on rides unless they were real gut busters. He had ventured unflinchingly onto roller coasters so violent as to turn away strong men, quaking in fear. He spotted one of his old favorites, an evil contraption known as the Whirligig Rocket Whip. We had been warned of its presence long before we arrived on the scene. Screams of horror and the flashing light of the emergency ambulance led us to the killer ride of them all.

At every fair or amusement park, there is one ride that is the yokel equivalent of the main bull ring in Madrid. This is where callow-faced youths and gorilla-armed icemen prove their virility to their admiring women. The Rocket Whip was a classic of its kind. It consisted of two bullet-shaped cars, one yellow, one red, attached to the ends of rotating arms. It revolved simultaneously clockwise and up and down. At the same time, the individual cars rotated in their own orbits. The old man, spotting the Rocket Whip, strained forward like a fire horse smelling smoke.

"Are you sure you should go on that?" My mother held back.

"Aw, come on. It'll do the kids good. Blow the stink off 'em." She didn't answer, just gazed up in fear at the mechanical devil that was now about to take on passengers. The yellow car rested near the ground, it's wire-mesh door invitingly open.

He bought three tickets from the operator, who sat near the turnstile in a rocking chair, the control lever at his side.

"Let's go, kids."

We piled into the car. It was simplicity itself; two hard metal seats and a bar that clamped down over the laps of the occupants, so that their bodies didn't become actually dismembered. We sat stationary for a long moment. High above us, the occupants of the red car gazed down at us—upside down—waiting for Thor's hammer to descend.

The man yanked the lever and it began. Slowly at first, we began to spin. The landscape outside our wire-mesh cage blurred as we gained speed. We leaped sky-ward, up, up; paused briefly at the top of the arc at what looked like thousands of feet above ground level, then plunged straight down. Just as we neared the earth, we were whipped upward again. By this time, the car, caught by enormous forces, had begun spinning centrifu-gally on its own. We were trapped in a giant cream sepa-rator.

There were brief flashes of dark sky, flashing lights, gaping throngs, my old man's rolling eyes, his straw hat sailing around the interior of the car.

"Oh, no, fer Chrissake!" he yelled. A shower of loose change—quarters, nickels, dimes, pennies—sprayed out of his pockets, filled the car for an instant and was gone, spun out into the night.

"Oh, Jesus Christ! No!" he yelled again, as his brown-and-white marbled Wearever fountain pen with his name on it, given to him by the bowling team, flew out of his pocket and disappeared into the night.

Higher and higher we flew, swooping low to scream upward again. My kid brother, chalk white, whimpered piteously. I hung onto the iron bar, certain that my last hour had arrived. My head thumped the back of the car steadily as it spun.

"Ain't this fun, kids? Wow, what a ride!" shouted

the old man, sweating profusely. He made a grab for his hat as it sailed past.

"Wave to Ma, kids! There she is!"

It was then that the operator turned the power on full. Everything that had gone before was only a warm-up. Our necks snapped back as the Rocket Whip accelerated. I was not touching the seat at any point. Jack-knifed over the bar, I saw that one of my shoes had been wrenched off my foot. At that moment, with no warning, my kid brother let it all go. His entire day's accumulation of goodies, now marinated and pungent, gushed out in a geyser. The car spun crazily. The air was filled with atomized spray of everything he had ingested for the past 24 hours. Down we swooped.

"My new pongee shirt!"

Soaked from head to foot, the old man struggled frantically in his seat to get out of the line of fire. It was no use. I felt it coming, too. I closed my eyes and the vacuum forces of outer space just dragged it all out of me like a suction pump. From a million miles away, I heard my old man shouting something, but it didn't matter. All I knew was that if I didn't hold onto that bar, it would be all over.

We gradually spun to a stop and finally the wire-mesh door opened. My feet touched the blessed earth. On rubbery legs, clinging weakly together, the three of us tottered past the turnstile as other victims were clamped into the torture chamber we had just left.

"Great ride, eh, folks? I left you on a little longer, 'cause I could see the kids was really enjoyin' it," said the operator, pocketing the last of my father's change as we passed through the turnstile.

"Thanks. It sure was great," said the old man with a weak smile, a bent cigarette hanging from his lips. He always judged a ride by how sick it made him. The nausea quotient of the Rocket Whip was about as high as they come.

We sat on a bench for a while to let the breeze dry off the old man's shirt, and so that our eyes could get back into focus. From all around us we could hear the whoops and hollers of people going up and down and sideways on the other rides.

There was one across from the Rocket Whip that my kid brother, who had great recuperative powers, *had* to go on. We didn't have the strength to stop him. It was a big barrel made out of some kind of shiny metal and it spun around like a cocktail shaker on its side. The people were screaming and yelling; their skirts were flying up, their shoes falling off. Randy loved it. We hung around and waited until they threw him out.

It was late now and getting a little chilly. It seemed like we had been at the fair for about a month. We sat on the bench while the crowd trudged past us, chewing hot dogs, lugging jars of succotash that they had bought at the exhibits, twirling sticks with little yellow birds on the ends of strings that we could hear whistling over the calliope on the merry-go-round, wearing souvenir Dr. Bodley's Iron Nerve Tonic sun visors, carrying drunken cousins who had hit the applejack since early morning, wheeling reeking babies smeared with caked Pablum and chocolate. Long-legged, skinny, yellow dogs with their tongues hanging out kept running back and forth and barking. It had been an unforgettable day.

"It sure feels good to just sit for a while," said my mother as she took off one shoe and dumped out some popcorn. The old man didn't say anything. The unlit cigarette still in his mouth, he just sat and watched the crowd move on, with his hat pushed back on his head. We sat like that for about 15 minutes, getting our wind back.

"Did you feel a drop of rain?" My mother looked up at the black sky and held out her hand.

The old man looked up. "Nah. You must be sweating."

"*I* felt a drop," I said, sticking my hand out.

The only one who didn't stick his hand out was my kid brother, who didn't care whether it rained or not. He just squatted at the end of the bench and went back to whining, which he always did when there was nothing else to do.

"Stop that! You're getting on my nerves!" said my mother, poking him in the ribs to shut him up.

"I'm tired." He had that high-pitched, irritating sound that he was so good at.

"You know, I think it *is* raining." The old man made it official.

People started to hold newspapers over their heads and duck under awnings and into tents.

"Well, we might as well call it a day," announced the old man as he stood up and stuck his shirttail back into his pants.

"Let's head for the car."

We were a long way from the parking lot, which was over on the other side of the race track, about four miles away. We slogged doggedly through drifting mountains of candy wrappers, cigar butts, apple cores and cow flop; past tents full of canned lima beans and crocheted doilies, sweetheart pillows and gingerbread men, past shooting galleries and harvester machines and, finally, as the rain was really beginning to come down hard, we reached the car. We joined the procession of mud-splattered vehicles inching painfully, bumper to bumper, toward the distant highway.

"Y'know, I think the fair was even better than usual this year." My father said the same thing every year.

"Yes, the quilts *were* better this year," my mother agreed. "I think Bernice should have won at least second prize, though. The quilt that won wasn't that good."

"Oh, well, you know there's a lot of politics in that quilt business." The old man always figured there was politics in everything.

"I'm hungry!" Randy was at it again. He'd had an empty stomach ever since the Rocket Whip.

"We'll all have meat-loaf sandwiches when we get home," said my mother, wiping the steam off the inside of the windshield with her handkerchief, so that she could see out.

. . .

A Right Guard commercial featuring two French Foreign Legionnaires hiding behind a sand dune snapped me back to the real world. I glanced at my watch. My

God! It was 20 after four. Another goddamn night shot in front of the television set.

The closing credits of the movie came on, superimposed over the never-never dreamworld of Dick Haymes' state fair. I stood up, my knees cracking like twin castanets —an occupational hazard of late-late movie addiction. Hobbling over to the set, I reached down and snapped it off. The picture quickly shrank to a tiny dot in the middle of the gray screen. It lingered for a moment, glowing at me accusingly, as though I had killed it, and then disappeared.

I was ready to hit the sack. Or was I? No, there was something I had to do. What was it? I felt a peculiar, unnamable yearning from deep within me, a gnawing emptiness. I smacked my lips, and suddenly I knew. Marching purposefully to the front closet, I threw on my coat and headed out the front door into the empty streets on a lonely quest. I had to have a taffy apple.

SCUT FARKAS AND THE
MURDEROUS MARIAH

"I'm going to throw this wagon out, George. You don't play with it anymore, you're a general now. It's just gathering dust in the cellar. And if you don't want that little hatchet you got for your birthday, I'll get rid of that, too. I don't want it just banging around the house. It's liable to cause more trouble."

I am hearing George Washington's mother speaking in a quavery, old-timy voice, filtering through the hazy mists of past ages. There in the case right in front of my eyes was a stylish, archaic, hunched-up kind of cart with big spoked wheels. You could even see vestigial flecks of ancient red paint. The card read:

TOY WAGON GENERALLY SUPPOSED TO HAVE BELONGED TO GEORGE WASHINGTON AS A CHILD. THIS PRICELESS RELIC HAS BEEN ALMOST CONCLUSIVELY AUTHENTI-CATED.

93

George Washington's little red wagon! My mind boggled at the thought of the Father of Our Country tugging his high-spoked wooden toy through the boondocks, his 18th Century overalls faintly damp, his 18th Century kidshoes trailing laces in the sand, on his way to becoming the most successful revolutionist in all history.

I moved among the museum exhibits, now deep in a maelstrom of contemplation, mining a new vein of thought that had never occurred to me. In the next case, resting on a chaste velvet-covered podium, lay a chewed and worn wooden top of the type commonly known among the wooden-top set of my day as a spikesie. For the unfortunates unfamiliar with this maddening device, which over the centuries has separated the men from the boys among kids, a spikesie is a highly functional top-shaped wooden toy, beautifully, malevolently tapered down to a glittering steel spikelike spinning surface.

I stopped dead in my tracks, unable to believe my eyes. I looked long and hard, peering intently into the shiny glass case at the squat toy that was displayed there. There was no doubt about it. This was no ordinary spikesie, but identical with a sinister breed of top that I myself had once encountered. Bending low over the exhibit, I examined the inscription:

UNUSUAL HANDMADE TOP. ORIGIN UNKNOWN. SAID TO HAVE BEEN OWNED BY THE YOUNG THOMAS JEFFERSON.

My God! Thomas Jefferson! The elegant, consummate product of the age of reason; architect, statesman, utopian, man of letters. I wondered modestly whether I could have shown Tom a thing or two about top spinning. After all, a Declaration of Independence is one thing; a split top is another. The top rested quietly on its podium, mute and mysterious. It was a dark, rich, worn russet color. I wondered what its name was and what battles it had fought for the framer of the American way of life, what battles it had fought in the distant past and perhaps would fight again.

As I gazed at the top, old spike wounds itched vaguely beneath my tapered Italian slacks—old wounds I had sustained in hand-to-hand spikesie combat with antagonists of my dim past. Well did I remember Junior Kissel's economical, slicing sidearm movement, his green top string snapping curtly as he laid his yellow spikesie down right on a dime with a hissing whir. Flick, on the other hand —more erratic, more flamboyant—had a tendency to loft his spikesie, releasing it after a showy, looping overhand motion a good two feet above the surface of the playing field. His top spun with an exhibitionistic, wobbling playfulness and usually bounced hesitantly two or three times before settling into the groove. I myself preferred a sneaky, snakelike, underhand movement, beginning at the hip, swinging down to around the knees, upward slightly, and then the quick release after a fast, whiplike follow-through. Flick was great to watch; Kissel, methodical and clean. I was deadly.

In my day, there were two types of top spinners: those who merely *played* with a top—dilettantes, haphazard, sloppy, beneath notice; and those to whom a top was a weapon in the purest sense, an extension of the will, an instrument of talent and aggression. Anything *but* a toy. I was one of that lonely breed. In combat, the top was used for only one thing: destruction. A top in the sweaty, tense hand of a real artist was capable of splitting his rival's top down the middle in the flickering of an eyelash.

I remember all too well the sinking sensation of total defeat when my first top skittered into the gutter, wobbling crazily like a drunken thing, in two distinct and irrevocable halves; and Scut Farkas, pocketing his sleek, ugly, black spikesie, strode away without so much as a backward glance. Then and there, the course of the next few years of my festering life was uncompromisingly set. In the secrecy of the basement, hour after hour, I clandestinely practiced every known motion, ranging from the rarely seen, difficult-to-master whiplash to the effete, delicate sidearm slice. Slowly my own true personal form began to emerge—until one spring day, in five minutes. I had halved the prized possessions of three of my closest friends. I knew then that I was ready for the big time.

Not quite. True, as a performer I felt fairly confident. It was the top itself that I lacked. To the untutored eye, I suppose, a top is a top—some red, some green, some blue. I find this hard to believe, but no doubt this is so to some. Ignorance may be bliss, but it is also pitiable. To the uninformed, all bats used by ballplayers look alike. This could not be further from the truth. Major-leaguers make annual treks to Louisville, Kentucky, for the sole and express purpose of selecting the seasoned lumber, the delicate taper, the precise finish and exquisitely calculated weight of the one thing that stands between them and anonymity. They guard their personal weapons with a fierce and unremitting jealousy. Long winter evenings are spent by internationally known sluggers resting before the fireside, carefully, endlessly rubbing next season's lumber with oily pork-chop bones, until finally, by opening day, the cleanup man steps to the plate, whipping through the ambient air a personal and completely assimilated fusion of man and device. Boog Powell's bat is as different from, say, Tony Conigliaro's as twilight is from dawn. They may look a little alike, but they don't feel the same.

Scut Farkas' top, known throughout the neighborhood as Mariah, had at least 50 or more confirmed kills to its credit, as well as half a dozen probables and God knows how many disabling gashes and wounds. Rumor held that this top had been owned by Farkas' father before him, a silent, steely-eyed, blue-jawed man who spoke with a thick, guttural accent. He ran a junk yard piled high with rotting hulks of deceased automobiles and rusting railroad-train wheels. Some said that it was not a top at all, but some kind of foreign knife, and not large, as tops go, being of a peculiar squat shape, a kind of small, stunted, pitch-black mushroom, wider above than most and sloping off quickly to a dark-blue, casehardened, glittering saber tip. Not only was the top strange in appearance; it spun with a mean, low humming—a truly distinctive, ominous note, a note that rose and fell, deep and rumbling, like the sound of an approaching squadron of distant Fokkers bent on death and destruction. Farkas, like all true professionals, rarely showed his top unless in anger. Skulking about the playground, his back pocket bulging meaningfully, just the trace of top string showing, Farkas was a continual, walking, living, surly challenge.

As a marble player, he had long since been barred from civilized games. His persistent use of blue-steel ball bearings, lightly polished with 3-In-One Oil, had reduced our heisty and spitsie games to a shambles, leaving the playground strewn with the wreckage of shattered comsies, precious aggies—and blasted hopes. Farkas played for keeps, in the truest sense of the word. An aggie belted by one of Farkas' cannonballs ceased to exist, dissolving in a quick puff of pulverized ash.

Farkas' secret was not in his choice of weapons alone. He had the evil eye. We all have seen this eye at one time or another in our lives, glimpsed fleetingly, perhaps, for a terrifying, paralyzing moment on the subway, among a jostling throng on the sidewalk in the midst of a riotous Saturday night, peering from the gloom through the bars of a deathhouse cell in a B movie at the Orpheum, or through the steamy, aromatic air of the reptile house. It is not easy to describe the effect that Farkas' eye had on the playground of the Warren G. Harding School. I know that such a thing is anatomically not possible, but Farkas' eye seemed to be of the purest silver-gray, totally unblinking and glowing from within with a kind of gemlike hardness. These eyes, set in his narrow, high-cheekboned weasel face above a sharp, runny nose, have scarred forever the tender psyches of countless preadolescents. Many's the kid who awakened screaming, drenched with cold sweat in the dead of night, dreaming wild nightmares of being chased over fences, under porches, through garages by that remorseless weasel face. The closest thing I have ever seen to the general quality, both physical and spiritual, of Scut Farkas was when, on a sunny afternoon on a Florida dock, I came face to face with a not-quite-deceased, eight-foot mako shark. Scut Farkas, at ten, was a man not to be trifled with.

He was the only kid I had ever heard of who rarely smoked cigars, cigarettes or corn silk. Farkas chewed apple-cured Red Mule Cut Plug. In class and out. As a spitter, Farkas unquestionably stands among the all-time greats. During class he generally used his inkwell as a target, while on the playground he usually preferred someone else's hair. Few dared to protest, and those who did lived to regret it. Farkas' glance boring gun-hard across the classroom carried a message to every male in the class, save one, at one time or another. It read: "I'll get you after school." The kid, knowing he was doomed, often wet his pants right there and then.

He had never been known to refer to *any* of his classmates by other than their last name only. The use of the first name somehow would have been a sign of camaraderie or weakness, and would have undermined his position as an unbending belligerent. The victim's last name was always followed by the same phrase: "Ya chicken bastard!"

His only known rival in pure thuggishness was the equally infamous Grover Dill. The two had formed an unspoken alliance, each recognizing the other as extremely dangerous—an alliance that held the rest of the kids in total subjugation.

As a competitive top spinner, Farkas was universally recognized as unbeatable. The combination of Mariah and Farkas' short, whistling three-quarter-lash movement was devastating. He sacrificed accuracy for sheer power, like a fast-ball pitcher with a streak of wildness. When Mariah hit, there was no return.

Occasionally a challenger, getting wind of Farkas' overpowering reputation at Warren G. Harding, would show up at recess from some foreign school. A ripple of excitement would move quickly through the motley throng as the two battlers squared off. There was a strong streak of chauvinism among the Warren G. Harding students. It could be said that we felt, "Warren G. Harding, right or wrong"—except when Scut Farkas was facing down a challenger from, say, St. Peter's parochial school, or George Rogers Clark. Farkas did not carry the colors of Warren G. Harding on his back. Like all true outlaws, the only color he recognized was blood-red. The other guy's, of course.

Week after week, month after month, we stood by helplessly as Scut Farkas and Mariah made wreckage of the best tops in Hohman, Indiana. Not only that; we were forced by a single scythelike sweep of his evil eye to applaud his victories. This was the unkindest cut of all. I remember the hated words rattling in my throat as I banged Flick on the back: "Old Farkas sure did it." Flick hollowly answering: ". . . Yeah."

Pocketing Mariah and hawking fiercely, Farkas would swagger sideways into the gloom of the boys' bathroom to look for somebody to hit. Another notch was added to his already well-notched belt.

This was the nature of my enemy as I practiced day after day in the basement next to the furnace, perfecting, honing, polishing my burgeoning technique. Why I did it, I cannot tell. Some men are driven to climb Everest, others to go over Niagara Falls in barrels or beach balls. Some are driven to wrestle crocodiles barehanded. I only knew that in the end there would be just Farkas and me, and our tops.

One thing was sure: To get hold of a top that could even stay in the same ring with Mariah, I would have to do better than the measly assortment that Old Man Pulaski kept in the candy case among the jawbreakers, the JuJu Babies and the wax teeth. Pulaski's tops were not fighting tops. They were little-kid playing-around tops; weak, defenseless, wobbly, minnowlike, they were even used by girls.

"Do you have any other tops but them little ones?"

"D'ya wanna top or don'tcha?" Old Man Pulaski glared down at me from behind his bloody butcher's apron while the jostling knot of Lithuanian and Polish housewives clamored for soup bones.

"Yeah, but I got that kind."

"Here, how 'bout a nice red one?" He reached into the case, trying to hurry the sale.

"Ya got any black ones?"

"Aw, for Chrissake, black tops! Come on, kid, I ain't got no time to fool around!"

"Scut Farkas got one."

"I told Scut Farkas if he ever came in again I'd kick his behind. He didn't get no black top here."

"Well, he's got one."

"Ask *him* where he got it." He roared off back to the meat counter.

Obviously, that was out of the question. Asking Farkas where he got Mariah was about like asking King Kong where he got his fangs. So I began methodically to visit candy store, dime store, toy store—any kind of store where they might conceivably have tops. Every day on my paper route I sniffed and hunted. From time to time I even bought what looked like a promising challenger, but I knew deep down in my heart that none of them came close to Mariah. Some were better than Pulaski's, some worse. I even discovered all sorts of tricky, effete, frilly tops I had never before seen or heard of. This went on well through spring. Then, late one balmy day, slowly pedaling home on my Elgin bicycle—the pride of my life—its foxtails hanging limply in the soft air, my mind a good five light-years away, I came unexpectedly to the end of my search.

I was at least four miles beyond my usual range, in a run-down, rickety tenement section of town, near the roundhouse. The steady crash and roar of switch engines, the shrieking and booming of Monon freight cars went on 24 hours a day, seven days a week in this country. Even when the sun was out brightly, the skies here were gray. I rarely got over this far. It was foreign territory. I pedaled aimlessly along the dingy, dark street, the curbs lined with elderly, disreputable automobiles, reading signs as I went. For the first few years after you really learn to read, you read everything in sight carefully.

BEECH-NUT TOBACCO . . . BULL DURHAM . . . FISK TIRES . . . ROOM FOR RENT—RAILROADERS WELCOME . . . COMMIT NO NUISANCE . . . CHILI PARLOR, HOT TAMALES . . . SHOESHINE . . . BARBERSHOP . . . SNOOKER TABLES . . . TOTAL VICTORY NEWSSTAND AND NOTIONS . . . LUMP COAL . . .

Wait a minute. TOTAL VICTORY NEWSSTAND AND NOTIONS. It was a tiny, dark sliver of a shop, wedged in between two gloomy red-brick buildings, about the size of those places where a man sells celluloid combs and hunches over a lathe making keys. I swung over to the curb, squeaked on the brakes and dropped the bike in back of a derelict Hudson Terraplane. In front of the Total Victory, a faded-red-metal slotted newspaper display case leaned against a locked Coca-Cola icebox. The window of the store was impenetrable by human gaze, covered with a rich, dank patina of locomotive smoke, blast-furnace dust and the fine essence of Sinclair Oil from the nearby refineries. Faded posters hawking Copenhagen

Snuff, Sweet Orr work gloves and Lava Soap, the mechanic's friend, completed the job. For a second or two, once inside, I couldn't see a thing, it was so dark and dingy.

"What d'ya want, sonny?" I peered around the high glass case containing stacks of snuffboxes and tablets, looking for the speaker.

"What d'ya want?" An ancient lady wearing a black shawl over her head, the way most Polish ladies did in our neighborhood, stared piercingly at me.

"Uh . . ."

"D'ya want some orange pop, sonny?" She spoke with the slightest trace of a European accent.

"You got any tops?"

"Why, yes, sonny."

She disappeared behind the counter for a long moment. The shop's air was heavy with the scent of cabbage, garlic, tobacco juice and old clothes. Outside, a diesel engine blatted its horn thunderingly, rumbling off into the middle distance.

"How about these, sonny?"

She hoisted a cardboard box of tops onto the counter. I might have known it. She must have got these tops from the same place Pulaski got his—weak-kneed trifles that you saw everywhere.

"Uh . . . is that all you got?"

"How 'bout a red one, sonny?"

"Uh . . . you got any other kind?"

"Other kind? These are good tops, sonny."

"Naw, I got one a them. 'Bye."

I started to leave, as I had done so many times in the past, from every dinky candy store in town. Just as I got to the door:

"Hey, sonny, come back here."

Vaguely uneasy, I turned, one foot out on the sidewalk, the other on the greasy floor, my Keds ready to spring for the Elgin. She had disappeared into the back of the store behind a beaded curtain. She re-emerged into the murky gloom, carrying a cardboard Quaker Oats box. She set it down on the counter and began fishing in it with a withered claw. I waited, figuring she was going to spring a yo-yo on me, a toy for boobs and idiots, a sop for the untalented.

She pulled out a tangled mass of rubber bands, string, a couple of old clothespins and what looked like a dead mouse. A switch engine breathed asthmatically in the ambient air outside—followed by muffled curses from the brakemen.

"Aha! Here she is!" She fished scratchingly, unable to grab whatever it was.

"I wouldn't sell this top to everybody, sonny."

"Yeah?" I was ready to jump.

"But I can tell you need a top, sonny." She cackled, her faint white beard glinting dully. Her hand snaked out of the can, clutching something round.

Great Scott! Cradled in her talons lay a malevolent duplicate of Scut Farkas' evil Mariah. A duplicate in everything—spirit, conformation, size, everything—except color. It was a dull, burnished, scuffed silvery-pewter, a color I had never seen on a top before. But then, except for Mariah, I had never seen a black one, either.

"It's been used, so it won't cost you much, sonny."

"How much?" I was almost afraid to ask.

"I'd say ten cents, sonny. It's imported. She's a Gypsy top."

I was In. It was one of those few moments when I was well-heeled, carrying a full 12 cents in my jeans. I forked over my two nickels as calmly as I could and took possession of what was to prove to be a historic find. I had at last come together with the greatest fighting top I had ever seen. It had an oily, heavy, solid feel, a nice comfortable heft like, say, a Colt snub .38 Special feels to the hand. I had already decided to call it Wolf.

"Good luck, sonny. Careful, she's a mean one."

Outside, the switchyard mumbled and muttered as a long, clanking string of flat beds rumbled toward the steel mill. With Wolf safely in my hip pocket, I pedaled furiously through the twilight toward Cleveland Street. The showdown had begun. I knew it. And somewhere in his lair, Scut Farkas must have known it, too.

That night after supper, under a dim yellow light bulb in the basement, next to the looming furnace that dominated the underworld below our house, I carefully wound my best top string around Wolf for the first time, pulling each loop hard and tight so that it lay flat against the preceding one, until finally Wolf was cocked and ready for action.

The string itself is highly important to a genuine expert. I preferred the hard, green, twisted cord that knotted solidly and got a good bite on the side of the top. This type of string was not easy to use, but once the technique was mastered, nothing could come near it. I had long since outgrown the standard wooden button for the end of the string, using instead a thin, one-inch mother-of-pearl button stolen from my mother's sewing basket. There were three extras stashed away in my dresser drawer for emergencies.

As the dim bulb illuminated a faint circle on the gray concrete floor, I scratched out a mark in the exact center of the pool of light for a target and stepped back into almost full darkness. I could smell the moldering old tires that my father kept hanging on the walls just in case someday he might pick up another Hupmobile, and the mildewed Sunday papers of years back that lay piled against the concrete-block walls, and the scent of countless generations of field mice who had lived out their lives in this basement, and the dusty Mason jars filled with grape jelly and strawberry preserves that lined the plank shelves under the steps, and the sharp rubber smell —bitter and strong—of the coiled garden hose under the workbench, and the more subtle but pervasive aroma of a half ton of damp soft coal in the pitchblack bin, all held together with the soapy dankness of the drains, covered with perforated iron lids, that every week carried the family's used wash water back into Lake Michigan.

Deliberately and meticulously, I set Wolf down on the concrete floor for the first time. We were made for each other, just the way Mariah was made for Scut. The personality of tops is an odd thing. Mariah spun with an angry ferocity, a carnivorous drive that was despised and feared by everyone who had the bad luck to see it in action. Wolf, on the other hand, was steadier, giving off a note higher in pitch than Mariah but in some ways even more deadly. Mariah was a hot-blooded animal; Wolf, cold-blooded, snakelike. It would be an interesting meeting.

Again I laid the top precisely on the mark I had made, getting the feel of it, gradually letting myself out, feeling the full flush of rising excitement and mounting confidence as I gradually mastered the sinister Wolf. Even from the start, however, I had the sneaky, uneasy feeling that somehow I didn't really *own* this top. At first I felt that it was just because I was not used to it, little suspecting how right I was.

For two weeks, every night, Wolf and I practiced together in the basement. I had decided not to show him to anyone until we could take on Farkas. No telling what might have happened if Farkas had heard of the existence of Wolf, and my plans, before I was ready to really give him a battle. Even at that, I knew very well that my chances of breaking even with Farkas, let alone defeating him, were as slim as the chances of that proverbial snowball in hell.

In public I began throwing my weight around with second-string tops, until the word slowly began to spread throughout the gym, the auditorium, the homerooms; till at recess time I could always draw a small claque of fans goading me on to belt some poor kid's top into the boondocks.

Since the day Farkas had publicly humiliated me, he no longer even deigned to note my topwork. Once, however, he paused briefly, while twisting Jack Robertson's arm behind him and belting him in the ribs with his free hand, to spit a thin spray of tobacco juice over my orange top, which had just landed neatly beside Delbert Bumpus' yellow ball-bearing spinner. He might have taken me on right then and there, but he was busy giving Robertson his refresher course. Periodically, Farkas treated every kid in the class to a good, brisk, tendon-snapping arm twist. He shoved the victim's wrist up between his shoulder blades, pushing up and twisting out, until the supplicant's face turned ashen, his eyes bugged out and his tongue lolled in agony, Farkas yelling: "C'mon, you son of a bitch. Say it!"

". . . Graaahhhkkk!"

"C'mon, say it! You son of a bitch." Farkas gives him two more degrees of twist and brings his knee smartly into contact with the tailbone of the sufferer.

"I said SAY it!"

The victim, looking piteously at the ring of silent, scornful watchers, including, no doubt, his ex-girlfriend, finally squeaked out: "I'm a chicken bastard."

"Say it again, louder."

"I'M A CHICKEN BASTARD!" With that, Farkas hurled the pain-wracked body violently into the stickers.

"Gimme a cigarette, Dill."

And the two of them would go skulking off toward the poolroom. He gave this refresher course about every six months, to all of us. We figure he kept a list and checked us off when our time came.

It was Friday. I knew that today would be the day. Somehow you know those things. It had rained all night, a hard, driving, Midwestern drenching downpour. Now, as I toyed with my Wheaties, I could feel the edge of danger mounting within me.

"Will you listen to me? I'm talking to you."

"Ah . . . what?"

"When I'm talking to you, I want you to listen. You sit there like you've got potatoes in your ears!"

My mother always had a thing about my not listening; also dragging my feet. That drove her crazy. She always yelled that I didn't walk straight, either.

"How many times have I told you not to slump like that while you're eating? It isn't good for your stomach."

I scrunched around in my chair, pretending I was listening to her.

"You'd better be home early this afternoon, because you've got to go to the store. I don't want to have to tell you again."

"Yeah, yeah."

"How many times have I told you not to say 'Yeah'?"

". . . Yeah."

This went on for about three hours or so, until I finally got out of the house, with Wolf stuck down deep in my hip pocket, with two other, lesser, tops in my front right-side pocket. I was loaded for bear.

It looked like rain as I walked through the alleys, over the fences, through the vacant lots on my way to the playground, kicking sheets of water up from muddy puddles, skipping bottle caps into new lakes as I moved toward the battlefield. A few other kids drifted in the same direction from the next block. The trees dripped warm water under the low, gray, ragged clouds. Off to the north, toward Lake Michigan, even though it was full daytime, the steel mills glowed dark red against the low-hanging overcast.

At last on the playground, I began my carefully thought-out scheme. "Hey, Kissel, how 'bout a little action?"

My top, the second-string orange one, whistled out and landed with a click on the asphalt.

"How 'bout it, Kissel?"

I scooped up the top, this time laying her down on one of the school steps, making it walk downstairs a step at a time, a neat trick from my basic repertoire. Finally goaded, Kissel pulled out of his pocket his lumpy little green top.

"I won't split it. Just nick it a little, Kissel. Don't worry."

A few onlookers had drifted into range, sensing something important afoot. I was deliberately overplaying my hand.

"I'll even let you go first, Kissel. Come on—chicken?" I spun my top temptingly in front of Kissel's Indian Tread tennis shoes. He couldn't resist any longer. He bit hard.

"All right, smart guy," he said, "take that!" His green top narrowly missed mine, bouncing on the asphalt and then settling down into its pedestrian buzz. Quickly I scooped up my top, wound it up and let him have it. His green toy careened drunkenly into the gutter.

"Sorry, Kissel. I just can't control it." I put my top back into my pocket, saying loudly:

"There's no good top men around here, anyway. Let's get up a game of softball."

I had made sure that before any of this happened, Grover Dill was in the throng. I knew only one thing could happen after such an outrageous remark. Even now his sloping shoulders, his thick neck, his ragged crewcut were disappearing in the direction of the alley behind the school where he and Farkas smoked cigars, chewed tobacco, hatched plots and went over their refresher-course check lists. I must admit that I felt no little nervousness at this point, but it was too late to turn back. The die was cast.

Nervously I fished a Tootsie Roll out of my pocket, and chewed furiously to cover up. Sure enough, not five minutes had passed—in fact, we were in the middle of choosing up sides for the softball game—when a tremendous wallop from behind sent me sprawling into a puddle. Instantly the mob surged forward. Looking up from the mud, I saw Farkas holding Mariah casually in his left hand, while spinning his greasy black top string like a lariat in his right. It whistled faintly.

"Get up, ya chicken bastard."

He quickly wound the string around Mariah and flicked it high into the air, catching it on his palm as it came down. She spun efficiently on his hand for a moment before he closed his talons over her.

"Come on, get up."

Slowly I arose, pretending to be contrite.

"What's the matter, Farkas? What did I do? Gee whiz!" A low snicker went through the multitude. They recognized the signs, the old familiar signs. To a man, they had uttered those words themselves from time to time. They enjoyed seeing others in the trap.

"Get out ya top."

"My *top?*"

"GET IT OUT!"

A few drops of rain had begun to fall, and it seemed to grow darker by the second. By now the crowd had grown, until we were ringed by a motley circle of non-committal faces. Every kid on the playground was in the crowd. The word was out. Farkas was getting someone, and Farkas demanded an audience. Nervously, I pulled out my poor doomed orange top. There was no hope for it once Farkas zeroed in his sights. I had carefully planned this sacrifice.

"We'll flip for firsties," Farkas barked, his eyes cold, Mariah resting at the ready.

"Flip, Dill. Heads."

His crony spun his famous two-headed nickel into the gray air.

"Heads. You win, Scut," Dill snarled in my direction.

The crowd murmured ominously, but stilled instantly when Farkas glanced quickly around to spot who the wise guys were.

"Spin, jerk."

I wound my orange top tightly, dug my feet as hard as I could down on the asphalt. Using my underhand sweep, fast and low, I laid her down a good 15 feet away.

Farkas half crouched, Mariah digging into his grimy thumb, the rusty metal washer he used for a button jabbing out between his fingers. His arm jerked down and out, the string snapped, black Mariah struck. That is, she missed, by less than an inch. The two tops spun side by side for a moment until I darted forward, scooped mine up and backed off. Before me, black Mariah sat toadlike, growling moodily, while Farkas watched with ill-concealed contempt.

I decided to go in for the kill. Again my arm dropped, the orange top streaked out, heading straight for black Mariah's vitals. It was a good shot. Farkas knew it. He snarled low in his throat. The crowd murmured excitedly as my orange top cracked smartly against Mariah—but wobbled off weakly among the feet of the onlookers. Mariah did not budge.

"Spin it again, ya chicken bastard."

Farkas picked up Mariah and waited for my next move. I knew this was it. I had missed my chance. But then, I wasn't counting on this poor top. My big move was on the way.

I spun. Then, with his accustomed sardonic ease, the showboat attitude he always displayed when picking up a scalp, Farkas neatly cracked my top into kingdom come, the deadly spike sending up a thin spray from the wet pavement.

By habit or tradition, the multitude indicated its approval of Scut's victory:

"Wow!"

"Holy smokes!"

"Gee whiz!"

"Whoooiee!"

And other sickening sounds.

Farkas casually picked up Mariah, turned his back on me and, followed by Dill, started to walk away, the crowd parting before them. It was *now!*

My hand whipped down into my back pocket, quickly snaked Wolf out into the open, and in the twinkling of a moment, I had him wound and instantly laid Wolf down hard and solid. Its high, thin note, steady as a dentist's drill and twice as nasty, cut through the falling rain and stopped Farkas in his tracks. He turned and stared for a long instant. His eyes seemed to widen and he actually, for a moment at least, appeared to grow pale—but even more baleful—as he recognized Wolf for what it was. Between us, the silver-gray top sang tauntingly. I didn't say a word. Wolf said it all.

The crowd, sensing that something had happened, became hushed and tense. Somewhere off in the south a mutter of thunder rumbled and stilled. Casually, Farkas wound his top string about Mariah and, without a word, laid it down with a hard, vicious, overhand, cracking shot that missed Wolf by the thickness of a coat of paint. The two tops spun together with no daylight between,

Mariah's bass rumble blending with the shuddering whine of Wolf in an eerie, angry duet.

Quickly I picked up Wolf, and this time, with all the force I had, I went in for the big one. A silver-gray streak, Wolf blurred out before me. The crowd gasped audibly. Scut peered sharply down at Mariah as Wolf screamed toward the *coup de grâce*.

I couldn't believe it! Moving like a shadow over Mariah, Wolf missed by the thickness of a hair. Instantly, with a cackle, Farkas gathered in Mariah and, with a guttural laugh, sent her down the rails to finish off Wolf. I had seen him really angry at an opponent before, but nothing like this. I was afraid to look, half turning away—but the roar of the crowd told me that, incredibly, Mariah had missed!

It was my turn now. For once in my life, my nerves were like steel. This time, with infinite deliberation, I aimed and carefully let fly, a little higher, with more lift, a more deadly trajectory. Wolf rose and came down like a fiend of hell, swooping out of the sky like some gray eagle. But at the last impossible instant, it actually seemed to change course in mid-air, grazing Mariah slightly and skittering off into a puddle.

Again and again we attacked each other, first Wolf, then Mariah. Over and over we drove at each other's vitals. Something was happening that slowly began to dawn first on Farkas and me and then on the crowd. Incredibly, these two tops seemed to be *afraid* of each other. Either that, or they were somehow, in some way, mysteriously jinxed.

My arm ached. Farkas paused only to blow his nose on his sleeve before going back to the attack. It was growing darker; and it became obvious to us that at this rate, neither of us was going to scalp the other. The two insane tops, grimy, covered with mud, leaped like live things—ricocheting, leapfrogging, hovering over each other, behaving in a way that no top before or since has ever acted. They hated each other; yet they seemed to be in league.

Dill, like all good toadies, tried everything he could to snaffle Wolf, kicking up mud when I spun, going even to the extent of nudging me violently on two occasions, hoping to tip the balance. Farkas was game but growing angrier and fiercer by the second, until finally he grabbed Mariah up from the scratched and scarred battlefield, looked at me with a long, searing gaze of hate and finally said, in a low boice:

"OK, ya chicken bastard. Let's play keepers."

Keepers meant that one kid would own *both* these tops, if his top could drive the other out of a circle made on the concrete with chalk. It was the final test of topping. Farkas was gambling Mariah against Wolf. Dill quickly drew a lopsided circle on the concrete sidewalk that paralleled the asphalt. The hard surface was perfect for keepers.

"You go first," Farkas commanded.

Under the rules of the game, you were not allowed to strike your opponent's top directly, so it really didn't matter who went first. The tops themselves fought it out, walking each other around the circle until one or the other was pushed out.

I spun Wolf—little realizing for the last time. It whistled out in a low arc, landing fair in the center of the circle. I put as much power on the spin itself as I could, cracking the string with a hard, flat snap. Wolf spun, waiting for Mariah, its spike ringing sharp and hard. Farkas spun Mariah, and the two tops hummed within an inch of each other. Slowly they walked, closer and closer, as the crowd closed in. Closer and even closer, then finally— tick . . . tick . . . tick—they touched. Locked in mortal combat, first Wolf and then Mariah, then Mariah and then Wolf, ticking, humming in rising and falling cadence as they edged toward the dreaded line. Which would go out first?

For a few moments it seemed as though Wolf was doomed, but then, righting itself, it shouldered Mariah closer. Impossibly, the two seemed to pick up speed as they spun. Angrier and angrier they grew, until suddenly, with a lunge, the two tops smashed together, both reeling in tandem in a mad, locked, spinning embrace *together* over the line and out of the circle. The rain, falling steadily, pattered down on the two hazy forms in the misty air.

Farkas, sensing victory, shouted: "YOURS IS OUT!"

He darted forward. The two tops continued to struggle and together they toppled over the curb, into the gutter, clicking, snarling crazily in the fast-running water, sending up sharp rooster tails of muddy foam. I moved as fast as I could to defend Wolf.

Suddenly, it was all over. The two tops, locked in mortal combat, disappeared down a sewer from which rose a deep roar of rushing water. They were gone. Never before had any of us seen tops behave like this!

Farkas, his face white, his eyes glazed, stared down into the raging flood through the grille of the drain. Then, without a word, he arose and, followed by Dill, walked off down the street in the rain. I knew I would never see Wolf again. But somehow I knew that neither Wolf nor Mariah were finished. They would go on. I don't know why I knew this, but I did, and I still do.

The crowd broke up into small knots. The great top days were over at Warren G. Harding School. A few weeks later, I rode over to the other side of town, looking for the Total Victory. One time, months later, I thought I saw it, but it turned out to be a place where they sold stuffed animals and rocking chairs. Off and on, for a while, I continued my search; but I never found it again.

OLLIE HOPNOODLE'S HAVEN OF BLISS

"Gosh, I don't think we'll be able to leave for the lake today. My stomach. . . ." Instantly, a chorus of self-pitying moans and whimpers drowns out the hapless TV daddy. His TV wife, surrounded by her rosy-cheeked brood and a mountain of tennis rackets, suitcases, water skis and all the other paraphernalia for an on-the-go family holiday, reaches into her Mexican handbag, pulls out a blue bottle and hands it to him.

"Here, take two of these."

"Well, OK, but it's no use. I've tried everything."

Popping the pills into his mouth, he smacks his lips a couple of times and says irritably, "Why, these taste just like—*candy*."

"There's no law that says medicine can't taste good," the family shouts in unison.

He swallows doubtfully, waits a moment for the little A's and B's to go to work, then breaks into a blinding

Ultra Brite smile. "Say, you're right. I feel *good* again."
Cheers.

"All right, then, let's get the show on the road," barks
the TV momma, herding the happy family out the door
toward the station wagon and vacationland.

My old man, I reflected gratefully as I snapped off the
set, was not a TV daddy. For one thing, I have never
heard one of them use anything like the language he
employed in moments of stress. Had he been playing that
same touching scene, it would have gone something like
this:

Quick medium shot of a fifth-hand Olds in the family
driveway. Close-up of the old man's face behind the
wheel.

"HOLY CHRIST, I'M GONNA HEAVE! WHAT THE
HELL WAS IN THAT RED CABBAGE?"

Quick pan to my mother, hair in curlers.

"What do you mean, red cabbage? Them seven
beers. . . ."

Back to the old man, face now turning green.

"Forget that crummy trip!"

Sudden uproar from kids in back seat, including me.
Quick cut to the old man.

"WHAT DID YOU SAY?"

Shot of his right hand sweeping the back seat like an
avenging boom, knocking heads together indiscriminately.
Pan to Mother:

"Here. Take a Tums."

Old man, bellowing:

"ARE YOU OUT OF YOUR MIND!"

Shot of door opening quickly, as he rushes into bushes. End of commercial.

That true-life vacation scene is all too reminiscent of the one we played out every year. The family took a vacation trip by car each and every time the earth completed its laborious cycle around the sun. It usually came in late July or the first two weeks in August, but it made no difference. It always went the same way. For 14 straight years, our vacations were spent in southern Michigan on the shores of colorful Clear Lake. Clear Lake—it was many things, but the one thing it wasn't was clear. In fact, it was never even clear why we went there, but we did. Such are the vacations of the humble.

From June on, five minutes after school let out, my kid brother and I were in a feverish sweat of anticipation about this annual pilgrimage. The old man, playing it cool, didn't get really heated up until maybe a month or so before the big day. My mother—who, incidentally, would never have made a TV momma—would begin laying in supplies. As far as I was concerned, the only thing that counted was my meager collection of dime-store fishing tackle and my BB gun. For weeks I gazed at fishhooks, rolled lead sinkers over my tongue, drenched my Sears, Roebuck 79-cent reel in 3-in-1 oil. To be honest, I don't think I could have made it as a TV kid. For one thing, there were the pimples; and for another thing, I had a tendency to smell in those days—as a result of a lot of time spent in alleys and under porches and crawling through bushes with Schwartz and Flick and Kissel and the motley collection of spotted dogs that always accompanied us wherever we went. Come to think of it, Schwartz and Flick and Kissel smelled, too; which may be why, to one another, none of us smelled. In any event, Right Guard was something we played, not something we squirted on ourselves.

About two weeks or so before the big day, the old man would take the Olds down to Paswinski's Garage for a tune-up, which in our case was purely a cabalistic ritual. It was like fingering a string of beads or burning incense. But southern Michigan was a long way from northern Indiana and the Olds was our only hope. She was a large, hulking four-door sedan of a peculiar faded green color that the old man always called "goat-vomit green." This was his big party joke. He always said it when everybody was eating. The Olds had been in the hands of at least four previous owners, all of whom had left their individuals marks on body and seat, fender and grille.

The week before vacation, the old man would go into high gear. On Monday of the last week, just after supper, he would make the Big Phone Call. Putting through a long-distance call to Michigan was not something that happened every day in our house.

"Is this long distance?" he shouted into the receiver. "Operator, I want to put through a long-distance call to Michigan." The rest of us sat in hushed excitement, trepidation and fear. This was crucial. Would there be a cabin available? The old man played it for all it was worth:

"Marcellus, Michigan. Ollie Hopnoodle's Feed and Grain Store. I wanna talk to Mr. Hopnoodle."

He listened intently, then put his hand over the phone and whispered:

"I can hear 'em ringing him! . . . Hello, Ollie? You old son of a bitch! Guess who this is. . . . Right! How did you guess? . . . We want the green one this year. . . . Yeah, the one on the other side of the outhouse. . . . You did? That's great!

"Ollie had two more holes put in the outhouse," he reported in an aside to us.

"OK, Ollie, see you next week."

The die was cast. We were on our way—almost. The week dragged by interminably—but finally it was Saturday night. All day, my mother had been cleaning up the house for the two-week hiatus, nailing down the screens, locking the basement windows, packing suitcases, trunks, cardboard boxes, laundry bags and wicker baskets with everything she could lay her hands on. The old man, who worked on Saturday, came roaring up the drive, the Olds already snarling in defiance over what was about to occur. He charged into the kitchen, his eyes rolling wildly, his very being radiating sparks of excitement.

"OK, now. This year we're all gonna get up early and we're gonna be on the road by six o'clock. No later! This time we're gonna beat the traffic!"

My mother, who had heard all this before, continued toiling stoically over her enormous pile of effluvia.

"When that alarm goes off at four-thirty," the old man said to no one in particular, "I don't want to hear no griping. OK, now, let's check the list."

Far into the night they went over every can of pork and

beans, every slice of bacon, every box of crackers, every undershirt and rubber band—even the jug of citronella, that foul, fetid liquid mystically (and erroneously) believed to be effective in warding off mosquitoes of the Michigan variety. Finally, sometime after midnight, the uproar slowly petered out.

A few minutes later, the alarm went off and my kid brother and I leaped out of the sack like shots. This was it! From the next bedroom came a muffled curse.

"Fer Chrissake, will ya shut that damn thing off!"

Mutterings from my mother as she put on her slippers in the dark.

"Don't worry," growled the old man in his familiar litany, "I'll get right up. I'm just resting."

More mutterings. "Look, I'm just resting my eyes! I'm getting right up!"

The vacation had begun as it always began. Already, not three minutes old and it was imperceptibly inching downhill. Five minutes later my mother, wearing her rump-sprung Chinese-red chenille bathrobe with tiny flecks of petrified egg on the lapels, her eyes puffed sleepily, peered down at a pot of simmering oatmeal in the clammy kitchen. Outside in the blackness, a few sparrows clinging to telephone wires chirped drowsily, pretending that they were real birds and not just sparrows living in a steel-mill town.

My kid brother and I ran insanely up and down the basement stairs, dragging stuff out of the coalbin that we figured we might need at the lake. For over a month I had been assiduously collecting night crawlers in a

Chase & Sanborn coffee can; I brought them up from the basement to be ready to pack when the time came. I toyed with my oatmeal, but it was such a great day that I actually went ahead and ate it.

My brother, who had been known to go for over two years without eating, was playing Pig in honor of the festive occasion. This was a game invented by my mother to euchre the little runt into eating. It consisted of my mother saying:

"Randy, how does the little piggy go?"

His nostrils would flare, his neck would thicken, his face, redden. He would grunt twice and look for approval to my mother.

"Nice piggy. Here's your trough."

He would give another snort and then shovel his snout deep into the red cabbage, mashed potatoes, oatmeal or whatever it was and slurp it up loudly. He wasn't a TV kid, either. This morning, in excitement, he polished off two troughs of Quaker Oats, usually his quota for a month. My mother, her hair curlers clinking, called out:

"Are you up?" Silence.

"Are you up?" Silence.

"It's getting late."

"SHUT UP, FER CHRISSAKE!"

Wearily, she bent back over the sink. She had been this route before.

Half an hour later, the sun streaming in through the kitchen windows finally flushed the old man out into the open. By now, the mound of impedimenta filled the kitchen and overflowed out onto the back porch. His B.V.D.s hanging limply, the old man weaved unsteadily between the piles and collapsed into a chair.

"Gimme some coffee."

He slumped unshaven, staring numbly at the kitchen table, until my mother set the coffee down in front of him. She did not speak. She knew that this was no time for conversation. He lit a Lucky, took a mighty drag and then sipped gingerly at the scalding black coffee, his eyes glaring malevolently ahead. My old man had begun every day of his life since the age of four with a Lucky and a cup of black coffee. He inhaled each one alternately, grimly, deeply. During this routine, it was sheer suicide to goad him.

The sun rose higher. And higher. It grew hotter and muggier, as only late July in northern Indiana can. The first faint whiff of oil-refinery smoke and blast-furnace dust eddied in through the screen door. Somewhere a cicada screamed into the brightening haze. Clotheslines drooped. My brother and I were busy carrying bags, suitcases and lumpy cardboard cartons tied with string out into the driveway. My mother wordlessly squeezed lemons for the lemonade we always carried along in our big two-gallon Thermos.

The old man stonily began his second cup. Halfway through it, he suddenly looked up, the sun now well over the high-tension wires and striking him full on his stubbled face.

"WELL!" he shouted. "ARE WE ALL SET TO GO?"

This was the signal that the *real* action could begin.

The old man was still alive for another day. It was vacationtime. He had been let out of the pen. My mother, picking up her cue, said:

"Well, everything's about set."

"OK, gimme that list."

He roared around the kitchen, his B.V.D.s flapping obscenely as he rechecked the pile of rubber ducks, beach balls, old inner tubes, spyglasses, straw hats, fielders' mitts —all of it. He rushed into the bathroom to shave and emerged a few minutes later with a wad of toilet paper plastered to a nasty gash on his chin. As I said, he was no TV daddy.

By now, we had moved perhaps a ton and a quarter of stuff out into the weeds of the back yard, which at this time of the year were usually knee high, filled with green caterpillars and millions of stickers. As always, Mrs. Kissel peered wistfully from her kitchen window next door. Since Mr. Kissel never worked, the Kissel family never took vacations.

The neighborhood dogs, sensing that something was afoot, scurried round and round the cardboard cartons, yipping. A couple of them did more than that. Piece by piece, carton by carton, every available inch of the back seat was packed solid. The old man had a Sears luggage rack clamped onto the roof of the Olds. The heavy stuff was loaded on top: comforters, folding camp chairs, beach umbrellas, his set of matched Montgomery Ward golf clubs—all piled high and held down with lengths of clothesline. Those wooden-handled, chrome-headed clubs represented his only foray into the magic world of the "Big People," as he called them, the ones who ran Chevy agencies and sauntered around the course on Sundays in checkered knickers.

At last he crawled in behind the wheel, rolled down his window and peered over a pile of junk next to him to see if my mother was in place. Back in the rear, my brother and I were wedged into two tiny cockpits burrowed into the wall of tightly packed essentials for living. My mother, for some reason, always pretended that going to Clear Lake was something like traveling to the North Pole. You had to be ready for anything. The doors were slammed, windows adjusted, and finally the old man gave his yearly cry:

"OK. Here we go!"

Outside in the yard, a motley collection of well-wishers had gathered, including Flick, Schwartz, Kissel and other smaller fry who moved in the substrata of kid life—nameless, noses running, never invited to play ball.

The old man turned the key in the dash and stepped on the starter. From deep within the bowels of the Oldsmobile came a faint click. He jabbed again at the starter. Another click. His neck reddened.

"Oh, fer Chrissake! That damn starter spring's stuck again!" The sun beat down mercilessly on our wheeled pyramid, the interior growing hotter by the second. Enraged, the old man threw the door open and rushed around to the front of the Olds, shouting:

"TURN THE KEY ON WHEN I JUMP UP AND DOWN ON THE BUMPER!"

He grabbed the radiator ornament, a shoddy copy of

the *Winged Victory*, climbed up on the bumper and began to bounce maniacally up and down. It was a routine we all knew well. The old man, his face beet red, the blood once again dripping from his gashed chin, hopped up and down in a frenzy. Once again, from deep within the Olds, came another faint click. Instantly, the old man shouted:

"DON'T NOBODY MOVE! SIT REAL STILL!"

He tore around the side of the car and eased himself into the driver's seat. It was a touchy moment. Carefully, so as not to create the slightest vibration, he pushed the starter button on the floor.

Gug gug gug gug. . . . It failed to catch.

The old man whispered hoarsely: "Don't nobody breathe."

He tried it again. G-gug gug . . . BBRRROOOOOO-MMMM!

The mighty six-cylinder, low-compression Oldsmobile engine rattled into life, rocker arms clattering, valve springs clanging, pistons slapping. After all, 142,000 miles isn't exactly around the block. He threw her into reverse and slowly she lumbered backward down the driveway, swaying under the immense load of half the available stock of the A. & P.

Safely out on the street, he threw her into first. Painfully she began to roll forward. I peered out of the tiny crack of window available to me, a square of glass no more than three inches across, and saw my assembled friends standing dumbly along the sidewalk. For a brief instant, I felt a deep pang of regret about all the great things that were going to happen in the neighborhood while I was gone. From somewhere off to my left, amid the rumblings of the Olds, I heard the first muffled squeakings of my kid brother.

Two minutes later, we turned down a side road toward the main highway that wended its way listlessly past junk yards and onion patches toward the distant, rolling, sandy hills of Michigan. It was Sunday and already a solid line of automobiles, bumper to bumper, stretched from one horizon to the other, barely moving. The old man, his eyes narrowed with hatred, glared through the windshield at his most ancient and implacable foe —the traffic.

"Damn Sunday drivers! Stupid sons of bitches!"

He was warming up for the big scenes yet to come. As traffic fighters go, he was probably no more talented nor dedicated than most other men of his time. But what he lacked in finesse he more than made up for in sheer ferocity. His vast catalog of invective—learned in the field, so to speak, back of the stockyards on the South Side of Chicago—had enriched every Sunday-afternoon drive we ever took. Some men gain their education about life at their mother's knee, others by reading yellowed volumes of fiction. I nurtured and flowered in the back seat of the Olds, listening to my father.

At least we were on our way. No one could deny that. We crept along in the great line of Sunday traffic, the Olds muttering gloomily as its radiator temperature slowly mounted. My mother occasionally shouted back through the din in our direction:

134

"Are you kids all right?"

All right? I was out of my head with excitement. I looked forward to this moment all year long; it made Christmas and everything else pale to nothing. I had pored over every issue of *Field & Stream* in the barbershop, dreaming about tracking beavers and fording streams and making hunter's stew. Of course, nobody ever *did* any of those things in Michigan, but they were great to read about. One time, our scoutmaster took us out on a hike through Hohman and painted moss on the north side of all the fireplugs, so that we could blaze a trail to the vacant lot behind the Sherwin-Williams sign. But that was about the extent of my expertise in nature lore.

Hour after hour we inched northward, and finally burst out of the heavy traffic and turned onto the rolling, open highway that led through the sandy hills to Marcellus, Michigan. By now it was well along in the afternoon and the temperature inside the car hovered at maybe 15 or 20 degrees below the boiling point. The Olds had a habit of hitting a thrumming, resonant vibration at about 50 that jiggled the bones, loosened the molars, rattled the eyeballs and made all talk totally impossible. But over the roar, a faint squeak filtered through the cartons to my left. My mother turned in her seat, took one look and shouted at the old man to stop the car.

"WHAT THE HELL NOW?" he bellowed, as he pulled over to the side of the road under a pair of great, overhanging Michigan poplars. Everywhere around us the yellow-and-dun fields, mottled with patches of grapevines, stretched out to the horizon.

My mother dashed around the side of the car to my brother's door. I heard him being hauled out of his tiny capsule. Oatmeal, Ovaltine, caterpillars—everything he had downed in the past couple of days gushed out into the lilies.

I sat in my slot, peering out of the window at the alien landscape, my excitement now at fever pitch. Randy always got sick at about this point. That meant we were halfway there. Ashen-faced, he was stuffed back into his hole. Once again, the starter spring stuck. Once again, the old man raged up and down on the bumper. We were off.

It was then that the bombshell struck. Oh, no! OH, *NO!* I slumped deep down into the seat, a two-pound box of rice sliding from the shelf behind me and pouring its contents down the back of my neck. The Oldsmobile boomed on toward Clear Lake and its fighting three-ounce sunfish, its seven-inch bluegills and its five-inch perch, all waiting for me under lily pads, beside submerged logs and in the weed beds. *Oh, no!* I had left all my fishing tackle in the garage, all piled up next to the door, where I had taken it the night before to make sure I wouldn't forget it! Every sinker, every bobber, every hook I had saved for, polished, loved and cherished stood all neatly piled up back home in the garage.

"DAD!" I cried out in anguish. The great thrum of the Olds drowned me out.

"HEY, DAD!"

He glanced into the rearview mirror. "Yeah?"

"I LEFT ALL MY FISHING TACKLE IN THE GA-RAGE!" That meant *his*, too.

"WHAT?!" He straighted up in his sweat-soaked pongee shirt. "YOU DID WHAT?!"

"I . . . I. . . ."

"Oh, fer CHRISSAKE! What next!" He spit through the open window into the onrushing hot air. It arced back into the rear window and missed my brother's head by an inch. My mother had been asleep now for some time. She never stirred through this disaster. Deep in my hole, I wept.

The steady, rumbling oscillation of the ancient Olds rolled back over me. Way down deep inside, the first faint gnawings of car sickness, like some tiny, gray, beady-eyed rat scurrying among my vitals, merged appropriately with the disappointment and the heat. A faint whiff of the sweetish-sour aroma of my kid brother filtered through the camp gear, drifted past my nose and out the window to my right. I stared with glazed eyes at the blur of telephone poles; at a barn with a huge Bull Durham sign on its side, with its slogan, HER HERO; at farmhouse after farmhouse; at a rusty tin sign with its faded message: HOOKED RUGS FOR SALE—ALSO EGGS.

The low hills, green, yellow and brown, wound on and on. I had wrecked the vacation. You might just as well tell Santa Claus to go to hell as leave your split-bamboo casting rod that you saved all year to buy and that had a cork handle and a level-wind Sears, Roebuck reel with a red jewel in the handle, and your Daredevil wiggler, so red and white and chromy, back in the garage amid the bald Goodyears and empty Simoniz cans. Oh, well, nothing ever works out, anyway. My little gray, furry rat reared on its hind legs, his fangs flashing in the darkness.

Over the steady hum of the mighty Olds engine I could hear the pitiful keening of my kid brother, who had now burrowed down to the floor boards in his travail. I stared sullenly out the window over a huge, rolled-up, dark-green comforter and an orange crate full of coffeepots and frying pans.

Suddenly: BA-LOOOMMMMPPP! K-tunk k-tunk kk-tunk k-tunk.

The car reeled drunkenly under the wrenching blows of a disintegrating Allstate tire. In the front seat, the driver wrestled with the heaving steering wheel. Overloaded by a quarter ton at least, the car continued to lurch forward.

Ding ding ding ding. It was down to the rim now. My father hauled back on the emergency brake. We slued up onto the gravel shoulder of the highway and rolled to a limping stop. He cut the ignition; but for a full 20 seconds or so, the motor continued to turn over, firing on sheer heat. Finally, she coughed twice and stopped. Dead silence enveloped us all. My father sat unmoving behind the wheel, his hands clenched on the controls in silent rage.

"Do you think it's a flat?" my mother chirped helpfully, her quick, mechanical mind analyzing the situation with deadly accuracy.

"No, I don't think it could be that. Probably we ran over a pebble." His voice was low, almost inaudible, drenched in sarcasm.

"I'm glad to hear that," she sighed with relief. "I thought for a minute we might have had a flat."

He stared out his window at the seared corn stalks across the road, watching the corn borers destroy what was left of the crops after the locusts had finished their work. We sat for possibly two minutes, frozen in time and space like flies in amber.

Then, in the lowest of all possible voices, he breathed toward the cornfield: "Balls."

Very quietly he opened the door, climbed out and stalked back to the trunk.

"ALL A' YA GET OUT!" he shouted.

My mother, realizing by this time that it hadn't been a pebble after all, whispered: "Now, don't get on his nerves. And don't whine."

The four of us gathered on the dusty gravel. Along the road behind us for a quarter mile at least, chunks of black, twisted rubber smoked in the sun and marked our trail of pain.

The old man silently opened the trunk, peered into the tangled mess of odds and ends that always filled it and began to rummage glumly among the shards. He removed the clamp that released the spare tire. In his world, spare tires were tires that had long since been given extreme unction but had somehow clung to a thread of life and perhaps a shred or two of rubber. Next, the jack.

We sat at a safe distance next to the cornfield, in the shade of an elm tree suffering from oak blight.

"Let's have a picnic while Daddy fixes the tire," suggested Mother cheerfully.

Daddy, his shirt drenched in sweat, tore his thumbnail off while trying to straighten out the jack handle, which was insanely jointed in four different spots, making it as pliable as a wet noodle and about as useful. While he cursed and bled, we opened the lunch basket and fished out the warm cream-cheese sandwiches and the lunch-meat-and-relish sandwiches.

"Gimme a peanut-butter-and-jelly sandwich," said my kid brother.

"We don't have peanut-butter-and-jelly."

"I want a peanut-butter-and-jelly sandwich."

"We have nice tuna and egg-salad sandwiches. On rye bread. You can pick the seeds out and have fun making believe they're little bugs."

"I WANT PEANUT-BUTTER-AND-JELLY!" Randy's voice was rising to a shrill pitch. Off in the middle distance, the jack clanked and rattled as the Olds teetered precariously on the flimsy metal support.

"GODDAMN IT! IN TWO SECONDS, I'M GONNA COME OVER AND BAT YOU ONE GOOD!" yelled the tire repairman.

Randy threw his tuna-salad sandwich out into the road, where it was instantly smashed flat by a Mack truck. Our little picnic went on. We drank lemonade, ate cookies.

Finally came the call: "OK. Pile in."

"How 'bout some music," my mother asked rhetorically as we rolled out onto the highway.

My father stonily drove on. Sometimes, after a particularly bad flat, he didn't speak to the family for upward of two weeks. I suspect that he always pictured heaven as a place where everybody was issued a full set of brand-new, four-ply U. S. Royal roadmasters, something he never in his life attained, at least on this earth.

My mother fiddled with the car radio, which hummed and crackled.

> *"Roll out the barrel*
> *We'll have a barrel of fun*
> *Roll out the barrel*
> *We've got the blues on the run. . . ."*

The Andrews Sisters were always rolling out barrels and having fun.

"Isn't that nice? Now, how 'bout playing a game, kids? What am I thinking of—animal, vegetable or mineral?"

We always played games in the car, like who could tell quicker what kind of car was coming toward us; or Count the Number of Cows; or Beaver, where the first guy who saw a red truck or a blue Chevy or a Coca-Cola sign could hit the other guy if he hollered "Beaver" first. Then there was Padiddle, which was generally played when there were girls in the car and had a complicated scoring system involving burned-out headlights, the highest point getter being a police car running one-eyed. But Padiddle was never played in cars carrying mothers and kid brothers.

"*NOW* what the hell!" My father had broken his vow of silence.

Ahead, across the highway, stretched a procession of sawhorses with flashing lights and arrows and a sign, reading: ROAD UNDER CONSTRUCTION—DETOUR AHEAD 27.8 MILES.

Muttering obscenities, the old man veered to the right, onto a slanting gravel cow path. Giant bulldozers and road graders roared all around us.

"Holy God! This'll kill that spare!"

The Olds crashed into a hole. The springs bottomed. She bellowed forward, throwing gravel high into the air. The trail wound through a tiny hamlet—and then, a fork, where a red arrow pointed to the right: CONTINUE DETOUR. The road to the left was even narrower than the other, marked with a battered black-and-white tin sign perforated with rusting .22-caliber bullet holes: COUNTY ROAD 872 (ALTERNATE).

We fishtailed to a stop, yellow dust pouring in the windows.

"Gimme that map!"

The old man reached across the dashboard and snapped open the glove compartment just as a truck rumbled past, raining gravel onto the windshield and along the side of the car.

"What the hell is THIS?" He yanked his hand convulsively out of the glove compartment. It dripped a dark, viscous liquid.

"OK," he said with his best Edgar Kennedy slow burn. "Who stuck a Hershey bar in the glove compartment?" No one spoke.

"All right, who did it?" He licked his fingers disgustedly.

"What a goddamn mess!"

The mystery of the Hershey bar was the subject of bitter wrangling off and on for years afterward. I know that *I* didn't stick it in there. If my brother had gotten hold of a Hershey bar, he would have eaten it instantly. It never did come out—but then, neither did the chocolate; forevermore, the Oldsmobile had a chocolate-lined glove compartment.

My father pored over the creased and greasy map. "Aha! Eight-seven-two. Here it is. It goes through East Jerusalem and hits four-three-eight. I'll tell you what. I'll bet we can beat this detour by crossing through four-three-eight to this one with the dotted red line, nine-seven-four. Then we'll cut back and hit the highway the other side of Niles."

Two and a half hours later, we were up to our hubs in a swamp. Overhead, four large crows circled angrily at the first disturbance their wilderness had seen in years. After backing and filling for half an hour, we finally managed to regain semisolid ground on the corduroy road that we had been thumping over for the past hour or so. None of us spoke. We long ago had learned not to say a word in times like these.

Our spattered, battered hulk hauled itself, at long last, back onto the main highway, after traveling over patches of country that had not been seen by the eye of man since Indian times.

"I knew I'd beat the damn detour." When my father *really* loused up, he always tried to pretend it was not only deliberate but a lot of fun.

"Did you kids see those big crows? Weren't they big? And I bet you never saw quicksand before. That was really something, wasn't it?"

Leaving a trail of mud, we rumbled along smoothly for a few minutes on the blessed concrete.

"How 'bout some of those Mary Janes? Would you kids like some Mary Janes?" He was now in a great mood.

My mother scratched around in the luggage a few moments until she found a cellophane bag full of the dentist's delight. "Be careful how you chew 'em," she cautioned us futilely, "because if you're not, they'll pull your fillings out."

The sound of our munching was drowned out by the RRRAAAAWWWRRRR of a giant, block-long truck as it barreled past our struggling flivver, eclipsing us in a deep shadow. As the truck roared past, inches away, sucking the car into its slip stream, an overwhelming cacophony of sound engulfed us—a sea of insane squawks and cluckings.

"Chickens!" Randy hollered ecstatically.

Thousands of chickens peered at us through the windows on our left side. Stretching for a mile back of us, a wall of Leghorns was going by. Then they were past us and the mammoth truck pulled into the lane directly ahead of us, shedding a stream of white feathers that struck the windshield and billowed around us and in the windows like a summer snowstorm. Almost immediately we were enveloped in a wrenching, fetid, kick-in-the-stomach stench; it swept over us in a tidal wave of nausea.

"When the swallows come back to Capistrano . . ." the Inkspots chimed in on the radio.

"Gaak! What a stink!!"

"Maybe you'd better pass him," suggested my mother through her handkerchief.

"Yeah. Here goes."

He floored the Olds, but nothing happened. She was already going her limit. Ahead, the driver of the chicken truck settled into the groove, a lumbering juggernaut rolling along at 55, spraying feathers and a dark-brown aroma over the countryside. Again and again, the old man edged out into the left lane, gamely trying to pass, but it was no use. The truck stayed tantalizingly just out of reach, the chickens squawking delightedly, their necks sticking out of the iron cages, their beady red eyes wild with excitement, as the driver happily headed to market. Occasionally, a stray egg whistled past or splashed into the radiator grille to join the dead butterflies, grasshoppers and dragonflies.

"I have to go to the toilet." Already we had stopped at 74 gas stations so that Randy could go to the toilet. His output was incredible.

"You'll just have to hold it."

It had begun to rain—big ripe summer drops. The

windshield wipers were stuck and now my father drove
with his head craned out the window in order to see.
Rain ricocheted off his face and splattered everything
within a two-foot radius. It carried with it chicken
feathers and other by-products that streamed back from
the truck ahead. But this was not the first time we had
been caught behind moving livestock. A load of ducks
make chickens a pure joy. And one time we had been
trapped for over four hours behind 37 sheep and at
least 200 exuberantly ripe porkers on U.S. 41.

The rain suddenly stopped, just when the menagerie
boomed into a turnoff, and peace reigned once again.
A few feathers clung to the headlights here and there,
but the last lingering aroma of the barnyard finally departed through the rear windows. Then:

"WAAAH! I GOTTA WEEWEE!"

"All *right!* But this is the last time, ya hear?"

No answer. Randy was promising nothing. Ahead, a
one-pump gas station crouched amid the cornfields next
to a white shack that had once been a diner but was
now sinking into the clay, carrying with it its faded red
sign with the single word EAT. Under a rusted soft-drink
cooler sprawled a mangy hound, who greeted our arrival
by opening one rheumy eye and lifting a leg to scratch
wearily and indiscriminately at his undernourished
room-and-boarders.

We pulled up next to the pump. A thin, creased, dusty
old man wearing a blue work shirt and faded jeans sat
chewing a toothpick beside the screen door on an old

146

wooden chair, with his feet on a "Phillips 66" oil drum. He didn't stir.

"Fillerup, bub?"

"The kid's gotta go to the toilet."

He shifted the toothpick. "Round the side, past them tires."

"You can check the oil while we're waiting."

Taking one foot off the oil drum, then the other, the man struggled to his feet with painful deliberation, shuffled over to the car and fiddled with the hood latch for a minute or so. Finally getting the knack of it, he yanked it open, leaned over the engine, pulled out the dipstick and held it up. It dripped rich, viscous sludge onto the gravel.

"Needs about two and a half quarts." It *always* needed two and a half quarts. "You want the good stuff or the cheap stuff?"

"The cheap stuff. Put in the heaviest ya got." The old crate burned oil like a diesel.

My mother and Randy were back in the car now. It was a typical pit stop on our long caravan route to Clear Lake and paradise.

Doggedly, we swung back out onto the highway. Randy relieved, the Olds refreshed. A mile up the road, my mother, making conversation, said:

"Why didn't you get gas?"

"I didn't want any of that cheap bootleg gas that guy had. I'm waiting for a Texas Blue Station."

"The gauge says empty. Maybe you shoulda got some."

"That gauge is cockeyed. When it says empty, there's

over an eighth of a tank left. There oughta be a Texas Blue station ahead."

Texas Blue was an obscure gasoline that had at one time sponsored the Chicago White Sox ball games on radio, thereby winning my father's undying patronage. If Texas Blue backed the White Sox, it was *his* gas. He would have used it if they had distilled it from old cabbages.

Thirty seconds later, the car sputtered to a stop, bone dry. After sitting stony-faced for a long time behind the wheel, the old man silently opened the door, got out, slammed it, opened the trunk, took out the red can he always carried and continually used, slammed the lid shut and set out without a word for the gas station we had left a mile and a half behind. He plodded over the horizon and was gone.

We played animal, vegetable or mineral and drank more warm lemonade while we waited in the steamy heat. Forty minutes later he returned, his two gallon can filled to the brim with gas so cheap you could hear it knocking in the container. He smelled heavily of both gasoline and bourbon. He poured the former into the tank and shortly thereafter we once again entered the mainstream of humanity.

A single red sign stuck in the road's shoulder at a crazy angle whizzed by; in white letters, it read: LISTEN, BIRDS. My father lit another Lucky and leaned forward on the alert, peering through the bug-spattered windshield.

THESE SIGNS COST MONEY. The second red-and-white

announcement flashed by, followed quickly by the third:
SO ROOST AWHILE.

The old man flicked his match out the side window,
his neck craning in anticipation of the snapper. We
drove on. And on. Had some crummy, rotten fiend stolen
the punch line? Another sign loomed over the next hill.
He squinted tensely.

GENUINE CHERRY CIDER FOR SALE.

"Fer Chrissake!" he muttered amid the thrumming uproar and the constant ping of kamikaze gnats and bettles
on the spattered windshield. But finally it came, half
hidden next to a gnarled oak tree at the far end of a
long, sweeping curve: BUT DON'T GET FUNNY.

I didn't get it. But then, I didn't get much of anything
in those days. A few yards farther on, the sponsor's name
flashed by: BURMA-SHAVE. Up front, the old man cackled
appreciatively; his favorite form of reading, next to the
Chicago Herald-American sports section, was Burma
Shave signs. He could recite them like a Shakespearean
scholar quoting first folios. He had just added another
gem to his repertoire. In the months to come, it would be
referred to over and over, complete to location, time of
day and pertinent weather information. In fact, he and
his pal Zudock even invented their own Burma-Shave
signs—pungent, unprintable and *single-entendre*. It would
have been a great ad campaign, if the Burma-Shave
company had the guts to do it.

It began to rain again. My father rolled up his window
part way. Normally, the atmosphere in the Olds in full
cry was a faint, barely discernible blue haze, an aromatic

mixture of exhaust fumes from the split muffler, a whiff of manifold heat, burning oil, sizzling grease, dust from the floor boards, alcoholic steam from the radiator and the indescribably heady aroma of an antique tangerine, left over from last year's trip, that had rolled under the front seat and gotten wedged directly in front of the heater vent. Now subtly blended with this oleo were the heavenly scents of wet hay, tiger lilies, yellow clay and fermenting manure.

Ahead of us, a house trailer towed by a Dodge drifted from side to side as they, too, rumbled on toward two weeks away from it all. The old man muttered:

"Lousy Chicago drivers"—a litany he repeated over and over to himself, endlessly, while driving. It must have had the same sort of soothing effect on him that prayer wheels and mystic slogans had on others. He firmly believed that almost all accidents, directly or indirectly, were caused by Chicago drivers, and that if they could all be barred at birth from getting behind a wheel, cars could be made without bumpers and the insurance companies could turn their efforts into more constructive channels.

"Look at that nut!" The old man muttered to himself as the house trailer cut across the oncoming lane and rumbled out of sight up a gravel road, trailing a thick cloud of yellow dust.

My mother was now passing out Wrigley's Spearmint chewing gum. "This'll keep you from getting thirsty," she counseled sagely.

We were doing well, all things considered, having

stopped for Randy at only 75 gas stations so far. After licking off the sweet, dry coating of powdered sugar, I chewed the gum for a while and leafed restlessly through a Donald Duck Big Little Book that I'd brought along to pass the time; but I was too excited and kind of sick to worry about old Donald and Dewey and Huey and Louie.

Suddenly the front seat was in a great uproar. I sat up. My mother screamed and shrank away toward the door. The old man shouted above her shrieks:

"Fer Chrissake, it's only a *bee*. It's not gonna kill you!"

A big fat bumblebee zoomed over the pots and pans and groceries, banging from window to window as my mother, flailing her tattered copy of *True Romance*, cowered screaming on the floor boards next to the gear-shift. The bee zoomed low over her, banked sharply upward and began walking calmly up the inside of the windshield, like he knew just what he was doing. Every year, a bee got in the car—the same bee. My mother had an insane fear of being stung. She had read in *Ripley's Believe It or Not!* that a bee sting had killed a man named Howard J. Detweiler in Canton, Ohio, and she never forgot it. The subject came up often around our house, especially in the summer, and my mother invariably quoted Ripley, who was universally recognized as an ultimate authority on everything. She screamed again.

"Goddamn it! Shut up! Do you want me to have an accident?" my father bellowed. He pulled off to the side of the road, flung his door open and began the chase.

"Gimme the rag outta the side pocket!" he yelled.

My mother, shielding her head with her magazine, interrupted her whimpering long enough to shriek: "Where is he? I can hear him!"

The bee strolled casually up the windshield a few inches farther, humming cheerfully to himself. The old man tore around to the other side of the car to get the rag himself. Sensing that he had made his point, the bee revved his motors with a loud buzz and was out the window. He disappeared back down the road into the lowering skies of early evening, obviously getting set for the next Indiana car to show up over the hill.

"He got away, the bastard!" My father slid back into his seat, threw the Olds into gear and pulled back out onto the asphalt.

"OK, he's gone. You can get up now." His voice dripped with scorn.

My mother crawled back up into her seat, flushed and shaking slightly, and said in a weak voice: "You never can tell about bees. I read once where. . . ."

My father snorted in derision: "Howard J. Detweiler! I'd like to know where that goddamn bee stung him that it killed him. I'll bet I know where it got him!" he roared.

"Shhhh. The kids are listening."

"Hey, look! There's Crystal Lake." My father pointed off to the left.

I sat bolt upright. Way off past a big gray farmhouse and a bank of black trees under the darkening sky was a tiny flash of water.

A gravel road slanted off into the trees, bracketed by a thicket of signs: BOATS FOR RENT BATHING FISHING OVERNIGHT CABINS BEER EATS. We were in vacationland.

Oh, boy! In the back seat, I had broken out into a frenzied sweat. In just a few minutes, we would be there at that one-and-only place where everything happened: Clear Lake! For months, when the snow piled high around the garage and the arctic wind whistled past the blast furnaces, into the open hearth and around the back porch, under the eaves and through the cracks in the window sills, I had lain tossing on my solitary pallet and dreaming of Clear Lake, imagining myself flexing my magnificent split-bamboo casting rod, drifting toward the lily pads, where a huge bronzeback—an evil, legendary smallmouthed bass named Old Jake—waited to meet his doom at my hands.

I would see myself showing my dad how to tie a royal-coachman fly, which I had read about in *Sports Afield*. He would gasp in astonishment. I also astounded my mother in these dreams by demonstrating an encyclopedic grasp of camp cookery. I had practically memorized an article entitled "How to Prepare the Larger Game Fish." The text began: "A skillful angler knows how to broil landlocked salmon and lake trout in the 25-to-40-pound weight range. . . ." I had never *seen*, let alone cooked, a salmon or a trout or a pike or anything else—except for little sunfish, perch, bullheads and the wily crappie—but I was ready for them.

We rounded a familiar curve and rolled past a green cemetery dotted with drooping American flags. Steaming, the Olds slowed to a crawl as we inched past the general store, with a cluster of yellow cane poles leaning against its wooden front amid a pile of zinc washtubs. We had arrived.

"Now, look, you kids stay in the car. HEY, OLLIE!" the old man shouted out of the side window toward the feed store. "HEY, OLLIE, WE'RE HERE!"

Through the rain-spattered windshield, we could see that a few lights were on here and there in the ram-shackle white-clapboard buildings overhung with willows and sweeping elm trees that lined the street. A tall figure in overalls strolled across the sidewalk and plunked his size-14 clodhopper on the running board, battered farmer's straw hat pushed to the back of his head.

"By God, ya made it." His Adam's apple, the size of a baseball, bobbed up and down his skinny neck like a yo-yo.

"Yep. We're here, Ollie."

"How was the trip?"

"Pretty good. Got a bee in the car, though."

"Back just before ya hit Crystal Lake?"

"That's right."

"Just before ya come to Henshaw's barn?"

"Yep."

"Gol durn. That son of a gun's been doin' that all summer. Got me twice."

Ollie owned six cabins on the shore of Clear Lake, which was rimmed solidly with a thick incrustation of summer shacks—except at the north end, where the lake was swampy and the mosquitoes swarmed.

"I saved the green one for you. She's all set. I emptied out the boat this morning."

A jolting shot of excitement ripped through me. The boat! *Our* boat, which I would row and anchor and bail out, and hang onto and cast my split-bamboo rod— My split-bamboo rod! I had forgotten for hours that I had left it all back in the garage.

"How's the fishing this year?" asked the old man.

"Well, now, it's a funny thing you asked. They sure were hittin' up to about a week or ten day ago. Guy from Mishawaka stayin' in cabin three got his limit a' walleye every day. But they slacked off 'bout a week ago. Ain't hittin' now."

"I guess I shoulda been here last week." It was always "last week" at Clear Lake.

"They might hit crickets. I got some for sale."

"I'll be over in the morning to pick some up, Ollie. I got a feeling we're gonna hit 'em big this year." The old man never gave up.

We turned off the main highway and drove along the beloved, twisting dirt road—now a river of mud—that led through cornfields and meadows, down toward the magical lake.

"Ollie looks skinnier," my mother said.

"He's just got new overalls," my father answered, sluing the Olds around a sharp bend. Night was coming on fast as it does in the Michigan lake country, black and chill. The rain had picked up. In the back seat, I was practically unconscious with excitement as the first cottages hove into view. Between them and the trees that ringed them was the dark, slate void of the lake.

"She looks high," my father said. He always pretended to be an expert on everything, including lakes. Already my mother was plucking at pickle jars, Brillo pads, clothespins, rolls of toilet paper and other drifting odds and ends of stuff that she had banked around her in the front seat.

Next to every cottage but one was a parked car pulled up under the trees. Down in the lake, I could make out the pier and the black swinging wedges of Ollie's leaky rowboats. A few yellow lights gleamed from the dark cottages onto the green, wet leaves of the trees.

"Well, there she is."

Our lights swept over the rear of a starboard-leaning, green-shingled, screen-enclosed cabin. Above the back door, painted on a weathered two-by-four, was the evocative appellation HAVEN OF BLISS. All of Ollie's other cottages had names, too: BIDE-A-WEE, REST-A-SPELL, DEW DROP INN, NEVA-KARE, SUN-N-FUN.

We inched under the trees. My father switched off the Olds. With a great, gasping shudder, she sank into a deep stupor, her yearly trial by fire half over. The rain was coming down hard now, pounding on the roof of the car and dripping off the trees all around us. I tumbled out of the back door—plunging into mud up to my ankles—and began sloshing my way down through the wet bushes and undergrowth to the lake. Behind me, I could hear my kid brother already whining that the mosquitoes were biting him. There at my feet, lapping quietly at the rocks, the black water faintly aglow, was Clear Lake.

In the darkness a few feet offshore, I could dimly make out our wooden boat, the waves slapping against its side.

K-thunk . . . K-thunk . . . K-splat . . . Plop . . . Plop. . . . One of the most exciting sounds known to man.

"Hey, come on! We gotta unload! Everything's getting wet!" my father shouted down through the trees.

I slogged back up the path, splopping and slipping and skidding and cracking my shins against tree stumps. My father and mother were tugging at the tarpaulin that covered the luggage rack on the roof. The rain poured down unrelentingly.

"Where the hell's the flashlight? Don't tell me we forgot the FLASHLIGHT!"

"I thought you brought it," my mother answered from the dark deluge.

"OH, JESUS CHRIST! WHAT THE HELL *DID* WE BRING?"

"Well, you made up the list."

"How the hell can your forget the FLASHLIGHT?"

"Well, if you had gotten up when you said you would, you—"

"SHUT UP! I don't have no time to argue. This stuff's getting soaked!"

My mother disappeared into the cabin. "The lights aren't working," she called out into the rain a moment later.

My father didn't even bother to answer that one. If

she had said the roof was gone and there was a moose in the bedroom, it wouldn't have surprised him. He staggered past me, reeling under an enormous cardboard box full of pots, pans, baking powder, rubber ducks and ping-pong paddles.

"Don't just stand around. *Do* something!" he bellowed to everyone within hearing. "DAMN IT, DO I HAVE TO DO *EVERYTHING?*"

I grabbed a beach ball from the back seat, waded through the clay and groped my way up the rickety back steps. Inside, the cabin smelled of rotting wood, wet shingles, petrified fish scales and dead squirrels. My father had struck a match, which dimly lit up the worn linoleum and bare boards of the kitchen.

"Why the hell didn't Ollie turn on the juice? That's what I want to know!" he raged, flicking his match around in the dimness.

"Hey, here's a kerosene lantern!" my mother said excitedly. Above the tin sink, on a shelf, stood a dusty glass lamp half full of cloudy yellow oil.

"OUCH! DAMN IT!" The match had burned down to the old man's thumb. Sound of fumbling and scratching and cursing in the darkness. Finally, another match flared.

"Gimme that lousy lamp."

He lifted off the black, smoky chimney and applied the match to the wick, turning up the knob on the side as he did so. It sputtered and hissed.

"DON'T BREATHE ON THE MATCH!" he yelled.

At last the wick caught hold and a steady blue-yellow flame lit up the primitive kitchen. We rushed out into the dark and for the next hour lugged wet sacks, bags, blankets, fielders' mitts, all of it, into the kitchen, until at long last the Olds, a ton and a half lighter, shook itself in relief and settled down for a two-week rest.

My mother had been sorting it all out as we dragged it in, carrying blankets and bedding into the little wooden cubicles that flanked the kitchen. When it was all indoors, the old man stripped off his soaked shirt and sprawled out on a lumpy blue kitchen chair.

"Well, here we are." He grinned, water dripping down over his ears. "Boy, am I hungry!"

My mother had already opened a can of Spam. We sat amid the boxes, downing two-inch-thick sandwiches.

"We gotta set the alarm, because we wanna get out real early to fish," announced the old man between bites.

My kid brother was already asleep in the next room.

"If ya wanna get the big ones, ya gotta get up early!" His eyes gleamed brightly in the glow of the kerosene lamp. "They always bite good after a rain. Yessir!"

But it was all back in the garage—my rod, my reel, my father's tackle box, his bobbers, his Secret Gypsy Fish Bait Oil that he had bought from the mail-order catalog.

"But, Dad, don't you remember I told you. . . ." I began miserably.

"So how come I found it on top of the car? I wonder who put all that fishing stuff on top of the car? Hmmmm . . . . I guess somebody must have snuck up and put it on top of the car when you weren't looking."

Ten minutes later, I lay in the dark, ecstatic with

relief and expectation, huddled under damp blankets and a musty comforter. The rain roared steadily on the roof— as it would for the next two weeks—and drummed metronomically onto the bare wooden floor beside my bed.

K-thunk . . . K-thunk . . . Plop . . . Plop . . . Plop. . . .

The boat called to me from the dark lake. From somewhere out in the woods, something squeaked twice and then was silent. My kid brother tossed and whimpered softly from beneath his pillow; and across the room, my father's low, muttering snores thrummed quietly in the night. We were on vacation.

THE STAR-CROSSED ROMANCE
OF JOSEPHINE COSNOWSKI

Lustiki! read the marquee in letters three feet high. Must be Lithuanian for lust, I mused, jogging from foot to foot to keep warm in the long line of Manhattan art-film fanciers in front of the East Side's smart new Cinema 69, their ascetic faces flushed in anticipation of another evening of artful montages, elegant pans, gracefully executed dissolves. I glanced at the posters that rimmed the box office. One of them read:

LESBIA, AN IDEALISTIC YOUNG PEASANT GIRL, TRAVELS TO THE BIG CITY IN SEARCH OF TRUTH. STARRING LUD-VICKA BELLICOSNICK AND DIRECTED BY MILOS PEDER-ASTINCKI, THE 13-YEAR-OLD SENSATION.
"A SEARING EXPERIENCE" . . . NY TIMES "SMASHING" . . . REX REED

Lesbia herself, bosoms ripe as Indiana cantaloupes, her peasant eyes widely spaced in her magnificent Slavic face, appeared to be enjoying a transcendental sexual climax with a Viet Cong irregular.

The throng around me looked like a Fellini crowd scene: squat females in leather jackets carrying bull-whips, coveys of razor-thin, trilling creatures of inde-terminate sex in velvet jerkins and elf shoes, a few scowling, bearded revolutionaries in full Zapata attire, their denim jackets abristle with OFF THE PIGS buttons. The light from the marquee glinted from the polished lenses of hundreds of pairs of rose and blue sunglasses, some as large as dinner plates. A sizable contingent of Shoshone Indians in beaded headbands and fringed deer-skin jackets exchanged mystic signs, their voices oddly Bronx-tinged as only CCNY braves' can be.

Others were clad in castoff costumes from Joan Craw-ford pictures: padded shoulders, frumpy skirts, sequined wedgies, ringlet curls and feather boas. Here and there a Grand Concourse version of Humphrey Bogart sneered condescendingly at the mob, cigarette drooping sardoni-cally from a lower lip. A few Belmondos and several Warhols added vivid accents to the mosaic. A Salvation Army Santa Claus at the curb, his Kriss Kringle costume hopelessly *démodé*, rang his bell listlessly above the clamor. I tugged at the bill of my Jackie Coogan tweed cap, setting it more firmly on my head as I shivered slightly under my Clint Eastwood paisano serape, my Fred Astaire two-tone patent-leather pumps pitifully in-adequate to the December slush.

After the show—which turned out to be a flawed but compelling black-comedic existential skin flick in the drolly amusing Sacher-Masoch genre—I eased into a booth at Le Bagel Vérité, a favorite haunt of cinemagoers in the neighborhood. Sipping a mug of mocha absinthe, described on the menu as the favorite of John Barrymore, I found myself studying a striking poster on the wall amid the likenesses of Paul Newman, Marlon Brando, Peter Fonda, Ché Guevara and Charley Brown. It was my old friend Ludvicka, "Don't I know you from someplace?" I reflected, the absinthe flowing like tepid laval through my veins.

Of course! It hit me. Every male I ever knew believed that foreign girls, even if they're just from the next town, were infinitely sexier than the ordinary homegrown product. I laughed ironically in my Sidney Greenstreet manner, as I often do when my mind takes a philosophical turn. Then, painfully, it all began to come back—my own almost forgotten adventure in alien sensuality, foreign passion, forbidden fruit.

It began innocently enough a couple of weeks before Christmas in the northern-Indiana steel-mill town where I festered as a youth. It was just before Christmas vacation, already deep into a bitterly cold winter, and I was shuffling idly through clots of drifted, soot-covered snow, my mind drifting aimlessly like a semi-deflated blimp. I was between romances. A brief, disastrous fling with Elizabeth Mae Longnecker had petered out in late November, when I discovered she wore earmuffs and galoshes with snaps. Somehow she had seemed *different* on the tennis courts.

I was coming home late from band practice, my

left shoulder still aching from the weight of my sousa-phone, lips tingling from the last 24 bars of *The 1812 Overture*, when I sniffed a pungent aroma that was to play a dramatic part in the erotic history of my kidhood. I sniffed again. It was vaguely familiar, yet strange—and mysteriously exciting.

The elusive aroma mingled with the rotten-egg smell of the Grasselli Chemical Works, the swamp-gas exhalation of the Sinclair refining plant, the smoldering, metallic miasma of the blast-furnace dust that formed our daily breathing air.

As I got closer and closer to home, the aroma grew even lustier.

It was then that I noticed *lights* coming from the Bumpus house next door. The infamous house had been empty since the moiling Bumpus clan, a mob that made Genghis Khan's hordes look like a Cub Scout Jamboree, had stealthily departed in the night with their blue tick hounds and their gallon jugs of corn likker, leaving unpaid rent and a yard full of garbage behind. I looked curiously at the lighted windows. After the Bumpus family, there was no telling *what* might show up. I went up our back porch and into the kitchen, already feeling a vague, rising excitement.

"HEY, MA. . . ."

"How many times do I have to tell you to take off your overshoes out on the porch?"

"Yeah. Ma, who . . . ?"

"I said take 'em off on the porch. Now! Look at my floor!"

I went back out on the porch, kicked off my overshoes and darted back into the kitchen. My kid brother sat at the kitchen table, glaring sullenly at an arithmetic book.

"Hey, Ma, who moved in next door?"

She didn't answer, being busy at the moment sliding a meat loaf covered with tomato sauce into the oven. The radio on the refrigerator whined:

> When the deep purpulll fallz
> Over sleepy garden wallllzz. . . .

"Would you turn that radio down? I can't hear a word you're saying."

Flushed after her usual struggle with the oven door, which had a bad catch and hardly ever closed right unless it was slammed four times, my mother straightened up and wiped her hands on a kitchen towel. I reached up and turned the radio down just as the back door opened and in came my old man, snow showering off him as he stamped and snorted.

"Holy Christ, it's cold enough to freeze off a brass monkey's. . . ."

"Please. The kids are listening." She caught him just in time.

"Hey, what the hell's that I smell? You cookin' somethin' new for supper?" he asked suspiciously, being strictly a meat-and-potatoes man who viewed all divergences from that basic menu as an effete affectation. He truly believed that the only food people really liked was meat and potatoes and that they just pretended to like other things in order to impress each other.

"It's coming from next door," my mother answered absently as she set the table.

"Next door? Y' mean they're actually cookin' supper over at the Kissels?" His voice rose in disbelief. Lud Kissel, our other next-door neighbor, had given up eating food years before, about the time he discovered bourbon, on which he subsisted entirely except for periods when he had to settle for gin. Since he had given up eating— and working—the rest of the family lived on cornflakes.

"No, from the Bumpus house."

"THE BUMPUSES!" He blew up, rushing to the window. "Don't tell me them bastards are back! Goddamnit, if I have to kick another of them lousy hounds. . . ."

One of his worst fears was that the Bumpuses would move back next door, just to drive him crazy. The memory of that shiftless swarm of tobacco-spitting, raw-boned, gimlet-eyed primitives was still an open wound in my father's psyche.

The heady aroma from next door filled our kitchen like a cloud of exotic gas. Suddenly, without warning, as the old man peered into the darkness, a loud musical thumping, heavy and rhythmic, added to the clamor.

"What the hell is that?" The old man's voice was tinged with trepidation. We remembered all too well the sleepless nights we spent while the Bumpuses' ever-twanging Victrola filled the night air with the nasal sounds of Ernest Tubb, the Delmore Twins and Cowboy

Copas. It was the first note of a barrage of thumpings that was to continue for some time.

"Well, here we go again." My father slumped into his chair at the kitchen table and opened a can of Atlas Praeger.

"I think I know what that smell is," said my mother with quiet authority.

"Yeah?"

"That smells to me like stuffed cabbage."

The old man looked up from his beer. "It does smell like stuffed cabbage. But there's somethin' else." He sniffed the air.

"I think they're cooking blood soup, too." My mother said it as if everybody cooked blood soup every night.

"*Blood* soup!" My father gagged briefly on his beer.

"AAAGGHH!" My kid brother had joined the discussion. He was a notoriously picky eater.

"Yes. Irma Kissel says they're Polish."

"Boy, that's a relief!" The old man said it like he meant it. "For a second there, I thought we had the Bumpuses back. Sometimes I get nightmares dreamin' about all that guitar playin' and them dogs yappin', and that old bastard spittin' tobacco juice into our driveway."

POLISH! I thought, suddenly alert. "Do they have any kids?" I asked.

"I'm not sure, but I think there's two or three boys. And. . . ." she stirred the mashed potatoes expertly, salting them lightly with her left hand, ". . . I believe there's a girl."

My father had lost all interest in the subject and was

deep in the sports page. As long as the Bumpuses weren't coming back, he didn't care who moved in.

A *girl!* A *Polish* girl! A wave of ecstasy shuddered through my frame. Our neighborhood was singularly lacking in girls of any kind. For some reason, practically every kid in the neighborhood was a male. The only place we ran into actual girls was at school, and they all lived in mysterious neighborhoods far from ours. Of course, there was Esther Jane Alberry, squat, truculent and morose; and there was Helen Weathers, who had hair like a football helmet and who weighed 200 pounds soaked in sweat, which she almost always was; and there was Eileen Akers, in her thick glasses, who spent all of her time at the library. But they didn't count. Though Schwartz, Junior Kissel and I talked a lot about girls, it was mostly hypothetical.

"Her name's Josephine," said my mother. "She's about your age. She goes to All Saints School."

I struggled to maintain my composure, but inwardly I reeled. My god, the jackpot! A Polish girl my age had moved next door to me!

A prime universal belief among my peers was that the girls of the next town, East Chicago, were fantastic, and that the most fantastic of all were Polish girls. There was never any scientific evidence. It wasn't necessary. It was just an established fact. Sometimes when Flick got his old man's car, we'd go to East Chicago to ride around with the windows open just *looking* at Polish girls walking around the streets. We'd holler out at them and ride around and around the block, jabbing each other in the ribs, swigging Nehi orange, gulping down White Castle hamburgers and blatting the horn. This sport was called skragging for some reason. We never actually talked to a girl, of course, or even really got near one; we just hollered, gunned the motor and stared.

"Josephine?" I tried to sound unconcerned, as though I hadn't caught the name.

My mother ladled out the gravy as she said, "They call her Josie. Their last name's Cosnowski. They come from East Chicago."

God almighty! Wait'll Schwartz and Flick hear about this! Josie Cosnowski from East Chicago! A new era had begun.

At lunchtime the next day, the following dialog took place at a fashionable greasy spoon called John's Place, which catered to the high school crowd and featured the gristliest hamburgers in Christendom:

SCHWARTZ (*mouth full of French fries*): "I bet you couldn't guess what I'm gettin' for Christmas."

FLICK: "This ketchup is rotten. It's all clotted on the bottom." (*Hollering loudly over general hullabaloo and 400 watts of jukebox.* "HEY JOHN, HOW ABOUT SOME FRESH KETCHUP HERE? THIS BOTTLE'S BEEN ON THE TABLE FOR SIX YEARS!"

SCHWARTZ: (*persistently*) "You wouldn't believe what I'm gettin' for Christmas."

FLICK (*standing up at his stool and waving ketchup bottle*): "HEY JOHN, KETCHUP OVER HERE FOR THE TROOPS!"

JOHN (*a short, swarthy man of uncertain parentage and evil temper due to a life of continual harassment by acne-plagued adolescents and a succession of short-order cooks who quit every three days*): "Who the hell's hollerin' for ketchup?"

FLICK: "Me. Over here." (*Ketchup in bottle, still being waved, suddenly unclots, spraying surrounding customers, including renowned defensive halfback who rises menacingly from his stool and then settles back, figuring it isn't worth it.*)

HALFBACK: "Watch it, punk."

JOHN: "I don't have ten arms, kid. Here's your damn mustard."

FLICK: "I wanted ketchup."

JOHN: "Oh, fer Crissake!" (*Disappears into smoky blue kitchen, where loud crash has just occurred.*)

SCHWARTZ: "Yep, this is gonna be some Christmas."

ME: (*hearing Schwartz for the first time through my daydream*) "Hmm?"

SCHWARTZ: "What's the matter with you? You got the crud or something?"

FLICK (*resigned to his fate, scooping mustard out of bottle with finger and smearing it on cheeseburger*): "You got the crud? Stay away from me, man! I don't need no crud."

ME: "Crud? Who's got the crud?"

JOHN (*reappearing from kitchen trailing sweat and lugging tray of hot roast-beef sandwiches*): "Who wanted the ketchup here?"

FLICK: "I had an uncle once almost died of the crud."

JOHN: "WHO WANTED THE KETCHUP?"

HALFBACK (*to Flick*): "Hey, Shrimp, you wanted the ketchup, right?" (*Grabs ketchup from John, pours half a bottle on Flick's cheeseburger.*) "That enough? Or wouldja like a little on top of yer head?"

ME: "Pass the ketchup, please."

HALFBACK: "You trying to get smart, kid?"

SCHWARTZ (*oblivious*): "I think my old man's getting me a power saw."

HALFBACK (*shoving ketchup bottle toward me*): "Just watch it, kid."

FLICK: "He caught it in Indianapolis, at the Y.M.C.A."

ME: "Caught what?"

SCHWARTZ: "Yessir, I'm gonna mount it on my workbench."

JOHN: "Which one a you gets the coffee malt?"

FLICK: "Here."

JOHN: "You two guys get the Cokes, right?"

ME AND SCHWARTZ: "Yeah."
(*BRIEF PERIOD OF GULPING.*)

ME: "You guys know the Bumpus house?"

SCHWARTZ (*chewing on an ice cube*): "Don't tell me?"

ME: "Tell you what?"

SCHWARTZ: "That good old Delbert Bumpus has moved back. One a them stinkin' Bumpus hounds bit me so hard one day on my paper route, I thought I'd die. That mutt hung onto my leg for two blocks."

ME: "No. Somebody else moved in." (*I paused dramatically, with impeccable timing.*) "A girl."

FLICK: "A what?"

SCHWARTZ: "That crummy hound waited for me every day and . . . a girl?"

ME (*nonchalantly sipping my Coke, milking the suspense*): "Yep. A girl." (*I bit off the end of a French fry.*) "She's Polish."

The effect was galvanic. Flick looked up from his malt, something he rarely did, face blank with wonder. Schwartz, his hand palsied, slopped Coke on the counter.

ME: "From *East Chicago*."

SCHWARTZ: "A Polish girl? From East Chicago? Next door to *you?*"

FLICK: "What's her name?"

ME: "Josephine. Josephine Cosnowski."

The three of us sat silently for a long moment, each lost in his private thoughts. Already, schemes and fantasies were rushing through our respective skulls.

HALFBACK: "Did you say Cosnowski, kid?" (*Obviously he had overheard our entire conversation.*)

ME: (*warily*): "Yeah."

HALFBACK: "That's what I thought you said." (*He took a huge swig of root beer, burped menacingly, hitched up his pants and swaggered out.*)

SCHWARTZ: "What was that all about?"

ME: "Search me."

FLICK: "You never can figure what them jocks are thinking. If anything."

That night after school, Flick, Schwartz, Kissel and I sauntered casually past the Bumpus house—as casually as we could with the temperature five below and the wind howling through the telephone wires like the sound effects on *I Love a Mystery*. We slogged along in our overshoes, pretending there was nothing at all unusual in the fact that we had paraded up and down in front of the Bumpus house 12 times in the last ten minutes.

"I'll bet she's fat," said Flick his breath swirling in the arctic air.

"You sure are lucky, living right next door. You can probably look right in her *bedroom*," muttered Schwartz bitterly.

I peered up at the house, hoping for a glimpse. I could still see the scuff marks on the front door where Floyd Bumpus had kicked it in the night he and old Emil, his father, had the fistfight that Emil won by hitting him with a tire iron. The place looked the same, but it was different, somehow. Now it was a *girl* house. It kind of radiated femaleness. The steady thump of polka records shook the frozen ground beneath our feet, and the seductive aroma of stuffed cabbage filled our nostrils. It was almost dark and the streetlights were coming on up and down the block when Junior Kissel made the first score.

Flick had just picked up a chunk of rock-ice and was about to throw it at a shivering sparrow huddled on top of a garage. I was busily trying to scratch my left shoulder blade because my sheepskin coat always itched through my shirt. Schwartz was bent over hooking his galoshes.

"There she is!"

We stood poised in the icy air, like some diorama of *Ancient Man at His Daily Tasks* in the Museum of Natural History. The side door of the Bumpus house had opened and two figures emerged into the gloom: a short, lumpy lady with a shawl over her head, and behind her, barely visible in the darkness—a girl! She had on a parka with those rope hooks which were very big that year. The lady picked up something next to the basement stairs, and together the two of them disappeared back into the house.

For a half-minute or so, nobody said a thing. Finally Flick tossed his ice chunk in the general direction of a streetlight and Schwartz whistled a low, quavering note.

"Well, I saw her first," said Kissel.

I didn't say anything. But I knew what I had to do. There was no turning back.

Every night before I did anything else, I had one chore to perform. I was supposed to go to Pulaski's store to buy whatever my mother put down on a list. It wasn't really every night: just whenever she didn't feel like doing the shopping herself in the afternoon; but it was often enough to be irritating. Tonight was a store night. On the way through the darkness, as I cut across a vacant lot, I imagined how I would meet Josie. She'd fall off a ladder and I'd catch her. I'd dribble a basketball in the gym and crash into the stands—right into her lap. Or a bus would run up on the sidewalk with a crazed driver at the wheel, and I'd scoop her up just as the wheels were about to. . . . Men think these things.

I went into Pulaski's store, still in a misty daze. The usual mob of steelworkers crowded the joint. Pulaski sold a lot of chewing tobacco and work gloves. Pulaski himself toiled behind the glass meat counter, his apron stained with grease and blood. Howie, his current clerk, a guy who used to work at the Esso station, glared at me from behind the grocery counter. Grubby kids huddled around the penny-candy case, as I had done in my long-gone youth. I had played softball with Howie before he had become permanently angry working at the gas station and Pulaski's. He didn't go to school anymore, just worked and drove around in Pulaski's panel truck, delivering potatoes and sacks of groceries.

"Whaddaya want? And be quick about it, fer Crissake."

He worked 19 hours a day, and everyone thought he

was lucky because he didn't have to go to school anymore. He had a thin, red, hawklike face. His hair was a kind of mustard yellow, and it stuck up all over his head like worn-out paint brushes. He was famous because he'd had to quit school over a girl. He had just made the basketball team in the middle of his sophomore year and then suddenly he had dropped out and gotten married. After that, he was always mad.

"Gimme a loaf of Silvercup." Pulaski's was not a self-service store. He kept everything safely out of everybody's reach.

"Large or small?"

"Large."

I read off the rest of the list and Howie packed everything into a paper sack as the crowd eddied around me.

"Oh, yeah. And a Mr. Goodbar." At that stage of the game, I was completely hooked on Mr. Goodbars. There was something about the way the chocolate mixed with the peanuts when you crunched your teeth down on it that got me where I lived.

Howie shoved the candy bar toward me. He knew I usually ate it on the way home, and it didn't go into the sack. I handed him the money and he savagely hit the keys on Pulaski's cash register.

"Goin' to the game Thursday?" I asked, passing the time of day.

"Are you kiddin'?" That was his standard answer to almost everything. I guess he felt that the world kidded him a lot.

My frozen feet propelled me unsteadily back toward

home. I had made this trip so many times that my body moved totally on its own. The street lamps were festooned with the plastic wreaths and electric candles that the town put up every year. Sometimes they didn't take them down until April. A giant semi boomed past, cascading gray slush up over the sidewalk.

I slogged across the street and began to cut through the vacant lot, thinking of the basketball game on Thursday, only four days away. Basketball is Indiana's true religion. Nobody thinks of anything else from the opening game of the season through the state finals, and then they argue about it all summer long. This was the big game with our hated rivals, the Whiting Oilers, a well-named team. They came from a school buried amid a jumble of refinery tanks and fumes. Understandably, they played a hard, vindictive game. I already had my ticket in my wallet. It was the big game of the year.

I was about halfway across the vacant lot, crunching contentedly and clumping along the well-worn path, when I saw something ahead of me in the darkness. I hardly ever met anybody on the path, so I stopped for a second. It looked like some kind of bear, a low dark blob in the gloom. I'd always felt that one day I'd meet a bear someplace, but I never thought it would be here in this vacant lot. I couldn't make out what the hell it was. It seemed to be sort of lunging around, making sounds. I was about 20 or 30 yards away from it, maybe a little less. Deep in my sheepskin pocket, I felt for my Scout knife and edged forward.

For a couple of seconds I had a powerful urge to turn

and run like hell, and then I saw what it was. It was somebody picking things up off the ground. I walked forward warily, because Grover Dill used this path, too, and he was dangerous in the winter because the cold made his teeth hurt.

It was a girl. It was Josie! It *had* to be. No girl in our neighborhood looked like *that*. She was bent over picking up cans and packages from the path and trying to stuff them into a torn paper bag. She looked up. The light from the neon sign at the Bluebird Tavern illuminated her face in a flickering radiance. I almost fainted. These moments are known to all men: the electric instant of manifest destiny: Ahab sighting Moby Dick, Tristan meeting Isolde, John meeting Yoko! She stuck a can into the tattered bag, and it rolled out into a snowdrift.

"Hi." It was all I could think of to say. She said nothing, just continued to scrabble among the weeds.

"I guess your bag broke," I said observantly. Still nothing. She struggled on in the snow.

"Here. I'll help you." It was the first coherent thought I'd had.

And then she spoke, her rich, sensual, vibrant voice coming from deep within her well-filled corduroy coat, from amid the mufflers and the red stocking cap; a voice which to this day I have never forgotten: "T'anks."

Together we packed the torn bag. Her groceries ran heavily to sausages and what smelled like sauerkraut. I could feel a surge of erotic tension warming my longjohns. Together we marched on through the darkness, occasionally dropping a can or a bottle.

"Uh . . . what's your name?" I didn't want to tip my hand and let her know I had been stalking her relentlessly for days.

"Josephine." She didn't ask mine—a bad sign.

"Where do you live?" She didn't answer, being busy at the moment retrieving a turnip that had rolled among a collection of beer cans.

"You want a piece of candy?" I asked, hoping to soften her up for the kill.

"What kind?"

"Mr. Goodbar. It's got peanuts."

"They stick in my teeth," she said, her breath making a misty, fragrant cloud.

I kept looking at her sideways, and every time the streetlight hit her I couldn't believe that such a girl had moved into our neighborhood. Her high, chiseled cheekbones, the dark hair trickling from under the stocking cap, the rounded slopes and valleys of her corduroy coat, the faint scent of cabbage—all were beginning to tell on my addled senses. But my mind was alert and sharp, guarding against a false move. I could sense that this voluptuous creature must be carefully handled. She could fly into the wilderness forever if I so much as struck a wrong note. With Esther Jane Alberry, it was a hit here, a kick there, a hurled snowball and nothing more. But I sensed something in Josephine that opened up pores in my soul I never knew I had.

"Boy, it sure is cold," I said finally. I figured I was

on safe ground. Somehow I knew I had to keep her talking.

"Yeah. I'm sure glad we don't have to go far," she answered, sniffing in the cold air. I saw my opening.

"Where do you live?" I tried to sound totally uninterested.

"Right down the street. Third house from the corner."

"Oh. . . ." I struck, hurling the harpoon with all my might. "Well, well. That sure is funny. I live in the second house from the corner. How come I never saw you before?" I lied adroitly.

"We just moved in from East Chicago."

"That's a nice town. What school do you go to?"

"All Saints."

"I go to Harding."

She didn't comment. We were nearing her house. I knew I had to make my move or all would be lost. I couldn't ask her to the basketball game, since I only had one ticket and they had been sold out for over 12 years for the Whiting game. How about the Orpheum? No, I was almost totally broke because of Christmas. I had bought a catcher's mitt for my kid brother.

I started to drag my feet and suddenly I became aware that she was giving me a long, intense stare, her magnificent crystal blue eyes catching the gleam of a passing headlight. I felt silly.

"Would you like to go to a party?" she said suddenly.

Good God! No girl ever asked *me* to a party before, except Helen Weathers once, and that didn't count because she was fat.

"A party? A party? Why, why, yes, sure, uh . . . Josie."

"I don't know anybody around here," she said. "I hope you don't get the wrong idea because I asked you."

"Heh-heh-heh. Why, of course not!"

I couldn't believe it. Polish girls really *were* everything I'd heard! Here I didn't even know her five minutes and she was asking me to a party. At last life had begun. This was it!

We trudged up the front steps of the Bumpus house to the sagging porch where the Bumpus hounds had howled and raged on many an afternoon of summers past and old Emil had fallen through the railing one night when he had a snootful. But I wasn't thinking about that now. She opened the front door and a great wave of warm air redolent with strange aromas—along with the rumble of recorded polkas—came flooding out onto the wintry porch.

"Don't forget the party," she said, holding the door partly closed with her free hand.

"Oh, I won't! I go to a lot of parties. When is it?"

"Thursday. Pick me up about eight."

"Why, I just happen to have Thursday open. Yessir, and. . . ."

She was gone. The door closed. It wasn't until I got back home with the groceries that I realized that she had said Thursday. THURSDAY! There were at least 12,000 people who would have given anything to have a ticket for the Whiting game, but suddenly basketball and the Oilers didn't seem as important as they had before. Sex will do that to you.

The next day I told Schwartz what had happened.

"Y'mean *she* asked *you* to a *party? You?*" He practically reeled.

"Yup."

"Boy, them Polish parties are really wild. Casimir told me about one once that went on for four days."

All day in school I drifted on a plane of ecstasy, floating high above the humdrum dronings of history teachers. All through geometry I wrote Josie, Josie, Josie in parabolic curves on the back of my notebook.

That night I began to plan my wardrobe. I laid the stuff out on my bed, checking it carefully. Let's see, I'll use the Old Man's Aqua Velva, and. . . .

The next essential was getting my father to let me use the car. A car was absolutely necessary for the operation that was beginning to evolve in my mind. In Indiana, male kids usually start driving at about ten, so I was an accomplished gravel-thrower and was well known at all the local drive-ins hamburger joints from Big Blimpie to the Route 41 Diner.

"Uh . . . Dad. Is there any chance of getting the Olds Thursday?" He was deep in the sports page, which I figured was as good a time as any to hit him for the car.

"Thursday?" He squinted at me, blowing smoke through his nose and letting it curl up in front of his eyes like a shifting curtain. If I hadn't known that he hated movies, I'd have sworn that he studied under Humphrey

Bogart. For all I know, Humphrey Bogart studied under him. The old man got around.

"Thursday . . . let's see. Thursday. What am I doin' Thursday?" He talked aloud to himself, toying with me. I knew Wednesday was his league bowling night and on Fridays he went to the wrestling matches with Gertz and Zudock. Saturday was usually up for grabs, with my mother usually winning when they drove over to visit her friend Bernice and her dumb husband, Elmer, who worked for the phone company.

"What do you have in mind for Thursday?" he asked, folding the paper over so that he could read the scores of the various bowling leagues. His life revolved around three things—the Chicago White Sox, bowling and the Oldsmobile, the order depending on the season.

"Well? What d'ya want the car for?"

Naturally I couldn't tell him what I *really* wanted it for. "Me and Schwartz are going to the Whiting game at the civic center, and Schwartz's old man's Ford is up on blocks."

"Whiting'll kill ya. That Zodnycki's got a jump shot from the keyhole that you can't block, and he hits from the outside, too. They'll murder you guys."

"Yeah?" was all I could say, knowing that the old man was probably right and also that I wouldn't be anywhere near the game, if things went right.

"OK. But be sure to fill the tank. Not like the last time, so you run out of gas in Blue Island and me and Heinie hafta chase all over the place before we find ya. If that wasn't stupid, tryin' to make it to Chicago and back on a gallon of Shell regular. Leave it to you and Schwartz."

He had opened an old wound: the memory of that miserable night when Schwartz had supplied a gallon of gas and I had supplied the car on a disastrous double date that ended with the four of us sitting in the car on a railroad siding at 15 below zero for two and a half hours. The two girls hadn't spoken to us then or since, and I didn't blame them.

"Don't worry. I'll fill it up. I learned my lesson."

"Yeah, I'll bet," was all he said as he went back to the scores.

Well, that took care of that. It was humiliating, but I had the car; that was the big thing. I went to my room and sat down at the desk that I used for my homework. My Aunt Glenn gave it to me for my eighth birthday. It was robin's-egg bue and had yellow bunnies painted on the side. I figured one day I'd paint it red or green, since the bunnies were beginning to be embarrassing. My aunt had a thing about bunnies. For every Christmas as long as I could remember, she'd given me bunny slippers and no doubt I'd get another pair this year, even though my shoe was a half-size bigger than my old man's.

I made out a list of what I had to do:

1. Get haircut.
2. Polish car.
3. Buy gas.
4. Gargle.
5. Squeeze blackheads.

The next day, which was Wednesday, was dark and windy with a lot of snow drifting down all afternoon. We had an auditorium session in which Jack Morton and Glen Atkinson and some other guy dressed up like Wise Men while our crummy glee club sang *We Three Kings of Orient Are.*

"Boy, you sure are gonna miss one hell of a ball game," said Flick as we hitchhiked home from school that night. "That better be some babe."

I said nothing, since it was obvious that Flick was jealous that I had a date with the greatest-looking girl for miles around. For a couple of days now there had been churning inside of me a molten excitement that was getting so hot I could hardly stand it. Every time I thought of her, it started again. I can't explain why, since I hardly knew her, but maybe that's the reason. You never feel that way over somebody you really know.

"Didja hear Zodnycki said the Wildcats are a bunch of overrated punks, and that he and four girls could beat 'em goin' away? I read it in the *Times*," Schwartz chipped in, blowing his breath in a big cloud as the cars rumbled past us. We were part of a tiny contingent of diehards who always hitchhiked the three miles back and forth to school, not only to save our bus money but also out of principle.

"That bum'll be lucky if he cans five points against Sobec," I answered, trying to sound like I cared about the game.

"Ah, I dunno. That bastard must be eight feet tall. And he looks like he's about 40 years old," Flick yelled over the roar of a passing diesel. He spoke the truth. Northern Indiana high school teams often resemble the best the Big Ten can field; 300-pound tackles, blue-jowled and squinty-eyed, are common. Their actual ages are as hard to tell as the sex of a clam. There are rumors that many promising players are not even enrolled in first grade till their 17th year, and by the time they're high school sophomores are grizzled veterans with large families and pro contracts from four leagues.

"Watch this baby." Schwartz waggled his thumb seductively as a knock-kneed Buick rattled toward us. It slowed to a stop. "GOT 'IM!" Schwartz hollered.

We piled into the amiable wreck, which was driven by a mammoth steelworker who was fragrant with beer and chewing tobacco. He spit a long amber skein out the window into the frigid air.

"If yer gonna get in, get in. I ain't got all day!"

The uproar inside the Buick was deafening. No muffler, bad shocks and a transmission that sounded as if it were made of a million cracked iron marbles. The floor of the car was ankle-deep in beer cans, cigar butts and rags—a real working car.

"Hey, Schwartz!" Flick yelled over the din.

"Yeah?"

"D' ya think Ace here is gonna score tonight?"

"I hear them Polish girls invented sex!" shouted Flick.

"You guys are just jealous!" I yelled as I struggled to keep from falling off the seat.

At that moment, I became aware that the driver was

peering intently into his cracked rearview mirror right at me. At the time, it had no meaning.

Just as we climbed out at the end of the roaring ride, the steel puddler spit another stream of tobacco juice and hollered over the clatter of his valves:

"You guys go to high school?"

"Yeah," Schwartz answered for all of us.

"You don't know when you're well off."

He spat again and drove off. It was a point we weren't prepared to accept. It was just before the dawn of the age of youth culture, and being a kid was just something you went through before joining the real world.

"Y' comin' over to the Red Rooster tomorrow night after your date?" Flick asked me. The Red Rooster was where everyone who was with it went after a big night.

"Are you kiddin', Flick?" said Schwartz, jabbing him in the ribs with a mitten. "He's gonna have a lot more to do besides sit around and eat cheeseburgers, right?"

"Now look, you guys, I don't know what you're thinkin' I'm gonna do, but. . . ." I tried to inject a note of dignity into the discussion.

"Don't worry. We know what you're gonna *try* to do. Oh boy! If I had a date with that doll, lemme tell you. . . ." Flick winked a large, lascivious wink.

"Don't worry. I can handle whatever comes up." More elbows in the ribs. I played the game.

I plodded home. There was time before supper to back the car out of the garage in the frigid air and to give her a coat of Duco Seven if I worked fast. I had polished that car so many times that I could do it in my sleep. I was already deep in the middle of a torrid embrace in my mind when I became aware, as my right arm buffed the hood, that a hulking shadow had darkened the gloom around me. It blotted out the distant glow of the open-hearth furnaces against the lowering clouds. As I glanced up, a rasping voice set my teeth on edge.

"Hey!"

A thrill of fear zipped through me. "Uh . . . yeah?" I managed to squeak, dropping my polishing rag into the slush.

"You the kid takin' Josie t' tha pardy t'morra?"

"Yeah."

"I t'ought so." He was wearing a checkered wool jacket about the size of a circus tent. He had on red earmuffs and no hat. He had a crewcut that looked like steel wool.

"Who're you?" I asked. It was a dangerous question, but I couldn't think of anything else to say.

"Whatsit to ya?" He leaned with one hand the size of a 12-pound ham on the fender of the Olds. I didn't like the way the conversation was going, and I wondered if I should make a break for the back door.

"I'm 'er brudder. I jus' t'ought I oughta see who was goin' out wit' Josie."

"Oh. Yeah. I heard of you. She's a nice girl. She sure is a nice girl. Yeah."

Words kept squirting out of me. He reminded me of

Alice the Goon from the Popeye comic strip. I could smell the faint aroma of a locker room.

"You play football," I said, trying to make contact.

"Dat's right, she's a nice girl." He ignored my latest remark as being too obvious to answer.

"Yep. She sure is. A real nice girl. Yep."

"You show her a nice time, y' hear? An' if anybuddy gives ya any trouble, tell 'em ya know Stosh." He made a sound that I guess was a laugh. It sounded like two angle irons clanking together.

"I sure will . . . Stosh."

He clanked again and shambled off into the darkness. I noticed that he had left a dent the size of an elephant's footprint in the fender of the Olds. I should have taken the hint.

Later that night at Pulaski's, I waited my turn amid a crowd of ladies who milled around the meat counter, watching Pulaski as he weighed pork chops. He was famous for his two-pound thumb.

"I said I didn't want 'em so fatty!" bellowed a hulking lady in a stocking cap.

"Whaddaya want from me, lady? I don't grow the pigs!"

An angry murmur arose among the throng as Pulaski held them at bay with his cleaver. Howie struggled past me, carrying a sack of potatoes on his shoulder.

"I hear you're goin' to the party," he said out of the side of his mouth as he hurried past.

"How'd you know?" I threw after him.

"I hear," he answered.

Finally, as I picked up my sack of groceries, Howie leaned over the counter and said: "You're takin' Josie, eh? Well, good luck." He said it in a kind of voice that could mean anything.

"Thanks," I answered in the same voice. He looked tired, as though he had worked 18 hours that day, which he had.

Sure enough, I met Josie on the way home again. This time she hung on my arm and brushed up against me as we struggled home with the grocery sacks.

"I hear you met Stosh." She spoke in a husky, throaty voice, not at all like her brother's.

"He came over when I was polishing the car."

"You'll like him."

"Yeah, sure."

"You'll like my uncles, too. They want to meet you." She snuggled closer as we sloshed through the slush. Somewhere a radio was playing *White Chrismas*, with old Bing Crosby crooning away. We never really had a white Christmas in northern Indiana, since the snow came down already gray from the steel mills, but it was a nice thought. Once in a while we had a fall of rust-colored snow, and that could be kind of pretty once you got used to it.

"Especially you'll like my uncle Stanley."

"Yeah, that'll be great." Inside my gut, those roaring waves of excitement crashed so loud that I didn't realize how sinister it was that all her uncles wanted to meet me. The streetlights played over her magnificent cheek-bones, her fantastic eyes, her coal-black hair. I felt hints

192

of her body, round and soft, through her corduroy parka and my sheepskin coat. I clutched desperately to my bag of groceries.

The great Atlantic salmon struggling thousands of miles upstream, leaping waterfalls, battling bears to mate is nothing compared to your average high school sophomore. The salmon dies in the attempt, and so, often, does the sophomore, in more ways than one. As we ambled on through the gloom, I didn't have the slightest hint of what was coming; neither, I suppose, does the salmon, just does what he has to do. So did I.

"Hey," I said just before we got to her house. "Where is this party going to be?"

She looked into my eyes with that gland-tingling look that can drive a man out of his skull—if he's lucky.

"It's a surprise. You'll have fun."

Instantly I pictured a mysterious, blue-lit den somewhere with writhing bodies and the distant thudding of orgiastic drums. Her smoldering gaze promised everything. I felt deep-down stirrings, and I was glad it was dark. A few snowflakes drifted down between us. She closed her eyes in the dim light. I leaned forward. Our lips touched. My ears roared. Passion rushed in a mighty torrent through my veins. . . .

RRRRRRRIIIIPPPP! I felt my bag of groceries give way. I grabbed frantically at a box of eggs as it hurtled to the frozen pavement, followed by a bottle of ketchup and a jar of strawberry jam. Crash followed crash.

Lightly she breathed, "I'll see you tomorrow . . . darling." And was gone.

Blindly I struggled amid the gray heaps of snow. I salvaged only a half-pound of sliced bacon, one No. 2 can of carrots and a loaf of rye bread. All the rest was ruined or lost. But it was only the beginning.

I was up at seven the next morning, nervous and excited. As I left for school after the usual oatmeal, I tried to catch a glimpse of Josie, but her house was dark and silent. All day at school the talk was about Zodnycki and what he had said about our ball club. Naturally, passions ran high. The Whiting Oilers had always been menacing, but with Zodnycki at the pivot and popping off like that, it was going to be a grudge match. I played it as cool as I could, pretending to be deeply involved in the game. It was a peculiar feeling, since I was normally a red-hot basketball nut and for the first time in my life something else was sneaking in by the side door.

"Hey, you want to sell your ticket?" Schwartz asked after school. "You got a date tonight, so what are you goin' to do with the ticket?"

"I may sell, if the price is right," I lied, since I knew that I never could sell a ticket to one of the big games of the year, even if I couldn't use it. Just *having* the ticket meant something.

"I know a guy who'll give you four dollars, in my biology class."

"Nah, I'll hang on." Tickets cost students a dollar and a half, so four dollars wasn't much of a deal, and I wasn't going to sell anyway.

"Well, you lucky fink, just don't catch anything I

wouldn't catch, ha-ha," Flick yelled out at me at the top of his lungs as I left the crowd on my way home.

"Where you takin' her?" asked Schwartz as the December wind sighed through the telephone lines and the branches of the trees creaked under the load of ice they carried. Just before Christmas, it gets dark early in the afternoon on the Indiana plains. School had just let out and already it was almost dark. Two kids struggled by, pulling a Christmas tree on a sled.

"How 'bout the Dreamland Roller Rink?" Schwartz sarcastically suggested. "Girls love roller skating."

I said nothing, just chucked a piece of ice in his direction and headed home.

"How come you're not eating the creamed onions?" my mother asked at the supper table.

"Uh . . . I'll have some later," I answered. I didn't want any onions lousing up the plans I had in mind. I wasn't hungry. I was out for big game tonight, and food meant nothing.

I went into the bathroom and carefully shaved, and as usual the mysterious Nicked Chin Law went into operation—a peculiar phenomenon that I was not yet familiar with but which later became part of my life. All men know of this and have pondered it. On the evening of every important date, the razor invariably bites deep, leaving rich geysers of spurting blood in its wake. I stuck bits of toilet paper all over my face, attempting to stanch the flow. They didn't help, so I splashed Aqua Velva on my raw jaws. My face sizzled like a halibut on the broiler.

"Yer sure shavin' close for a basketball game," the old man tossed at me as he peered in the bathroom to see how much longer I'd be. He liked to finish the paper in there every night after supper.

"I'll be right out," I said noncommittally.

"Well, just don't take all night," he said, rattling the editorial page.

After the shave I doused myself with Bloode Of The Sheik, a spectacular cologne that my father had won on a punchboard and that came in a bottle shaped like an Arab riding on a glass horse. The label, in jade and gold, read:

"LOVE ELIXIR OF THE EAST . . . 47% PERCENT ALCOHOL."

I sloshed it over my head and down my chest, and instantly an explosive aroma filled the bathroom and clouded the mirror. For a few seconds my head reeled out of control as the love elixir did its seductive work. I staggered out into the fresh air. The mixture of the cologne with Aqua Velva was irresistible.

Meticulously I got dressed, making sure that my T-shirt and Jockey shorts were snowy, my mauve-colored Tony Martin roll-collar sport shirt tucked carefully into my best slacks. Everything had to be absolutely right. This was a historic night. Never again would I suffer the guilt of knowing that I had never really done much with a girl except smooch with her in the balcony of the Orpheum.

I examined myself in the mirror in my room. A magnificent specimen of sophomoric manhood. Bits of toilet paper still clung to my chin. The rich exhalations of the mysterious East rose about me in a purple haze. I was loaded for bear.

Slipping into my mackinaw, I clamped my green earmuffs on my head, wound my precious eight-foot purple-and-white scarf around my neck 36 times—purple and white being our school colors, a combination so adroitly selected as to make all acne-ridden complexions look leprous by day and absolutely necrotic in gymnasium lighting. Casually, yet with a touch of stealth, since the old man had been known to change his mind without warning, I picked up the car keys from the dining room table.

"Don't forget to fill the tank," he bellowed from the next room. I went out into the icy darkness and over to the garage. Tonight I had a date with an actual girl from East Chicago. An East Chicago *Polish* girl. At last, after a measly lifetime of basketball games and double features and French fries at the Red Rooster and Monopoly games with Schwartz and Flick, I was in the big time! I put the key into the ignition and the Olds started instantly, as if it, too, sensed impending ecstasy.

Since Josie lived next door, it wasn't much of a drive over to her house, but I hummed happily all the way as waves of excitement coursed up and down to every nerve ending. The Olds had a gasoline heater that, when it was in the mood, was hotter than the hinges of Hell. I flipped it on. Immediately a great flood of scorching air engulfed my feet and steamed the windows. Hot dog! Everything is going great! I pounded my mittens on the steering wheel in a frenzy as I eased out of the driveway and up to the curb in front of Josie's house. Life stretched before me, a vast unexplored continent of voluptuous abandon. With throttle wide open and a full head of steam, I hurled myself full tilt toward the unknown, little suspecting what lay ahead.

For a full half-minute I sat in the darkness, peering up at the porch through the frosted window of the Olds, composing my mind for the opening ploy. The heater roared. The car felt richly warm and dark. Straightening my earmuffs, I swung out into the cold, leaving the engine running.

I knocked on the front door and waited. Inside, all was silence. I peered in through the heavy curtains that hung at the front windows. Pitch darkness in the parlor, where once the Bumpuses had spent their squalid hours amid pig and chicken, dog and mule, guitars twanging at all hours, hawking and snorting and squatting amid old Montgomery Ward catalogs.

I knocked again, louder. Something seemed to be moving inside. The door opened a tiny crack.

"Who you vant?" A beady eye peered out at me.

"Uh . . . I come for Josie."

Silence. The eyeball glinted piercingly in the streetlight.

Finally: "Josie?"

"Yeah. Me and Josie are going to a party."

"You vait." The eye disappeared.

I stood alone on the windswept porch. For a brief moment, I had the wild urge to flee into the night. In fact, I was just about to turn and make a break for it when the door opened to a larger crack and the same voice, possibly female, said, "You come in. She not ready."

I found myself in the black parlor and was aware of dim, blocky shapes of furniture set with geometric precision about the room. A crucifix gleamed dully from atop an upright piano flanked by what looked like stone urns. I was led through the house and into the darkened kitchen. The overpowering aroma of Polish cooking engulfed me like an octopus. Coming from a family where Franco-American spaghetti was considered an exotic dish, this was enough to make me stagger slightly as I felt my way past the redolent stove.

The figure ahead moved steadily to the cellar door and we descended the steps. Fear clutched at my vitals. At that time I was deep in the works of Sax Rohmer, the illustrious author of *The Claw of Fu Manchu, The Insidious Doctor Fu Manchu,* beside which Ian Fleming and his insipid Dr. No pale to the pasteboard figures that they are. Well I knew that Dr. Petrie had been many times lured into sinister traps down just such a passageway as I was traversing now. We reached the first landing. If I was going to escape at all, it was now or never. But like C. Nayland Smith himself, I allowed myself to be lured into the spider web of foreign intrigue.

For a moment, I was blinded by the bright light of the cellar.

"You sit. You eat."

For the first time I saw that my guide was a short stocky woman wearing a black shawl over her head, her cheeks bright red with peasant health, her eyes a brilliant china blue.

"Me Josie's mother."

A heavy-set man sat at the table, huge shoulders bulging under his uncomfortable-looking shirt. He wore suspenders, something I thought only firemen did. He had a handlebar mustache of such magnificence and daring that he would have been an instant hit in any of today's hippie communes. His thin blond hair was parted in the middle.

"You take Josie to party," he said, his voice heavy and blocklike, like chucks of iron ore clanking out on the table. I recognized instantly that I was in the presence of a first-class open-hearth worker. [Polish steelmen are legendary, and in fact the Paul Bunyan of the Gary mills was a Pole. This could have been Joe Magerac himself, a man capable of personally rolling out hot ingots between the palms of his hands.]

I squatted at the table, surrounded by dishes loaded with boiled potatoes and slices of dark home-made Polish bread. Josie's mother, beaming, shoved a huge white plate of thick foreign china in front of me.

"You like cabbage, yes?"

Josie's father, as I suspected he was, dug into his own plate, a fine spray of juice rising about him as he tucked into his nightly meal. I looked down at my plate, and there before me was a mountainous, steaming portion of God knows what.

"But I already had supper," I protested weakly.

"You eat," she repeated, still beaming happily.

There was no way out. But if this was what I had to do for a night of passion, it was worth it. Taking a deep breath, I took a bite. For a moment, the heady mixture of cabbage, spice and meat was a great, wet wad in my mouth, and then its haunting, incandescent succulence, inevitability and *rightness* hit me where I lived. My God, I had never eaten anything in my life that came anywhere near this; even the chili mac at the Red Rooster, which had seemed to me to be the ultimate in cuisine, wasn't in the same league with this incredible concoction. Across the table from me, Josie's father attacked his second platterful, washing it down with a stein of dark beer. As I wolfed the cabbage down, it was like some long-contained dammed-up secret part of me had broken into the open and was on the hunt.

As I ate I glanced around, noticed chair, tables, couches, chests—a whole *house* in the basement. It was the first time in my life that I had met anyone who lived in the basement and kept the upstairs of their house, I later learned, for state occasions such as weddings, funerals and visits from the taxman. They had painted the furnace, which loomed at the far end of the basement like some multi-armed fairy-tale monster, a bright robin's-egg blue. All the furniture—the wooden tables and chairs and benches—was the same Easter-egg color.

"Josie almost ready," her mother said, pressing a half-dozen Polish pickles on me. Gripped by an uncontrollable rapacious hunger, I ate and ate, spurred on by the slurpings and fork scraping of Josie's father.

"You have good time. You good boy. You like cabbage?" she asked, forking a potato scented with bay leaves onto my plate.

"Cabbage good. I like." I found myself picking up the cadence of their speech.

A huge belch welled its way up from the dark hidden caves of my body. I couldn't control it. It rumbled deep in my throat like a passing freight train laden with smoked hams and late fall turnips. My fellow eater burped amiably through his handlebar mustache and gulped down another two liters of beer.

"You good eater," he rumbled, and I hate to use that word because people are always "rumbling" things in bad books, but he *really* rumbled, the way only a Polish open-hearth worker can.

"Pickle, potato good, too," I mumbled between bites, elbow-deep in cabbage juice and beating down an insane desire to lick the plate.

The next moment my eyeballs were straining at their moorings like two barrage balloons. Josie was with us. She had come down the stairs while I was in mid-burp and sucking a fugitive bit of cabbage from under a back tooth. She wore a dirndl skirt, which at that time was a big deal among high school girls, but she wore a dirndl the way a tiger wears its skin. Her narrow waist flared suddenly into broad, sculptured peasant hips. Above a wide dirndl belt, her embroidery-laced puffed-sleeved blouse—stuffed fuller than the cabbage—billowed and rippled like the heavy white clouds that scud over Warsaw in the spring. I have heard stories of German soldiers after World War Two refusing to leave Poland, being literally dragged home by their heels, protesting every inch of the way. I can understand them. It isn't often that a kid in the sophomore class has a date with an earth mother.

It's hard to explain the combination of the basement, the blouse, the stuffed cabbage, the handlebar mustache and the mysterious shrouded parlor furniture, but all of it made me feel that I was in some kind of exotic delirium. Was the cabbage drugged? Were these actually highly trained dacoits in the pay of a power-mad Oriental? Their eyes *did* look strange, not like Esther Jane Alberry's wholesome Sunday School orbs.

"Hi," was all she said, her voice rich and low like the waters of the Danau flowing past the ancient bridges of medieval Europe.

"Hi," I answered, my rapier wit honed to its finest cutting edge.

"I see my mother's been feeding you," she said, smiling in a way that made my socks itch deep inside my Thom McAn saddle shoes.

"Yeah. It sure was good. Boy. Yessir."

"Josie good cook," said her mother, clearing away the dishes and preparing to serve what appeared to be a plate of spectacular plum dumplings topped with sour cream. "She make cabbage."

"*Josie* cooked the cabbage?" I said stupidly, struggling

to get to my feet and finding, unaccountably, that I seemed to be carrying several cast-iron bowling balls under my waistband.

"She make good wife one day." A claw gripped at my intestines. There was something in Mrs. Cosnowski's eye that I had never seen in the eye of a mother before. I would learn to know that look well in later years. At the time, I thought it was just the cabbage clouding my eyesight.

"Well, what do you say? Shall we go?" Josie asked lightly, touching my arm suggestively with the tips of her fingers.

"You come next, we play pinochle?" Her father stood up, towering above me like a stone god from Easter Island, his head bowed under the ceiling. Seated, he was a human being; standing he became a monument of 6′5″ or 6′6″, wearing what must have been a size-75 shirt with probably a 22-inch neck.

"I play pinochle good," I answered, which was the truth. We shook hands, or rather I stuck my tiny fist into the vise for a moment or two. My knuckles clattered and snapped.

"Next time Josie fix whole meal. You like." Her mother seemed to think only of food. Josie put her coat on and we climbed the basement steps, groped our way through the darkened parlor and were out on the porch, Mrs. Cosnowski clucking behind us in her native tongue.

At last we were in the Olds, warm and redolent with muffler fumes. I felt her hand resting on my arm as I shoved it into first gear. I had no idea where we were going.

"They liked you," Josie said, her hand squeezing my arm affectionately as she snuggled closer.

"Yeah, they were sure great." I wanted to ask her about the basement scene, but I figured what the hell, live and let live.

"Did you really cook that cabbage?" I asked, struggling with the defroster. She said nothing, but her grip on my arm tightened perceptively.

"Gee, I'm glad you got the car," she sighed. What was she trying to tell me? I detected a double meaning in every syllable, every intake of breath.

"Yeah, my old man lets me have it any time I want." This, of course, was a bald-faced lie. If I had gotten the car every time I wanted it, the old man would have had to walk to work, which was five miles away.

"Well, heh-heh-heh. Where to? Let's get over to that party."

"Turn right on California and I'll let you know when to turn next."

"Who's throwing this party?"

"Ooh, look at the Santa Claus." She ignored the question, peering through the clouded window at a hulking electrical Santa in a store window who seemed to be alternately hitting croquet balls and picking his nose.

We drove on. My anticipation over the approaching party was almost uncontainable. I'd always heard about great parties that other guys went to. They always described them in the clinical detail of a sex manual.

I had even pretended to have been to a few myself, which of course, like most of my life, was a sham and a fraud. The parties I had been to consisted mostly of shoving, standing around and drinking Cokes, turning up or turning down the record player and constantly going out for more potato chips. This pulsating creature next to me, so full of life and stuffed cabbage, obviously offered far more than potato chips.

The Olds banged along as it always did, bottoming familiarly in and out of potholes.

"Turn right!" she said suddenly. Her hand clutched sensually at my arm as I wheeled the Olds into a lumbering right turn, clunking over the rutted ice. I couldn't figure out where she was taking me. I didn't know anybody from school who lived in this neighborhood. We rolled past the Ever Rest Funeral Parlor And Furniture Store, its green-and-red neon sign glowing bleakly onto the snow.

"Tell me when," I said, trying to sound like Robert Cummings.

"Turn left here." Like most girls, she gave directions in retrospect, invariably telling you to turn just after you've almost passed the street. I spun the wheel wildly. A scurrying panel truck bounced in and out of the ruts, trying to avoid me. I caught a brief glimpse of a swarthy face mouthing obscenities. We crawled up a darkened street.

"OK. You can park here."

Cars were parked on both sides of the street and in a parking lot on my left. I eased into a slot. For a brief moment, I squeezed her hand in the dark, and her lips brushed my ear. Then we were out in the cold and going up some kind of gravel walk between snow-covered shrubbery. I could see in the darkness a great stone-turreted building. I thought, God almighty, I've hit the jackpot! I could see the headline: "ORGY AT WEALTHY HOME. TEENAGERS ARRESTED." I saw other people going in a side entrance, and brief flashes of light from within. We stood now in the gloom cast by a vast stone façade. Gargoyles leered from black nooks wearing tiny caps of crusted ice. Josie's eyes gleamed with an exalted light. NO! I thought, it CAN'T be!

It was. The heavy wooden door swung open and we stepped into the vestibule of St. Ignatius R. C. Church. A throng of pious merrymakers eddied somberly around me. I had been euchred beyond human depravity. I had been tricked into a church Christmas party, something I had avoided like the plague for all of my atheistic years.

"Ah, my son, we haven't met you, have we?" A bald priest wearing gold-rimmed glasses leaped forward, taking my hand and clinging to it for a long, agonizing moment.

"Ah, I see you're with our little Josephine. Ah, yes, I remember her baptism, and now she's a grown lady and bringing her young man here for us to meet. Well, we'll grow to know each other well, my son, and. . . ."

Her young man! We'll grow to know each other well! What is this? Our little Josephine stood at my side, her arm linked in mine, eyes shining.

"Yes, Father, he could hardly wait to get here."

I looked her full in the face, expecting to see a wink, some sign that she was kidding, but no! A look of benign piety glowed on her magnificent face. I began to feel like the worm in the apple, a butterfly on the pin. The crowd moved forward, the priest greeting newcomers and pointing me out. I heard snatches of conversation: "Josie's young man," "My, one minute they're babies and the next you're marrying them. . . ."

Heavy men with mustaches and ladies with shawls beamed at me. Hundreds of little kids bumped and milled at my knees. From somewhere in the bowels of the church, I heard a deep steady thumping. We moved on in the great throng, downstairs, through corridors, the thumping growing louder and louder. Again I was seized by a paroxysm of fear, some instinct telling me to flee before it was too late.

And then it *was* too late. We were in a huge room heavy with the scent of sweating bodies and Polish cooking. The heavy rhythmic thumping made the floors jar, the walls shudder. Sweat coursed down my shoulder blades. Josie grasped my right hand.

"Darling, do you dance?"

I was known as a particularly tenacious dancer in my somewhat limited set, but I had never seen anything like this. On a stand on one side of the room, dressed in suspenders, funny pants, embroidered shirts and plumed derbies, were Frankie Yankovic and His Polka All Stars, thumping out the *Dawn Patrol Polka,* a particularly insistent and violent example of the genre. I was yanked almost off my feet by a single powerful motion of Josie's left arm. Her beautiful feet thumped the floor maniacally. I bobbed up and down like a yo-yo on a tight string. Elbows jabbed me in the ribs, deep and hard. I caught brief images of sweating faces, clumping feet. Frankie Yankovic and His All Stars—led by Frankie himself, playing a mother-of-pearl accordion—rose to thunderous heights that would have made coleslaw out of the most powerful electronic rock groups. Every third beat, feet rose and fell like great balls of concrete.

For some unaccountable reason, I discovered I was a consummate polka dancer. The polka is a true soul dance. You don't learn it; it engulfs you and sweeps you on in a flood of braying cornets and tootling clarinets and the thundering syncopation of bass drums and cymbals. The drummer, a heavy-set Pole, squatted like a toad and his equipment, operating with the machinelike precision of a pile driver. I bounced and sweated, Josie clinging and hopping, ducking and bobbing as one born to the beat. As we danced she seemed to grow progressively more alien and foreign.

In the midst of the 23rd chorus of the *Stars and Stripes Polka*, as we swirled past a group of shawled ladies standing like vultures along the wall, I caught a glimpse of a pale, harassed, hawklike face. We swirled around the floor again like a merry-go-round out of control. Deedledeedle *BOOM* Boom deedle deedle *BOOM* Boom! The drummer's heavy foot rose and fell like an air hammer, booming out the bass notes.

Again I saw that white, pinched face staring directly at

me like some despairing ghost. It was Howie. *Howie!* Our eyes met. He was trying to tell me something. I saw a round little fat girl clinging to his elbow and around them, like so many toadstools around a rock, three other short, squat children, noses running, some crying, some yelling, all with the look of Howie around the eyes. Old Howie, who could handle a basketball like Bob Cousy. Howie, who had worked 18 hours a day at Pulaski's, lugging potatoes and weighing salami, ever since he married his Polish girlfriend.

It was then that I knew I had to get out of there fast. Josie was wearing some kind of perfume that must have been brewed by the Devil himself. The more she danced, the headier it became; but I was impervious to its siren lure, for every time we spun around, I saw Howie standing there like a dead man stood among the shawled women with his round little wife and his brood.

Frankie Yankovic did a rippling riff on his squeezebox to signal a brief break in the gymnastics. Even though I was in top shape and had been playing basketball, football and Indian wrestling for months on end, I was wheezing badly.

"I'm so glad we came. You're going to like the Father. He's a wonderful man." I saw large numbers of the celebrants pushing their way into the next room, where there seemed to be some sort of table set up.

"Uh . . . I'll get us a drink or something, OK?"

Josie was now in confidential conversation with a girlfriend. They appeared to be talking about me. Her girlfriend nodded in what looked suspiciously like approval.

"I'll get a couple of Cokes. And one for your friend."

Josie smiled. Like a greased pig. I darted off through the doorway, threading my way through the crowd like a half-back on an off-tackle slant. I edged past a table where nuns were selling gingerbread men and cider. Again I caught a glimpse of Howie, who looked more harassed than ever as he handed doughnuts around to his crowd of kids. It was a sight that chilled the marrow. I worked my way up a stairway against a stream of people who were working their way down. I was in the vestibule, moving like a shadow. And now I was at the door.

Suddenly, without warning, a heavy weight descended on my left shoulder from behind. For an instant I thought I was having a paralytic stroke brought on by too much dancing. Some immense force spun me counterclockwise. A great hulking form blocked out the rest of the room from my vision.

"Uh . . . hi, Stosh."

He looked at me with a kind of joyous hunger flickering ing in his beady eyes, the way a Kansas City lineman must look when he's closing in on Joe Namath.

"Yuh havin' a good time wit' Josie?" he asked rhetorically.

"Yeah! Sure! Great!"

It was then I became aware that he was not alone. He had a friend with him. He looked vaguely familiar.

"This is Josie's fella." He introduced me. "I want you to meet Uncle Stanley."

"Pleasta meetcha," the stranger muttered, sticking out a gigantic mitt. Something in that voice rang a bell. Good

Lord, no! It was the steel puddler from the Buick! He looked at me with cool, malevolent eyes, and then I remembered that brilliant conversation in the back seat of that wreck he drove, about *scoring* and all that!

Uncle Stanley looked down at me and for a second or two I hoped he didn't recognize me. "Howya doin', kid?" The way he said it, I knew he knew, and it didn't sound good. "Hey, Stosh, where's Josie? I wanna talk to her." Uncle Stanley sounded like he meant it.

They both turned to look for Josephine. I saw my chance and took it. Like a flash, I was out the door. Behind me I could hear the Polka All-Stars going into high gear for the second set. I darted across the crusted ice, catching a fleeting impression of the door slamming open against the wall behind me as Stosh, all his magnificent killer instincts turned up to full, lumbered into the backfield. I knew I'd have to come back for the car later. Around a concrete wall I shot, Stosh huffing behind me, through a hedge, across a street, down an alley, through a used-car lot, past the Ever Rest Funeral Parlor And Furniture Store, down another alley and then a long, dark street. Stosh moved surprisingly well for a giant, but after what seemed hours, he finally gave up the chase. I continued to run, blindly, hysterically, sensing that I was running not from just Stosh or Stanley but from what happened to Howie, from the doughnuts, the toadstools, the ladies with the shawls—all of it!

I found myself in a familiar neighborhood. There was another huge building with thousands of cars and gleaming yellow lights. The Civic Center! The Whiting Oilers!

The big game! I ran up the long concrete steps, gasping for breath, fumbled through my wallet at the turnstile and found my ticket.

"What quarter is it?" I asked the doorman.

"Just beginning the third."

"What's the score?"

"Sixty-five–sixty-three. Whiting."

From deep inside the arena I heard great roars. I was safe! Back home! I struggled to my reserved seat: Seat 6, Row G, Section 21. At last I found it. Empty. Inviting. Waiting for me. The great scoreboard with its flashing yellow and red lights loomed reassuringly overhead.

Next to me was Schwartz. We had bought our tickets together. And on the other side of him was Flick. My chest was heaving and sweat poured down my face. A five-mile run in the snow brings roses to the cheeks.

"Boy, that must have been some date!" Schwartz stared at me admiringly. A hooting roar came from the crowd. Flick hollered: "Zodnycki canned another one! Look at that bastard hit them hook shots!"

Oblivious, Schwartz dug his elbow in my ribs. "How was she?"

"Fantastic! Unbelievable! There's no way I can tell you about it. Them Polish girls are somethin' else!"

That night a legend was born. I stood tall among my peers. Naturally, I've left many of the details hazy and embellished others, but that's the way you do in life. Suffice it to say that I never saw Josie much after that. It's not easy to see much of someone when you wear sunglasses to school and sneak home every night after dark through the cellar window.

DAPHNE BIGELOW
AND THE SPINE-CHILLING SAGA OF THE
SNAIL-ENCRUSTED TINFOIL NOOSE

Why does a man become a revolutionary? Just when is that precise instant of stark realization when he perceives with unmistakable clarity that he is but a humble tenpin in the cosmic bowling game of life? And that others are balls in that game? Look closely into the early private life of any great revolutionary and you will find a girl. Somewhere along the line, a pair of elfin eyes put Karl Marx down so decisively that he went home and wrote the first words of his *Manifesto*. I well remember my own turning point. Like most pivotal moments in our lives, it came unexpectedly and in the guise of rare good fortune. Her name was Daphne Bigelow. Even now, ten light-years removed from the event, I cannot suppress a fugitive shiver of tremulous passion and dark yearning. Her skin was of the clearest, rarest form of pure, translucent alabaster. She had no "eyes" in the mundane sense, but rather, she saw the world, or the world saw her, through twin jade-green jungle pools, mirrors of a soul that was so mysterious, so enigmatic as to baffle ninth graders for yards around. I hesitate to use such a pitifully inadequate word as "hair" to describe the nimbus of magic, that shifting cloud of iridescence that framed a face of such surpassing beauty that even Buddha would have thought long and hard before staring straight into it. Why I go on with this self-flagellation I do not know. Nevertheless, I cannot but continue.

There was something else about her, something I am not quite sure I can adequately convey through the sadly lacking means of imperfect human language. Daphne walked in a kind of soft haze of approaching dawn. A suggestion always lingered about her that she wasn't there at all. Rosy gold and blue tints flushed and were gone; soft winds blew. Somewhere exotic birds called out in their sleep as Daphne drifted into Biology I, trailing mimosa blossoms and offering ecstasies not yet plumbed by human experience.

Way down deep among the lower one third of the class, amid that great rabble of faceless mankind who squat among the rancid lunch bags and musky galoshes of academe, who are forever condemned to view the great pageants of life from parked third-hand jalopies amid the apple cores and beer cans of drive-in movies, I sat hardly daring to hope—from over a gulf so vast as to make all earthly distances pale to triviality—and devoured her daily with my eyes from behind a Biology I workbook.

Throughout the entire first semester after she came to Hohman High, my wonder grew like some dank, unclassi-

fied toadstool in the coalbin of my subconscious. At first,
dimly and with naïve joy. I believed myself to be secretly
blessed. I watched for her face everywhere: in the halls,
on the stairways, in auditorium crowds, in the sullen
herd who waited numbly outside the doors to be admitted in the early-morning hours, in the rumbling
hordes who poured out of school after the last classes.
Everywhere. From time to time, she would drift briefly
into view and then disappear. Her name never appeared
on those lists of kids involved in what are known as
"activities." She was above that. As day after day faded
forever into history, as my intricately contrived glandular
system ripened and matured, so my carefully concealed
passion for Daphne Bigelow burgeoned, until finally it
engulfed me and I was swallowed up like Jonah into
the inky blackness of the whale's belly.

The midsemester exams came and went. Over Christmas vacation I had been haunted by nameless fears,
since Daphne was out of my sight. Now a new terror—
would I be assigned to the same biology class with
her next semester? Finally, the dread day arrived. I
could scarce credit my senses. Not only had Daphne
Bigelow condescended to remain among us; our new
biology teacher—a dapper gentleman wearing rimless
glasses, black shellacked hair and squeaky shoes, named
Mr. Settlemeyer—had, in an exquisite moment of insight
and compassion, assigned Daphne Bigelow to me as my
Biology II lab partner! Together we would investigate
the mysteries of the great animal kingdom of which we
were but a small part.

217

Well do I remember that blissful afternoon when, together, Daphne and I pinned a limp, formaldehyde-dripping frog to a cork specimen board and I, being the man of the house, bravely took up scalpel and showed her the stuff of which I was made. At the head of the class, Mr. Settlemeyer, pointer in hand, described various portions of frog anatomy, while beside me Daphne smiled with the faintest suggestion of approval, of perhaps even admiration, as I rose to magnificent heights of skill and daring. She averted her eyes delicately as I performed the autopsy. Her tiny *moues* of girlish fright and squeamishness drove me on to even greater pinnacles as I laid bare the vitals of the unfortunate amphibian. We both received an A+ for the afternoon's work.

From that deceptively unprepossessing yet starkly symbolic beginning, our love took root and grew. By the end of the third week we were on a first-name basis. This may seem a small achievement, but it is not every man who is privileged to call a genuine goddess by her first name, and to be answered in kind.

I learned more about her every day, but mostly from outside sources. She spoke little of her home life, her joys, her aspirations, her dreams. While I, being a male, babbled on endlessly, weaving about both of us a rich cocoon of myth and gradiose philosophical generalities.

As winter silently faded into the soft sensuality of early spring, my resolve strengthened and took specific form, though I never saw Daphne outside of biology class. Officially, that is. Unofficially, I shadowed her like a maniacally devoted dacoit, one of the sinister footpad tribe of early India. Watching her from afar, I cataloged her every movement. I covertly made a note of every article of clothing she wore; her wardrobe was immense and infinitely varied. My maroon corduroy slacks, meanwhile, a holdover from the Christmas before, grew increasingly repugnant to me. My purple pullover sweater, with its faded, block-lettered "H," somehow did not sing to me as it used to.

Daphne never rode the school bus or the streetcar, or hitchhiked home like me and Schwartz and Flick. She just magically disappeared. One day I thought I saw a fleeting form enter a long, black, waiting Cadillac down the block from the school, but I could not be sure it was she.

When we passed in the halls, I always wore my carefully rehearsed, debonair Fred Astaire smile, evincing private amusement at this unexpected coincidence. But she always smiled back even more enigmatically as she drifted past—always alone and aloof from the grubby, normal kid hoopla of high school life.

The time for the spring dance was fast approaching. It was the custom for dates to exchange invitations well before the event. Posters appeared. Mickey Iseley a big-name local band, was engaged to officiate. I decided to lay the groundwork for a move so daring, so hazardous that if I had ever confided my scheme to Schwartz or Flick, they would have immediately wrestled me to the ground, hollering that I had finally completely gone off my nut. But I had not breathed to a soul, even to myself, that I had designs on the most magnificent woman in all of Hohman High, if not of the known universe. Few common gophers ever entertained designs on prize-winning, thoroughbred fillies. I did, and learned a lesson that I have never forgotten.

One night, while safely huddled in the familiar lumpiness of the bed I had slept in ever since I had first crawled out of the playpen, staring up into the blackness—the faint sounds of distant, romantic whistles on trains bearing magic people off into the mysterious outside world drifting in through the cracked window shades and limp curtains of my bedroom—I decided to bestow my invitation to the big spring dance on Daphne Bigelow. My mind reeled with the mere thought of it! Craftily I began to piece my plan together. First I must have a date—a casual, everyday date—with her, and from there, inevitably, I would lead her to that dazzling ballroom where our love would finally be consummated in the throes of a dance I had zealously perfected in long hours of loose-limbed, sweaty practice, a dance that I knew neither Daphne nor any other woman alive could ever resist: the lindy. Among my peers, those who really appreciated subtle creativity, the beauty of the withheld statement, my lindy knew no rivals.

The next day my sardonic, martini-dry wit during Biology II flickered like a flame as Daphne hunched next to me over a huge night crawler that together we were dissecting, the heady aroma of her exotic French perfume blending provocatively with the rich fumes of preserving alcohol and dead worm. My courage grew as my bons mots became more and more epigrammatic. Oscar

Wilde would have stood tongue-tied in my presence. And then, casually, amid a brilliant analysis of Mr. Settlemeyer's teaching deficiencies, I prepared to drop my bomb.

"Oh, say, Daphne—heh, heh—pass me another round-head pin."

Snakily I watched her from the corner of my eye as she turned her gaze away from the benighted night crawler and reached her delicate hand, with infinite grace, over to the pin box. For a moment, panic almost stilled me. Her beauty was such that it took the breath away. Rallying quickly, however, I plunged on:

"Ah—heh, heh—"

I took the pin from her hand, the light brush of her fingers over mine sending goose-pimples all the way down to my Argyle socks and out the ventilation ports of my Keds. Without thinking, I did it. It came out in a rush.

"Howaboutyouanmehavinadate?!"

Instantly, I bent over my friend, the deceased denizen of the underground, a distinct ringing in my ears as the classroom faded from my consciousness and I stood alone, unafraid, in the bull ring. From somewhere off in the hazy distance I heard a flutelike voice say softly:

"What?"

Did I detect a note of incredulity, or was it my imagination? I repeated my question, not daring to so much as glance at her. After a three-century pause came the answer.

"When?"

From a distant auditorium, the school band struck up

The 1812 Overture. Cannons roared; bugles blew. I had scored beyond my wildest dreams! The rest of the conversation went by and is now mercifully lost from memory. But I remember mumbling something about a John Wayne movie, and that I would pick her up. She told me where she lived. The next night, a blessed Friday, was going to be *it!*

Realizing that there was much to be done and no time to lose, like an arrow loosed from the bow, I shot homeward the instant the doors of our pen were grudgingly thrown open. Closeting myself immediately in the bedroom, the scene of so many sweaty erotic daydreams, I went over every item in my vast wardrobe, carefully calculating piece by piece how best to achieve the magnetic effect I knew was necessary. Overlooking nothing, including my American Legion Ball left fielder's uniform, I considered, weighed, rejected, wavered; selected each tiny link in my crucial costuming for what was to prove a fateful night. Individual socks were pored over with infinite care, held up to the light, smoothed and laid reverently aside for a final screening.

Through my locked door filtered the usual family sounds: pots banging, my kid brother's occasional whimper, and finally, the roar of the old man's Olds up the drive. The shadows darkened and lengthened. At last my ensemble was complete. If the outward man has any shield against the slings of outrageous fortune, I was more than ready.

Now I was at the supper table, ready to let the family in on what could very well be a turning point in all our lives. My old man, seated to my left in, as usual, his long underwear, dug lustily into his meat loaf—which, as usual, he chopped up into small pieces, the better to mix with his mashed potatoes and peas, over which he splashed a heavy puddle of lush, piquant Heinz tomato ketchup.

My kid brother, his snout buried deep in his plastic Mickey Mouse Drinkee Mug, slurped noisily at his Cocomalt, which he attacked with a venomous hatred, recognizing the stuff for what it was—a cheap trick to get him to drink milk. The nightly fight that preceded this ritual had come and gone before my arrival at the table. As he drank, he performed the daily rite that my mother referred to as "playing with your food." For some obscure reason, he had found that mashed potatoes, meat loaf and red cabbage tasted better when molded into the shape of an inflated football. He occasionally varied this pattern by constructing other symbolic structures such as propellers, and once even a fairly good likeness of Tillie the Toiler. He then asked everybody:

"What does this look like?

Nobody ever told him. Our family did not use that kind of language at the table.

My mother shuttled between the stove, the sink and her chair, wiping up debris from around my brother, refilling my old man's coffee cup and in general keeping the action going. In the midst of all this, I asked casually, of no one in particular:

"Do you remember one time I told you about Daphne Bigelow? In Biology II?"

My mother, not accustomed to actual conversation from

anybody, at first did not grasp the meaning of what I had said, thinking that I had asked for more gravy. The old man, who rarely listened to anything said in the kitchen, banged his cup down with a clank on the white-enamel table as a signal for more coffee, a beverage to which he was passionately dedicated. I began again:

"She sure is a great girl."

Behind me, the refrigerator chugged and squeaked to itself, a sound that provided night and day a musical obbligato to our lives. My kid brother had extended his tongue to its fullest length, at least a foot and a half. He was using it to make great sworls in his red cabbage.

"Stop playing with your food!"

My mother slapped him smartly on the arm with a wet dishcloth and shoved a fork into his greasy mitt. Silently he glowered straight down into his plate to announce that it was going to be another of those nights. There were times when he was fed through the use of a funnel and a ramrod, my father prying his teeth apart with a screwdriver while my mother poured the turnips into him. Absent-mindedly, my father, glancing up from the sports page, said:

"Girl?"

"Daphne Bigelow."

My mother, now seated and trying to wrench the Mickey Mouse cup from my brother, who had placed it atop his head, asked:

"Who?"

"Daphne Bigelow."

"STOP FOOLING AROUND AND EAT!"

My father raised his head again and asked:

"What about her?"

Bracing myself for the big plunge, I looked meaningfully around the table at our tiny brood wallowing happily at the trough.

"Well, me and Daphne Bigelow are going on a date. I'm going to take her to the Orpheum to see John Wayne in *Hearts Aflame at the Old Corral*. She's really a great girl."

It was out! Irretrievably!

"I'm going to take the bus and go over—"

The old man cut in:

"The *bus?* Where does she live?"

No kid in the neighborhood had ever dated anyone who lived more than 150 feet away from his own warren. The idea of taking a bus to a girl's house was a truly revolutionary concept, and I knew it. Picking my words carefully, I laid the javelin home.

"Oh, she lives over on Waverly Street. On the North Side." The North Side! In one breath I had evoked an image of a land, a world so remote from ours, so inaccessible as to be almost outside the realm of reality. I might as well have said the North Pole. The North Side was a legendary fairyland of vast lawns, great elm trees and sprawling fiefdoms reached only by winding private drives through landscaped wonderlands.

My father, recognizing instantly the emergence of a new and possibly dangerous generation being nurtured in the bosom of his own home, was now alert and intensely interested. My mother lay back, suspecting a trick.

He asked:

"Did you say Daphne *Bigelow?*"

"Yeah."

"On *Waverly* Street?"

I had struck pay dirt. I played him like a rainbow trout on opening day.

"Yeah. She's in my Biology II class."

My mother, not fully realizing the import of what she had heard, fuzzily threw in:

"What happened to Esther Jane?"

The faintest trace of an enigmatic smile curled the corners of my lips. My father carefully smoothed out his *Chicago Herald-American*. He folded and refolded it with exaggerated care, and then said:

"Daphne Bigelow. I wonder if she's the daughter of Mr. Bigelow over at the Second Calumet Region National Bank?"

"Isn't he that tall, thin man at the second cage?" asked my mother. My father, radiating disbelief from every pore and speaking with some wonder, said:

"No. He's the chairman of the board."

This was news to me! But at the time I did not fully grasp what *kind* of news it was. I was to find out all too soon.

At the time, I thought a chairman was somebody who sat at a desk holding a gavel. I had no idea what a board was, other than the two-by-fours that Flick and I stole from time to time to use in various ways.

"Maxwell Bigelow is the guy who gave that ice-skating

rink to the park," said my old man. He was looking at me now with a very funny expression on his face.

"Oh, it can't be the same one. Does anybody want any more mashed potatoes before I put them back on the stove?" When confronted with inexplicable developments, my mother often pretended that they didn't exist.

"You've got a date with his daughter?" My father slowly stirred his coffee, steaming and black.

"Yep. We're going to a show."

"How did you get a date with her?" my mother asked.

"She's in my biology class. I asked her."

With infinite care and deliberation, the old man placed his cup on the tabletop. He was not a veteran Edgar Kennedy fan for nothing.

"You mean to sit there and tell me"—he paused dramatically—"that you just *asked* her?"

"Yep."

"Maxwell Bigelow's daughter? Maxwell Bigelow from the Second Calumet Region National Bank's daughter? You just *asked* her for a date?"

"Yep."

"Well, I'll be damned!"

Upward mobility had at last hit Hohman. It was the first recorded instance in Indiana of its occurring at the grassroots level.

My mother, who had been gradually sucked into what she now saw was a situation that even more mashed potatoes would not change, decided to go along with it.

"Well, you be *nice* to her parents."

I never quite understood what she meant by this advice—which she always handed out over the years. On various occasions she had advised me to "be *nice*" to teachers, to people on my paper route, to steel-mill foremen, and later even to first sergeants; all people or institutions that she recognized to be in absolute authority.

She continued: "I don't want anyone to think you weren't well brought up."

"Well, I'll be goddamned!" The old man, who had played such a large role in Bringing Me Up Well used this favorite expression to cover all occasions.

"Yep, I'm taking her to the Orpheum. And the Red Rooster afterward."

"Well, don't you keep her out too late so that her mother and father will worry." With that, my mother concluded her entire catalog of counsel about life and its problems. She took it as it came, and felt that as long as you were nice along the way, things would work out fairly well, provided you got home early enough.

All through dessert—her famous rhubarb rice pudding —technical matters of transportation, dress and behavior were discussed. Obviously I had scored heavily, and the awe that they felt about this unparalled achievement slowly gave way to righteous pride.

My old man unbuttoned the top of his long underwear and began to talk of great dates *he* had had in his feckless youth. In sullen silence, my mother cleared the dishes off the table and resumed her old station, hanging over the sink, Brillo pad in hand, amid the lingering aroma of red cabbage, meat loaf and coffee grounds. The squeaking of the refrigerator blended with the sound of Bing

Crosby singing about some Hawaiian babe from the radio in the next room. I began to feel my new status.

By bedtime, as I checked over my outfit for the great adventure. I found myself—for the first time in my life—a full-fledged hero in my own home, not an experience one has often, I have later found. But being a kid, of course, I was under the impression that this was only the natural state of affairs.

Later, in the dark, incredibly witty things to say to Daphne tumbled end over end through my churning mind. I sifted through my assortment of jazzy stories, which I had picked up from the ball field and the gym. In the dark I could see my lean-flanked figure escorting Daphne to a seat in the fabled lushness of the Orpheum. And then—whisked magically—we were in the number-one booth next to the jukebox at the Red Rooster. Casually I drop a coin in the slot, and amid admiring bursts of applause, I demonstrate my matchless lindy, waving casually for Bucky the counterman to knock together another of my specials. Daphne, her eyes shining in unabashed adoration, poured out her heart to me. Squeezing her hand, looking deep into those jade-green jungle pools, I knew at last the meaning of true soul communication. The night was full of laughter, song, dance and awakening love, all against the backdrop of soft spring skies—and, of course, the clean thrust of my chiseled jaw.

Waves of ecstasy coursed up and down my body as I tossed on my monastic pallet. Outside in the darkness, a few distant rumbles of early spring thunder mingled with the soughing of the eternal train whistles reaching into the dark, going away, coming closer, going away again. A few drops of rain pattered on the rusty screen outside my bedroom window. Gradually I fell asleep, but not without a struggle.

At first, as I awoke in the gray-green light that trickled in through the battered window shade and the roar of sparrows holding their morning orgy filled the room with whooping and hollering, I did not remember what day this was. Then I noticed my Number-One, Heavy-Artillery, Important-Occasion Sports Coat hanging on the back of my bedroom door, and I knew. This was D day.

I dressed absent-mindedly in my school clothes, my mind deep in scheming. At the breakfast table the aura of wonder was still rich and ripe. As I spooned in the oatmeal, my kid brother abortively tempted to wrest from me the glory that was rightfully mine by relating some trivial cock-and-bull story about a silly pumpkin he had drawn at school and that was being hung on the bulletin board. I smiled tolerantly and headed off for school.

That morning, when I joined my hitchhiking companions, my fellow freeloaders who every day pocketed—and squandered—the dime that was given to them by their parents to ride the school bus, it was all I could do not to tell them that although I was briefly among them, I was no longer *of* them. Flick particularly, that morning, seemed to be not only disrespectful but somewhat insolent. He had gained some degree of fame on the hitchhiking corner by an alleged exploit which, at least according to his overblown account, he had shared with a certain Juanita Clobberman. I, naturally, did not pull him up short, knowing full well that when the word got out that I had had a date with Daphne Bigelow—in full public view—there would be no question as to who was who and what was what among the hitchhikers.

I approached biology class, however, with certain trepidations. Perhaps she would chicken out. But no, it was like any other day, a routine class. As I crouched over our pickled grasshopper, Daphne was as cool and detached, as chillingly beautiful as ever, but now, deep inside myself, there was a mounting conspiratorial excitement that could not be denied. Almost at the very end of that session, in my most urbanely offhand manner. I came straight to the point:

"Uh—heh, heh—what time shall I pick you up? Ah . . ."

She smiled that faint extra-dry lemon twist of a smile, which to this day I remember above all smiles that have ever been aimed in my direction.

"Tonight?" she asked. An ice pick of fear jabbed up my spinal cord. She paused and went on:

"Oh, any time."

"Ah—how 'bout after supper?"

"Supper?"

Without knowing why, I knew that already I had ticked off a foul ball.

"Oh, you mean *dinner*," said Daphne.

Dinner? Dinner was something we had in the middle of the afternoon, on Sundays, Thanksgiving, New Year's

Day and Christmas. It was always eaten with the sun high, around three P.M., after which, immediately, my old man, his belt opened, lurching across the living room, burping loudly and bellowing, "Boy, am I stuffed!," would topple over on the sofa and instantly plunge into a snoring coma. I did not, therefore, see how I could pick Daphne up after dinner, and decided to play it safe.

"Well, uh—how about seven-thirty? We can catch the eight-twenty show."

"That'd be nice."

She smiled, and we returned to the world of the grasshopper, the cricket and the cockroach. The rest of the day passed in a kind of dreamy delirium. Bells rang, chalk scratched, basketballs swished through hoops, papers were passed from hand to hand, poems were read, questions asked. School droned on.

At last I was home. Into my bedroom I went. Every item of clothing I had selected the night before I carefully rechecked twice, going back over my entire wardrobe to be sure that in my enthusiasm I had not committed a sartorial *faux pas*. I hadn't.

"NOW DON'T ANYBODY TOUCH ANY OF THIS STUFF!" I shouted out into the hall.

My mother's pans rattled; my brother stolidly threw a ball against the side of the house out in the driveway as I went into the bathroom to begin the meticulous ritual of ablution that would result in a vision of masculine beauty so blinding that there could be no conceivable chance for anything but a spectacularly triumphant evening.

232

Carefully examining my face, the door locked tightly behind me, I worked with a surgeon's dispassionate skill over my usual blossoming array of bruises, blackheads and what my father called "old juicers." Applying steaming hot water between operations, I worked steadily, until finally there shone out of the bathroom mirror the fresh, pink, beaming image of dynamic handsomeness.

I leaped into the shower. This was an important enough occasion to warrant a second shower for the week. The water roared, and I spread a thick, vibrantly aromatic layer of pungent Lifebuoy lather over my Olympian torso. I had read enough ads to know what happened to those who Offend. I took no chances. The water ran alternately hot and cold, until finally I stood as pure and clean as the driven snow in the heady steaminess of the bathroom, buffing myself down briskly with a terrycloth towel. Reaching up to the top shelf of the medicine cabinet. I took down my father's can of Old Spice talcum powder, a gift that he had received many Christmases before and never, to the best of anyone's knowledge, used. I shook billowing clouds of its cloying sweetness down over me; dusting, brushing here and there, smoothing, anointing myself.

Stealthily using his heavily guarded razor, I then shaved myself to the veritable quick. All 17 of my downy golden fibers, undiscernible to the naked eye, washed down the drain with the shaving lather and warm water. My leonine mane of manly auburn hair, which had been thoroughly shampooed, I now massaged with a heavy elixir of what my father scornfully called "bear grease," a concoction put out by Vaseline to abet the ambitions of countless generations of Midwestern Lotharios. Its scent was more of a direct statement than a suggestion, being violent, highly volatile and—some said—inflammable when in close quarters.

Now came the most crucial task of all. I was known far and wide for my "cute wave," which did not come easily. Dragging a comb through my greasy locks, I began to mold my classic Grecian coiffure. Time and again I redid my masterpiece, only to be driven, as the true artist always is by the elusive dream of perfection, to start anew.

At long last, there I stood: the finished product, American manhood at its ultimate. Teeth agleam, seven pounds of carefully sculptured hair, exuding all the aromatic mystery of a thousand mingled scents enveloped in a palpable nimbus of pure Lifebuoy, the soap of those who care for others. As a final fillip, I gargled at great length, swirling it about my mouth voluptuously—a generous draught of Listerine. Well I knew of The Pitfalls of Halitosis, a dread disease that had struck down many a burgeoning romantic career at its very inception.

Springing light as a gazelle into the bedroom, I began to don my armor. Layer upon layer, I carefully girded my loins. Zero Hour was rapidly approaching. Tonight I would skip supper. First, a crisp new pair of Jockey shorts that I had kept concealed in my drawer for just such a state occasion. I debated briefly about whether or not to wear a T-shirt, finally deciding that I was sexier without. My white-on-white dress shirt, which I had received as a birthday present and worn only for genuinely high moments in life, was painstakingly unbuttoned. I admired its vast, razorsharp, seven-inch-long collar points, its Tony Martin high-rise, its crackling, crisp French cuffs. Pulling it on inch by inch so as not to create the slightest wrinkle, I buttoned it, using only the tips of my sanitary fingers. Then, reaching into my dresser drawer, I brought out the most effective weapon of my arsenal, a pair of magnificent bull's-eye cuff links, each link a great bull's eyeball outlined in dazzling gold. I loved to hold them in certain lights; they seemed to glow—a malevolent, baleful, virile shaft of masculine aggression. True, they made movement of the arm rather difficult, since their combined weight was several pounds, but it was worth it.

Now the tie. A thing of transcendent beauty. It had been given to me as a graduation present from eighth grade by my Aunt Clara. Tying my widest, fattest, sharpest Windsor knot—about the size of a man's fist—I drew it up under my collar with geometric precision. A glittering opalescent silver-gray, 100-percent satin, five and a half inches wide at its fulcrum, it bore in its center the hand-painted image of a beautiful red snail, and hung tastefully well below my belt. It was the greatest tie I had ever seen.

My slacks were a rich chocolate brown, high and pinch-waisted, beginning just under my armpits. They cascaded down over my loins, my kneecaps, and finally clung tenaciously to my ankles. Billowing, pleated, alligator belted, they were the slacks of a man who worked in the lindy as other artists worked in marble. I thought briefly of wearing my golden key chain with the emerald initials, but decided tonight I would underplay. Voluptuously, I then drew on my gray-and-maroon Argyle socks, and then neatly tied a perfect bow on each lace of my perforated, Scotch-grained-leather, full-dress, blunt-toed, crepe-soled bluchers; burnished to a high gloss, the rich dark-red Thom McAn cordovan leather glowed in the gloom of my bedroom.

There are moments of dramatic climax in the rite of dressing. Mine came when I donned my greatest pride— my sports coat. With infinite care, so as not to wrinkle my cuffs, I drew each waffle-weave woolen sleeve down clutched by the fingers, tugged at its low, sweeping hem, squared its massive, looming, horse-hair-packed shoulders, straightened its fashionable six-inch delta-wing lapels, and finally fastened its tasteful mother-of-pearl button. It lit up the entire room, its unique electric-blue shade sending off a lambent radiance of such promise, such rare, delicate aesthetic excitement as to crown my entire ensemble.

Rummaging through my socks in the little drawer of my dresser where I kept my secret papers, I hauled out my invitation to the spring ball. Carefully I tucked it into the inner pocket of my coat. After all, this was the reason for it all. Tonight I would present Daphne with the ultimate gift!

Walking carefully so as not to disturb a hair of my billowing pompadour, I ambled into the kitchen—not without some difficulty, since I had to inch sideways through my bedroom door to squeeze my enormous padded shoulders into the next room. The applause was deafening.

"Wow!"

My kid brother, openly awed at my entrance, raised his head dripping from the mound of creamed chipped beef into which he had burrowed—chipped beef being the regular Friday-night chef-d'oeuvre of our weekly menu. My familiarity with this epicurean dish was to prove invaluable basic training for my later years in the Army.

As I walked in—a veritable human Christmas tree—the pulse of family life noticeably quickened.

"My, you certainly look nice." My mother approved.

"Do you think you'll see Mr. Bigelow tonight?" my father asked, always hoping for an opening, some slight crack in the wall between us and real life outside.

"I don't know," I answered, breathing Pepsodent, Listerine and Sen Sen into the already rich mixture left permanently in the air of the kitchen by millions of boiled cabbages, fried bacon, souring milk and moldering dishrags.

"See if he looks like he does in the pictures in the paper," the old man said.

"Well, I better get going."

I glanced up at the clock hanging over the stove, a clock of purest white plastic made in the form of a large chicken, with two red hands. It didn't have actual numbers to mark the hours; instead, golden plastic letters marched around the rim spelling out: "It hasn't scratched yet." My mother had gotten the clock by saving Bon Ami cleanser labels. It was considered the most beautiful thing in that part of the house.

"Well, I'll see you."

My father smiled proudly; my mother smiled proudly; my kid brother stared blankly, chewing slightly. With a casual flick of my left hand in farewell, I slipped out into the night. It was a cool evening, with just the slight edge of winter coldness to it, the kind of night made for warm bodies snuggling together, for dark exchanges of deep thoughts, out of the wind, away from the unfriendly night.

Under the streetlight two blocks away, I waited for the cross-town bus, little realizing that a man named Charon would be at the controls. As I waited, not daring to move lest I disturb a crease, a button, a single undulating wave, I watched the mundane neighborhood life go on around me. The Bluebird Tavern halfway up the block flung open its doors briefly. A flash of light and Mr. Kissel reeled out into the darkness, his unmistakable starboard list instantly recognizable even at 200 yards. And there was Pulaski's Bull Durham sign on the wall of the old candy store (where I had spent many an hour of my callow youth in mortal combat with Old Man Pulaski over the purchase of jawbreakers, JuJu Babies and root beer barrels), looming high against the glow of the steel mills on the horizon. I could barely make out the familiar slogan under the massive bulk of that subtly humorous old bull on the sign: HER HERO. I looked up at him; he looked down at me. We were both in the same business.

The bus slammed to a stop, breathing out hot air and carbon monoxide. In I went, dropping my fare into the box with the practiced nonchalance of the true sophisticate, a man of the world out on the big town. There were no other passengers in the bus that night: I had my choice of seats. I sat immobile, protecting my razor crease, for the entire journey—through darkened streets, traffic, long stretches of used-car lots, junk yards, machine shops, car barns, gas stations, gray battered houses huddled in the shadow of monstrous gasworks. On and on.

Gradually the neighborhoods changed, until at last I was on the North Side. The bus rarely stopped now. Few got on or off except an occasional maid or elderly people carrying little bundles. Somehow the night was different over here: darker and yet more exciting. I watched the trees grow thicker and higher outside the bus window— hedges and graveled walks, until finally we reached my stop. I got off, and the bus roared on. Again I was alone under a streetlight. There were no Bull Durham signs. Mr. Kissel was light-years away. Even the street sign was different from those on the other side of town; a kind of carved Olde English sort of plaque swung in the breeze under the short, stubby little street lamp: WAVERLY STREET.

Daphne had told me that her house was the third one from the corner, on the right. I followed the broad, grass-lined sidewalk into the night. The air fragrant with well-tended lawns, rare budding tulips, freshly graveled drives. Here the houses were not hard by the street but, rather, buried deep in the velvety blackness; a glowing yellow light through the trees, here a glint of silver

239

there a splash of blue. I drifted on, knowing that at last I had reached a safe harbor, the world I had always known was mine.

There is something about the smell of well-being that is a balm for the most savage of souls, and yet contains the vaguest whiff of nameless dread. Now I stood at the foot of a curving asphalt ribbon that wound through a grove of overhanging trees, weaving between sculptured beds of rich loam. A small white sign read simply, BIGELOW. No street number, no explanation; just BIGE-LOW. The lure of the unknown, Circe calling from the rock, enticing ancient sailors to their doom—it was all there, beckoning; but in the American night, what 15-year-old with seven dollars in his pocket knows of this? Or cares?

It was one of those porches modeled loosely after the Lincoln Memorial: Neo-Greek and noble. I felt the tiniest twinge of fear, like the faint beginnings of a toothache. Never, outside of a Viven Leigh movie, had I seen anything like this. A bronze lantern hung amid the snowy vastness, casting a soft amber glow on the welcome mat before a stained-glass door—carved, sparkling, gleaming. The rest of the veranda trailed off into the blackness to the left and right.

I knocked. Nothing happened. I knocked again, peering through the colored panes into a hall; dimly lit, arched and vaulted, silent. I knocked again. It seemed as though I had been under that amber lantern for perhaps a month, maybe more, before I noticed a tiny carved-ivory button sunken into one of the fluted Doric columns that framed the vast doorway. A doorbell. I pressed. After a discreet interval, floating as if from a vast distance away, came the sound of two chimes. Then silence. I waited. The sound of approaching footsteps. Finally the door swung open and an elderly man dressed in black stood in the gloom.

"Master Shepherd?"

"Yeah . . . I . . ."

"Miss Daphne is expecting you."

I followed him down a short, wide flight of stairs to a vaulted hallway lit by a giant crystal chandelier and then through two sliding oak doors into an enormous, darkened chamber lit here and there by glowing bronze lamps.

"Won't you sit down? Miss Daphne will be down presently. I'll tell her you're here."

"Uh—thanks."

He disappeared. I sat on the edge of a high-backed leather chair that looked as though it had been hand-carved by a Spanish conquistador. I looked around. Books with leather binding, thick and wide, ran from floor to ceiling, fading off into the distance. A mammoth carved desk of black wood lit by a small green lamp stretched along one wall. Above it, a tall man with white hair, wearing a black suit, holding a book in one hand, his other resting on a dark-brown globe, looked down at me with a faint, familiar smile from a gigantic painting. I looked again. It was Daphne's lemon-twist smile.

A distant voice filtered down the curved, arching staircase that disappeared upward in the hall. Somewhere a light went on. I caught a glimpse of a long table, sparkling crystal, snowy-white linen, the kind of table and glassware I had seen only in the movies.

Then, suddenly, through the door came a tall, gray, dignified man. For a minute I thought he was the one in the portrait, but no, not quite. I rose. For the first time, I noticed that my shoes squeaked. His face was jovial, pink, a few white hairs over the ear, his suit brown, striped, elegant.

"Hi there. You're here for Daphne, aren't you?" he asked, sticking his hand out toward me, thumb skyward. It was the first time a grownup had ever offered to shake hands with me.

I yanked my mitt out of my right pocket, spraying change all over the Oriental rug. Nickels, dimes, streetcar tokens and a rare bottle cap I had been saving softly distributed themselves in artistic patterns among the furniture legs. He laughed as he shook my sweaty hand. We both bent simultaneously to pick up my dropped effluvia. My sports coat hunched up over my shoulders, burying my ears deep in horsehair. Together we scavenged about under rich cordovan leather, behind carved-ebony claws holding cut-crystal orbs.

"By George, this is interesting," he said as he scooped up my Magic Tom Mix Good-Luck Charm with the embossed secret Tom Mix TM Bar password.

"Heh, heh . . . yeah . . ." I replied.

I tried to hide the bottle cap, but it was no use. Three times I dropped my rare collector's item before I finally got it back into my pocket.

"You're Shepherd, aren't you, son?" His voice was yeasty, deep; it bounced off the oil portrait.

"Yeah. Heh, heh . . ."

"Sit down, my boy. Care for some sherry?"

"Uh . . . yeah. Heh, heh . . . I really liked cherry pop. How did he know? He pulled a cloth cord on the wall. A minute later, the old guy who had let me in appeared in the door.

"You rang, sir?"

"Yes, Drew. Bring us some of the sherry, will you? Well, young man, it certainly is tiresome waiting for the womenfolk, isn't it?"

"Yeah. It sure is. Heh, heh. It sure is . . ."

"Say! . . ." He looked at me with great interest, his white brows arched, his magnificent teeth glowing healthily. "Aren't you one of the Pittsburgh Shepherds?"

"Uh . . ."

He continued: "The Pittsburgh *steel* Shepherds?"

I could feel, actually *hear*, my face getting beet red. The Pittsburgh STEEL Shepherds! All I knew about Pittsburgh was that the Pirates came from there, but I did have an uncle who worked in the 40-inch soaking pits at the steel mill. I couldn't see how Mr. Bigelow would know him.

"Well, yes . . . I guess so. I do have some relatives in steel."

He slapped his knee and laughed.

"By George, I thought you looked like old Googie! I haven't seen the old rascal since our class reunion at New Haven! The next time you see him, tell him Max

Bigelow said—now get this, he'll know what it means—Bango!" He roared.

"Heh, heh. I sure will."

"Don't forget, boy. Bango!"

Over his shoulder, off in the middle distance, I saw a maid moving back and forth along the immense table, touching a glass, arranging a napkin. A huge grandfather clock, seven feet tall, all brass and dark wood, ticked quietly in the rich air.

The old guy shoved a silver tray under my nose and smiled. Panicky, I reached for the thinnest, tiniest glass I had ever seen. It looked like my Uncle Carl's eyecup, only tinier. I had it for a brief instant between my thumb and forefinger, its stem barely discernible. And then, suddenly, it tipped over and the warm amber fluid soaked into my best slacks, dripping down inside over my kneecap and down my leg, to be absorbed by my Argyles.

"Oops!" Mr. Bigelow bellowed. "Bad luck!" Immediately, the old guy was back with another glassful. I took it and held it tight.

"Cheers!"

"What?"

"In your eye!"

"What?"

It was then that I think he began to suspect. He sipped his drink and watched me narrowly as I raised my glass to my mouth and drained it in a single gollop. A raging bolt of fire streaked downward.

"Gaaahhhkkk!"

"What did you say, boy?"

". . . Gork!" My eyes watered, my throat burned. Deep in my stomach a pot began to boil. Never in my life had I had anything stronger than a fleeting sip of my Uncle Tom's homemade root beer.

Mr. Bigelow settled back in his deep leather armchair and for the first time really looked at me. It was then, inexplicably, that my sports coat began to glow in the dark. His beautifully cut muted mocha creation looked like no suit I had ever seen before. It was not a Cleveland Street pick-'em-off-the-pipe-rack special. Even I knew it. My father's only good suit was a kind of yellowish color with a tasty kelly-green plaid. Its lapels, high and sweeping, jutted out like the mainsails on a Spanish galleon. He always wore his lodge button stuck in the left sail, a pin the size of a nickel made in the shape of a Sacred Beaver. He belonged to the Royal Order of the Beaver, Dam 28. Mr. Bigelow wore no pins.

Stealthily, I tried to hide my left cuff link, which had somehow begun to send a shaft of purple light to the ceiling. No sooner had I gotten it under my electric-blue sleeve than the other one switched on even brighter. I pulled it out of sight and sat with both arms clamped behind me, my French cuffs crinkling. Then I noticed that my beautiful shoes were getting wider; the soles of which I was so proud had grown thicker and squeakier. I tried to hide my Argyles by tucking my bowling balls under the chair. Mr. Bigelow watched, but said nothing. Finally he called out:

"Daphne. Your . . . *date* is here." His voice had changed.

"Well, have fun," he said to me. "Don't stay out too late." He smiled, again that lemon twist that Daphne used, then rose and left the room.

Almost on cue, Daphne appeared atop the broad, sweeping balustrade and glided gracefully down the thick, carpeted stairs. I stood, my cuff links jangling, my shoes squeaking, the bottle cap in my pocket clanking loudly against my Tom Mix lucky charm, my enormous padded shoulders swinging back and forth. But I was not at a loss for words.

"Heh, heh . . . Hi, Daphne."

"So glad to see you."

"Yeah. Likewise."

"Well, shall we go?"

We moved from room to room, down the marble entrance hall and finally out onto the dark, amber-lit veranda.

"Dad said we could use the car."

"The car?"

A long black Cadillac gleamed like an ebony crypt in the driveway, the one I had half seen near school. A man in black darted out of the bushes and opened the back door with a sweep. Daphne stepped in. In my panic, I cracked my shin such a thump against the doorsill that my teeth rattled for an instant.

"Heh, heh . . . By George!" I hadn't lost my presence of mind.

I hobbled into the car, stumbled across a deep wall-to-wall rug and groped my way to the back seat, my leg throbbing dully. A thin trickle of blood oozed down my shin.

We waited in the drive. In the front seat, the man who had opened the door sat quietly. After what seemed like 20 minutes. Daphne finally came out with:

"Well?"

"Well, it sure is a nice night out." I was really sharp tonight.

The driver turned and said, "Where to?"

Daphne waited. The Cadillac waited. The driver waited. Fuzzily suspecting they were waiting for me, I took the plunge:

"Uh . . . the Orpheum."

The driver said, "The *Orpheum?*" with a rising inflection that was familiar. Many teachers had used it on me before, an effective oleo of dignity and scorn. Daphne, her voice calm, said quietly:

"Yes, Raymond. The Orpheum." The note of stainless-steel authority was one she did not use in Biology II. I had not seen this side of Daphne. It interested me.

Silently, the car began to roll. We wound through the trees, past the flower beds and out into the great night through the tunnel of green, past looming hedges, wrought-iron gates, antique lanterns, and finally into the street.

I flayed my jelly-like mind for something to say. Where was my agile whipcord brain? What had happened to my famed cool irony? Finally, I quipped:

"Boy, it sure is nice out."

"Yes, it is a lovely evening."

"It sure is. Boy."

A flash of inspiration percolated through the coffee grounds of my cranium: "Old Settlemeyer's really a gasser, isn't he? Boy!"

"He *is* . . . amusing."

I did not know till that moment how wide, how vast, car seats could be. Daphne was at least 30 yards out of field-goal range, perched miles away from me on the billowing dove-gray cushion we shared. Raymond, two and a half miles ahead of us, was obviously clearly out of earshot.

Dauntless, I wondered how she would react to a quick clinch. I watched her out of the corner of my eye to see whether there were any outward signs of passion yet. It was hard to tell at that distance. Finally, I decided once again to play it safe, a tendency that has cursed me all of my life.

We were now in the streetcar—hot-dog-stand-neon-sign belt. As the terrain became more and more jazzy, more familiar, my courage rose. I was just on the point of making a quick grab for her delicately turned ankle and risking the whole caper on one shot in the dark when we drew up before the Orpheum. Such was my frenzy that I was caught off guard and didn't notice that the car had stopped and Raymond was holding the door open for our descent back into the real world.

"Well, here we are," said Daphne pointedly.

Coming to, I stepped out of the limousine, cracking my good ankle heavily against the curb. Where I came

from, cars had running boards. Raymond, alert, shot
a hand out as I pitched forward, grabbing my left shoulder
pad in an iron grip like a quarterback about to throw a
60-yard pass. Of course, all he got was a handful of
the horsehair, excelsior and tiny bedsprings with which
my coat was equipped to give me the stylish Chicago
Bears lineman look that was so admired in the sophomore
class. A few threads snapped and gave, but I stood upright.

"Are you all right, sir?"

"I was just kiddin' around."

I playfully belted him in the ribs. He coughed slightly
and drew back, his eyes flat, opaque.

"Just havin' a little fun, Raymond."

He did not laugh.

Daphne joined me on the sidewalk under the brilliant
glare of the white lights of the friendly old Orpheum
marquee. The usual motley rabble that hung around the
Orpheum entranceway every night—to watch the girls go
in or just to look at the red-and-yellow posters displaying
sinister Japanese soldiers tying Merle Oberon to 500-
pound bombs—openly gawked at the black land yacht,
Daphne, and my electric-blue coat. Quickly I scanned
the crowd, hoping for at least one envious face. There
was none. I bought the tickets and we passed inside. Mr.
Woscowski, who had replaced Mr. Doppler as manager
after the infamous Orpheum gravy-boat riot of my youth;
took the two tickets, ripped them across and dropped
them in the slot with one motion. I tried to catch his eye

in order to let Daphne know how widely known I was, but he ignored me.

Into the blackness we went. Some of the more meaningful moments of my life had been spent in this dark, warm cocoon. The Orpheum had always seemed to me one of the greatest places in the world. With suave assurance I convoyed Daphne safely down the littered aisle, popcorn crunching underfoot, ankle-deep in candy wrappers, to my favorite row of seats in the left-hand section halfway down. We sat directly behind a couple who, if not engaged in actual copulation, were certainly doing a good impersonation of it. On the screen a 75-foot John Wayne glared stonily into the rolling hills.

Since I had seen the picture twice before, I hoarsely outlined the part we had missed into Daphne's fragrant, shell-like ear. But I got the distinct impression of a lack of concentration on her part. Ahead of us the two seats squeaked and groaned. The girl, if that's what she was, giggled briefly as they battled on. A masculine voice in the darkness ahead mingled with the sound track overriding it sharply:

"Aw, for Crissake, Nan, come on!"

"Stop it!"

The slap of flesh sharply striking flesh, followed by a burst of raucous laughter.

I became aware of a movement behind as a large knee crept up the back of my seat and rested on my right shoulder. It pushed forward, tilting my seat three or four inches nearer the combatants ahead. I turned and said politely into the darkness:

"Do you mind removing your knee?"

A blast of alcohol engulfed me.

"WHO'S GONNA MAKE ME, YOU SON OF A BITCH?"

Now, in the Orpheum under normal circumstances, this was a direct cue for action. For a moment I almost forgot myself. Fighting for control, however, I forced myself to ignore the outrage and said to Daphne through clenched teeth:

"John Wayne is sure good."

She said nothing. She was sitting bolt upright, a rare sight in the Orpheum, and seemed to be peering around in the darkness at the huddled figures that surrounded us.

"Who ya lookin' at, baby?" a merry-making steelworker asked bluntly. Another challenge.

Daphne, tilting her head gracefully, whispered into my ear:

"This is a very *interesting* place."

It had never occurred to me that the Orpheum was a very interesting place, at least not the way she put it.

"Yeah. It's great. Really great."

Somewhere far off to our right, someone unleashed a gigantic, resonant burp, after a prolonged rasping gurgle, a guy really dredging it up from the bottom. Scattered applause and laughter followed. From the balcony a shower of Cracker Jack drifted down over the center section, accompanied by three folded airplanes that danced briefly in silhouette over the Western prairies.

"Wouldja like some popcorn?" I asked.

"No, thank you."

"How 'bout a Coke?"

"Maybe later."

We sat numbly together in the rickety seats. Comparative calm reigned for half a reel or so, and then the final collapse of the evening began. During a tense moment on the screen—in dead silence as John Wayne waited for the attacking rustlers to come over the hill, the audience crouching forward in nervous anticipation. Daphne herself showing discernible signs of interest—a low rumbling began. At first I thought it was a DC-3 flying over on its way to Chicago. It got closer and closer, louder and louder. It seemed to come from all directions at once, a low bass thrumming. It grew in volume. In the dark, my palms turned to ice. Oh God no, not now!

My stomach was rumbling! It was a great joke in the family that when I missed supper, or a meal was late, the old gut would bang it out like an anvil. As the roaring gurgle sighed off into the distance like a freight train crossing a viaduct, the voice behind me, still on the muscle, barked out:

"Cut it out, ya slob!"

More cackles. Daphne cleared her throat.

"Excuse me," I said.

After all, I didn't want the Bigelows to think I wasn't well brought up. My gut settled down to its regular idle after the first clarion blast and continued muttering throughout the movie.

I had always taken the Orpheum for granted. All of it. But now I began to notice things that I had never been aware of. Somewhere off behind us there was a continual flushing of plumbing. I could hear the projector whirring, accompanied by the low-voiced, nonstop argument between the two operators. I hoped Daphne didn't notice. But she caught something else.

"Certainly smells funny here."

"What d'ya mean?"

"You don't notice?"

"Oh, yeah. Yeah. Sure."

After all these years coming to the Orpheum, how was it I had never before been aware of all those feet? I sat quietly, sorting out scent after scent, hoping desperately that Daphne didn't recognize most of them.

The picture neared the end. John Wayne told Charles Bickford, the cattle baron, how he'd have to move on 'cause he was the roamin' kind. I knew it was now or never. My fingers crept softly over my knee, over the armrest, poised in the dark for a moment and then dropped slowly over Daphne's exquisitely modeled hand. For a few seconds we sat unmoving; her fingers, cool and smooth, nestled in my sweaty palm. I stared straight ahead, afraid to break the spell. Even my stomach stopped rumbling out of respect for this magic moment. Ahead of us, the tangled couple had fallen into a comatose state, lulled perhaps by satiation or maybe by the tender sentiments of *Hearts Aflame at the Old Corral*. Thus we sat to the final frame, the last slanting rays of the Western sun outlining a lone rider galloping into the distance.

The lights came up. Unfastening our hands, we moved

together back up the aisle and out into the glare of the marquee. Welders, steam fitters, kids, old men wearing black hats pushed and shoved around us. The Cadillac waited. Raymond at the wheel. Daphne said the first thing either of us had uttered for hours, it seemed:

"That was certainly a very interesting place. I'm really glad you brought me to it. Do you come here often?"

"Nah. I just thought you might find it interesting."

"Well, it certainly was."

We were back inside the chariot. Already its rich dove-gray aroma seemed homey and familiar to me. I was about to instruct Raymond to wheel us down to the old Red Rooster when Daphne said in a small voice:

"It's certainly late, isn't it? I had no idea how late it was."

Raymond, without a word, turned his battleship against the traffic and we headed back toward the North Side. For a few moments nothing was said, as the limousine hummed silently along. The heady excitement of social triumph surged through me. Stealthily my hand crept like a predatory spider over the soft mohair, closer and closer to Daphne, as I whistled a few snatches from the Hohman High Victory Song. Raymond tooled on, coolly, discreetly, as the trees grew higher, the privet hedges appeared and the neon signs receded.

Closer and closer. We touched! For a single quivering instant, and then quietly she drew her hand away, laying it in her mysterious lap.

"Did you finish that caterpillar drawing?" she asked.

"Caterpillar drawing?"

"In lab."

"Oh, yes. You can copy it Monday."

We rode on in silence. I groped frantically for some feeble straw, some last bit of flotsam to cling to, to keep the conversation going. It was no use.

"I sort of like Mr. Settlemeyer," she said finally.

"He's all right, I guess."

We pulled in the drive, up to the veranda and stopped. Raymond whipped the door open. This time I knew how to get out. Daphne took my hand and shook it, the second time it had happened in the same night!

"I've had a very lovely time, and I want to thank you."

"I had a great time, too. It sure was great."

"Raymond would be glad to drive you home."

"Oh, no, I'll walk. I live just a few blocks over, on Harrison," I lied spectacularly.

"Well, see you in class. Good night."

She was gone.

"Sure you don't want a ride, Bud?" Raymond had changed.

Without a word, I turned and walked down the long curving asphalt drive between the flower beds, under the trees, past the stone sundial, the iron gates, the white sign that read BIGELOW, out into the night, walked in my electric-blue sports coat, my hated, rotten, crummy electric-blue sports coat, its padding squishing and banging against my shoulder blades, its hem flapping against my knees, walked with my long, fluttering tinfoil noose with its monster snail crawling up and down—my despised, ridiculous tie—walked in my booby, pleated, sacky clown pants, walked in my Tony-Martin-collared, French-cuffed, miserable, jazzy shirt. Walked and walked.

I had struck out. My old man had struck out. My mother had struck out. Even my kid brother had struck out. I sailed my Tom Mix lucky charm off across the street toward a delicate, lacy gazebo and walked on, mile after mile, through leafy streets, under catalpa trees, eventually past lurking pool halls, taverns, junk yards, used-car lots. I never knew it was so far to the North Side. Finally I walked under the Bull Durham sign, past the Bluebird, up the back steps, through the screen door and into the kitchen. It was then I remembered for the first time that the invitation to the spring ball was still in my pocket.

I breathed in the aroma of red cabbage, spilled ketchup, fermenting Brillo pads, my mother's Chinese-red chenille bathrobe. Opening the refrigerator, I peered into the yellow, fragrant interior. A dish of peas from last week, a meatball with a bite out of it, what was left of a baked ham, a plastic container with some pickled beets. Home. Smelly home.

Grabbing the meatball, I stuffed it in my mouth, washing it down with milk from the bottle, and was about to rip off a piece of ham when the kitchen light blasted on. Her hair in curlers, her bathrobe hanging limply, my mother beamed sleepily.

"Did you have a good time?"

"Sure did."

"Were you nice to them?"

"Yep."

"Well, that's nice. I don't want them to think you aren't well brought up. Well, hurry to bed."

"OK. Night."

I finished the food, snapped off the light, stumbled through the dark into my bedroom, removed my repulsive sports coat and my pleated slacks—smelling faintly of sherry—and threw them in the corner next to my baseball bats. I sat on the edge of my bed in the dark. A sparrow rustled under the eaves outside the window. In the next room my kid brother muttered in his sleep. The sink burped moodily. The refrigerator chugged and squeaked. I thought briefly of that long table, with all the crystal and the maid touching things here and there. I wondered idly if Esther Jane Alberry had gotten her invitation to the spring ball yet. Then I lay back on my lumpy mattress and finally fell asleep, but not without a struggle.

THE RETURN OF THE
SMILING WIMPY DOLL

"Kongratulations upon buying such a fine products! You have choosed wisely upon procuring our very fine patented (Pend.) devices. The guarante which accompanies herein is unquestionably good for one year or less. If fuse is not twisted? Note base of green color is not easily found to be crackable. To operate correctfully merely plug into standard U.S. (A.C.) two pronged electrics (110 V.). Immediately your Deluxe Yule A-Go-Go Tuneful Musical Revolving Puncture-Proof Table-Model Aluminum Xmas Tree should begins function. (Deluxe Model 2-A is capable of being folds. If excessive care is observed. This provide storage.)"

I reread the directions, which must contain somewhere a clue to the technical trouble I was experiencing with my sparkling little Japanese-made aluminum beauty, a triumph of modern science over the tuneless, nonreusable, old-fashioned Christmas tree of yesteryear. The only trouble was, the damn thing squatted there dark, mute and unrevolving in the middle of my winter-streaked picture window overlooking my beloved wasteland of Manhattan, even though I had taken every precaution to make sure it was plugged into the correct electrics. Maybe my Yule A-Go-Go is polarized, I thought, with my usual technical know-how, on which I pride myself as an ex-GI.

Dropping to my knees, I crawled laboriously behind my Danish Folding Swing-A-Ding Coucherama, inching forward toward the only electrical outlet that my entire high-rent, three-and-a-half-room apartment supported. I plunged my hand into the giant rat's nest of three-way, five-way, nine-way extensions and plugs, by dint of which I managed to squeeze out enough electricity from my one outlet to run my entire life. From somewhere in the distance, deep in some murky air shaft, came the faint strains of recorded Christmas music. I jiggled the plugs, reversed the green one from my Yule A-Go-Go and crabbed backward from behind the couch.

Nothing. Returning to the tree, I picked it up and examined it from all sides in the gray light that filtered in from what passes for a winter sun in the big city. There were no knobs, no switches, no unseemly mechanistic protuberances. Aha! Again my brilliant technical mind leaped in excitement as I spotted on the underside of the Christmas-green polyethylene base what appeared to be the head of an embedded fuse. Quickly I scanned again the thinner-than-tissue-paper sheet of instructions. A single phrase leaped out at me: "If fuse is not twisted?" Do they mean to *twist* the fuse or *not* to twist the fuse? Since my Yule A-Go-Go wasn't yet playing carols and suffusing my apartment with a festive aura of soft Christmas lighting the way the ad said it would, I deduced that they must mean to *twist* the fuse.

Squinting closely at the base, I observed that the fuse was recessed well below the surface. It would require more than my fingernails to do the job. In a frenzy of creativity, I rushed out into my kitchen, where I kept my meager supply of tools, fished out my dime-store pliers and reurned to the fray. As I grasped the base firmly in one hand, the pliers in the other chomped solidly onto the head of the fuse. I gave it a smooth and clean twist.

For a single instant I felt the Christmas tree stir under my grasp, its tiny red, yellow, blue and green lights flaring brightly. The high, thin notes of "I'm dreaming of a white Christmas" bounced off the ceiling. Then a dull, roaring sensation boomed up my arm, crashed into my shoulder, down my spine, hovered for a moment in my pelvic region and then whinged out through my other arm. For a moment, I stood frozen; then I toppled through a cloud of billowing smoke—striking my head smartly against the arm of my burnt-orange Naugahyde Barcalounger—and lay for a full minute, during which I had the clear impression of being on a skiing trip in the Alps, which is rather odd, since I am resolutely anti skiing. Tentatively, my mind gradually groped back into focus and I knew the worst. I had just voided another guarantee.

I crawled to my feet, my silken dressing gown still smoldering slightly, and staggered over to the couch. I sat down heavily, flicking my wrists, attempting to restore some circulation. It was a little early in the morning for shock therapy, I reflected. Christmas decorations lay scattered about me. Absent-mindedly, I examined a plastic bag containing two sprigs of neoprene mistletoe. In red, Christmasy lettering, PLASTOKISS splashed across the gay bagging. Well, at least you don't have to plug this stuff in, I mused.

Little did I realize that this fiasco was but a prelude to an electrifying pre-Christmas trauma that would set the tone for the entire yuletide fortnight. Wisps of blue-gray electrical smoke eddied about my bookshelves. The shock had given me a more than moderately nasty headache, which, piled on top of my usual Saturday-morning hangover, should have been enough hint of impending events. But we live from moment to moment, rarely perceiving the vaster plans that contrive to undo us.

The doorbell rang. My mind, slowed by its unexpected jolt of Con Ed juice, at first did not respond. It rang again. Finally, I heard a disembodied voice that I dimly recognized as mine call out:

"What do you want?"

From beyond the door, I heard the surly, guttural tones of the doorman: "A package."

A package? Instantly the cobwebs fled. There is nothing that brings the roses to the cheeks of a man quicker than to announce he is receiving a package. Leaping to my feet, I lurched forward, barking my shins against my free-form coffee table, and limped to the door, oblivious of the thin crimson trail of blood I left behind me.

LIFE—THE COMPLETE CEREAL. Sweat poured down my

brow as I read the green block letters printed on the huge, lumpy, battered cardboard carton as I struggled to drag it over the sill of my apartment door. Slowly I inched the monster burden over my $700-a-yard, mocha-shaded wall-to-wall carpeting and into the living room, my Sulka dressing gown sopping wet with honest perspiration. Even the monogram drooped.

Painfully, I toppled the hulking mass end upward, hearing from inside a muffled clinking and clattering, a tinkling, rolling, sifting, grating mélange of sound from within the battered carton. Even as I eased myself down into my magnificent alligatorskin Pakistani sling chair to rub my shattered shin, which was now beginning to throb, the box continued to emit muted noises, like sand filtering down through a mess of broken Christmas-tree ornaments. From deep inside came the low whir of a spring suddenly uncoiling. It stopped, ticked twice and was silent. Somehow, that spring and the sound it made were vaguely familiar. Then began a faint, derisive quacking, as of some demented duck calling to its lascivious mate. Instinctively, I struck out at the carton with my clenched fist. The duck quacked once again and the giant carton lapsed into an ominous silence. Only the sound of distant sirens, keeping the citizenry at bay, drifted in from the outside world.

I knew that damn duck! Which is not an easy fact to accept before lunch. Awkwardly, I struggled out of my chair and stood looking down at my prize. For the first time, I noticed that there was an envelope taped on the top. It was addressed to me, hand-written in a familiar script:

> Merry Christmas. I was cleaning out the basement the other day and I came across all kinds of junk you had when you were little. I figured rather than throw it out, I'd send it on to you. A lot of it is still good and you might want to play with it, especially the Kangaroo Spring-Shus that Aunt Min gave you for Christmas.
>
> Love,
Mom

With an involuntary groan, I plumped down on my rickety camel-saddle seat and read the letter again, finally letting it fall to the floor between my feet. Seven tons of kid effluvia! What a master stroke of sadistic Christmas gift giving! Already my apartment was loaded to the gunnels with *grown-up* mementos—my complete library of first-edition *Peanuts* paperbacks, my matched set of souvenir pillows from 37 Army camps west of the Mississippi, my matchless, nationally known collection of rare swizzle sticks, all personally earned. My life was already overflowing. And now this! I thought briefly of throwing the whole mess down the air shaft.

Then, from deep inside the box came another sound, a faint honking, as of some ancient flivver caught in a long-forgotten traffic jam. It stopped. Maybe it was the duck, maybe the horn, maybe Christmas itself; but I found myself rising slowly from the camel seat, picking up my pair of shears and standing over the vast carton. From some remote apartment came the unmistakable beat of that new smash Christmas hit *The King Wenceslaus Rock* by the Bullwhip Four. Taking a deep breath, I plunged the shears into the top of the box. There was no turning back. As I sawed away, I began to be conscious of a rising twinge of apprehension. What was in this box? After all, as a kid, I had had a lot of things in my possession at one time or another that I would not want my mother to know about. Furthermore, it came as a somewhat nasty shock that this stuff was still in existence.

Finally, the shears chewed through the last strand of baling wire and the top of the battered receptacle stood ready for the final assault. Unflinching, I grasped the flaps and ripped. Instantly, an odd, indefinable odor rose from the muddled moil: musty, basementy, a slight touch of rust. I think I detected even a bit of residual ancient sweat mixed with other scents so subtle and ephemeral as to be unclassifiable.

Inside the cover, my mother had crumpled large sections of the editorial page and want-ad columns from an old copy of the *Chicago Tribune* that she had picked up, probably, from a pile of old newspapers in the basement. One faded headline read: "B-24 SQUADRON HITS SICILY IN DAYLIGHT RAID; REPORT SUCCESS; THREE PLANES LOST." The crumpled panels of a comic strip caught my eye. I smoothed it out and once again was face to face with Harold Teen. He was trying to get Lillums, his little lettuce leaf, to go to Pop Jenks' Sugar Bowl with him. Then Beezie Jenks said something that will be forever lost, since that part of the strip was ripped away. I noticed that Terry had not made second lieutenant yet but was still a struggling air cadet. Ruthlessly, I crumpled the papers, tossed them aside and peered down into the gloomy morass within the box. It was worse than I thought. A rich, moldering compost heap lay like some archaeological treasure-trove before me. For a fleeting instant, I felt like King Tut would feel if he came back and somebody insisted he take a tour through the Egyptian section of the Museum of Natural History to look at all his junk in the glass cases.

Gingerly, I reached down into this sorry mess of pottage—I must admit, with a certain amount of uneasiness, because there was no telling what was in there, and I've always been worried about getting bitten by things. Warily I grasped a round, furry projection that barely topped the surface of this sea of trivia and slowly began to pull from the rubble a battered, fuzzy, brownish, truncated form, which, as it began to emerge from the wreckage, I recognized with growing horror. Great Scott! There, staring insidiously up at me, hanging from my fingers by one ear, was something from so far gone in my dim past that at first I thought this was just some nasty trick of my mother's. But no, I knew it was mine.

I don't know how to say this, but there, right in my apartment in midtown Manhattan, surrounded by my paperbacks of Kafka, Nietzsche and Rona Jaffe, was—please don't think too harshly of me—my Teddy bear. Yes, I confess it. There was a period in my life when I would no sooner have gone to bed without Brownie than I would have thought of saying bad things about Santa Claus. And there he was, looking up at me, one black button eye hanging loose, the other peering right through me with the steadfast, baleful glare of one who knew me when and knew me all too well. And clinging to him, so help me, was the faint but unmistakable aroma of what is euphemistically called baby "urps"— vague remains of ancient Pablum, petrified oatmeal and insinuating touches of Fletcher's Castoria.

I held Brownie out at arm's length before me. He dangled, revolving slowly in the ambient air—immutable, imperishable, eternally cuddly, wanting only to comfort me in the dark hours of slumber. Discreetly, I turned his good eye away from me, since he seemed to be trying to tell me something, laid him down on the sofa and wandered over to the window to stare for a long, gloomy moment out over the teeming city. If the word ever got out in certain circles that my pad housed a Teddy bear named Brownie, it would do me no good at all. The mere fact that I had ever *owned* a Teddy bear would have been enough in some quarters!

Bracing myself with a drink, I returned to the box. Taking a little more care this time to guard against undue shock. I slowly withdrew from the entanglement a flat, stuffed, cutout figure made of colored oilcloth. It stood approximately 12 inches high. For a long moment, this strange apparition and I confronted each other without a spark of recognition. Dusty, a bit faded, a little round oilcloth man wearing a derby and sporting a ragged mustache and a potbelly, he smiled enigmatically over my shoulder toward the kitchen. Somehow he looked familiar, and yet. . . . Then, from some far-off rubbish heap of memory, I heard a voice, a cracked, comical voice on the radio, asking, beseeching, demanding, wheedling, whimpering for more hamburgers. My God! Hurray! It's my Wimpy doll!

It will surprise many historians to learn that at one point in American history there was actually a Popeye radio program. Popeye, Olive and Castor Oyl, Ham Gravy, Wimpy and the whole crowd came into the living room every day. They offered you a choice of a Wimpy doll, a Popeye doll, an Olive Oyl doll or an Alice the Goon doll if you ate enough soup and sent in the labels. We were a canned-soup family, so there was no problem collecting enough labels, but I was probably the only kid in the United States who didn't order a Popeye doll; I went for Wimpy, a down-at-the-heels moocher who lived only to stuff his gut with hamburgers. I identified with him; and I'll never forget the day my Wimpy doll arrived. He immediately outranked Brownie; and for one hectic era, I was one of the very few Americans who went to bed every night with a guy wearing a derby and smoking a cigar. I must admit I was glad to see the old freeloader again. His oilcloth was a little seedy; the stuffing was edging out of his frock coat, but somehow that was as it should be for Wimpy. Carefully, I laid him alongside his old rival and returned to the hustings.

A thin leatherette strap caught my eye and carefully,

so as not to break any of these precious artifacts, I dragged forth a strange, dusty, dangling black object covered with snaps and buckles and exuding the heady aroma of musty sheepskin. Faint silver letters could be seen through the basement patina of grime. Dipping a finger in my drink, I carefully wiped off the grease and dirt. B-U—one letter was missing—K—another missing letter—O-G-E. . . . Bless my buttons! My genuine Buck Rogers Space Helmet! For intergalactic flight. With sheepskin lining and—uh-oh, don't tell me! My old lady's lost them or thrown them out! I hurriedly scrabbled through the tangled mess and, with a great sigh of relief, pulled out my precious space goggles. Oh, wow! Their scratched, yellowed plastic lenses were curling at the edges, but I reverently pulled them down over my head and snapped them into place—after first carefully shaking out three dead cockroaches and an elderly retired moth. I tugged at the ear flaps of my space helmet, squeezing it down over my cranium, marveling at how it had shrunk. Finally, I snapped the chin strap shut and rushed into my bedroom to admire myself in the mirror, as I had done so many times in the past. Ah, yes, the same intrepid traveler to the 25th Century, the fearless, flinty-red protector of the beauteous Wilma, old Dr. Huer's trusted friend, stared back out at me. But there was one thing missing.

Instantly, I was back at the box—and, sure enough, there it was, a little rusty, a little pock-marked, but still excitingly dangerous-looking. Made of imitation blue steel, it was my faithful Flash Gordon Zap Gun, the same gun that had destroyed Ming the Merciless with its deadly Disintegrator Rays. I leveled it at my Black Forest Persian Water Clock and pulled the trigger: Twa-aaannng! The achingly familiar sound of the deadly rays with which I had gunned down my kid brother, disintegrated Flick, Kissel and Schwartz thousands of times over echoed weakly in the room. The scratchy sheepskin tickled my ears the way it had so often in the past. This helmet and I had been through hell together—not to mention giant snowstorms through which I had burrowed, trusty goggles protecting my eyes, as I pretended that I was on a space flight to Venus, Buck Rogers Space Rockets strapped to my back, on my way to trap the vile Black Barney, who was now in league with Zog, evil master of the Swamp Planet, to subjugate the entire known universe.

Faintly, through the leatherette, the sounds of the *1812 Overture* from my stereo-FM tuner reminded me of one of the bloodiest battles I had ever fought in my kidhood. It directly involved the honor and reputation of my idol Buck Rogers. Without provocation and entirely without grounds, Schwartz had alleged that Flash Gordon could take Buck Rogers any day and that if it wasn't for Flash, Ming the Merciless of the planet Mongo would have us all in his clutches. This slander could not be brooked by any Buck Rogers fan, so we mixed it up under Schwartz' front porch for the better part of an hour, rolling in the dirt, tearing our shirts, banging each other's heads on the rocks, sweating and crying. But he didn't convince me and I didn't convince him. In any case, it was good to have this helmet back. You never know when it might come in handy.

I knew that somewhere in that pile of kid junk there must be the Buck Rogers Spaceship that I had gotten from the Buck Rogers radio program. It was made of lead and attached to a long string, which you were supposed to tie to a chandelier; given the proper shove, the spaceship would then twirl around the room, making a high, whistling sound. Which it did, until one night when my old man got it in the eye in the dark and ripped it down, tearing half the chandelier off the ceiling.

Reverently, I removed my helmet and goggles, laid aside my zap gun and reached once again into the grab bag. After fumbling around for a moment or two, I felt a round metallic object, which I at first thought was my beloved Mickey Mouse watch, a beautiful timepiece whose dapper yellow gloves occasionally pointed to more or less the correct time. But it wasn't. Corroded, its gilt finish peeling, it was the size of a watch, but beneath its glass top I could see the number 227.4. I scraped off some of the grime and read the embossed inscription—OFFICIAL JACK ARMSTRONG WHEATIES PEDOMETER.

From out of the wind tunnel of my mind, a commanding voice dramatically intoned: "Fellas and gals, with the Official Jack Armstrong Pedometer, you can tell just how far you walk every day, how far it is to school, how many miles it is to the store or the scout meeting. You'll never be lost if you wear your Jack Armstrong

Pedometer at all times. For just one Wheaties boxtop and twenty-five cents mailed to Jack Armstrong in care of this station. . . ." This was an important find. I examined the pedometer closely, ticking the counter lever with my thumb. It still worked. It still made that telltale click at each revolution. I remembered great herds of kids wearing corduroy knickers drifting schoolward through the boondocks, clicking as they went. The whole neighborhood sounded like an enormous flock of crickets, day and night, as kids measured how far it was to everywhere. I could still see the funny look on Miss Shields' face as, one day in fourth grade, I got up, on direct orders, to go to the blackboard to demonstrate my grasp of the multiplication table.

"What's that clicking?" asked Miss Shields.

"I'm measuring how far it is from my seat to the board," I said.

"Give me that," is all she said as she stuck the eighth pedometer of the day in her bottom drawer.

Pulling up my pajamas, I strapped the pedometer to my right knee, got up and carefully paced the distance to my bar, returned to my seat and took a reading. Hasty calculations revealed that six martinis would result in traveling one twelfth of a mile. Happy as a clam, I dug back into the box and unsuspectingly unearthed a shadowy horror out of my past that caused me to rock back in my chair in a wave of terror. My God! The evidence still exists! The crime had lain dormant in the back of my mind for years, gnawing at my conscience like some dry rot in the foundations of a haunted house.

Furtively, I examined my find, shielding it in my hand so that if by remote chance there were onlookers, they would not see the incriminating cellophane envelope that I held. That old sick nausea of fear of discovery, of the unmasking of my calumny, the exposure of my rottenness, hit me again. I am not proud of what I had done, but I was young and unformed. Youth is always immoral, but if I had it to do over again, I know I would do the right thing. I held it up to the light, and there they were within the envelope—yellow and green, light blue, triangular-shaped, the collection of "Rare exotic hard-to-find Foreign stamps," which, in a headstrong moment of criminality, I had once sent away for—on approval. On approval meant you sent them your dime *after* you got the stamps. I do not have to tell you that I not only never sent in the dime, I never intended to. I remember the letter that came from Kansas City a month later, threatening my father with jail and me with a criminal record that would last throughout my life if I didn't ante up. I almost passed out when I read that; and after carefully burning it in the furnace, I decided I'd better pay. But I never did. I never heard from them again, although for years I had fleeting impressions of men in dark coats and Homburgs shadowing me wherever I went.

I tucked the stamp collection well back under the middle sofa cushion and moodily sipped my drink. Maybe that was the first misstep, I thought. Maybe if I had paid for those stamps, I could have marched through life clear-eyed, clean, honest, straight to the

White House. I'll bet Lyndon Johnson paid for *his* stamps! On second thought, however. . . .

It was with an effort that I returned to my investigation, fishing up next a collection of thin sheets of paper bound together with a crusty old rubber band that broke in my hand immediately, spilling the crinkly slips out over the floor. Cockamamies! I had unearthed some unused gems from the precious collection that I had bought over the years at Old Man Pulaski's. He really hated the times when we would come in to buy these tissue-paper tattoos that dissolved in water.

"All right, you kids, I ain't got no time for foolin' around. Either ya want pictures or ya don't."

Schwartz, Flick, Kissel and I, peering in through his glass case, would finally, after great soul-searching, decide on which magnificent artistic views of Old Faithful we wanted. I picked up from the floor a cockamamie showing a Marine in a green helmet sticking a bayonet into the thorax of a bright-yellow Jap soldier. A great fountain of crimson blood squirted out over the M-1. The Jap's eyes were slanted evilly, his mouth contorted as he hurled an Oriental obscenity at the square-jawed Marine. The caption read: "GUNG HO!" It was a beautiful picture, and I remember the day I bought it, my mother wouldn't let me put it on.

Here was my chance. I licked the ancient decal, tasting the old familiar glue flavor that I knew would not leave my mouth for a month, and meticulously smoothed the soggy cockamamie onto the back of my left hand, blowing on it expertly, as I had done so often in the past, to dry it off. Now for the delicate part. With the skill of a surgeon, I slowly peeled off the moist backing. There, in four beautiful colors on my left hand, was as magnificent a representation as I have ever seen of a Jap corporal going to his just rewards. I wondered what the gang at the office would say to me *now?* I knew that I would be the envy of all eyes and that it would especially impress the typing pool. I held my hand out admiringly, knowing that if I didn't wash my hands, I could keep it intact for at least a month.

By now, I must admit, I had been sucked bodily into this sobering and edifying dissection of my yeasty formative years. Old excitements and cravings, fugitive passions and desires crowded in upon me. With gusto, I drained off what remained of my bloody charlie and prepared to push on through the undergrowth of my childhood, little realizing the pitfalls and traps, the traumas that lay ahead.

My cockamamie had hardly dried when I found myself holding in my hand as sinister an object as I had ever owned, an object with a history of the sort that is rarely whispered in mixed company and that could and did make strong men weep. It was a penknife, but a penknife with a difference. Shaped like a lady's leg, no less—a lady's leg wearing a chromium-plated high-heeled shoe. The mother-of-pearl calf bulged enticingly and tapered off just above the knee. It carried two blades: one for ordinary cutting, the other for snipping off the butt ends of long black cigars. As I inspected it, the vision of an early but decisive humiliation sprang out from the knife directly into my consciousness.

My knees cracking warningly as I arose, I carried the grizzled weapon to the window. Holding it at the proper angle as I had done in the past, I looked for the silver shield embedded in the mother-of-pearl calf. Ah, yes, it was still there. I raised the knife to eye level, peering deep into the tiny hole in the shield, upward at the watery sun. There she was. My old paramour, who had contributed to many a sweaty evening and feverish dream, her grass skirt provocatively parted at mid-thigh, her roguish gypsy eyes glowing as brightly as ever, her ample and bare bazooms still in full, magnificent, flesh-colored bloom. She was the lady who had caused my disgrace and eventual court-martial from the Moose Patrol, Troop 41, Boy Scouts of America.

For months I had whined and cajoled, trying to pry out of my parents the price of an official Boy Scout knife. No one in our troop had a complete uniform. Some wore only khaki knickers; others sported only the broad-brimmed campaign hat; one or two had just a canteen; I owned only my purple neckerchief with the gold letters B.S.A. I wanted a knife to hang from my belt, like Flick had. My Uncle Carl, who spent the entire Depression playing his banjo and going in and out of pool-rooms, hearing of my burning desire, one day fulfilled my wish. I distinctly recall the conversation. He wasn't wearing his false teeth that day, but he did have on his straw hat.

"I hear ya want a knife."

"Yeah."

"How would ya like this knife?" He fished out of his pocket the lady's leg in question.

"WOW!"

"Wait'll they see that at the Scout troop. That's better than any old Boy Scout knife," said Uncle Carl.

I held it in my hand for the first time. He bent over and whispered into my ear, his beery breath enveloping me in warmth and suds. "Look into that hole on the side. And don't tell your mother." That was the beginning. The next week, she was an instant smash hit at Troop 41's meeting. And two weeks later, I was drummed out in disgrace when Mr. Gordon got wind of what the Moose Patrol was cackling about.

I put my trusty knife into the pocket of my dressing gown and returned to the fray. An angry gust of December wind rattled my window as I wallowed among Christmases past, days of Ovaltine and morning-glories. I found myself holding a singular object that at first I did not recognize. In fact, it was so grotesque that it was hard to believe that the human mind could conceive of such a surrealistic *object d'art*—a gently curved, warted, plastic, winged golden pickle, imprinted with the cabalistic symbol "57." The number had a curiously familiar ring: 57 what? Operative 57? No, that didn't sound right. And why the pickle? Then it hit me. Heinz' 57 Varieties! Sponsored by the pickle company, Colonel Roscoe Turner and his famous Flying Corps, of which I was a fully licensed and qualified member, had appeared in a comic strip that ran under *Tillie the Toiler* back in the days when Jiggs was hitting the corned beef and cabbage hard and Maggie was hitting Jiggs even harder. Turner's creased, intrepid face with the dashing Errol Flynn mustache had been the very embodiment of flying. His only passenger was a lion cub named Gilmore. I pinned the wings over my left breast and decided to have an extra shot of catsup with my hamburger that night, for old time's sake. There was a time when I devoutly believed that when I grew up, I would not only be a pilot but would own several pairs of beautifully tailored, whipcord pilot-type riding breeches. With put-tees. Here I am, grown up as much as I'll ever be, and all I've got are a couple of pairs of baggy Bermuda shorts, and I don't even know where I could lay my hands on as much as a single puttee if I had to. They don't even *name* guys Roscoe anymore. He did more for the canned-soup and piccalilli industries than Billy Graham has done for evangelism.

The next 15 minutes I spent happily working the plunger on my Captain Midnight Ovaltine Shake-Up Mug, which I immediately saw would be handy in whip-ping up a batch of gibsons. I next blew several high, piercing blasts from my Captain Midnight Three-Way Mystic Dog Whistle, causing 17 mutts in apartments as far as two blocks away to howl and bark frantically as I communicated to them in Captain Midnight's secret code, the same code that I had used to send secret messages across the back yards and alleys to Flick and Kissel.

Unexpectedly, I then ran across a veritable fortune

in unrealized assets. Here, for years, I had been moderately wealthy and did not know it. I discovered seven—that's right, *seven*—unredeemed Good Humor Lucky Sticks, each good for one free Good Humor bar any time I cared to cash them in. I could not figure how I had let them go by the boards when I was a kid; but then it slowly came back to me—the summer I had hoarded them for my old age. I had read a story in a comic book about an old man who didn't save when he was a kid and now was reduced to begging on street corners. The moral was to Save For A Rainy Day. It scared me so much that I began to lay away uncashed pop bottles, Lucky Sticks and slugs for free games on the pinball machine. Vestiges of chocolate syrup remained on the valuable premiums. I wondered briefly whether I could cash the whole lot in with Emile, the bartender at the Existentialiste du Morte, for an Irish coffee.

With moist eyes, I riffled through my prized collection of Fleer's bubble-gum cards, illustrating great moments in American history. There was good old Washington still crossing the Delaware, Paul Revere galloping over the countryside on a green horse, Abraham Lincoln making a speech. Dog-eared, thumbed, well worn and faithful, my collection—one of the world's most valuable of its kind—was completely intact. As I glanced at them, my jaw hinges ached dully from countless pounds of obscenely pink bubble gum that I had pulverized to get these cards. One card, in particular, told a story. It showed Robert Fulton waving a flag from the deck of his steamship. That card had cost me four fillings in one chomp of the gum; the sickening crunch of a mouthful of silver as the bubble gum did its deadly work is a feeling not soon to be forgotten.

The next item plunged me into such a funk as to necessitate an immediate trip to the sideboard for two fingers of the straight stuff. At first glance, it was a supremely innocent artifact. But to me, who lived through it, who suffered with it and was irrevocably scarred for life because of it, it was far more than a ten-cent package of nasturtium seeds. I looked at the brilliantly colored picture of gigantic prize-winning blossoms shown on the slender envelope of rattling seeds. It all came back —that grim week long ago that began with such high hopes and that ended in a black despair that had forever made me quail at the word "salesmanship."

Miss Shields that spring had enlisted us to sell seeds in the neighborhood in order to buy a set of World Books for the Warren G. Harding School. Her stirring, impassioned speech—exhorting us to get out and sell the seeds to "all your friends and neighbors who are waiting for you to deliver them"—had stirred me to sign up for a whole box of 12 envelopes. I ran all the way home, eager to hit the trail. My first jaunty knock was on the door of the gray house by the corner. A haggard, sleepy lady peered out of the darkness at me."

"What d'ya want?"

"Uh—d'ya want to buy any seeds?"

"Any what?"

"Seeds. I have marigolds, pansies, hollyhocks. . . ."

"*Seeds!*" The lady's red eyes glared out at me.

". . . Nasturtiums, morning-glories."

The door slammed shut. Miss Shields had not mentioned this possibility. At the next house, a large brown dog, closely related to the jaguar, chased me around the garage four times before I made it over the fence. Next door, a lady holding four babies and surrounded by a moiling thicket of wailing urchins peered dimly out at me, shaking her head silently.

House after house it went like this, until finally, at the end of four miles of humiliating defeat, I emerged a bent, stooped, tiny, wizened, nine-year-old Willy Loman —footsore and weary, without so much as a single seed sold. Finally, weeks later, various aunts paid for my stock, but I was left with this last unsold package of nasturtiums.

As that old sensation of self-pity overwhelmed me, my knuckles ached once again from knocking on unyielding doors as I stared through misty eyes at those brilliant nasturtiums. For some reason, I found myself wondering whether the seeds would actually grow and what they would produce if they did. I have heard that ancient grains of wheat taken from the tombs of Pharaohs have been made to sprout and prosper. Tenderly, I placed my remaining stock of seeds next to Wimpy. For a moment, I thought perhaps I might go out this afternoon, knock on a few apartment doors on my floor and maybe make a sale. But then the old fear took over and I knew I couldn't do it.

Right on the heels of the nasturtiums, as if by evil design, I came across a mint-condition flat-white can of

White Cloverine Brand Salve, another relic of my ill-fated career as a boy salesman. The ad in the comic book had read: "Kids! YOU may be the one to win this beautiful SHETLAND PONY! He will be awarded, along with thousands of other prizes, to winners in our big Sales Sweepstakes. Just help distribute to your friends and neighbors that old family stand-by White Cloverine Brand Salve." It pictured a smiling, freckle-faced, red-headed kid holding the reins of a brown-and-white Shetland. I clipped the coupon. God only knows what horrors would have descended on the household if I *had* won a pony.

Shortly thereafter, an enormous case full of White Cloverine Brand Salve arrived, and another trial by fire began. Once again, I was tested and found wanting. After 17 giant suppertime fights, and after I had sold only three cans of salve—one to my mother, one to Mrs. Kissel and one to me—my father wrapped the whole thing up and sent it back to the Cloverine people, hollering: "LET THE BASTARDS SUE! THEY CAN'T GET BLOOD OUT OF A ROCK! IF YOU EVER SEND ANOTHER DAMN COUPON IN, YOU WON'T SIT DOWN FOR A MONTH!" That ended that, technically, but nothing had ever sealed the ugly gash in my soul.

Next came my battered, rainbow-tinted Official Tournament Model Duncan Yo-Yo, its paint worn smoothly away along the groove from endless hours of Walking the Dog, its string knotted and blackened, trailing off into the mass of memorabilia. I pulled and tugged at it.

Something was attached to it. Out of the depths it came like a struggling freshwater catfish, glinting dully in the faint gray light of my apartment. I held it up, suspended from the yo-yo string, to examine it. Slowly spinning before my eyes was one of the true treasures of my youth, my Melvin Purvis G-Man Badge. I searched quickly and discovered, still intact and ready for action, its matching set of Melvin Purvis G-Man Escape-Proof Handcuffs, just like the ones John Dillinger had slipped out of so many times. I knew that somewhere down in the tangle must be my Melvin Purvis G-Man Book of Instructions on HOW TO STOP CRIME. It was. I glanced at the first page, entitled "HOW TO TELL A CROOK": "G-Men have found that crooks cannot look an honest man in the eye. Always look at the eyes of suspects for the telltale evidence." I remember the day I tried it on Grover Dill. "What are *you* lookin' at?" was all he said before he hit me in the mouth. I guess Melvin Purvis never had to deal with anybody like Grover Dill.

As you have no doubt deduced, there was a period in my life when I was an implacable foe of crime. Every week I listened intently as Warden Lawes of Sing Sing intoned on the radio: "Attention! All citizens be on the lookout for Harry Rottenstone, known as Harry the Fink, wanted for armed robbery in Oklahoma. He is five feet, eight and one half inches tall, usually of mean disposition, a diagonal scar running from left ear to jaw, steel-blue eyes, tattoo on right forearm of red heart: MOTHER. This man is armed and presumed dangerous. Notify the police. Do *not* attempt to take him singlehandedly.

Notify your local law-enforcement office. This is Warden Lawes saying 'Good night.'"

Every day after that, I coolly surveyed all passing strangers for telltale scars. Eventually it had to happen, and it did. I spotted a thickset steelworker getting on a bus and ten minutes later reported him to the big cop who helped kids across the street in front of Warren G. Harding School. The feeling of stark righteousness and bravery that I experienced at that moment, coupled with my natural fear of cops, is still fresh in my memory.

"Officer! I just saw Harry the Fink! He got on the Island Steel bus!"

"Harry who?"

"Harry the Fink! I heard about him on the radio. He robbed Oklahoma!"

"Oh, for God sake! You're the ninth kid today that's seen Harry the Fink! Last week it was Iron-Lip Louie. They oughta make listening to that damn Sing Sing program against the law. I'll Harry-the-Fink you! Get in school. You're late."

Between Warden Lawes and Mr. Keene, Tracer of Lost Persons, the cops must had had their hands full night and day. Mr. Keene was always announcing about how somebody had wandered away from his wife and seven kids in Minneapolis and was last seen wearing a blue suit and driving a black Plymouth with the name "Bubbles" written on the trunk. A population with its eye peeled for runaway husbands and escaped embezzlers did not make things easy down at the old precinct house.

I knew that somewhere under this pile of junk must be my FBI in Peace and War Official Fingerprint Kit, for which I had sent in two Lava soap wrappers. You *needed* Lava soap to get that crummy, sticky black ink off your fingers after you got the kit. I remember running the rubber roller, loaded with ink, right up the back of my kid brother's neck, a dismal incident that could well have been one of the contributing factors that led directly to World War Two.

A flash of red caught my eye and another trophy of another long-lost afternoon confronted me, a battered, bright-red plastic fireman's hat bearing the motto: ED WYNN TEXACO FIRE CHIEF. For one brief, feverish season, this Fire Chief hat was an absolute *must* for every right-thinking kid. Ed Wynn came on the radio with that big old siren, with the fire bells banging, wearing a hat exactly like this beauty. They gave them away at the Texaco station to anybody who could afford gas, and also at the World's Fair.

Gingerly, I placed it atop my head to see if it still gave me that old feeling of pizzazz. I arose, walked to the window and, for reasons that are obscure to me, raised the glass and stuck my head out, high over the roaring canyon of the Manhattan street. The sun bore down weakly as I said to myself:

"You are absolutely the only guy in all of New York that is wearing an Ed Wynn Fire Chief hat at this minute. You are unique. Hurray!"

At that instant, a gust of frigid wind struck me smartly on the left side of my cranium. I felt the Fire Chief hat lift slightly, and in an instant it was gone. I stared as it turned over and over, drifting down toward the traffic jam, a tiny, red, uproarious Ed Wynn horselaugh volplaning down to the sidewalk.

In a panic, I rushed into the kitchen and pressed the button on the phone that connected me with the doorman far below. His voice filtered up through the hum.

"Yeah?"

"MY FIRE CHIEF HAT JUST FELL OUT OF THE WINDOW!"

"Yer what?"

"My, uh—" I suddenly realized what I was saying. "My, uh—my Fire Chief hat."

"Fire Chief hat—out the window."

"It's red! It says Ed Wynn on it."

"Ed who?"

"WYNN! ED WYNN!" I was shouting.

"Don't he live on the third floor? In 3-C?"

"NO! ED WYNN, THE FIRE CHIEF!"

"You got a *fire?* You want me to call—"

"LOOK, GODDAMN IT! THERE'S A RED FIRE CHIEF HAT ON THE SIDEWALK IN FRONT OF THIS BUILDING, GET IT AND BRING IT UP TO ME!"

There was a long pause, until finally: "OK. If you say so. . . ." He hung up. I rushed back to the window to peer down. Sure enough, I could see the midget figure of the doorman far below, looking up and down the street. My God! A tiny kid had my hat on his head! Without thinking, I shouted down 16 floors:

"GIMME BACK MY HAT, KID!"

Instantly, dozens of passers-by peered up, hoping to
see another suicide. I saw the doorman tangle with the
struggling kid far below. A few shadowy faces appeared
at apartment windows across the avenue. Stealthily, I
pulled down the window and hid behind my madras
drapes. What am I doing? Skulking back to the sofa—
my Jack Armstrong Pedometer clicking, the cockamamie
on my left hand glowing brightly—I sat down and tried
to get a grip on myself. I know what I'll do. I'll wrap
all this junk up, throw it in the back of the closet, get
dressed and go down to P.J.'s. The hell with this. I'm
a grown-up man. What do I want with an Ed Wynn
Fire Chief hat?

It was no use. I couldn't kid myself. I wanted my hat
back. For years I had never once thought of my hat
and didn't even know I still had it, and now I wanted
it more than anything in the world. Even my cutout
cardboard Grumpy mask, which I got from *Pepper
Young's Family*, didn't seem to help. I stuck my nose
through the cutout hole in the mask and snapped the
two cracked rubber bands over my ears, my eyes staring
bleakly out through the slits in Grumpy's map.

I sat for a moment, wanting to go back to the window
to see how the doorman was doing but afraid they'd
spot me across the way. Suppressing the thought, I returned to the box and resumed my excavations. Rummaging about, I next rediscovered my old blue-steel bicycle clip for my pants. I snapped it on the left leg of my
pajamas to see if my ankles had gotten fatter. It was

then that I noticed my old canvas delivery bag from the time I had a magazine route: COLLIER'S, LIBERTY MAGAZINE WAS emblazoned in red letters on the side. Tucked in the bag was an old Nabisco Shredded Wheat Color Card. I could see where I had badly colored Niagara Falls with Crayolas. I pulled the shoulder strap down over my neck and was amazed to find that the bag came up under my armpit. It used to hang down around my knees. It must have shrunk. I was attempting to adjust it when my doorbell rang.

He's got it! I leaped to the door, flinging it open. Al, the Ukrainian doorman, stood in the hallway, holding my Ed Wynn Fire Chief hat.

"You got it! GREAT!"

"That kid sure put up a fight." He extended his paw, holding the battered plastic helmet.

"He can get his *own* hat!" I hissed. I noticed that Al had an odd look on his face.

"How come you're wearin' that mask, mister?"

I had forgotten completely about my false face, which I was still wearing. I figured I'd better play it cool:

"Oh. that's Grumpy. I'm doing a little work here this morning."

"Oh, I see," he said, backing off a bit as he noticed my bicycle clip and my *Collier's* delivery bag.

I reached out for the Fire Chief hat and knew immediately that I had made another mistake. The screaming yellow Jap on my hand, his blood gushing forth, lit up the entire hallway. Al started slightly and said:

"I never knew you was in the Marines. I was in the

Navy. You oughta see the tattoo I got on my backside!
Gung Ho!"

"Oh, that. I was just doing a little painting around
here."

As I took the precious Fire Chief hat from his grubby
claw, he noticed the Jack Armstrong Pedometer that
hung from my right knee.

Retreating hastily—clicking with each step—I mumbled
my thanks and slammed the door. There was no doubt
about it. I knew I would have to move. When the doorman told this story around, I would be cooked.

Pouring myself a neat brandy, I began to straighten
up the joint, ruffling through the still-untapped drift
of effluvia that remained in the box. What further horrors
lay here entombed? What as-yet-unrealized embarrass-
ments? There was my Joe Palooka Big Little Book, my
Junior Birdmen of America Senior Pilot's License, even
the four-color Magic Slide Rule Patented Piano Lesson
that had guaranteed to teach me to play in just seven
minutes. There was my Mystic Ventril-O, with which I
had unsuccessfully attempted to mystify my friends by
throwing my voice into trunks, hollering in a comb-and-
tissue-paper voice: "HELP! Let me out!" There was my
Charles Atlas Dynamic-Tension Muscle-Building and
Chest Expanding Course, my periscope, my match-cover
collection, the magnifying glass with which I had set
Helen Weathers on fire. It was all there.

Gingerly I tilted the huge box over onto its side. A
tinkling, squeaking, musty avalanche spilled out over the
floor—and my benighted youth lay shimmering before me

like some surrealistic collage of adolescent dreams: my Tom Mix Whistling Ring, which never whistled; my Captain Midnight Photomatic Code-O-Graph badge and Secret Squadron Bomber Wings, which lost their pin the very first instant I tried to attach them to my pullover and caused a fit of hysterics that has become legendary in my family, a fit that resulted in my mother banning *Captain Midnight* listening in our house for almost a month. Rolled in a sad little ball were the tattered remains of my Jack Armstrong pennant from Hudson High, a school that, by an odd coincidence, flew the same colors as the orange-and-white Wheaties box. I thought for a moment how well it would look over my desk at the office, and then sadly dismissed the thought. Lovingly, I fingered my Huskies Club pin, an athletic organization sponsored by the people who manufactured Grape-Nuts, a cereal that I remembered chiefly for its ability to crack false teeth. For a moment I stared off into the middle distance, seeing with stark clarity that dramatic instant when my grandmother's dentures shattered with a loud report on a mighty spoonful of that nutlike cereal, known for its gentle laxative action. Grandma was never quite the same after that. Lou Gehrig, who was the president of the Huskies Club, maintained in many a comic-strip advertisement that it was because of Grape-Nuts that he was able to follow Babe Ruth in the Yankee batting order.

A tiny, shriveled square of cloth next caught my eye. Great balls of fire! My Sky Blazers Arm Patch, which proved conclusively that I ate two slices of Wonder

Bread every day. Tom Mix Straight Shooter premiums, long forgotten but never forgiven, emerged; and a Tom Mix Special Sun Watch, to be used when lost in the jungles of Yucatán, a place I have always half suspected I would end up in, anyway. If you're lost in the head-hunter-ridden jungles, you'd better know what time it is. My pulse quickened as I extracted from the grisly array a device that could come in even handier: my Tom Mix Periscope Ring. I dusted it off and slipped it on my pinkie. Holding it up to my eye, I could see in hazy outline the bathroom door—*behind* me! The uses for such a device are obvious, especially around an office filled with ambitious, bushy-tailed young executives on the make.

Did mine eyes deceive me? No. Beneath a pair of Tom Mix spurs lurked my most occult treasure, a genuine Mystic Voodoo Skull Ring, with genuine simulated emerald eyes—a ring designed to put curses on your enemies. There is no doubt that such a ring could still have its uses. I slipped it carefully into my pocket, already formulating plans. Next came an *objet* of such poignant personal meaning that instinctively I turned my eyes away from it. Its very presence brought back an afternoon that even today rankles in my soul as one of those really terrible things that happen to all of us. My Uncle Ned had given me a dollar bill for my ninth birthday. Crisp, clean, of a beautiful green color, I held it for an all-too-brief time. Minutes later, I stood in front of a diabolical machine at the candy store, a machine filled with such tremendous bonanzas as Brownie cameras, wrist watches and cigarette lighters embossed with naked ladies; flash-lights made in the form of tiny revolvers, all floating in a sea of multicolored candy BBs. All you had to do to get one of these treasures was to skillfully operate two chromium handles, which in turn maneuvered the claw of a tiny steam shovel inside the case. Nickel after nickel I poured into this monster, growing more nervous and sweaty as each time the claw didn't *quite* grab the Brownie. Finally, after 85 cents had gone down the drain, it threw me a contemptible lead watch fob bear-ing the likeness of Myrna Loy.

I sucked moodily on my long-lost Dr. Christian Bubble Pipe. An angry wind laden with sooty ice crystals banged briefly at the windows of my apartment. It was getting colder. Sadly I returned it to the dusty magic mountain of illusion—lost and gone, grieved by only the wind. I had had enough. Back into the box I stuffed Brownie, Wimpy, Grumpy, Ed Wynn, Roscoe Turner, Jack Arm-strong, Melvin Purvis, Buck Rogers—the whole teeming throng of them from out of the past. Over this communal crypt I laid the Dead Sea Scrolls—carefully smoothed newspaper fragments bearing the faded face of Harold Teen, and Perry Winkle's round sailor hat, and the yel-lowed headline "DAYLIGHT RAID ON NORMANDY PORTS. B-17S BOMB COAST."

Replacing the cover, I twisted the wires back together, binding the whole thing in place. For a fleeting moment, I considered shoving the whole sorry mess out onto the garbage landing. But I chickened out. Staggering under

the load, I dragged my childhood to the hall closet.
With an enormous effort, I got it up to the top shelf.
Mysterious rattles and tinkles and squeakings continued
for a few seconds. Then, silence—except for the muffled,
jaunty quackings of my old rubber duck. I read the
lettering on the box again: LIFE—THE COMPLETE CEREAL.
I wondered whether my mother had picked that box
purposely. You never know about mothers.

Outside, the long December afternoon was darkening
into night. It wouldn't be long before the crowds of
Christmas shoppers and Rockefeller Center holiday rubes
would give way to the big-time, out-on-the-town crowd.
Across the avenue, Christmas trees glowed through Vene-
tian blinds. From the apartment next door drifted the
nasal tones of a 12-year-old protest caroler singing *Jesus
Don't Love Me Anymore, but I Got You, Babe,* the
current spiritual smash, to the accompaniment of his
electric tambourine.

I sat for a long moment in the gathering gloom and
then suddenly noticed the huddled form of my little
green aluminum Japanese Christmas tree. On impulse, I
fished around in the rubble on my coffee table and
came up with a thin, dime-sized copper disk with the
faded inscription POPEYE SPINACH EATERS' LUCKY PIECE.
Cradling it in my sweaty palm, I picked up the Christmas
tree and gingerly unscrewed the fuse that I had twisted
to death. With my forefinger, I carefully inserted my
old badge of spinach addiction and Popeye fandom.
Magically, the thin but unmistakable notes of "I'm dream-

ing of a white Christmas" filled the room and the tiny tree began to pirouette, its hidden mechanisms working flawlessly, its miniature red and green, blue and yellow candles sending out a dazzling rainbow of soft Christmas cheer. Lovingly, I place it on the window sill for the world to see. Popeye had saved the day again.

WANDA HICKEY'S NIGHT
OF GOLDEN MEMORIES

Puberty rites in the more primitive tribal societies are almost invariably painful and traumatic experiences."

I half dozed in front of my TV set as the speaker droned on in his high, nasal voice. One night a week, as a form of masochistic self-discipline, I sentence myself to a minimum of three hours viewing educational television. Like so many other things in life, educational TV is a great idea but a miserable reality: murky films of home life in Kurdistan, jowly English authors being interviewed by jowly English literary critics, pinched-faced ladies demonstrating Japanese brush techniques. But I watch all of it religiously—I suppose because it is there, like Mount Everest.

"A classic example is the Ugga Buggah tribe of lower Micronesia," the speaker continued, tapping a pointer on the map behind him.

A shot of an Ugga Buggah teenager appeared on the

screen, eyes rolling in misery, face bathed in sweat. I leaned forward. His expression was strangely familiar.

"When an Ugga Buggah reaches puberty, the rites are rigorous and unvarying for both sexes. Difficult dances are performed and the candidate for adulthood must eat a sickening ritual meal during the postdance banquet. You will also notice that his costume is as uncomfortable as it is decorative."

Again the Ugga Buggah appeared, clothed in a garment that seemed to be made of feathers and chain mail, the top grasping his Adam's apple like an iron clamp, his tongue lolling out in pain.

"The adults attend these tribal rituals only as chaperones and observers, and look upon the ceremony with indulgence. Here we see the ritual dance in progress."

A heavy rumble of drums; then a moiling herd of sweating feather-clad dancers of both sexes appeared on screen amid a great cloud of dust.

"Of course, we in more sophisticated societies no longer observe these rites."

Somehow, the scene was too painful for me to continue watching. Something dark and lurking had been awakened in my breast.

"What the hell you mean we don't observe puberty rites?" I mumbled rhetorically as I got up and switched off the set. Reaching up to the top bookshelf, I took down a leatherette-covered volume. It was my high school class yearbook. I leafed through the pages of photographs: beaming biology teachers, pimply-faced students, lantern-jawed football coaches. Suddenly, there it was—a sharply etched photographic record of a true puberty rite among the primitive tribes of northern Indiana.

The caption read: "The Junior Prom was heartily enjoyed by one and all. The annual event was held this year at the Cherrywood Country Club. Mickey Eisley and his Magic Music Makers provided the romantic rhythms. All agreed that it was an unforgettable evening, the memory of which we will all cherish in the years to come."

True enough. In the gathering gloom of my Manhattan apartment, it all came back.

"You going to the prom?" asked Schwartz, as we chewed on our salami sandwiches under the stands of the football field, where we preferred for some reason to take lunch at that period of our lives.

"Yep, I guess so," I answered as coolly as I could.

"Who ya takin'?" Flick joined the discussion, sucking at a bottle of Nehi orange.

"I don't know. I was thinking of Daphne Bigelow." I had dropped the name of the most spectacular girl in the entire high school, if not the state of Indiana itself.

"No kidding!" Schwartz reacted in a tone of proper awe and respect, tinged with disbelief.

"Yeh. I figure I'd give her a break."

Flick snorted, the gassy orange pop going down the wrong pipe. He coughed and wheezed brokenly for several moments. I had once dated Daphne Bigelow and, although the occasion, as faithful readers will recall, was not a riotous success, I felt that I was still in the running. Several occasions in the past month had led me to believe that I was making a comeback with Daphne. Twice she had distinctly acknowledged my presence in the halls between classes, once actually speaking to me.

"Oh, hi there, Fred," she had said in that musical voice.

"Uh . . . hi, Daph," I had replied wittily. The fact that my name is not Fred is neither here nor there; she had *spoken* to me. She had remembered my face from somewhere.

"Ya gotta go formal," said Schwartz. "I read on the bulletin board where it said you wear a summer formal to the prom."

"No kidding?" Flick had finished off the orange and was now fully with us. "What's a summer formal?"

"That's where you wear one of those white coats," I explained. I was known as the resident expert in our group on all forms of high life. This was because my mother was a fanatical Fred Astaire fan.

"Ya gotta rent 'em," I said with the finality of an expert.

Two weeks later, each one of us received a prim white envelope containing an engraved invitation.

> *The Junior Class is proud to invite you to the Junior Prom, to be held at the Cherrywood Country Club beginning eight P.M. June fifth. Dance to the music of Mickey Eisley and his Magic Music Makers.*
>
> *Summer formal required.*
>
> *The Committee*

It was the first engraved invitation I had ever received. The puberty rites had begun. That night around the supper table, the talk was of nothing else.

"Who ya gonna take?" my old man asked, getting right to the heart of the issue. Who you were taking to the prom was considered a highly significant decision, possibly affecting your whole life, which, in some tragic cases, it did.

"Oh, I don't know. I was thinking of a couple of girls." I replied in an offhand manner, as though this slight detail didn't concern me at all. My kid brother, who was taking all this in with sardonic interest, sneered derisively and went back to shoveling in his red cabbage. He had not yet discovered girls. My mother paused while slicing the meat loaf.

"Why not take that nice Wanda Hickey?"

"Aw, come on, Ma. This is the prom. This is important. You don't take Wanda Hickey to the *prom*."

Wanda Hickey was the only girl who I knew for an absolute fact liked me. Ever since we had been in third grade, Wanda had been hanging around the outskirts of my social circle. She laughed at my jokes and once, when we were 12, actually sent me a valentine. She was always loitering around the tennis courts, the ball diamonds, the alleys where on long summer nights we played Kick the Can or siphoned gas to keep Flick's Chevy running. In fact, there were times when I couldn't shake her.

"Nah, I haven't decided who I'm gonna take. I was kind of thinking of Daphne Bigelow."

The old man set his bottle of Pabst Blue Ribbon down

303

carefully on the table. Daphne Bigelow was the daughter of one of the larger men in town. There was, in truth, a street named after her family.

"You're a real glutton for punishment, ain't you?" The old man flicked a spot of foam off the table. He was referring to an unforgettable evening I had once spent with Daphne in my callow youth. "Oh, well, you might as well learn your lesson once and for all."

He was in one of his philosophical moods. The White Sox had dropped nine straight, and a losing streak like that usually brought out his fatalistic side. He leaned back in his chair, blew some smoke toward the ceiling and went on: "Yep. Too many guys settle for the first skirt that shows up. And regret it the rest of their lives."

Ignoring the innuendo, my mother set the mashed potatoes down on the table and said, "Well, I think Wanda is a very nice girl. But then, what I think doesn't matter."

My mother had the practiced turn of phrase of the veteran martyr, whose role in life is to suffer as publicly as possible.

"I gotta rent a summer formal," I announced.

"Christ, you gonna wear one a' them monkey suits?" the old man chuckled. He had never, to my knowledge, worn anything more formal than a sports jacket in his entire life.

"I'm going down to that place on Hohman Avenue tomorrow with Schwartz and see about it."

"Oh, boy! Lah-di-dah," said my kid brother with

characteristically eloquent understatement. Like father, like son.

The next day, after school, Schwartz and I went downtown to a place we both had passed countless times in our daily meanderings. Hanging out over the street was the cutout of a tall, creamfaced man dressed to the nines in high silk hat, stiff starched shirt, swallowtailed coat, striped morning trousers and an ivory-headed walking stick held with an easy grace by his dove-gray gloved hand. In red, sputtering neon script underneath: AL'S SWANK FORMALWEAR. RENTED BY THE DAY OR HOUR. FREE FITTINGS.

We climbed the narrow, dark wooden steps to the second floor. Within a red arrow painted on the wall were the words SWANK FORMAL—TURN LEFT.

We went past a couple of dentists' offices and a door marked BAIL BONDSMAN—FREEDOM FOR *you* DAY OR NIGHT.

"I wonder if Fred Astaire ever comes here," Schwartz said.

"Oh, come on, Schwartz. This is serious!" I could feel excitement rising deep inside me. The prom, the engraved invitation, the summer formal; it was all starting to come together.

Al's Swank Formalwear turned out to be a small room with a yellow light bulb hanging from the ceiling, a couple of tall glass cases containing suits on hangers, a counter and a couple of smudgy full-length mirrors. Schwartz opened negotiations with a swarthy, bald, hawk-eyed, shirt-sleeved man behind the counter. Around his neck hung a yellow measuring tape. He wore a worn vest with a half-dozen chalk pencils sticking out of the pocket.

"Uh . . . we'd like to . . . uh . . ." Schwartz began confidently

"OK, boys. Ya wanna make it big at the prom, am I right? Ya come to the right place. Ya goin' to that hop out at Cherrywood, right?"

"Uh . . . yeah," I replied.

"And ya wanna summah fawmal, right?"

"HEY, MORTY!" he shouted out. "HERE'S TWO MORE FOR THAT BASH AT CHERRYWOOD. I'D SAY ONE THIRTY-SIX SHAWT, ONE FAWTY REGU-LAH." His practiced eye had immediately sized us correctly.

"COMIN' UP!" Morty's voice echoed from the bowels of the establishment.

Humming to himself, Al began to pile and unpile boxes like we weren't even there. I looked around the room at the posters of various smartly turned out men of the world. One in particular, wearing a summer formal, had a striking resemblance to Cesar Romero, his distinguished gray sideburns and bronze face contrasting nicely with the snowy whiteness of his jacket.

There was another picture, of Tony Martin, who was at that time at the peak of his movie career, usually portraying Arab princes who disguised themselves as beggars in order to make the scene at the market place. He was always falling in love with a slave girl who turned out to be a princess in disguise, played by Paulette Goddard. Tony's roguish grin, somewhat flyspecked, showed that he was about to break into *Desert Song*.

Schwartz was busily inspecting a collection of bow ties displayed under glass in one of the showcases.

"OK ON THE THIRTY-SIX SHAWT, AL, BUT I'M OUTA FAWTIES. HOW 'BOUT THAT FAWTY-TWO REGULAH THAT JUST CAME BACK FROM THAT DAGO WEDDING?" shouted Morty from the back room.

"CUT THE TALK AN' BRING THE GOODS!" Al shouted back, straightening up, his face flushed.

"THE FAWTY-TWO AIN'T BEEN CLEANED YET!" came from the back room.

"BRING IT OUT, AWREADY!" barked Al. He turned to me.

"This suit just come in from anotha job. Don't worry about how it looks. We'll clean it up an' take it in so's it'll fit good."

Morty emerged, a tall, thin, sad man in a gray smock, even balder than Al. He carried two suits on hangers, draped them over the counter, gave Al a dirty look and stalked back into the shadows.

"OK now, boys. First you." Al nodded to Schwartz. "Take this and try it on behind the curtain. It should fit good. It's maybe a little long at the cuffs, but we'll take them up."

Schwartz grabbed the hanger and scurried behind the green curtain. Al held up the other suit. In the middle of a dark reddish-brown stain that covered the entire right breast pocket was a neat little hole right through the jacket. Al turned the hanger around and stuck his finger through the hole.

"HEY, MORTY!" he shouted.

"WHAT NOW?"

"HOW 'BOUT THIS HOLE INNA FAWTY-TWO? CAN YA FIX IT BY TONIGHT?"

"WADDAYA WANT, MIRACLES?" Morty whined.

"Don't worry, kid. We can fix this up good as new. You'll never tell it ain't a new coat."

Schwartz emerged from the fitting room shrouded in what looked like a parachute with sleeves.

"Perfect! Couldn't be bettuh!" shouted Al exultantly, darting from behind the counter. He grabbed Schwartz by the shoulders, spun him around and, with a single movement, ran his hand up into Schwartz' crotch, measured the inseam, spun him around again, made two pencil marks on the sleeves—which came almost to his finger tips—yanked up the collar, punched him smartly in the kidney, all the while murmuring in a hoarse stage whisper:

"It's made for you. Just perfect. Couldn't be bettuh. Perfect. Like tailormade."

Schwartz smiled weakly throughout the ordeal.

"OK, kid, take it off. I'll have it ready for you next week."

Obediently, Schwartz disappeared into the fitting room. Al turned to me. "Here, slip on this coat." He held it out invitingly. I plunged my arms into its voluminous folds. I felt his iron grip on my shoulder blades as he yanked me upward and spun me around, his appraising eye darting everywhere.

"Just perfect. Couldn't be bettuh. Fits like a glove. Take it in a little here; pull in the bias here. . . ."

He took out his chalk and made a few marks on my back.

"OK. Slip outa it."

Al again thrust his finger through the hole.

"Reweave it like new. An' doan worry 'bout the stain; we'll get it out. Musta been some party. Here, try on these pants."

He tossed a pair of midnight-blue trousers over the counter at me. Inside the hot little cubicle, as I changed into the pants, I stroked the broad black-velvet stripe that lined the outer seam. I was really in the big time now. They were rumpled, of course, and they smelled strongly of some spilled beverage, but they were truly magnificent. The waist came to just a shade below my armpits, beautifully pleated. Tossing the curtain aside, I sashayed out like Cary Grant.

"Stand up straight, kid," Al breathed into my ear. An aromatic blast of pastrami and pickled herring made my head reel.

"Ah. Perfect. Just right. Put a little tuck in the waist, so." He grabbed several yards of the seat. "And a little in here." A sudden thrill of pain as he violently measured the inseam. Then it was all over.

"Now," he said, back behind his counter once again, "how do ya see the shirts? You want 'em straight or ruffled? Or pleated, maybe? Very smart." He indicated several shirts on display in his grimy glass case. "I would recommend our Monte Carlo model, a real spiffy numbah."

We both peered down at the shirts. The Monte Carlo number was, indeed, spiffy, its wide, stiff, V-cut collar arching over cascading ribbons of razor-sharp pleats.

"Boy, now that's a shirt!" Schwartz breathed excitedly.

"That what *I* want," I said aloud. No other shirt would do.

"Me, too," Schwartz seconded.

"OK now," Al continued briskly, "how 'bout studs? Ya got 'em?"

"Uh. . . . what?"

He had caught me off guard. I had heard the word "stud" before, but never in a tailor shop.

"OK, I guess not. I'll throw 'em in. Because you're high-class customers. Now, I suppose ya wanna go first-class, right?"

Al directed this question at both of us, his face assuming a look of concerned forthrightness.

"Right?" he repeated.

"Yeah." Schwartz answered uncertainly for both of us.

"I knew that the minute you two walked in. Now, I'm gonna show you somepin that is exclusive with Al's Swank Formalwear."

With an air of surreptitious mystery, he bent over, slid open a drawer and placed atop the counter an object that unfocused my eyes with its sheer kaleidoscopic brilliance.

"No place else in town can supply you with a genuwine Hollywood paisley cummabund. It's our trademark."

I stared at the magnificent band of glowing, scintillating fabric, already seeing myself a total smash on the dance floor.

"It's only a buck extra. And worth five times the price. Adolphe Menjou always wears this model. How 'bout it, men?"

We both agreed in unison. After all, you only live once.

"Of course, included for only half a dolla more is our fawmal bow tie and matchin' booteneer. I would suggest the maroon."

"Sounds great," I answered.

"Isn't that everything?" asked Schwartz with some concern.

"Is that all! You gotta be kiddin', sonny. How do you expect to trip the light fantastic without a pair a black patent-leatha dancin' pumps?"

"Dancin' what?" I asked.

"Shoes, shoes," he explained irritably. "And we throw in the socks for nuttin'. How 'bout it?"

"Well, uh. . . ."

"Fine! So that's it, boys. I'll have everything all ready the day before the Prom. You'll really knock 'em dead."

As we left, another loud argument broke out between Morty and Al. Their voices accompanied us down the long flight of narrow stairs and out into the street.

Step by step, in the ancient tradition, the tribal ritual was being acted out. The prom, which was now two weeks off, began to occupy our minds most of the waking

311

day. The semester had just about played itself out; our junior year was almost over. The trees and flowers were in blossom, great white clouds drifted across deep-blue skies and baseball practice was in full swing—but somehow, this spring was different from the rest. The prom was something that we had heard about since our earliest days. A kind of golden aura hung over the word itself. Every couple of days, the P.A. at school announced that the prom committee was meeting or requesting something.

There was only one thing wrong. As each day ticked inexorably by toward that magic night at the Cherrywood Country Club, I still could not steel myself to actually seek out Daphne Bigelow and ask her the fatal question. Time and again, I spotted her in the halls, drifting by on gossamer wings, her radiant complexion casting a glow on all those around her, her brilliant smile lighting up the corners of 202 homeroom. But each time, I broke into a fevered sweat and chickened out at the last instant.

The weekend before the prom was sheer torture. Schwartz, always efficient and methodical, had already made all his plans. We sat on the back steps of my porch late Sunday afternoon, watching Lud Kissel next door struggle vainly to adjust the idling speed on his time-ravaged carburetor so that the family Nash didn't stall at 35 miles an hour. He had been drinking, of course, so it was quite a show.

"How ya doin' with Daphne Bigelow?" asked Schwartz sardonically, knowing full well the answer.

"Oh, that. I haven't had time to ask her," I lied.

"Ya better get on the stick. There's only a week left."

"Who *you* got lined up?" I asked, tossing a pebble at old Lud, who was now asleep under his running board.

"Clara Mae Mattingly," Schwartz replied in a steady, expressionless voice.

I was surprised. Clara Mae was one of those shadowy, quiet girls who rarely were mentioned outside of honor rolls and stuff like that. She wore gold-rimmed glasses and still had pigtails.

"Yep," Schwartz added smugly, gratified by my reaction.

"Boy, she sure can spell." It was all I could think of to say that was good about her, other than the fact that she was female.

"Sure can," Schwartz agreed. He, too, had been quite a speller in our grade school days; and on more than one occasion, Clara Mae had demolished him with a brilliant display of virtuosity in a school-wide spelldown, a form of verbal Indian wrestling now almost extinct but which at one time was a Waterloo for many of us among the unlettered. Clara Mae had actually once gone to the state final and had lost out to a gangly farm girl from downstate who apparently had nothing else to do down there but read *Webster's* through the long winter nights.

"You gonna send her a corsage?" I asked.

"Already ordered it. At the Cupid Florist." Schwartz' self-satisfaction was overflowing.

"An orchid?"

"Yep. Cost eight bucks."

"Holy God! Eight bucks!" I was truly impressed.

"That includes a gold pin for it."

Our conversation trailed off as Lud Kissel rose heavily to his knees and crawled off down the driveway on all fours, heading for the Bluebird Tavern, which was closed on Sundays. Lud always got restless in the spring.

A few hours later, after supper, I went out gloomily to water the lawn, a job that purportedly went toward earning my allowance, which had reached an all-time high that spring of three dollars a week. Fireflies played about the cottonwoods in the hazy twilight, but I was troubled. One week to go; less, now, because you couldn't count the day of the prom itself. In the drawer where I kept my socks and scout knife, buried deep in the back, were 24 one-dollar bills, which I had saved for the prom. Just as deep in my cowardly soul, I knew I could never ask Daphne Bigelow to be my date.

Refusing to admit it to myself, I whistled moodily as I sprayed the irises and watched a couple of low-flying bats as they skimmed over the lawn and up into the poplars. Mrs. Kissel, next door, creaked back and forth on her porch swing, a copy of *True Romances* open in her lap, as she waited for Lud's return with his usual snootful. My kid brother came out onto the porch and, from sheer habit, I quickly shot a stream of water over him, catching him in mid-air as he leaped high to avoid the stream. It was a superbly executed shot. I had led him just right. He caught it full in the chest, his yellow polo shirt clinging to his ribs wetly, like a second skin. Bawling at the top of his lungs, he disappeared into the house and slammed the screen door behind him. Ordinarily, this small triumph would have cheered me up for hours; but tonight, I tasted nothing but ashes. Suddenly, his face reappeared in the doorway.

"I'M GONNA TELL MA!" he yelled.

Instantly, like a cobra, I struck. Sweeping the stream quickly over the screen door, I got him again. Another scream of rage and he was gone. Again, I sank into my moody sea of reflection. Was I going to boot the prom?

Flick had asked Janie Hutchinson, a tall, funny girl who had been in our class since kindergarten. And Schwartz was lined up with Clara Mae; all he had talked about that week had been that crummy orchid and how good a dancer he was. Flick had stopped asking me about Daphne ever since the past Wednesday, when I had gotten mad because he'd been needling me. All week, I had been cleaning up my Ford for the big night. If there was one thing in my life that went all the way, my only true and total love, it was my Ford V8, a convertible that I had personally rebuilt at least 35 times. I knew every valve spring personally, had honed each valve, burnished every nut and bolt she carried. Tuesday, I had simonized her completely; Wednesday, I had repeated the job; and Thursday, I had polished the chrome until my knuckles ached and my back was stiff. I had spent the past two days minutely cleaning the interior, using a full can of saddle-soap on the worn leather. Everything was set to go, except for one thing—no girl.

A feeling of helpless rage settled over me as I continued spraying the lawn. I flushed out a poor, hapless caterpillar from under a bush, squirting him mercilessly

315

full blast, until he washed down the sidewalk and disappeared into the weeds. I felt a twinge of evil satisfaction as he rolled over and over helplessly. It was getting dark. All that was left of the sun was a long purple-orange streak along the western horizon. The glow of the steel mills to the north and east began to light up the twilight sky. I had worked my way down to the edge of our weedy, pock-marked bed of sod when, out of the corner of my eye, I noticed something white approaching out of the gloom. I sprinkled on, not knowing that another piece was being fitted into the intricate mosaic of adolescence. I kicked absent-mindedly at a passing toad as I soaked down the dandelions.

"What are you doing?"

So deeply was I involved in self-pity that at first my mind wouldn't focus. Startled, I swung my hose around, spraying the white figure on the sidewalk ten feet away.

"I'm sorry!" I blurted out, seeing at once that I had washed down a girl dressed in white tennis clothes.

"Oh, hi, Wanda. I didn't see you there."

She dried herself with a Kleenex.

"What are you doing?" she asked again.

"I'm sprinkling the lawn." The toad hopped past, going the other way now. I squirted him briefly, out of general principles.

"You been playing tennis?" Since she was wearing tennis clothes and was carrying a racket, it seemed the right thing to say.

"Me and Eileen Akers were playing. Down at the park," she answered.

Eileen Akers was a sharp-faced, bespectacled girl I had, inexplicably, been briefly in love with in the third grade. I had come to my senses by the time we got into 4-B. It was a narrow escape. By then, I had begun to dimly perceive that there was more to women than being able to play a good game of Run Sheep, Run.

"I'm sure glad school's almost over," she went on, when I couldn't think of anything to say. "I can hardly wait. I never thought I'd be a senior."

"Yeah," I said.

"I'm going to camp this summer. Are you?"

"Yeah," I lied. I had a job already lined up for the summer, working for a surveyor. The next camp I would see would be in the Ozarks, and I'd be carrying an M-1.

Wanda swung her tennis racket at a June bug that flapped by barely above stall speed. She missed. The bug soared angrily up and whirred off into the darkness.

"Are you going to college when you graduate next year?" she asked. For some reason, I didn't like the drift of the conversation.

"Yeah, I guess so, if I don't get drafted."

"My brother's in the Army. He's in the Artillery." Her brother, Bud Hickey, was a tall, laconic type four or five years older than both of us.

"Yeah, I heard. Does he like it?"

"Well, he doesn't write much," she said. "But he's gonna get a pass next September, before he goes overseas."

"How come he's in the Artillery?" I asked.

317

"I don't know. They just put him there. I guess because he's tall."

"What's that gotta do with it? Do they have to *throw* the shells, or something?"

"I don't know. They just did it."

Then it happened. Without thinking, without even a shadow of a suspicion of planning, I heard myself asking: "You going to the prom?"

For a long instant she said nothing, just swung her tennis racket at the air.

"I guess so," she finally answered, weakly.

"It's gonna be great," I said, trying to change the subject.

"Uh . . . who are you going with?" She said it as if she really didn't care one way or the other.

"Well, I haven't exactly made up my mind yet." I bent down unconcernedly and pulled a giant milkweed out by the roots.

"Neither have I," she said.

It was then that I realized there was no sense fighting it. Some guys are born to dance forever with the Daphne Bigelows on shining ballroom floors under endless starry skies. Others—well, they do the best they can. I didn't know that yet, but I was beginning to suspect something.

"Wanda?"

"Yes?"

"Wanda. Would you . . . well . . . I mean . . . would you, you see, I was thinking. . . ."

"Yes?"

Here I go, in over the horns: "Wanda, uh . . . how about . . . going to the prom with me?"

She stopped twitching her tennis racket. The crickets cheeped, the spring air was filled with the sound of singing froglets. A soft breeze carried with it the promise of a rich summer and the vibrant aromas of a nearby refinery.

She began softly, "Of course, I've had a lot of invitations, but I didn't say yes to any of them yet. I guess it would be fun to go with you," she ended gamely.

"Yeah, well, naturally, I've had four or five girls who wanted to go with me, but I figured that they were mostly jerks anyway, and . . . ah . . . I meant to ask you all along."

The die was cast. There was no turning back. It was an ironclad rule. Once a girl was asked to the prom, only a total crumb would even consider ducking out of it. There had been one or two cases in the past, but the perpetrators had become socials pariahs, driven from the tribe to fend for themselves in the unfriendly woods.

Later that night, hunched over the kitchen table, still somewhat numbed by the unexpected turn of events, I chewed thoughtfully on a peanut-butter-and-jelly sandwich, while my mother, hanging over the sink in her rump-sprung Chinese-red chenille bathrobe, droned on monotonously: "You're just going to *have* to stop squirting Randy."

"Yeah," I answered, my mind three light-years away.

"You got his new Flash Gordon T-shirt all wet."

"Sorry," I said automatically. It was a phrase I used often in those days.

"It shrunk. And now he can't wear it."

"Why not?" I asked.

"It comes up around his chest now."

"Well, why can't he stretch it?"

"You just stop squirting him, that's all. You hear me?"

"It's a silly T-shirt, anyway," I said truculently.

"You heard what I said. No more squirting." That ended the conversation.

Later, in bed, I thought briefly of Daphne Bigelow, but was interrupted by a voice from the bed on the other side of the room.

"You rotten crumb. You squirted my T-shirt!"

"Ah, shaddup."

"You wait. I'm gonna get you!"

I laughed raucously. My kid brother wailed in rage.

"SHUT UP, YOU TWO! CUT OUT THE FIGHTING OR I'LL COME IN THERE AND DO SOME HEAD KNOCKING!"

The old man meant what he said and we knew it. I promptly fell asleep. It had been a long and tumultuous day.

I broke the news to Schwartz the next morning, after biology. We were hurrying through the halls between classes on our way to our lockers, which were side by side on the second floor.

"Hey, Schwartz, how about double-dating for the prom?" I asked. I knew he had no car and I needed moral support, anyway.

"Great! I'll help you clean up the car."

"I've already simonized her. She's all set."

"Are you gonna send Daphne an orchid, or what?"

"Well, no . . ." I said lamely, hoping he'd forget what he asked.

"What do you mean? Ya gotta send a corsage."

"Well, I *am* going to send a corsage."

"I thought you said you weren't."

I just couldn't shake him off. "I never said I wasn't gonna send a corsage."

"Are you nuts? You just said you weren't gonna."

"I'm not gonna send a corsage to Daphne Bigelow. You asked me if I was gonna send a corsage to Daphne. I'm not."

"She's gonna think you're a real cheap skate."

It was getting ridiculous. Schwartz was being even more of a numskull than usual.

"Schwartz, I have decided not to ask Daphne Bigelow to the prom."

He looked directly at me, which caused him to slam into two strolling freshman girls. Their books slid across the floor, where they were trampled underfoot by the thundering mob.

"Well, who *are* you taking?" he asked, oblivious to their shrieks of dismay.

"Wanda Hickey."

"Wanda Hickey!"

Schwartz was completely thrown by the bit of news. Wanda Hickey had never been what you could call a major star in our Milky Way. We walked on, saying nothing, until finally, as we opened our lockers, Schwartz said: "Well, she sure is good at algebra."

It was true. Wanda was an algebra shark in the same way that Clara Mae was a spelling nut. Maybe we both got what we deserved.

Later that day, in the study hall, after I had polished off a history theme on some stupid thing like the Punic Wars, I got to thinking about Wanda. I could see her sitting way over on the other side of the room, a dusty sunbeam filtering through the window and lighting up her straw-colored hair. She was kind of cute. I'd never really noticed it before. Ever since second grade, Wanda had just been there, along with Eileen Akers, Helen Weathers and all the other girls who—along with me and Schwartz and Flick and Jossway and the rest—had moved together step by step up the creaky ladder of education. And here I was, at long last, taking Wanda Hickey—*Wanda Hickey*—to the prom, the only junior prom I would ever attend in my life.

As I chewed on the end of my fake-marble Wearever pen, I watched Wanda through half-closed eyes in the dusty sunbeam as she read *The Lady of the Lake*. Ahead of me, Schwartz dozed fitfully, as he always did in study hall, his forehead occasionally thumping the desk. Flick, to my right, struggled sullenly over his chemistry workbook. We both knew it was hopeless. Flick was the only one in our crowd who consistently flunked everything.

The prom was just five days away. This was the last week of school. Ahead our long summer in the sun stretched out like a lazy yellow road. For many of us, it was the last peaceful summer we were to know.

Mr. Wilson, the study-hall teacher, wandered aimlessly up and down the aisles, pretending he was interested in what we were pretending to be doing. From somewhere outside drifted the cries of a girls' volleyball game, while I drew pictures of my Ford on the inside cover of my three-ring notebook: front view, side view, rear view, outlining the drawings with ink.

That morning, on my way to school, I had gone down to the Cupid Florist Shop and ordered an orchid. My 24 dollars were shrinking fast. The eight-dollar bite for the orchid didn't help. Schwartz and I were going to split on the gas, which would come to maybe a buck apiece. After paying for the summer formal I'd have a fast ten dollars left for the night. As I sat in study hall, I calculated, writing the figures down, adding and substracting. But it didn't come out to much, no matter how I figured it.

Schwartz passed a note back to me. I opened it: "How about the Red Rooster afterward?"

I wrote underneath, "Where else?" and passed it back. The Red Rooster was part of the tribal ritual. It was *the* place you went after a big date, if you could afford it.

I glanced over across the room at Wanda and caught her looking at me. She instantly buried her head in her book. Good old Wanda.

On the way home from school every day that week of course, all we talked about was the prom. Flick was double-dating with Jossway and we were all going to meet afterward at the Rooster and roister until dawn, drinking deeply of the sweet elixir of the good life. The only thing that nagged me now was financial. Ten bucks didn't look as big as it usually did. Ordinarily, ten bucks could have gotten me through a month of just fooling around, but the prom was the big time.

Friday night, as I sat in the kitchen before going to bed, knocking down a liverwurst on whole wheat and drinking a glass of chocolate milk, the back door slammed open and in breezed the old man, carrying his bowling bag. Friday night was his big night down at the Pin-Bowl. He was a fanatical bowler, and a good one, too. He slid the bag across the floor, pretending to lay one down the groove, his right arm held out in a graceful follow-through, right leg trailing in the classic bowling stance.

"Right in the pocket," he said with satisfaction.

"How'd you do tonight?" I asked.

"Not bad. Had a two-oh-seven game. Damn near cracked six hundred."

He opened the refrigerator and fished around for a beer, then sat down heavily, took a deep drag from the bottle, burped loudly and said:

"Well, tomorrow's the big day, ain't it?"

"Yep," I answered. "Sure is."

"You takin' Daphne Bigelow?" he asked.

"Nah. Wanda Hickey."

"Oh, yeah? Well, you can't win 'em all. Wanda's old man is some kind of a foreman at the mill or something, ain't he?"

"I guess so."

"He drives a Studebaker Champion, don't he? The green two-door with the whitewalls."

The old man had a fine eye for cars. He judged all men by what they drove. Apparently a guy who drove a two-door Studebaker was not absolutely beyond the pale.

"Not a bad car. Except they burn oil after a while," he mused, omitting no aspects of the Studebaker.

"They used to have a weak front end. Bad kingpins." He shook his head critically, opening another beer and reaching for the rye bread.

I said nothing, lost in my own thoughts. My mother and kid brother had been in bed for an hour or so. We were, for all practical purposes, alone in the house. Next door, Mrs. Kissel threw out a pail of dishwater into the back yard with a swoosh. Her screen door slammed.

"How ya fixed for tomorrow night?" the old man asked suddenly, swirling his beer bottle around to raise the head.

"What do you mean?"

"I mean, how are ya *fixed?*"

My father never talked money to me. I got my allowance every Monday and that was that.

"Well, I've got about ten bucks."

"Hm." That was all he said.

After sitting in silence for a minute or so, he said, "You know, I always wished I coulda gone to a prom."

How can you answer something like that? He had

barely gotten out of eighth grade when he had to go to work, and he never stopped for the rest of his life.

"Oh, well, what the hell." He finally answered himself.

He cut himself a slice of boiled ham and made a sandwich.

"I was really hot tonight. Got a string of six straight strikes in the second game. The old hook was movin', getting a lot of wood."

He reached into his hip pocket, took out his wallet and said:

"Look, don't tell Ma." He handed me a $20 bill.

"I had a couple of bets going on the second game, and I'm a money bowler."

He was that. No doubt of it. In his early teens, he had scrounged out a living as a pool shark, and he had never lost the touch. I took the $20, glommed onto it the way the proverbial drowning man grabs at a straw. I was so astounded at this unprecedented gesture that it never occurred to me to say thanks. He would have been embarrassed if I had. A miracle had come to pass. There was no doubt about it—the prom was going to be an unqualified gas.

The next day dawned bright and sunny, as perfect as a June day can be—in a steel-mill town. Even the blast-furnace dust that drifted aimlessly through the soft air glowed with promise. I was out early, dusting off the car. It was going to be a top-down night. If there is anything more romantic than a convertible with the top down in June going to a prom, I'd like to hear about it.

Cleopatra's barge couldn't have been much more seductive.

My kid brother, his diminutive Flash Gordon T-shirt showing a great expanse of knobby backbone and skinny belly, yapped around me as I toiled over the Ford. "Look what you done to my T-shirt!" he whined, his runny nose atrickle. He was in the midst of his annual spring cold, which would be superseded by his summer cold, which lasted nicely to the whopper he got in the fall, which, of course, was only a prelude to his winter-long *monster* cold.

"Stay away from the fender. You're dripping on it!" I shouted angrily, shoving him away.

"Flash Gordon's only about an inch high now!"

I couldn't help laughing. It was true. Flash had shrunk, along with the shirt, which Randy had earned by doggedly eating three boxes of Wheaties, saving the boxtops and mailing them in with 25 cents that he had, by dint of ferocious self-denial, saved from his 30-cent weekly allowance.

"Look, I'll get you another Flash Gordon T-shirt."

"You can't. They're not givin' 'em away no more. They're givin' away Donald Duck beanies with a propeller on top now."

"Well, then, stretch the one you got now, stupid."

"It won't stretch. It keeps getting littler."

He bounced up and down on a clothes pole, joggling the clothesline and my mother's wash. Within three seconds, she was out on the back porch.

"CUT IT OUT WITH THE CLOTHES POLE."

327

Sullenly, he slid off onto the ground. I went back to work, until the Ford gleamed like some rare jewel. Then I went into the house to begin the even more laborious process of getting *myself* in shape for the evening ahead. Locking the bathroom door, I took two showers, wearing a brand-new bar of Lifebuoy down to a nub. I knew what happened to people who didn't use it; every week, little comic strips underneath *Moon Mullins* told endless tales of disastrous proms due to dreaded B.O. It would not happen to me.

I then shaved for the second time that week, using a new Gillette Blue Blade. As usual when an important shave was executed, I nicked myself nastily in several places.

"Son of a bitch," I muttered, plastering the wounds with little pieces of toilet paper.

Carefully, I went over every inch of my face, battling that age-old enemy, the blackhead, and polished off the job with a copious application of stinging Aqua Velva. Next I attacked my hair, combing and recombing, getting just the right insouciant pitch to my pride and joy, my d.a. cut. Tonight, I would be a truly magnificent specimen of lusty manhood.

Twilight was fast approaching when I emerged from the bathroom, redolent of rare aromas, pink and svelte. But the real battle had not yet begun. Laid out on my bed was my beautiful summer formal. Al was right: The elegant white coat truly gleamed in virginal splendor. Not a trace of the red stain nor the sinister hole could be detected. The coat was ready for another night of celebration, its lapels spotless, its sleeves smooth and un-creased.

Carefully, I undid the pins that festooned my pleated Monte Carlo shirt. It was the damnedest thing I had ever seen, once I got it straightened out: long, trailing gauze-like shirttails, a crinkly front that thrummed like sheet metal and a collar that seemed to be carved of white rock. I slipped it on. Panic! It had no buttons—just holes.

Rummaging around frantically in the box the suit came in, I found a cellophane envelope containing little round black things. Ripping the envelope open, I poured them out; there were five of them, two of which immediately darted under the bed. From the looks of the remaining three, they certainly weren't buttons; but they'd have to do. Although I didn't know it at the time, I had observed a classic maneuver executed by at least one stud out of every set rented with a tux. Down on my hands and knees, already beginning to lose my Lifebuoy sheen, sweat popping out here and there, I scrambled around for the missing culprits.

The ordeal was well under way. Seven o'clock was approaching with such rapidity as to be almost unbe-lievable. Schwartz, Clara Mae and Wanda would *al-ready* be waiting for me, and here I was in my drawers, crawling around on my hands and knees. Finally, amid the dust and dead spiders under my bed, I found the two studs cowering together behind a hardball I'd lost three months earlier.

Back before the mirror again, I struggled to get them in place between the concrete slits. Sweat was beginning to show under my arms. I got two in over my breastbone and now I tried to get the one at the collar over my Adam's apple. It was impossible! I could feel from deep within me several sobs beginning to form. The more I struggled, the more hamfisted I became. Oh, no! Two blackish thumb smudges appeared on my snowwhite collar.

"MA!" I screamed, "LOOK AT MY SHIRT!"

She rushed in from the kitchen, carrying a paring knife and a pan of apples. "What's the matter?"

"Look!" I pointed at the telltale prints.

My kid brother cackled in delight when he saw the trouble I was in.

"Don't touch it," she barked, taking control immediately. Dirty collars were her métier. She had fought them all her life. She darted out of the room and returned instantly with an artgum eraser.

"Now, hold still."

I obeyed as she carefully worked the stud in place and then artistically erased the two monstrous thumbprints. Never in my life had I experienced a collar remotely like the one that now clamped its iron grasp around my windpipe. Hard and unyielding, it dug mercilessly into my throat—a mere sample of what was to come.

"Where's your tie?" she asked. I had forgotten about that detail.

"It . . . ack . . . must be . . . in the box," I managed to gasp out. The collar had almost paralyzed my voice box.

She rummaged around and came up with the bow tie.

It was black and it had two metal clips. She snapped it onto the wing collar and stood back.

"Now, look at yourself in the mirror." I didn't recognize myself.

She picked up the midnight-blue trousers and held them open, so that I could slip into them without bending over.

True to his word, Al had, indeed, taken in the seat. The pants clamped me in a viselike grip that was to damn near emasculate me before the evening was out. I sucked in my stomach, buttoned the waistband tight, zippered up the fly and stood straight as a ramrod before the mirror. I had no other choice.

"Gimme your foot."

My mother was down on all fours, pulling the silky black socks onto my feet. Then, out of a box on the bed, she removed the gleaming pair of patent-leather dancing pumps, grabbed my right foot and shoved it into one of them, using her finger as a shoehorn. I tromped down. She squealed in pain.

"I can't get my finger out!"

I hobbled around, taking her finger with me.

"STAND STILL!" she screamed.

I stood like a crane, one foot in the air, with her finger jammed deep into the heel.

"RANDY! COME HERE!" she yelled.

My kid brother, who was sulking under the day bed, ran into the room.

"PULL HIS SHOE OFF, RANDY!" She was frantic.

"What for?" he asked sullenly.

"DON'T ASK STUPID QUESTIONS. JUST DO WHAT I SAY!"

I was getting an enormous cramp in my right buttock.

"STAND STILL!" she yelled. "YOU'RE BREAKING MY FINGER!" Randy looked on impassively, observing a scene that he was later to weave into a family legend, embroidering it more and more as the years went by—making himself the hero, of course.

"RANDY! *Take off his shoe!*" Her voice quavered with pain and exasperation.

"He squirted my T-shirt."

"If you don't take off his shoe this instant, you're gonna regret it." This time, her voice was low and menacing. We both knew the tone. It was the end of the line.

Randy bent over and tugged off the shoe. My mother toppled backward in relief, rubbing her index finger, which was already blue.

"Go back under the day bed," she snapped. He scurried out of the room. I straightened out my leg—the cramp subsiding like a volcano in the marrow of my bones—and the gleaming pumps were put in place without further incident. I stood encased as in armor.

"What's this thing?" she asked from behind me. I executed a careful 180-degree turn.

"Oh, that's my cummerbund."

Her face lit up like an Italian sunrise. "A cummerbund!" She had seen Fred Astaire in many a cummerbund while he spun down marble staircases with Ginger Rogers in his arms, but it was the first actual specimen she had ever been close to. She picked it up reverently, its paisley brilliance lighting up the room like an iridescent jewel.

"How does it work?" she asked, examining it closely. Before I could answer, she said, "Oh, I see. It has clips on the back. Hold still."

Around my waist it went. She drew it tight. The snaps clicked into place. It rode snugly halfway up my chest.

She picked up the snowy coat and held it out. I lowered my arms into it and straightened up. She darted around to the front, closed the single button and there I stood—Adonis!

Posing before the full-length mirror on the bathroom door, I noted the rich accent of my velvet stripes, the gleam of my pumps, the magnificent dash and sparkle of my high-fashion cummerbund. What a sight! What a feeling! This is the way life should be. This is what it's all about.

I heard my mother call out from the next room: "Hey, what's this thing?" She came out holding a cellophane bag containing a maroon object.

"Oh, that's my boutonniere."

"Your what?"

"It's a thing for the lapel. Like a fake flower."

It was the work of an instant to install my elegant wool carnation. It was the crowning touch. I was so overwhelmed that I didn't care about the fact that it didn't match my black tie, as Al had promised. With the cummerbund I was wearing, no one would notice, anyway.

Taking my leave as Cary Grant would have done, I sauntered out the front door, turned to give my mother a jaunty wave—just in time for her to call me back to pick up Wanda's corsage, which I'd left on the front-hall table.

Slipping carefully into the front seat with the cellophane-topped box safely beside me, I leaned forward slightly, to avoid wrinkling the back of my coat, started the motor up and shoved off into the warm summer night. A soft June moon hung overhead. The Ford purred like a kitten. When I pulled up before Wanda's house, it was lit up from top to bottom. Even before my brakes had stopped squealing, she was out on the porch, her mother fluttering about her, her father lurking in the background, beaming.

With stately tread, I moved up the walk; my pants were so tight that if I'd taken one false step, God knows what would have happened. In my sweaty, Aqua Velva-scented palm, I clutched the ritual largess in its shiny box.

Wanda wore a long turquoise taffeta gown, her milky skin and golden hair radiating in the glow of the porch light. This was *not* the old Wanda. For one thing, she didn't have her glasses on, and her eyes were unnaturally large and liquid, the way the true myopia victim's always are.

"Gee, thanks for the orchid," she whispered. Her voice sounded strained. In accordance with the tribal custom, she, too, was being mercilessly clamped by straps and girdles.

334

Her mother, an almost exact copy of Wanda, only slightly puffy here and there, said, "You'll take care of her now, won't you?"

"Now, Emily, don't start yapping," her old man muttered in the darkness. "They're not kids anymore."

They stood in the door as we drove off through the soft night toward Schwartz' house, our conversation stilted, our excitement almost at the boiling point. Schwartz rushed out of his house, his white coat like a ghost in the blackness, his hair agleam with Brylcreem, and surrounded by a palpable aura of Lifebuoy.

Five minutes later, Clara Mae piled into the back seat beside him, carefully holding up her daffodil-yellow skirts, her long slender neck arched. She, too, wasn't wearing her glasses. I had never realized that a good speller could be so pretty. Schwartz, a good half head shorter, laughed nervously as we tooled on toward the Cherrywood Country Club. From all over town, other cars, polished and waxed, carried the rest of the junior class to their great trial by fire.

The club nestled amid the rolling hills, where the Sinclair oil aroma was only barely detectable. Parking the car in the lot, we threaded our way through the starched and crinolined crowd—the girls' girdles creaking in unison—to the grand ballroom. Japanese lanterns danced in the breeze through the open doors to the garden, bathing the dance floor in a fairytale glow.

I found myself saying things like, "Why, hello there, Albert, how are you?" And, "Yes, I believe the weather is perfect." Only Flick, the unregenerate Philistine, failed to rise to the occasion. Already rumpled in his summer formal, he made a few tasteless wisecracks as Mickey Eisley and his Magic Music Makers struck up the sultry sounds that had made them famous in every steel-mill town that ringed Lake Michigan. Dark and sensuous, the dance floor engulfed us all. I felt tall, slim and beautiful, not realizing at the time that everybody feels that way wearing a white coat and rented pants. I could see myself standing on a mysterious balcony, a lonely, elegant figure, looking out over the lights of some exotic city, a scene of sophisticated gaiety behind me.

There was a hushed moment when Mickey Eisley stood in the baby spot, his wavy hair shining, before a microphone shaped like a chromium bullet.

"All right, boys and girls." The metallic ring of feedback framed his words in an echoing nimbus. "And now something really romantic. A request: *When the Swallows Come Back to Capistrano*. We're going to turn the lights down for this one."

Oh, wow! The lights faded even lower. Only the Japanese lanterns glowed dimly—red, green, yellow and blue —in the enchanted darkness. It was unquestionably the high point of my existence.

Wanda and I began to maneuver around the floor. My sole experience in dancing had been gained from reading Arthur Murray ads and practicing with a pillow for a partner behind the locked door of the bathroom. As we shuffled across the floor, I could see the black footprints before my eyes, marching on a white page: 1-2-3; then the white one that said, "Pause."

336

Back and forth, up and down, we moved metronomically. My box step was so square that I went in little
right angles for weeks afterward. The wool carnation
rode high up on my lapel and was beginning to scratch
my cheek, and an insistent itch began to nag at my
right shoulder. There was some kind of wire or horsehair or something in the shoulder pad that was beginning
to bore its way into my flesh.

By now, my dashing concrete collar, far from having
wilted, had set into the consistency of carborundum, and
its incessant abrasive action had removed a wide strip of
skin encircling my neck. As for my voice—due to the
manic strangulation of the collar, it was now little more
than a hoarse croak.

"When the swallows . . . retuuurrrrn to Capistraaaa-
aaaano . . ." mooed the drummer, who doubled as the
band's romantic vocalist.

I began to notice Wanda's orchid leering up at me
from her shoulder. It was the most repulsive flower I
had ever seen. At least 14 inches across, it looked like
some kind of overgrown Venus's-flytrap waiting for the
right moment to strike. Deep purple, with an obscene
yellow tongue that stuck straight out of it, and greenish
knobs on the end, it clashed almost audibly with her
turquoise dress. It looked like it was breathing, and it
clung to her shoulder as if with claws.

As I glided back and forth in my graceful box step,
my left shoulder began to develop an itch that helped
take my mind off of the insane itch in my right shoulder,
which was beginning to feel like an army of hungry

soldier ants on the march. The contortions I made to relieve the agony were camouflaged nicely by a short sneezing fit brought on by the orchid, which was exhaling directly into my face. So was Wanda, with a heady essence of Smith Brothers cough drops and sauerkraut.

"When the deeeep purpulllll falllllls . . . Over sleeeeepy gaaardennnn wallllls . . ." warbled the vocalist into his microphone, with which he seemed to be dancing the tango. The loudspeakers rattled in three-quarter time as Wanda started to sweat through her taffeta. I felt it running down her back. My own back was already so wet you could read the label on my undershirt right through the dinner jacket.

Back and forth we trudged doggedly across the crowded floor. Another Arthur Murray ad man, Schwartz was doing exactly the same step with Clara Mae directly behind me. We were all in a four-part lock step. As I hit the lower left-hand footprint in my square—the one marked "Pause"—he was hitting the upper right-hand corner of his square. Each time we did that, our elbows dug smartly into each other's ribs.

The jungle fragrance of the orchid was getting riper by the minute and the sweat, which had now saturated my jockey shorts, was pouring down my legs in rivulets. My soaked cummerbund turned two shades darker. So that she shouldn't notice, I pulled Wanda closer to me. Sighing, she hugged me back. Wanda was the vaguely chubby type of girl that was so popular at the time. Like Judy Garland, by whom she was heavily influenced, she strongly resembled a pink beach ball—but a *cute* beach ball, soft and rubbery. I felt bumpy things under her taffeta gown, with little hooks and knobs. Schwartz caught me a nasty shot in the rib cage just as I bent over to kiss her lightly on the bridge of her nose. It tasted salty. She looked up at me, her great liquid myopic eyes catching the reflection of the red and green lanterns overhead.

During a brief intermission, Schwartz and I carried paper cups dripping syrupy punch back to the girls, who had just spent some time in the ladies' room struggling unsuccessfully to repair the damage of the first half. As we were sipping, a face from my dim past floated by from out of nowhere—haughty, alabaster, green-eyed, dangerous.

"Hi, Daph," I muttered, spilling a little punch on my gleaming pumps, which had turned during the past hour into a pair of iron maidens.

"Oh, Howard." She spoke in the breathy, sexy way that such girls always have at proms. "I'd like you to meet Budge. Budge Cameron. He's at Princeton." A languid figure, probably born in a summer formal, loomed overhead.

"Budge, this is Howard."

"Hiya, fella." It was the first time I had heard the tight, nasal, swinging-jaw accent of the true Princetonian. It was not to be the last.

They were gone. Funny, I couldn't even remember actually dating her, I reflected, as the lights dimmed once again. We swung back into action. They opened with *Sleepy Lagoon*. 1-2-3-pause . . . 1-2-3-pause.

It was certain now. I had broken out in a raging rash.

339

I felt it spreading like lava across my shoulder blades under the sweat. The horsehair, meanwhile, had penetrated my chest cavity and was working its way toward a vital organ. Trying manfully to ignore it, I stared fixedly at the tiny turquoise ribbon that held Wanda's golden ponytail in place. With troubles of her own, she looked with an equally level gaze at my maroonwool carnation, which by this time had wilted into a clump of lint.

All of a sudden, it was all over. The band played *Good Night, Sweetheart* and we were out—into a driving rain. A violent cloudburst had begun just as we reached the door. My poor little car, the pride and joy of my life, was outside in the lot. With the top down.

None of us, of course, had an umbrella. We stood under the canopy as the roaring thunderstorm raged on. It wasn't going to stop.

"You guys stay here. I'll get the car," I said finally. After all, I was in charge.

Plunging into the downpour, I sloshed through the puddles and finally reached the Ford. She must have had at least a foot of water in her already. Hair streaming down over my eyes, soaked to the skin and muddied to the knees. I bailed it out with a coffee can from the trunk, slid behind the wheel and pressed the automatic-top lever. Smooth as silk, it began to lift—and stuck halfway up. As the rain poured down in sheets and the lightning flashed, I pounded on the relays, furiously switched the lever off and on. I could see the country club dimly through the downpour. Finally, the top groaned and flapped into place. I threw down the snaps, rolled up the windows and turned on the ignition; the battery was dead. The strain of hoisting that goddamn top had drained it dry. I yelled out the window at a passing car. It was Flick in his Chevy.

"GIMME A PUSH! MY BATTERY'S DEAD!"

This had never, to my knowledge, happened to Fred Astaire. And if it rained on Gene Kelly, he just sang.

Flick expertly swung his Chevy around and slammed into my trunk as I eased her into gear, and when she started to roll, the Ford shuddered and caught. Flick backed up and was gone, hollering out the window:

"SEE YOU AT THE ROOSTER."

Wanda, Schwartz and Clara Mae piled in on the damp, soggy seats and we took off. Do you know what happens to a maroon-wool carnation on a white-serge lapel in a heavy June downpour in the Midwest, where it rains not water but carbolic acid from the steel-mill fallout? I had a dark, wide, spreading maroon stripe that went all the way down to the bottom of my white coat. My French cuffs were covered with grease from fighting the top, and I had cracked a thumbnail, which was beginning to throb.

Undaunted, we slogged intrepidly through the rain toward the Red Rooster. Wedged against my side, Wanda looked up at me—oblivious to the elements—with luminous love eyes. She was truly an incurable romantic. Schwartz wisecracked in the back seat and Clara giggled from time to time. The savage tribal rite was nearing its final and most vicious phase.

We arrived at the Red Rooster, already crowded with other candidates for adulthood. A giant red neon rooster with a blue neon tail that flicked up and down in the rain set the tone for this glamorous establishment. An aura of undefined sin was always connected with the name Red Rooster. Sly winks, nudgings and adolescent cacklings about what purportedly went on at the Rooster made it the "in" spot for such a momentous revel. Its waiters were rumored really to be secret henchmen of the Mafia. But the only thing we knew for sure about the Rooster was that anybody on the far side of seven years old could procure any known drink without question.

The decor ran heavily to red-checkered-oilcloth table covers and plastic violets, and the musical background was provided by a legendary jukebox that stood a full seven feet high, featuring red and blue cascading waterfalls that gushed endlessly though its voluptuous façade. In full 200-watt operation, it could be *felt,* if not clearly heard, as far north as Gary and as far south as Kankakee. A triumph of American aesthetics.

Surging with anticipation, I guided Wanda through the uproarious throng of my peers. Schwartz and Clara Mae trailed behind, exchanging ribald remarks with the gang.

We occupied the only remaining table. Immediately, a beady-eyed waiter, hair glistening with Vaseline Hair Oil, sidled over and hovered like a vulture. Quickly distributing the famous Red Rooster Ala Carte Deluxe Menu, he stood back, smirking, and waited for us to impress our dates.

"Can I bring you anything to drink, gentlemen?" he said, heavily accenting the gentlemen.

My first impulse was to order my favorite drink of the period, a bottled chocolate concoction called Kayo, the Wonder Drink; but remembering that better things were expected of me on prom night, I said, in my deepest voice, "Uh . . . make mine . . . bourbon."

Schwartz grunted in admiration. Wanda ogled me with great, swimming, lovesick eyes. Bourbon was the only drink that I had actually heard of. My old man ordered it often down at the Bluebird Tavern. I had always wondered what it tasted like. I was soon to find out.

"How will you have it, sir?"

"Well, in a glass, I guess." I had failed to grasp the subtlety of his question, but the waiter snorted in appreciation of my humorous sally.

"Rocks?" he continued.

Rocks? I had heard about getting your rocks, but never in a restaurant. Oh, well, what the hell.

"Sure," I said. "Why not?"

All around me, the merrymaking throng was swinging into high gear. Carried away by it all, I added a phrase I had heard my old man use often: "And make it a triple." I had some vague idea that this was a brand or something.

"A *triple?* Yes, sir." His eyes snapped wide—in respect, I gathered. He knew he was in the presence of a serious drinker.

The waiter turned his gaze in Schwartz' direction. "And you, sir?"

"Make it the same." Schwartz had never been a leader.

The die was cast. Pink ladies, at the waiter's suggestion, were ordered for the girls, and we then proceeded to scan the immense menu with feigned disinterest. When the waiter returned with our drinks, I ordered—for reasons that even today I am unable to explain—lamb chops, yellow turnips, mashed potatoes and gravy, a side dish of the famous Red Rooster Roquefort Italian Cole Slaw—and a strawberry shortcake. The others wisely decided to stick with their drinks.

Munching bread sticks, Wanda, Schwartz, Clara and I engaged in sophisticated postprom repartee. Moment by moment, I felt my strength and maturity, my dashing bonhomie, my clean-cut handsomeness enveloping my friends in its benevolent warmth. Schwartz, too, seemed to scintillate as never before. Clara giggled and Wanda sighed, overcome by the romance of it all. Even when Flick, sitting three tables away, clipped Schwartz behind the left ear with a poppyseed roll, our urbanity remained unruffled.

Before me reposed a sparkling tumbler of beautiful amber liquid, ice cubes bobbing merrily on its surface, a plastic swizzle stick sporting an enormous red rooster sticking out at a jaunty angle. Schwartz was similarly equipped. And the fluffy pink ladies looked lovely in the reflected light of the pulsating jukebox.

I had seen my old man deal with just this sort of situation. Raising my beaded glass, I looked around at my companions and said suavely, "Well, here's mud in yer eye." Clara giggled; Wanda sighed dreamily, now

344

totally in love with this man of the world who sat across from her on this, our finest night.

"Yep," Schwartz parried wittily, hoisting his glass high and slopping a little bourbon on his pants as he did so.

Swiftly, I brought the bourbon to my lips, intending to down it in a single devil-may-care draught, the way Gary Cooper used to do in the Silver Dollar Saloon. I did, and Schwartz followed suit. Down it went—a screaming 90-proof rocket searing savagely down my gullet. For an instant, I sat stunned, unable to comprehend what had happened. Eyes watering copiously, I had a brief urge to sneeze, but my throat seemed to be paralyzed. Wanda and Clara Mae swam before my misted vision; and Schwartz seemed to have disappeared under the table. He popped up again—face beet-red, eyes bugging, jaw slack, tongue lolling.

"Isn't this romantic? Isn't this the most wonderful night in all our lives? I will forever treasure the memories of this wonderful night." From far off, echoing as from some subterranean tunnel, I heard Wanda speaking.

Deep down in the pit of my stomach, I felt crackling flames licking at my innards. I struggled to reply, to maintain my élan, my fabled *savoir-faire*. "Urk . . . urk . . . . yeah," I finally managed with superhuman effort.

Wanda swam hazily into focus. She was gazing across the table at me with adoring eyes.

"Another, gents?" The waiter was back, still smirking.

Schwartz nodded dumbly. I just sat there, afraid to move. An instant later, two more triple bourbons materialized in front of us.

Clara raised her pink lady high and said reverently, "Let's drink to the happiest night of our lives."

There was no turning back. Another screamer rocketed down the hatch. For an instant, it seemed as though this one wasn't going to be as lethal as the first, but the room suddenly tilted sideways. I felt torrents of cold sweat pouring from my forehead. Clinging to the edge of the table, I watched as Schwartz gagged across from me. Flick, I noticed, had just chugalugged his third rum and coke and was eating a cheeseburger with the works.

The conflagration deep inside me was now clearly out of control. My feet were smoking; my diaphragm heaved convulsively, jiggling my cummerbund; and Schwartz began to shrink, his face alternating between purple-red and chalk-white, his eyes black holes staring fixedly at the ketchup bottle. He sat stock-still. Wanda, meanwhile, cooed on ecstatically—but I was beyond understanding what she was saying. Faster and faster, in ever-widening circles, the room, the jukebox, the crowd swirled dizzily about me. In all the excitement of preparations for the prom, I realized that I hadn't eaten a single thing all day.

Out of the maelstrom, a plate mysteriously appeared before me; paper-pantied lamb chops hissing in bubbling grease, piled yellow turnips, gray mashed potatoes awash in rich brown gravy. Maybe this would help, I thought incoherently. Grasping my knife and fork as firmly as I could, I poised to whack off a piece of meat. Suddenly, the landscape listed 45 degrees to starboard and the chop I was about to attack skidded off my plate—plowing a swath through the mashed potatoes—and right into the aisle.

Pretending not to notice, I addressed myself to the remaining chop, which slid around, eluding my grasp, until I managed to skewer it with my fork. Hacking off a chunk, I jammed it fiercely mouthward, missing my target completely. Still impaled on my fork, the chop slithered over my cheekbone, spraying gravy as it went, all over my white lapels. On the next try, I had better luck, and finally I managed to get the whole chop down.

To my surprise, I didn't feel any better. Maybe the turnips will help, I thought. Lowering my head to within an inch of the plate to prevent embarrassing mishaps, I shoveled them in—but the flames within only fanned higher and higher. I tried the potatoes and gravy. My legs began to turn cold. I wolfed down the Red Rooster Roquefort Italian Cole Slaw. My stomach began to rise like a helium balloon, bobbing slowly up the alimentary canal.

My nose low over the heaping dish of strawberry shortcake, piled high with whipped cream and running with juice, I knew at last for a dead certainty what I had to do before it happened right here in front of everybody. I struggled to my feet. A strange rubbery numbness had struck my extremities. I tottered from chair to chair, grasping for the wall. There was a buzzing in my ears.

Twenty seconds later, I was on my knees, gripping the bowl of the john like a life preserver in pitching seas. Schwartz, imitating me as usual, lay almost prostrate on the tiles beside me, his body racked with heaving sobs. Lamb chops, bourbon, turnips, mashed potatoes, cole slaw—all of it came rushing out of me in a great roaring torrent—out of my mouth, my nose, my ears, my very soul. Then Schwartz opened up, and we took turns retching and shuddering. A head thrust itself between us directly into the pot. It was Flick moaning wretchedly. Up came the cheeseburger, the rum and Cokes, pretzels, potato chips, punch, gumdrops, a corned-beef sandwich, a fingernail or two—everything he'd eaten for the last week. For long minutes, the three of us lay there limp and quivering, smelling to high heaven, too weak to get up. It was the absolute high point of the junior prom; the rest was anticlimax.

Finally, we returned to the table, ashen-faced and shaking. Schwartz, his coat stained and rumpled, sat Zombie-like across from me. The girls didn't say much. Pink ladies just aren't straight bourbon.

But our little group played the scene out bravely to the end. My dinner jacket was now even more redolent and disreputable than when I'd first seen it on the hanger at Al's. And my bow tie, which had hung for a while by one clip, had somehow disappeared completely, perhaps flushed into eternity with all the rest. But as time wore on, my hearing and eyesight began slowly to return; my legs began to lose their rubberiness and the room slowly resumed its even keel—at least even enough to consider getting up and leaving. The waiter seemed to know. He returned as if on cue, bearing a slip of paper.

"The damages, gentlemen."

Taking the old man's $20 out of my wallet, I handed it to him with as much of a flourish as I could muster. There wouldn't have been any point in looking over the check; I wouldn't have been able to read it, anyway. In one last attempt to recoup my cosmopolitan image, I said offhandedly, "Keep the change." Wanda beamed in unconcealed ecstasy.

The drive home in the damp car was not quite the same as the one that had begun the evening so many weeks earlier. Our rapidly fermenting coats made the enclosed air rich and gamy, and Schwartz, who had stopped belching, sat with head pulled low between his shoulder blades, staring straight ahead. Only the girls preserved the joyousness of the occasion. Women always survive.

In a daze, I dropped off Schwartz and Clara Mae and drove in silence toward Wanda's home, the faint light of dawn beginning to show in the east.

We stood on her porch for the last ritual encounter. A chill dawn wind rustled the lilac bushes.

"This was the most wonderful, wonderful night of my whole life. I always dreamed the prom would be like this," breathed Wanda, gazing passionately up into my watering eyes.

"Me, too," was all I could manage.

I knew what was expected of me now. Her eyes closed dreamily. Swaying slightly, I leaned forward—and the faint odor of sauerkraut from her parted lips coiled slowly up to my nostrils. This was not in the script. I knew I had better get off that porch fast, or else. Backpedaling

349

desperately and down the stairs, I blurted, "Bye!" and—fighting down my rising gorge—clamped my mouth tight, leaped into the Ford, burned rubber and tore off into the dawn. Two blocks away, I squealed to a stop alongside a vacant lot containing only a huge Sherwin-Williams paint sign. WE COVER THE WORLD, it aptly read. In the blessed darkness behind the sign, concealed from prying eyes, I completed the final rite of the ceremony.

The sun was just rising as I swung the car up the driveway and eased myself quietly into the kitchen. The old man, who was going fishing that morning, sat at the enamel table sipping black coffee. He looked up as I came in. I was in no mood for idle chatter.

"You look like you had a hell of a prom," was all he said.

"I sure did."

The yellow kitchen light glared harshly on my muddy pants, my maroon-streaked, vomit-stained white coat, my cracked fingernail, my greasy shirt.

"You want anything to eat?" he asked sardonically.

At the word "eat," my stomach heaved convulsively. I shook my head numbly.

"That's what I thought," he said. "Get some sleep. You'll feel better in a couple of days, when your head stops banging."

He went back to reading his paper. I staggered into my bedroom, dropping bits of clothing as I went. My soggy Hollywood paisley cummerbund, the veteran of another gala night, was flung beneath my dresser as I toppled into bed. My brother muttered in his sleep across the room. He was still a kid. But his time would come.

350